One of the oldest and simplest spells—and most powerful. Powerful enough, I fear, to work even here.

"Once a human seizes upon the Sword, he will begin a transformation. A metamorphosis into a monster whose only food is the flesh of the humans who were once his own kind, and whose only desire is to retain possession of the Sword. A reasonable desire, that, as once the transformation takes place, the Sword is the only thing that can kill him."

"What about an atomic grenade?" asked Philip.

"Have you *got* an atomic grenade, Philip?" asked Jane.

"The only thing," Melior repeated. "Not fire, not sorcery, not boiling lead nor cold iron. The Sword alone will slay the *grendel*."

"So you're saying that whoever has that sword of yours will turn into a cannibal monster?" asked Naomi.

"No. Only any human who seizes it. Against the Morning Lords this magic will have no effect. At the time, it was thought to be a security measure," Melior said disgustedly.

"Okay, one monster. Height, weight, distinguishing marks? Last known address?" asked Michael.

"If I knew where it was, Friend Michael, I would go there and take the Sword back. Each hour it possesses the Sword renders it more powerful. And each kill. As it kills—and feeds—this human will begin to grow, and change. You will know the *grendel* because it will not look elvish or human. And because it will be trying to kill you. . . ."

THE SWORD OF MAIDEN'S TEARS

The First Book of
The Twelve Treasures

Rosemary Edghill

DAW BOOKS, INC.
DONALD A. WOLLHEIM, FOUNDER
375 Hudson Street, New York, NY 10014

ELIZABETH R. WOLLHEIM
SHEILA E. GILBERT
PUBLISHERS

First Printing, October 1994

2 3 4 5 6 7 8 9

DAW TRADEMARK REGISTERED
U.S. PAT. OFF. AND FOREIGN COUNTRIES
—MARCA REGISTRADA HECHO EN U.S.A.

PRINTED IN THE U.S.A.

AUTHOR'S NOTE

Many things can happen in the time it takes to write a book. For example, when I began this one, the Columbia Library School was still open and the underground sections of the World Trade Center were still intact. If I had to try to revise these sections to reflect the Real World of Now, this book would have been set somewhere else.

And so I beg your readerly indulgence. The heart has its raisins which the kumquats know not of, as the French don't say.

Special thanks to:
Neil Christiansen
Kate Elliott
Bonya Far-Rider
Esther Friesner
Nicole Jordan
Daniel Sifrit
and the Ladies' Proofreading
and Cookery Consumption Society
(you know who you are)
without whom this book
would have more commas.

Contents

Chapter 1

Never Trust Anyone Over 30

It was April 30th and it was raining. Naomi was at kendo, Michael was at the gym, Philip was (probably) torturing small animals, and Jane was at New York Public doing passionate in-depth research on a subject of which nobody'd ever heard, and about which she would insist on telling all of them the next time Naomi made dinner. Which would be, now that Ruth came to think about it, tomorrow.

As for Ruth, Ruth was alone.

Ruth was tall and blue-eyed, brown-haired and sensible, with a face, as Naomi often said, which made her look like the better class of Flemish Madonna; oval and even, with regular unexciting features and a small pink mouth. Ruth was rather vain of that mouth, and bought it lipstick far in excess of that which is deemed needful by proto-Librarians.

People had told Ruth she was sensible from the moment she had first fallen into the toils of the educational system; so much so that by now Ruth was ready for actions senseless and insensible.

Unfortunately, she didn't seem to have any talent for them at all. After all, wasn't she on her way toward a Master's in library science—*library science,* for God's sweet sake, was there anything more sensible than that?

Sensible Ruth.

Sensible Ruth was out walking in the rain. Today was her birthday, and Ruth was thirty. Thirty. All alone, and on the threshold of the rest of her entire life, which would be spent solitary, virginal, and depressed in some minuscule upstate New York library where the book was on view between the hours of three and three-fifteen every other Wednesday.

Such a depressing future called for ice cream at the very least, and there was a Häagen-Dazs shop on Broadway.

Ruth's Columbia-sponsored housing was on 116th Street between Broadway and Riverside Drive, but the streets were

fairly safe this close to the college, even at night. Marooned
by the changing demographic currents of New York City,
Columbia University stood like a last bastion of Gilded Age
Gotham in a sea of late-twentieth century chaos surrounded
by a moat of chichi restaurants and donut shops.

Ruth hesitated between ice cream and going to the Hunan
Balcony and really pigging out, but when Naomi got back
from her martial arts class she sometimes liked to cook. So
Ruth contented herself *(sensibly!)* with a pint of something
that ought by rights to be called *Death by Chocolate* and
turned back toward the apartment.

The fine spring rain haloed everything and dampened her
skin and clothes like heavy dew. It made the slope of 116th
Street slippery as glass, and Ruth's attention was divided
neatly between her footing and the ice cream as she wended
along.

But a New York pedestrian is nobody's fool. She had
enough attention left over to spot the body.

Ruth Marlowe, after some practice, was a good New
Yorker. She'd lived in New York since she'd come to Columbia three years ago with a fistful of equivalency credits that
let her collect a shatteringly inconsequential BA in History
on her way to the Master's of Library Science that might actually let her earn a living. She knew the rules: If you see a
supine-or-prone body, run—or at least walk fast—in the opposite direction. Never interfere. James T. Kirk would not
have found a lot of sympathy here in New York City for his
darling habit of breaking the Prime Directive.

But this body was different.

For one thing, it didn't look like your average muggee.
Even from here, in the rain-misted streetlamp light, Ruth
could see he *(he?)* was dressed in a bright-colored tunic and
boots—maybe a medievalist wandered over from St. John
the Unfinished, and thus more likely to respond favorably to
an offer of help.

Unless he was dead.

Ruth tried not to think about what she'd do if he were
dead, but as she minced closer she saw that he was breathing. He'd crawled out of—or into?—the narrow alley that
ran between her building and the one behind it. If he hadn't
been so fair, she might not have seen him.

So fair—and dressed in linen and cramoisie, though the
linen was stained and there was blood in the long silver-

blond hair. She crouched and leaned forward, shying away
from touching him for fear of hurting him further. Her heart
hammered with near-exposure to violence. But at least he
was alive.

He rolled over on his back then, moaning, and with the
improved angle and visibility Ruth could see that his skin
was not only fair, but albino-fair. He wore a belt and baldric
of silver-studded leather, luxurious and theatrical.

His ears were pointed.

Good makeup, but not period costume, Ruth was thinking,
when he opened his eyes.

They were bright leaf green, and when the pupils contracted in the streetlamp's glare she could see that the pupils
were slitted. They flashed in the dark like a cat's.

*Ohboyohboyohboyohboy. Jane is going to kill me for be-
ing here instead of her,* Ruth thought automatically.

His hands roved over his body, obviously in search of
something. Ruth repressed a wince of sympathy—they
looked like they'd been stepped on.

Mugged. Definitely.

Whatever he was looking for, he didn't find. His eyes focused on her and he moved, painfully, to sit up.

"My sword," the stranger said. "Where is it?"

Ruth stared into his eyes and couldn't think of a single
thing to say.

Mistaking her silence for a number of things it probably
wasn't, the stranger-elf began the laborious process of attempting to get to his feet. Ruth backed away and looked
wildly around for someone, anyone, even Philip, to enlist in
the solution of her peculiar problems. Finding none, she
looked for the sword.

Ruth's experience with swords was not as limited as that
of other women her age. She'd never joined the Society for
Creative Anachronism (though Naomi, who cooked for the
local revels, had suggested it often) but Ruth had been a medievalist by inclination all her life—and she'd practically
lived in the Hall of Arms and Armor at the Met.

So Ruth looked around for a two- to four-foot piece of
metal with a handle, with X- or cross- or basket-shaped hilt,
in a scabbard or without one, covered with gold and jewels
and enamel or just very plain.

She saw nothing fitting the description.

When she looked back at him, the elf was standing. He was taller than she was but not as tall as Michael, which was a good height to be. Standing, his clothes were covered with a long dark cloak, making his face seem to float unsupported in the shadows. He met her eyes.

Fair, that face; fair as a flower despite the puffiness around the jaw, the split and still bleeding lip. Fair, and age-less as a nun's.

"It isn't here, is it, human girl?" The elf brushed back his hair and winced. A large plain ring on his finger flashed mirror-bright. His hand came away wet with blood, black under the streetlamps.

"Are you hurt?" Ruth asked, since one must say some-thing, no matter how stupid. The elf sighed.

"I am hurt; I am slain; I am— Where am I, precisely?"

Reality, Ruth kept herself from saying. "New York."

"Ah."

Plainly this meant nothing to him. He looked around again—looking up, as no native-or-acculturated New Yorker would think to, and his mouth settled itself into harsh lines having little to do with the drubbing he'd received. For a moment Ruth saw the world through his eyes: a perfidious Albion of dark satanic mills, frighteningly alien.

"It seems a large place," he said. He tried to keep his voice even, but the sound of it made Ruth revise her esti-mate of his age downward. Younger than she, and therefore less threatening.

"Eleven million plus people—as of the last census."

He looked quickly at her, as if hoping to catch her in a lie, and she saw the quick cat-in-darkness flash of his eyes.

It was the eyes, perhaps, that decided her, with the back-ward wistful logic of *"If a mad ax-murderer pretending to be an elf has gone to all the trouble of getting mirrored tinted contact lenses, why don't I let him get away with it?"*

That, and the fact that it was her birthday, and she was thirty, and all her hopeful attempts to climb up to the imag-ined sanity and perks of the adult world didn't seem to be worth the trouble. Like Oakland, California; when you got there, there was no there there. Or so Gertrude Stein had said.

"Look," said Ruth, with firm calmness. "Why don't you come back to my apartment? You can at least get cleaned up. I'll make you a cup of tea."

"I thank you, mortal girl." He looked pleased, but not surprised—and more relieved than pleased, as if good manners would have kept him from asking for what he desperately hoped for.

"Ruth," said Ruth steadily. And besides, she could always hit him with one of Naomi's *shinai*.

"I am . . . Melior." He hesitated over the name, as if there had been going to be more. "Melior," he repeated firmly. He shook his head and winced.

"Come on." Ruth, belatedly awakening to the fact that where there had been muggers there could still be muggers, glanced up and down the hill. She took a few steps toward home and sanity, meaningfully. Melior followed.

He had long since lost track of how long he had sought the Sword, for the time changed with each Borderland he crossed, but he thought it had been long indeed. But never yet, in all his years of war and wandering, had Rohannan Melior of the House of the Silver Silences been so caught between joy and despair.

Despair, because the Sword was lost to him again. For a brief moment he had held it in his hands, and even though it had been spellbound to carry him into this city of dreadful night, Melior had found and passed many Gates, and with the Sword's aid he could win free of even the Last World itself.

But through foolishness, through inattention, through the cursed luck that had dogged every step of his quest, the Sword was ravished away, stolen by a brace of common footpads.

If that were all, despair would be his only companion. But there was Ruth.

He had never known her name until this moment, but it seemed to him that he had always known her face. It had been his companion on the blood-soaked battlefields of his homeland; a promise that he had once been too young to understand. Her image had burned in his heart like the brief bright lives of humans, only awaiting her presence to kindle itself past all extinction.

But to find her here, in this world, human and mortal and with no idea of the greater worlds that held her own in nested embrace—

It was difficult at times, Melior reflected, to know when

you were well off. Was it better to search for his heart's-ease forever, or to find her like this?

And the worst of it was, she did not know him.

The lobby of the building that held Ruth and Naomi's shared apartment was one of those typical New York glass air locks, requiring for its navigation two different keys and the agility required to ski through a revolving door. Melior acted as if he'd never seen one before, which made things difficult. He watched Ruth's every movement with a grave courtesy, as though he expected to be quizzed on them later.

The building's elevator alternated between dysfunctional and homicidal, and the apartment was only on the seventh floor. Ruth opted for the stairs. Melior followed her, limping slightly, the authentic signs of a recent beating turning flushed and red.

Deliberately she did not think. Why borrow trouble when the universe gave so much of it away free? She achieved her door (7A), unlocked two more locks, and was in.

One carpet, indifferent khaki. The entryway was a clutter of inadequate mismatched bookshelves covered with trinkets, souvenirs, and just plain junk. The living room was an antiseptic horror of "furniture-provided-by-the-college"; vinyl-covered and mended in tape. She and Naomi had put throws on the couch and chairs; fake fur and patchwork, tie-dye and corduroy. Melior stepped into the middle of it like an insulted cat, senses straining at normalcy.

In the overhead light of her own living room, Ruth got her first good look at her rescue project. Forced herself to look; confronting the unwelcome head-on with iron determination, just as she had every day for the last four years. Beyond which point lay that undiscovered country from which no traveler returneth, thank you very much, and this was a hell of a time for her thoughts to lead her down *that* particular primrose path. She turned her attention back to her guest.

This was nothing ordinary in the way of Upper Manhattan mugging victims. Where it wasn't bruised, Melior's skin was as smooth and blemishless as a child's; pale as the lily. He looked foreign to this place, but whether his own place was Graustark or Elfland Ruth wasn't prepared to say.

It began to seem even less likely that this was a long, careful entrapment, a way to gain access to a woman alone, and Ruth felt herself begin to relax.

"Make yourself comfortable," Ruth said. Belatedly she became aware of half a pint of Häagen-Dazs, unconsumed, slowly melting in her hand. "I'll put on tea," she said, retreating.

The kitchen, bereft of elves, was soothing. She put the ice cream carton into the tiny freezer compartment of the antique refrigerator and put the kettle on the stove, then sluiced one tea towel to sopping and filled another with ice cubes. She put both into a bowl and returned, reluctantly, to the living room.

Melior was standing in the middle of the living room, his back to her. He'd removed his cloak and belt, and had pulled up his shirt to inspect reddened ribs that would probably be gloriously black by morning. When he heard her come in, he smoothed his clothes down and turned to greet her.

"Ah," he said, eyes on the bowl. "Probably more than I deserve."

"You're lucky you weren't stabbed," Ruth said. The words came out more harshly than she intended. She skirted around him and put the bowl on the table.

Now that he'd removed his cloak, Ruth could see him better. Melior looked gaudily medieval in red tunic and white undertunic and high leather boots, but slender rather than broad; a dancer's body. He picked up the towel full of ice and pressed it gingerly to his jaw.

"I'll get the tea," Ruth said, and fled.

Back in the safety of her kitchen—*Oh, Ruth, this is NOT a good idea*—Ruth concentrated on providing tea. Besides, she was safe, Naomi would be home soon, and Naomi was authentically dangerous with hockey stick or frying pan.

And Melior *was* hurt. You couldn't spend your entire life not helping people out of stark raving cowardice—

But was it cowardice or common sense?

Tea. Probably-still-okay milk and Demerara sugar. Big stoneware mugs. The kitchen supplies were Naomi's: if Ruth was sensible, Naomi was competent. Perhaps Naomi and Michael should get together and beget a master race of tidiers; perfect secretaries and chiefs of staff.

Ruth found half a Zabar's cake and sliced it. She puttered desperately in the kitchen, unwilling to go back to the living room and Cope once more.

Who was he? What did he want? How much of her scant

time, money, and emotional energy was he going to need—and how guilty would he feel if she didn't provide them?

The teakettle shrilled. Ruth dumped loose Russian Caravan into the pot and poured water over it. Anonymous white stoneware, safe to drop.

But that meant the tray was loaded and the Minotaur must be faced. Ruth went back into the living room.

Melior was sitting at the table by the window now—the one she and Naomi used both as dining table and desk-by-courtesy. His skin was reddened from the application of ice packs, but he looked better. He looked up as she entered with the tray, and not the shadow of a suspicion crossed his face that he should leap across the room and take the tray from her. She set it down on the table. Melior looked at it.

"I guess you'd better tell me what you were doing just before you got jumped," Ruth said grudgingly.

"Gladly. But first—forgive me if I offend—is it possible, in this establishment, to bathe?"

Ruth poured out tea, black and fugitively iridescent.

"You want to take a shower?"

"Yes, if— If that is traditional," Melior said hesitantly.

Ruth spooned two heaping servings of Demerara rock into Melior's tea—*for treatment of shock, give sweetened hot liquids and wrap up warm*—and pushed it toward him. He took it and sniffed at it cautiously, then sipped.

"If it is an imposition—" he began.

"Oh, sure. I mean, no. Go ahead—I'll get you some fresh towels and stuff." Ruth fled once more.

Why does he make you so nervous? You're the one who invited him in. Ruth rummaged through the closets to find something he could wear when he came out of the shower. After some thought, she sacrificed Naomi's black kimono to the Cause. Naomi was tall, and the kimono was wide. It should do.

Because he's going to be trouble. I know he is. And my capacity for handling other people's trouble is somewhat overextended just now.

Ruth took the kimono and towels into the bathroom and piled them precariously on the edge of the sink. She made one quick tidying swipe and caught a snapshot glimpse of her reflection in the mirror: long brown hair worn in a fashion ten years out of date hanging sheepdog over her eyes;

blue eyes the only vivid thing in her face, which was pleasant, sensible, and unexciting.

You're the one who was tired of being sensible, her mind maliciously reminded her.

But that was before she'd met elves, or persons purporting to be elves.

When she went back to the living room, the cake, the milk, and most of the sugar was gone. Melior was standing, looking out the window, through which could be seen Riverside Drive, the Hudson River, and (in daylight) Fort Lee, New Jersey.

"I have to find it," he said without turning around.

"Your shower's ready," Ruth said. She pointed. He walked past her into the bedroom, picking up his cloak and swordbelt as he went. There was a suitable interval, and then Ruth heard the sound of the shower. Apparently he'd figured out how to work it—assuming he didn't really know how.

She tiptoed to the bedroom door. Ruth might know armor in passing, but her real passion was clothes. She would have embraced far more socially risky acts than inviting a strange elf in for a shower, just to be alone with his clothes.

His clothes—*garb,* the SCA always called it—was laid out neatly on one of the twin beds: cloak, tunic, pants and boots (on the floor nearby), all from the later TSR period. Gloves—well, one glove anyway; the other must have been lost. For undergarments there were a pair of knee-length drawers knitted out of a soft shiny beige yarn, knee socks and muscle shirt of the same material, and a long-sleeved shirt with a shorter hemline than the tunic. The shirt was the pale beige color of real linen and embroidered around the sleeves with an entire wildflower garden in silk floss; the front was smocked to narrowness with a thousand tiny tucks.

She turned all three pieces of knitted underwear inside out and found neither seam nor maker's mark: apparently it had been knitted all of a piece, and to size. She set them aside.

The smocked shirt yielded more clues: hand-sewing, and of a sort that ought by rights to have driven an entire convent blind. Nothing storebought or modern about this.

The pants were—it took her a moment to make up her mind—leather. Buckskin, she thought, and soaking wet, but buckskin was famous for retaining its flexibility no matter what you did to it. They'd still been making men's trousers out of it as late as the English Regency—those snow-white inexpressibles so beloved of Beau Brummell. This particular pair was flapped at the front and closed with four sterling silver buttons set with small sapphires.

Ruth sat back, aware of the chilly buzzing in her head that she associated with late nights and too much coffee—a dizzy dazzled vacation from common sense. Silver jeweled buttons?

Pointed ears?

Maybe they'd wash off while he was in the shower.

Speaking of which, she'd better hurry up.

The scarlet tunic was wool—that was an easy one—with appliques of felt and leather on the breast and at the elbow-length sleeves. The front laced shut, the vexed grommet question having been settled by interleaving a thin piece of punched leather between the two layers of wool so that the rawhide thong wouldn't cause the wool to stretch. Once more the fabric was sumptuous, the workmanship superb. As in "several thousand dollars of custom tailoring" superb, and even if you could afford to buy it, who could you find to do it?

It was too much money to spend playing dress-up for a joke.

She turned her attention to the cape.

It was a dull blotchy thing, green and gray and brown, contemptible until you realized that pure white wool had been carefully painted with these very colors, because a man wearing such a cape—no matter how scarlet his tunic—would not be visible in a woods or from any great distance. It was half-lined with sheepskins and fastened shut halfway down its length by a system of horn buttons and leather loops sewn to the inside face. It was thick as a blanket in her hands; she could not imagine how Melior could have stood up in it, especially once it had gotten wet. Carefully she spread it over the back of a chair to dry and turned to the boots. High soft Errol Flynn style boots, reaching above the knee and notched so they could be folded over to cuff in proper buccaneer style. Soft and silky as a well-oiled Coach bag.

And strapped to instep and heel, spurs of bronze and jeweled gold.

She was sure about that. Ruth had haunted enough craft fairs to know the look of handmade jewelry. She set the boots down carefully, soberly, heels together.

That left, for her delectation, a baldric and swordbelt, both top-grade harness leather. The belt was at least six inches wide and riveted with small silver roundels, each of which supported a silver ring. The forsoothly equivalent of the sadly-defunct Banana Republic photojournalist's vest: a ring for everything, and everything on its ring. A regular utility belt.

Still attached to rings were a knife in a metal scabbard and a small pouch. Reluctantly forsaking the knife—which looked to be lovely with enamel work and rock crystal—Ruth opened the pouch.

"Were you afraid I couldn't pay for my lodging?" Melior said behind her.

Ruth jumped back, agonized. "I was just—"

"Searching my possessions," Melior finished.

Naomi's black kimono came very close to not meeting in front at all. Wearing it, Melior looked like some perilously exotic Kabuki dancer; a paragraph from the lost language of cranes.

"Let me help you."

He took the pouch from her nerveless fingers and upended it on the bed.

"Signet ring—useless—sixteen *taels* in copper for chummage—useless—a useless earring, a map of no place I'm ever likely to see again, flint and steel, tinderbox, perfume, dice—useless.

"All useless. Have it if you like," he said in a deadly tired voice.

Ruth was saved from having to answer by the jingle of keys in the lock.

"Ruth?" Naomi called.

Naomi Nasmyth was about Ruth's age, but then, Naomi was deep in the toils of acquiring a Doctorate in Library Science and had been at Columbia, woman and girl, since the age of eighteen: BA in English, Master's in Library Science, Teaching Certificate, and now back to the erebean regions of the Library School's Doctoral Program.

As was often the case with roommates thrown together by fate, Naomi was all that Ruth wished to be: tall and vivid and poised and serene and organized. Black hair and hazel eyes and sangfroid that Emma Peel would envy—not to mention good at games. Ruth could have easily hated her, if not for the fact that Naomi had looked her up and down on the day she moved in and decided Ruth was in need of tidying, thereby smoothing Ruth's way enormously through the freshman maze. If there were two kinds of people in the world—Teflon and Velcro—then Naomi was definitely a Teflon person, the sort to whom trouble never stuck.

Ruth hoped it wouldn't stick now.

"She's back from the dead and ready to party! Ruth! You here?" Naomi called cheerfully.

Ruth could see the reflection of Naomi's voice in Melior's eyes. And to their mutual surprise it was Melior who moved, sliding away from one confrontation into another. Ruth barely had time to register his absence before she was moving herself, following him. She looked past his shoulder into Naomi's eyes.

Naomi's face was utterly still, entirely calm.

"Are you all right, Ruth?" she said.

Ruth stared at her, as dumbstruck as if she hadn't been hoping all night that Naomi would come back. Melior stepped aside so that Naomi could see her clearly.

"Speak, Ruth. Your friend desires to know if I have harmed you."

"He's an elf," Ruth blurted out, and the rest of her strange stasis was swamped in a burning sea of humiliation. "I mean, he was mugged, Naomi."

"Right the first time," Naomi said.

"And the second," Melior said. "I was 'mugged,' if that is the word for being assaulted by priggers and cutpurse varlets."

And that was why you decided to take up cross-dressing. Ruth could almost hear the words, but Naomi didn't say them.

"Well," said Naomi, "Maybe we can help. Right, Ruth?"

Ruth swallowed hard. "Right."

Naomi heard the story of how Ruth had found him. She heard Melior's story—which, now that Ruth had a chance to hear it over a second time and while being told to someone else, consisted of little more than his name and the statement that he had been mugged and his sword stolen. After he had told Naomi that much, Melior retreated into the bedroom and emerged a few minutes later in his white undertunic, buckskins, and boots. Naomi looked at his clothes, and at Ruth's face. She did not ask any further questions.

"Looks like the first thing you need is some more inconspicuous clothes," Naomi said. "And anyway, I'm making ginger stir-fry chicken; you'll have to stay for that, so why don't I see if Michael's home and can loan you a sweatsuit or something?"

It was Ruth's personal belief that if the Creature from the Black Lagoon itself showed up in the living room gnashing its gills and dripping slime, Naomi would hand it a towel. Ruth had seen her outface most of the forms of street weirdness that New York had to offer, as well as a number of the more offensive forms of college bureaucracy, and had yet to see Naomi flapped—if that was what you called the opposite of being unflappable. Melior gave Naomi a smile that instantly made Ruth unreasonably jealous and inclined his head.

"I would indeed be churlish did I despise such well-captained hospitality," Melior said gravely. "I pray you, Lady, be aware that I only bring peace to this house."

"That's fine, then," Naomi said. "Kitchen's too small for three, so why don't you make yourself comfortable in the living room—and get ready to tell your life story once more with feeling."

"I am utterly at your disposal," said Melior, with only the faintest hint of mockery. Ruth,. absorbed in their interplay, actually jumped when Naomi took her arm in a firm grip and pulled her toward the kitchen.

Once there, Ruth was occupied—in the same sense that an enemy city in wartime is occupied—with the task of chopping fresh ginger root into even, coin-thick slices. Naomi took the wok from the top of the refrigerator and set it on the stove. Formidable cleaver in hand (and incidentally barring Ruth's escape), Naomi set about reducing an entire helpless chicken to raw boneless gobbets suitable for stir-frying.

"So," Naomi said over the metronomic thud of the cleaver on the chopping block, "what is it this time?"

You would think to hear her talk, Ruth thought with a flash of unreasonable irritation, *that I was forever getting into predicaments that Nai was getting me out of!* She allowed several slices of ginger to elapse before she answered:

"I was up to the Häagen-Dazs on Broadway, and when I came back I found him lying in that alley behind the building."

"Dressed like that?"

"No," Ruth snapped, "I took him shopping before I brought him home."

Naomi's only comment to that was a faint snort and a raised eyebrow that made Ruth unreasonably cross with herself. "And?" Naomi prompted.

"He said his name was Melior, he said he'd been mugged, he said they'd taken his sword." *And he asked where he was, just as if he didn't know, and his ears are pointed, and his eyes glow in the dark.* "So I brought him back here," Ruth said, beginning to feel that this course of action was hardly defensible. "And he asked if he could take a shower. He really *was* mugged, Nai—he's all over bruises."

"And he's got genuine Mr. Spock ears that don't come off with water," Naomi said flatly. She took a double handful of chicken gobbets and dropped them into the wok, then scooped the remaining debris into a plastic bag and knotted it shut before dropping it into the trash can. Plop-whick-thump-bang. "And you're usually more careful than that. So what do *you* think is going on, Ruth?" Naomi turned back to the refrigerator and began divesting it of scallions, garlic, bok choy. She pulled out a bottle of peanut oil and sprinkled it generously over the chicken, and then lit the gas stove.

"Ready for the ginger in a minute," Naomi warned.

Ruth continued her careful cutting. "I don't know what's going on," she finally said. "If I said I thought he was a Tolkien elf, you'd say I was crazy. There isn't any such thing as an elf," Ruth added, carefully grammatical.

"There are more things in Heaven and Earth, Horatio—as the actress said to the bishop," Naomi said cheerfully. She swiped the pile of ginger from beneath Ruth's knife and dumped it on top of the chicken. "Watch that for a minute, will you? I'm going to go call Michael."

Michael Harrison Peacock—to give him his full name, rank, and title—was not the sort of person who would be called "Mike," even if you knew him very well. He sometimes remained Ruth of an enormous friendly dog—a black-haired, green-eyed, friendly dog with eyelashes much longer than hers, far too ebullient to be contained by anything less than a full two-syllable "Michael" (or, as was often the case, "Oh, MI-chael, HON-estly").

Michael was somewhere around Ruth's age, which was

oldish for a Master's program, and stood out by being one of the few men in her Lib Sci classes, but Michael would have stood out in any lineup—except, perhaps, a Chippendale's revue. Michael was six feet, two inches tall, had a body purchased by extended work at the gym several nights a week (and in fact Michael worked there four mornings a week as one of the instructors), and a face so flawlessly gorgeous that it was always a surprise that he could speak intelligible English. He was far too imposing for any normal woman to entertain thoughts of having a romantic relationship with him, and if Naomi hadn't been assigned as his Student Adviser, Ruth could easily have gone through her entire two years at Columbia without ever speaking to him—which would have been her loss, as Michael was genuinely, uncomplicatedly nice.

As for why he was in library school instead of working as a model, gigolo, or exotic danger, Ruth couldn't imagine—nor why he was studying for an M. L. S. at the age when he ought by rights to have been clawing his way up the corporate ladder somewhere.

She'd even asked him once, and only days later realized that "I'm trying a number of different things and this one was next," was hardly an informative answer. But Michael managed to make even mysteriousness seem wholesome, and once Ruth had managed to stop being dazzled by his wholesale gorgeousness, she found that Michael made a perfectly nice friend and study partner.

If he had any flaws at all, Ruth reflected, it was only that he was a little *too* nice and accommodating. There was, after all, the fact that Michael let Philip hang around with him.

"Got him!" Naomi announced triumphantly. "He'll be over here in about— Ruth! I told you to watch that!" She deftly elbowed Ruth out of the way and began stirring furiously at the smoking wok. "Well. Not *too* much harm done. But honestly, Ruth—"

"If God had meant me to cook, She would not have invented the telephone," Ruth said solemnly. "I could start the rice," she added, knowing what the answer would be.

"Oh, no you can't. *You* can go out and be nice to our guest. *I* will preserve my remaining pots from Grievous Bodily Harm. Go."

Thus dismissed, Ruth went back to the living room. And the elf.

Melior was sitting at the table by the window, his back to her and his attention concentrated on the window. Ruth knew that he must know she was there, but he didn't move a muscle in acknowledgment.

"Ahem," Ruth said. Melior turned his head.

"What a wonderful place your new York city is," he said disparagingly. His voice stressed the name in odd places. "Come, sit, and peruse it with me, mortal maid."

"Naomi wants to know who you really are," Ruth said, sitting down opposite him.

"And you do not? It must be wonderful to be incurious—I wish I had been born so."

"If you're going to be nasty, you can leave," Ruth said sharply.

Melior turned and looked at her. As his head moved, Ruth saw the iridescent flash of cat's eyes, and watched, fascinated, as the pupils contracted to vertical ovals in the lamp's glare.

"I am sorry, mortal maid—Ruth. My temper is not good—through my own stupidity I have lost so much more than belongs to me alone that I am sick with it. But you are not my enemy."

"Who is? What have you lost? If you tell me, maybe I can help," Ruth said.

Melior smiled. "I owe you the round tale—I do not see where the harm in the telling lies, only the urgent need. But that may wait until this "Michael" the warrior-maid Naomi has summoned comes to us. It is not in me, I think, to tell this tale twice."

Ruth smiled, a little distantly, wishing someone would call *her* a "warrior-maid." But Melior, apparently, called them as he saw them, and Ruth knew perfectly well that she was nobody's idea of an Amazon. The conversation flagged. Melior went back to gazing out the window. From the kitchen Ruth could hear the incomprehensible sounds of culinary sorcery.

Just about the time Ruth suspected she'd been dismissed, Melior swung around sharply to stare in the direction of the hallway. As Ruth gazed at him blankly, there was a familiar banging on the door.

Michael. Someone must have left the street door open

again—that's why he didn't buzz. Melior must've heard him. Ears like a cat, too.

But even convinced it was Michael, Ruth looked out through the peephole first. And saw what she had subconsciously expected to see. And sighed. And opened the door.

"Come on in, guys. Nai! Michael's here—and with Philip." *Quelle surprise.*

Michael came in, smiling at Ruth and looking around until he saw Melior. Tucked under one arm, football-wise, Michael held a brown plastic trash bag, undoubtedly full of clothes.

Philip scuttled past Michael and flung himself onto the couch, from which he surveyed the room through white-reflecting round glasses—bifocals, in fact, and only one of the many surprises Philip held in store for the uninitiated. Ruth looked at Philip, who gazed blandly back before devoting himself to the portable computer that he usually—and tonight was no exception—carried with him.

Ruth didn't much care for him and they both knew it, but Philip LeStrange was a de facto part of their group, grandfathered in under the umbrella of Michael's indiscriminate good will and Naomi's optimistic tolerance.

"Hi, Ruth," Michael said. "You must be Melior," he added, looking past her. He held out his hand.

Melior stood, and gazed at Michael's outstretched hand in the blankly helpless fashion with which polite people greet the unfamiliar. As Ruth had originally estimated, he was not quite as tall as Michael, and the sight of the two of them together—dark and fair, fantastic and mundane—made Ruth imagine a weird sort of mirror that reflected opposites. After a pause too slight to be insulting, Melior stepped forward and grasped Michael's hand above the wrist in an oddly formal gesture.

"And you are Michael, whom Naomi has summoned," Melior said.

"And this is Philip." *Whom Naomi has NOT summoned,* added Ruth with mental uncharity. "Philip, this is Melior."

"Okay," said Philip. He glanced up and then away, the flash-flash of the overhead light on his steel-rimmed glasses making a jarring cross-reference to Melior's cat-glowing eyes. Oblivious to the social graces, Philip went back to tap-tap-tapping on his computer, a true wannabe-cyberpunk, poised to leap right into the future.

"Naomi says you got pretty beat up. I know a little bit about sports medicine—I can at least tell you if you're going to need to make a trip to the emergency room," Michael, all shining rational competence, said. "And I brought some street clothes for you to try." Michael jerked his head toward the bedroom, whole body language indicating that Melior should accompany him. After another socially-baffled pause, Melior acquiesced gracefully and was led away.

Which left Ruth alone with Philip—which was the same as alone, unless Philip was in one of his chatty moods. Well, worse, actually. Ruth liked being alone, which was more than she could say for being with Philip.

Ruth Marlowe was a charter member of the sane, reasonable, people-can-get-along-if-they'll-just-try contingent of the Silent Majority, and having never been really popular in her life, saw no reason to disparage people simply because they weren't cool enough to hang with. But there were, she felt, limits to that kind of social tolerance.

Putting up with Philip, in Ruth's opinion, was carrying tolerance to self-destructive extremes.

Philip LeStrange (Jane had told her—and God alone knew how Jane had found out—that his middle name was Leslie, and Ruth hoarded this information against a day of great need) was weedy, blond, short, twenty-two, and the product of respectable (and, Ruth felt, overindulgent) parents who were sure that his health was too delicate for anything more than a quiet respectable career as a librarian. It was something to do with a heart murmur, Michael had told her once, and if she had been Philip's parents and in possession of this knowledge she would have encouraged her only chick and child to take up lumberjacking.

Philip LeStrange had pale blue eyes and no mercy and if he did not idolize Michael he would have been impossible to tolerate. As it was, he was merely difficult. Philip was wonderfully ill-suited to the library field, having no particular interest in any writing that did not appear on a computer screen, and was already planning to specialize in the electronic databases that were encroaching (like mold) on the traditional library resources—for in his own small and illegal way Philip was brilliant.

At least, amended Ruth, Philip was illegally brilliant if you believed half of what he said about his computer hacking and other anarchic activities, but since she had no talent in that realm herself and did not take any particular vicarious delight in random lawbreaking, she had no idea how much of what he said he did Philip actually did and how much was just retold urban folklore with himself cast in the starring role: an amoral Robin Hood of cyberspace, unfailingly successful.

It was a pity he was so unprepossessing. Perhaps that was why Michael put up with him—and why Ruth herself did. Philip rapped the rap of a darkling prince of the city, soigné and dangerous, when what he resembled was a pink-eyed laboratory rat, sickly, hopeful, and fatally out of synch with true hipness. Clothes that would look gloriously macho on Michael—blue jeans, black high-tops, white T-shirt, and red (James Dean) Lands End windcheater (not that Philip had ever heard of James Dean)—made Philip resemble some alien life-form unconvincingly impersonating a Real Human Being. But Philip's utter inhumanity did not breed compassion in Ruth's bosom—which was odd, considering what she put up with from Jane.

"Somebody want to set the table?" Naomi called from the kitchen.

"I don't suppose you want to help?" Ruth said punctiliously to Philip.

"No," said Philip, smiling his most irritating smile.

Naomi, on the whole, handled Philip better. She was perfectly willing and able to make him look ridiculous—a talent Ruth lacked, and the only thing Philip hated enough to mind. When Ruth went into the kitchen to collect five plates, Naomi sailed out the other way, and when Ruth came back into the living room, Philip had just finished dragging the table into the middle of the room and was flipping the tablecloth over it.

"Hi, Ruth," he said, as if he'd just now seen her for the first time.

Ruth set the plates on the table and dealt them like a poker hand. "Hello, Philip; suborned any good governments lately?" The trouble was, she *ought* to like Philip; she never had to define the words she used for him.

"Nope. Been down at the dump, shooting rats." Philip smiled, nasty-sweet.

"That's not original," Ruth said. The trouble was, she didn't like Philip. Plain and simple, and somewhere underneath it all she felt it was her social duty to *try,* as if any-

thing she did or didn't do could change the future course of
Philip LeStrange's theatric self-referential life.

"But it's good."

"The trouble is," Ruth observed to the ceiling, "that the
good parts aren't original and the original parts aren't good."

Philip walked off into the kitchen. He came out again with
a large bowl of rice, following Naomi who bore a large bowl
of ginger stir-fry chicken that smelled wonderful at eleven
o'clock at night and far too many hours after a supper Ruth
hadn't eaten anyway. The table service was assembled with
the ease of long practice; Naomi liked to cook and the rest
of them liked to eat, and that—as much as any mysterious
agenda—was what held the five of them together.

That, and, perhaps, the fact that all of them were equally
unsuited, somehow, for the space and time they were in now.
Even Jane. Or maybe especially Jane.

"Michael!" Naomi called. "Food!" ("Slop the hogs,"
Philip muttered. "Oh, shut up, wetbrain," snapped Ruth.)
The bedroom door opened, and Melior emerged, the gorgeous embroidered linen shirt replaced by one of Michael's
navy and khaki striped rugby shirts, making Melior look
even more exotic, if possible. Michael followed, no sign of
unease visible.

"Ribs cracked, maybe, but the rest is just bruises," Michael announced to the room at large with a charming lack
of self-consciousness. "Ro here was real lucky." Ruth saw
Melior's mouth curve in on itself, ever so slightly. Melior
didn't think he was lucky.

And no one among these lunatics she called her friends
had said anything about cat's eyes, pointed ears, or any elvish thing whatever. Ruth began, ever-so-slightly, to doubt
her personal grip upon sanity.

Seating five at the table meant using the two chairs, the
step stool from the kitchen, the high stool with the straw seat
from the living room, and arranging the table so that someone could perch precariously on the arm of the couch. Out
of consideration for Melior's ribs, he was given one of the
chairs. Ruth had the other.

"Just a minute," said Michael, before they were all settled.
He got up, went into the bedroom, and came back bearing a
bottle. "Happy birthday, Ruth," he said, grinning.

Ruth felt her eyes begin to tear; she forced her mouth into
a smile before it could bend in another direction.

"Bet you thought we'd forgot," crowed Naomi.

"I didn't," Ruth protested. "But I didn't tell anyone."

"I hacked into your records," Philip explained. *"Thirty . . ."* he let his voice trail off, as if unable to imagine such senescence.

"Someday, my son, you, too, will be thirty—maybe," Michael said to Philip.

"Well, open it and let's eat," Naomi said briskly. "And for dessert, there's birthday cake. I hid it behind the real food in the freezer because you and the roaches never look there."

The wine was poured—even Philip took a little, and Philip disliked alcohol in all its forms.

"A toast," Michael said, when the glasses were ready, but it was Melior who stood and raised his glass.

"To the Beltaine child," Melior said. "May she find what she seeks."

Ruth felt rather as though she had been given a very great gift—and one that she didn't know how to unwrap. *That's right*, Ruth thought. *It's Beltaine. May Eve—the 30th of April. Walpurgisnacht. But if he's from Elfland, how did HE know?*

Then Melior drank, and the moment of strangeness passed.

"Now the story," Naomi said to Melior, once the dishes were scraped and the cake was sitting on the table thawing.

"Lose the ears," Philip suggested. Melior raised an eyebrow in Philip's direction but said nothing. He looked around at the other three.

"Is it your will that this tale be told?" he asked. "For know ye this: Rohannan Melior of the House of the Silver Silences is a prince and a king's son, and the son of a prince and a king's son and so on to the beginning of time, and the words that he speaks are not without power in whichever of the worlds he speaks them."

Philip smirked, caught Naomi's eye, and didn't say anything.

"I think we all appreciate that, uh, Melior," Michael said courteously. "Why don't you tell us what happened, and maybe we can do something to help."

Melior stretched—and winced—and smiled ruefully. "Very well, Friend Michael. But this is not a tale for high words, as it is not a tale of high deeds, merely of stupidity, overconfidence, and pride."

"That we can handle," Naomi said.

Philip leaned forward—really paying attention, Ruth realized, and not out of a desire to help, but more because if he were asked to help it would give him a chance to do what Philip loved to do best—meddle with permission.

"Well, then," Melior said. "First the tale, then you may ask what you will—for as strange as you are to me, I warrant you have never seen my like as well."

"Not since *Star Trek* was canceled," Philip said. Ruth kicked him.

Melior began to speak. He spoke as clearly and as fluently as if he were reciting an old and familiar story. The others became as still and silent as an audience spellbound by a play, and soon, listening, Ruth lost all sense of anything beyond the tale he told.

CHAPTER 2

The Elf-Lord's Tale

"My name is Rohannan Melior of the House of the Silver Silences, and that House is one of the seven Great Houses of the Twilight which rule a land so far from this land that the World of Iron in which you dwell is barely a myth for our scholars. As we rule over the Men of our land, so does a High King rule over us, and that he shall have died is the cause of tragedy both in my world and your own.

"Yet it is not the death of the one who is known now in death as Rainouart the Beautiful, High King of Chandrakar, which is the tragedy, though the Sons of the Morning and the Daughters of the Evening Star do not die in the time and season of Men. The tragedy came once the funeral games were ended, and Rainouart's funeral boat was set upon the bosom of the wave, and it was time to say who from among the Seven Houses would be High King thereafter, for Rainouart had ruled long and left no son or daughter behind him, and of the Lords Temporal, our Barons, there was none among them whose puissance and courtois was greater than his fellows'."

("I saw the miniseries," Philip said under his breath. Ruth put her foot on top of his and pressed.)

"At first it seemed that all might be settled with reasoned council—that it was not, you may know when I tell you the High King died when my mother was but a child, and from that time until I grew to manhood his successor was not chosen.

"The way of it was this:

"There was a lady among the Houses whose name was Hermonicet, who was the most beautiful lady born to the Houses of the Twilight in the memory of the Morning Lords or the reckoning of bards. To the sorrow of all and the envy of some, her father had betrothed her when only a child to the Lord of the Western Marches, who lived in wild solitude at the very edge of the sea.

"That her father was wise and kind the barons only knew later. Then, they knew that the Marchlord her husband had lately died, and so the Lady Hermonicet was free to remarry how she would.

"Many hopes were pinned upon her choice—for I have seen her, and I tell you truly she is all they said she was; as beautiful as the stars, and as cold. And when it seemed that the Barons—among them my father—might come to agreement on who now would rule them, the Lady spoke from her sea-tower and said she would take no one to spouse save he who would now be High King, and open the gates of her tower never, save to that one lord.

"The lords who were met in council at the place of the High King's death tarried not one moment more over their deliberations but went forth to arm and to raise their troops, and there was thereafter in that time such a war and travail that it set brother against brother and father against son— aye, and sister against brother, and cast-out Lady against her once-loved Lord—and none of this for the High Kingship, nor any reward more lasting than the sea-cool kisses of a heartless elphen jade with nothing in her save trouble and despite."

("So there was a war," Philip said.

"How long did it last—and what happened next?" asked Michael.)

"At last, and this an undertaking of years, and with many good men slain, Lord Baligant, a younger son from an un-distinguished house, and not even of the line of one of the Treasurekeepers, took the High Kingship—by force and by guile, and partly, so I believe, because all who might depose him were sick and weary with war, and took good care that they should not come again to the sea-tower and there be-come englamoured of Hermonicet's beauty once more. So Eirdois Baligant of (by courtesy) the House of Vermilion Shadows became High King-Elect over the Houses of the Twilight and future husband to Hermonicet the Fair.

"But the wounds of that long war were not healed, nor was Baligant a forgiving suzerain, and despite the fact that law and custom compels that the High King may not go to war with any of the Great Houses, nor condemn a Son of the Morning without a trial before all his peers, I fear me that

Eirdois Baligant has found a way to punish those he will not forgive."

(Here Melior paused for a long moment, and refilled his glass, and drank. Ruth, roused by the silence, glanced quickly to right and left, but the others were merely listening, as nonjudgmental as a movie audience.)

"And the way of that is this: In our land are Twelve Treasures: Sword and Cup; Lance and Shield; Harp; Mirror; Cauldron; Comb; Cloak; Horse; Book; and Crown. Each is a talisman of surpassing magical power; all conjoined defend us from our enemies and ensure the peace and fertility of the land. Each one of these Treasures is separately entrusted to one of the noble families of Chandrakar for safekeeping, lest, possessing them all beneath his own hand, the High King's power grow too great and his spirit too haughty. No one of the Great Houses may have more than two in its keeping for the same cause; should such a thing fall out through death or wedding, the present guardian of the Treasure must find someone willing to guard that which he has guarded.

"Line Rohannan is guardian to the Sword, called the Sword of Maiden's Tears, which renders its possessor infallible in battle, with an insight into his enemy's heart as keen as a sword's edge."

("Excuse me, Melior, but that really doesn't explain how you came to be mugged on 116th Street," Naomi said. Melior nodded. "Forgive me, Mistress Naomi, but I had rather tell too much than not enough—and this is not a tale I care to tell twice.")

"Be such things as they will—the Treasures are twelve and in the wardship of the Seven Houses of the Twilight, and the particular care of Line Rohannan of the House of the Silver Silences is the Sword.

"But never had I seen the Sword, though I was much past the age when its secrets ought to have been entrusted to me. Our land had been at war, and lest any be tempted to bring the Treasures to the field of battle and use them, brother against brother, they were hidden away in various wise, and only a few knew their hiding.

"So Baligant was proclaimed, and the date for his wedding and accession set, and those with Treasures in their care set themselves to retrieve them, as my father set me.

"And thus was Baligant's subtlety and guile made patent,

and the way to his revenge made clear, because the Kingmaking is a ritual that requires all the Twelve Treasures to be present, and the lineage that does not come before the High Seat upon that day with the Treasure entrusted into its care may never come before it again: all rank and seizin are forfeit, and that line is forever banished from the Twilight Lands."

("And when you got to the wherever-it-was, your sword wasn't there, right?" Michael said. Melior nodded.

"I could write this turkey by mail," Philip said.

"Get a new scriptwriter, Philip," Ruth said.

"Now, children," Naomi said.)

"The Sword of Maiden's Tears was not where my father had left it. I sought it within and without the land, always aware that the time draws near that Line Rohannan will be called upon to present it to the High King, and aware of what will befall us do we not.

"And thus, in the end, such fear made me overhasty. I achieved the Sword at last, but in my haste allowed myself to be whelmed by magic and cut loose from the worlds; so loosed, I fell, as I must, down through the worlds until I reached the World of Iron, than which there is none lower that we know of.

"The Sword fell with me; such is its magic that even then all was not lost—though the way be filled with hazard, it was not impossible that in the end I would regain my own fair Chandrakar."

("But you were mugged," said Ruth, speaking out for the first time.)

"But I was mugged, as you say, when I was not above half-an-hour in this world, and the villains, charmed by what ill stars I know not, took from me the one thing I would not willingly have given them.

"And here, in the ruin of all my hopes and the destruction of my Line, begins your own horror, my mortal friends.

"The Sword of Maiden's Tears is forged with a great magic, that no one save the Morning Lords can wield it. Yet it has been taken from me by a man of mortal kind, and so I tell you that soon he will begin to prey upon his former kindred, shunning the light, and unslayable save by that very sword which shall be until his death his dearest treasure.

"There are no others of my kind in this world, I fear, yet only my blood may wield the Sword safely. I do not speak of the disaster fallen upon Line Rohannan, for its weaving none of the Seven Houses had a hand in and that weaving may even now be past all unraveling. I speak only of the evil to fall upon your kind, here and now in this new York city, should the Sword remain in those hands which have stolen it, and do I fail to recover it.

"Do I not regain the Sword of Maiden's Tears, my friends, your race is doomed."

CHAPTER 3

Ruth Amid the Alien Corn

"Great going, guy—and I bet Ruthie here believes every word," Philip said, with a wholly spurious enthusiasm. "So you're an elf with a magic sword, huh?" he added, smiling patronizingly.

Ruth prepared to leap to Melior's defense, but she needn't have bothered.

"Were I an elf *with* a magic sword, young Philip, I would have no despite save that my visit to your pleasant realm was to be so short. And do you choose to call Rohannan Melior liar and *warlock,* pray do so openly, lest he call you coward."

"Hey, nothing personal, Elfie," Philip said, holding his hands up in a mocking gesture of surrender.

"Get a life, Philip," Naomi said without heat. "Now, Melior, as far as I understand it, you aren't here by choice. You ran into a booby trap of some kind that dropped you in the middle of New York, and then you got mugged, and when you were mugged you lost this ceremonial sword which, according to you, will do something pretty awful to whoever has it."

"That is the essence of my tale, Mistress Naomi. I must regain the Sword, before it is too late. And then I must try to return to my own place—before it is too late."

"I think the cake's defrosted," said Philip ingenuously. He bounded to his feet, the image of helpfulness, and sprang off to the kitchen in search of plates and forks.

"Have you any ideas about how to, uh, regain this sword?" Michael said carefully. Ruth, looking at him, had no idea how much he believed of Melior's story—but *she* believed, defiantly determined to hold Melior to it no matter what mundane apostasy he contemplated.

"In the lands I know I would seek aid at the nearest castle. Were I within the boundaries of a town, there would be magistrates to enquire of—as well as taverns, and receivers of stolen goods who might inform upon their patrons. Here—" Melior sighed, and bowed his head, suddenly looking very tired. "Here every building is a castle, and I know not where to begin."

"There is also the possibility that the magic doesn't work here, Melior," said Naomi, very gently.

The elf-lord looked up at her through ice-crystal lashes. "And perhaps I am no prince of Chandrakar, but a mad mountebank trying your charity," he finished. "But no."

He slipped off his ring and set it on the table. Ruth picked it up. Instead of the carved intaglio suitable for sealing letters that she had expected to see, all she saw was a round-edged rectangle of some mirror-black stone.

Hematite? "Signet ring?"

"Here." Melior ran his thumb over the stone. For a moment colored lights sparkled just beneath the surface, then faded away again.

All of them had seen it. Melior turned back to Naomi.

"There is too much iron in the air for this small a magic to work. But the Sword was enchanted with a greater magic than any living thing can wield; if the ring works even so much as this, the Sword will work well indeed."

Michael picked up the ring next, and when Philip came back with plates and forks, Michael flipped it at him. Philip looked inquiring.

"It lights up," Michael said.

Philip tapped with a thumbnail; weighed it in his hand.

"No, it doesn't," he said positively.

"It's magic," said Naomi helpfully.

There was a knock at the door.

"I'll get it," said Ruth to no one in particular.

"It's the Thought Police," said the door when she approached it. Ruth took a quick peek through the peephole, then opened the door.

"Hi, Jane."

"I hope it isn't too late. I know it's one in the morning, but I saw your lights, and anyway, it's May Day and I forgot your birthday, so I thought I'd bring you some flowers," Jane said, still hovering on the doorstep, daffodils outstretched rather in the manner of one offering a poisonous snake.

"Come on in. Everyone's here—Naomi made me a cake—

and there's someone here I'd like you to meet," Ruth said, quasi-mendaciously, falling back full-length on trite, time-worn, hackneyed clichés. She accepted the flowers with an overpowering sense of *cusp*; she'd thought no one remembered her birthday and it seemed that everyone had, and if she'd known in advance that they would, would she have gone out at all—and if she hadn't gone out, would Melior even have been there?

Flowers in hand, Ruth went off to the kitchen. There must be a carafe somewhere in there that she could use for the daffies. *Daffies, daffodils, daffy-down dillies....* She saw the container she sought, high on the topmost shelf, and strained, tiptoe, to reach it.

"Let me." Melior, behind her. He reached past her, over her shoulder, and plucked the vase down deftly. She turned. He held it out to her, brows quirking.

"And are you sorry, now, that you rescued me? And do you think me, as the others claim to, mad, or misled, or larcenous?" Melior said softly.

Ruth took the vase. "I think you're a long way from home. And I think the first thing to do is get back your sword." She filled the vase and put the daffodils in it, and stared firmly at Melior until he moved and let her go back out into the living room.

Michael and Philip, heads together, were conferring over the mysterious signet ring. Jane was sitting in the chair Ruth had occupied, back perfectly straight (rather as if she were auditioning for a role as one of the better class of Egyptian hieratic statues) while Naomi, draped over the couch, filled her in on the evening's events with swooping theatrical gestures.

Melior brushed past Ruth and walked out to join Philip and Michael. Jane looked up as he approached, face carefully neutral, and Ruth was seized by a sudden, heart-clutching, irrational panic—a panic that somehow this was the last good moment they would all have together, that, irrespective of normal fears of madmen and con artists, somehow an evil angel was watching over everyone here, marking them for his own.

Honestly, Ruth, you'd think the lights were going out all over Europe or something. It's late, that's all.

Shrugging her shoulders at her own silliness, Ruth walked over to the table.

"Oh, good," Naomi said, "Michael, go get another plate, there's a good lad, and then we can cut the cake and decide what we're going to do with Ro, here." Naomi, unflappably competent.

"Melior is my name," Melior corrected her gently. "My Line is Rohannan."

"Chinese," Jane said cryptically.

Another plate was brought, and another glass, and the more-chocolate-than-thou cake was scrupulously divided into six enormous pieces—which might not go with red wine in anybody else's opinion, but Ruth found nothing to complain of.

"What were you doing out so late, Jane?" Naomi asked around a mouthful of cake.

"Whatever it was, you shouldn't do it." Michael said firmly. "And don't the dorms have curfews? You could get mugged, you know."

Jane elevated one shoulder, face studiously blank. It didn't matter what you said to Jane: if she listened, it was because she already intended to do what you were telling her anyway; if she did not have such an intention, it was a waste of time. Ruth had found that out a long time ago; she saved her breath.

"I was mugged," Melior offered with wary pride. "And I a blooded warrior of Line Rohannan."

Jane gazed at him for a moment, thinking it over.

"Yeah," she finally said. "But you're from out of town."

Philip whooped with laughter, spraying crumbs.

"Anyway," Michael said with firm persistence, "Ro—*Mel* and I will walk you back to the dorm. I thought he could stay with me; I've got the most room."

And are of the right gender, Ruth added mentally. Michael lived alone in off-campus student housing; Ruth wasn't sure where Philip lived, but she knew it was with several other people. She and Naomi were overcrowded as it was, and Jane lived in the dorm, expensive and cramped though it was, because with one thing and another, at nineteen to Philip's twenty-two, she was the youngest of them, the result of skipped levels in grade school.

From the vantage point of eleven years' seniority Ruth was not sure that all that skipping had been a good idea, no matter how gifted and accelerated Jane was. Jane was glib, Jane was verbal, Jane was never at a loss for a witty rejoin-

der, but Ruth suspected that the child Jane had been had suffered from being forced into adulthood too soon. Emotion-
ally she lagged far behind the people with whom she had
been thrust, willy-nilly, into peerdom, and coped with this
estrangement by permitting herself no emotions at all, lest
they turn out (incomprehensibly) to be the wrong ones.

Jane, in short, had perfected the fine art of glib superfici-
ality. Bring on what elves you chose, they would not faze
Jane Treasure Greyson of Patroon County, New York. She'd
be too certain it was some form of extended malicious practical joke. And Jane, so far as Ruth could tell, had wit but
no real sense of humor. Which made her a refreshing change
from Philip, in case anyone was interested.

One would think, all things taken into account, that Jane
and Philip would consider themselves soulmates. One would
be wrong. If there was one person in her circle of acquaintance whom Jane bestirred herself to have open feelings
about, it was Philip. And the feeling was murderous revulsion, which was too bad as everyone else thought they
would be perfect for each other.

They were, after all, both short and blond with bad eye-
sight, Jane slightly plump and moon-faced to Philip's thin
and weedy, but with nice gray eyes behind the ghastly horn-
rimmed thick-lensed glasses. And, Ruth thought wearily, if
she would wear clothes fashionable or even suitable she
would look very well.

But either she didn't care or she didn't notice: Jane was
still wearing the shetland sweaters, plaid pleated skirts, and
poly-cotton blouses with Peter Pan collars that her mother
had picked out for her in high school, and she would probably still be wearing them when she went for her first job interview. Jane came for a family that could (and did) trace its
lineage back to the Signers (of the Declaration of Indepen-
dence) on both sides and who (Ruth gathered, mostly by
omission) felt that a library degree was the height of intellectual attainment for womankind; their collective psychic
feet firmly mired in a past where the two professional tracks
for nonmarrying daughters were nurse and librarian.

So here Jane was, massively unready to cope with Real
Life in any form, and being hustled neatly down a greased
chute to neuterhood and intellectual stagnation.

Ruth looked at her wineglass suspiciously. Surely she
hadn't had *that* much to drink?

It's turning thirty. That's what it is. Oh, Ruth, you ARE a goon.

"—and then tomorrow after class we can roust some of the local pawnshops," Michael was saying, "and I'll ask the Scadians on campus—not making out like it was stolen, you understand, just misplaced."

"Your kindness does you much honor, Michael Peacock, but I fear you draw that covert in vain. Who takes the Sword will not relinquish it, did his dearest kinsman beg him for it," Melior said sadly.

"Yeah, well, you don't know earthlings very well, Elfie. Probably he ditched it in the trash somewhere after he pried all the jewels out of it. But if you want to offer a reward or something like that for it, I could post it on the Internet and some of the local BBSs."

BBS stood for Bulletin Board System, and there Ruth's knowledge of cyberspace ended.

"He hasn't got any money, Philip," Ruth said, all the while calculating how much cash she could divert from her overtaxed savings account to cover reward, and food, and the dozen hundred things Melior would need.

"But if there are pawnbrokers in this city, I can get money, Ruth," Melior said. "If your world still trades in gold and precious gems, I have that which I can sell."

Ruth thought of that exquisite earring; the spurs; the delicate wicked crystal and enamel knife. "I'll buy them," she began.

"Get together what you want to hock," Michael said, interrupting her. "I'll take it and get it valued—then Ruth gets first crack at it. Philip, you can post a reward of twenty for information leading to, and fifty for the thing itself."

"That's too low!" wailed Philip, rather as if he were hoping to claim the reward himself.

"Yeah, well, if you offer more than twenty you're going to have to chase down a lot of false leads, and if you offer fifty for the return you'll at least get people negotiating," said Michael, as if he did this all the time.

"Settled, then," said Naomi briskly. Briskly was the way Naomi did things, keeping meetings and discussions and planning committees moving steadily forward, never getting mired in attitude and argument. "Today's Friday, right?"

"Six more weeks of class," Jane said, as if announcing the weather.

"But none tomorrow. So I'll see everybody here for dinner."

And that was that.

It was about two o'clock Saturday morning when Michael, in the company of Rohannan Melior, left Naomi's apartment for his own. He carried all of Melior's worldly possessions bundled under one arm in the bag he'd brought his own clothes to Naomi's in. Their study might prove something. Then again, it might not. Michael was prepared to withhold judgment indefinitely in default of cold hard proof. *Just the facts, ma'am.* And meanwhile, the guy *had* been beaten and *did* have to sleep somewhere.

Michael wasn't worried about trouble from his chance-met houseguest; Michael knew his own worth; the worth of 200 pounds of well-sculpted beef on the hoof. A big impressive body, so that nobody, ever, would try to start up something with him. And so nobody would ever get hurt.

Michael not only abhorred violence, he dreaded it, with the fey certainty of all his Irish blood that the thing which had already destroyed his life once beyond all recovering must certainly come again.

But not tonight. And not for him. And not from some wimp elf-wannabe that talked like a cross between Alistair Cook and the *Lais* of Marie de France.

But Ruth, now. . . .

Michael liked Ruth. Michael had always liked Ruth, from the moment Naomi had first introduced them, banging them together repeatedly like half-spheres of plutonium which refused, stubbornly, to react. There was something about Ruth that was less-than-right, but it did not affect any of the fundamental Ruth-qualities that Michael liked, and everyone, God knew, was entitled to his own secrets. But maybe not now.

Michael regarded his companion. Melior walked unselfconsciously beside him, eyes flicking left and right, scanning the territory before him as if he thought that at any moment it might burst out into violence. There was something familiar about that, and after a moment Michael identified what it was.

The cop look. Melior had it. Whoever he was. *Whatever* he was.

And that made things, if possible, worse. Ruth had it bad

for this guy; Michael could see that even if nobody else could. Had it bad for Mel the Elf, who, bad actor or no, had blown into town like some sort of con man, telling them there was trouble right here in River City, roping them all in and stringing them along in the name of some kind of obscure payoff.

A psychic payoff, maybe. Contracts signed in blood.

Michael shivered.

It didn't matter—or, maybe, the worst of it was—that Mel the Elf really was authentically strange. Pointed ears and glowing eyes, maybe he was just a space alien who thought he was an elf. (As if that were a more sensible approach to the problem.)

"There are more things in heaven and earth, Horatio, than are dreamt of in your philosophy," Michael quoted to himself. "We're here," he said aloud.

Michael's apartment was small (which is to say, large by New York standards) and neat, paid for by scrupulous saving and a number of rotating part-time jobs (including one summer that had indeed been spent dancing in an all-male revue) that—along with his life in New York City—would be over by graduation. In six weeks' time (without elvish intervention) he would be a new-made Master of Library Science with a major in children's literature, ready to take some library somewhere by storm.

There were few enough men in the field—and the bad old sexist bias so strong—that even in today's "recovering" economy Michael Harrison Peacock, Male Librarian, could very nearly take his pick of jobs. He had six interviews scheduled for the last two weeks of June, and after that he'd know.

It wasn't the future he'd wanted, but it was the future he was going to get. And Michael had seen enough of real life to be grateful rather than disappointed.

He stood back as Melior entered the apartment, watching for some clue that would tell him more about Melior. Crazy or just lying?

Or, worse, real?

Melior walked to the center of the living room and looked around himself, then back at Michael. Michael closed the door and locked it three ways: chain, snap-bolt, and the deadbolt he'd bought after the first week because the other two wouldn't stop a professional housebreaker more than ninety seconds.

"And?" Melior asked, when Michael turned back. Michael raised an eyebrow.

"There must be more, Michael-my-friend. You have said so little before opening your home to me." Melior watched him narrowly, and Michael found himself looking for the iridescent flare of light reflecting silver-green off the retina, scientific cause for the folk belief that cat's eyes glowed in the dark.

But human eyes didn't.

"I think your story's bunk," Michael said bluntly.

"Ah." Melior might not understand the word, but the tone was clear enough. Nevertheless, he did not seem to be particularly hurt by Michael's disbelief. "Would that I could string a convincing warp of fancy for you. I cannot."

"What is it you really want?" Michael asked.

"I want the Sword," Melior said simply. "I want to take it to my own hall. And I should like a private word with he who stands as High King," he added mildly.

"Violence never solved anything," Michael said, and regretted it as Melior turned and stared right into his eyes.

Green and silver, flickering like flames. Like flames ... Like FLAMES—

"You know better, warrior," Melior said flatly. Michael, released from whatever spell Melior had cast, looked away, shaking with reaction.

Lucky guess. Lucky question. Gypsy tricks. Leave it. "You can have the couch; I'll get out the extra blankets. Tomorrow we can see about getting you some clothes that fit a little better—" Michael talked on, filling the air with words, putting space between himself and the ancient scar that Melior had so casually ripped open.

And somewhere inside himself, Michael Peacock began to believe.

Ruth lay awake after everyone was gone, gazing out of westward windows while the sky slowly paled toward dawn. Saturday. May Day. And maybe Melior had already vanished with the dawn. Maybe the whole evening had been some bizarre form of hallucination caused by turning thirty.

Because if it hadn't been—if the world had suddenly turned into the sort of place that could encompass both war in the Balkans and war in Elphame; pipe bombs and fairy knights with gilded spurs—Ruth wasn't sure she really wanted to have anything to do with it.

At last she gave up trying to sleep at all. Rising quietly, tiptoeing past the other bed where Naomi slept as sweetly as if she had not been hostess just last night to an elf-lord from nowhere, Ruth gathered up skirt and sweater and sensible walking shoes and slipped into the living room to dress.

The living room window shades were half-drawn, and the early morning light sliding beneath them made the room mauve and chilly. Michael had taken away Melior and all his possessions; there was nothing here to prove either that he existed or didn't. *"And I awoke and found me here on the cold hill side."*

Ruth struggled quickly into her clothes; thrift shop and antique store finds, they saved her from the need to confront the twentieth century head-on. Wearing secondhand cashmere and heirloom lace, she was saved from defining herself by this retreat into others' definitions and others' selves. And—sensible Ruth!—a cashmere twin-set was undeniably warm, warm enough, even, for a chilly, early-morning May.

Soft blue sweaters and retro kiltie skirts; sometimes Ruth wondered if there was as much difference between her and Jane as she thought. But she had chosen her own clothes, piece by piece, out of her own needs for her own purposes, and the clothes Jane was wearing were not her own; new in themselves, but fostering a secondhand image—sense of other, not of self.

Selfness was very important. To be yourself. Even if, as it turned out, you didn't like who that was, you just couldn't live your life to suit someone else's definition of who you were.

And if that meant coming down four-square in favor of reckless insanity, then that was what it meant. Ruth slung her purse over her shoulder and took her keys firmly in hand. She closed the door very quietly as she went out.

Michael lived twenty blocks south, on Riverside at 96th. It was not, Ruth insisted to herself, that she was going there—who'd be up, at quarter to six in the morning?—but rather that it made a convenient destination. Down to 96th, back up on Broadway, coffee and a bagel somewhere along the way as reward for the early morning walkabout. And besides, the walk would clear her head.

Elf or not? The morning air was sharply cold, with only the faint promise of later warmth to make it bearable. Regretting her absence of coat, Ruth walked faster. Elf or not?

Magic or not? Ruth amended conscientiously, thinking of Edward Eager, of children's books fame, whose characters always seemed to be getting into situations just like this. Only Eager's creations were fictional children, not real adults, and their imaginary garden of bright images had no room for the thousand razor-edged horrors of contemporary urban life.

But Melior seemed so reasonable, so radiantly sane. . . .

Ruth walked faster.

This section of Riverside Drive still echoed some of New York City's lost gentility. Across the road there was a grassy berm sloping toward the fence which guarded balls and small children from the precipitous drop to the river; where they hadn't been vandalized into oblivion, park benches stood, facing the water. Some were occupied by sleeping homeless, some by early joggers doing stretches.

A forty minute walk brought Ruth to the block that Michael's apartment was on. She looked up but wasn't sure which windows were his. Time to cut over to Broadway, in search of that bagel that was her ostensible reason for coming out.

Melior was sitting on one of the park benches.

At first she wasn't sure it was him. In New York such brilliantly silver hair was not uncommon, even if achieved by unnatural means. But she felt compelled to make sure, and by the time she crossed the street he had turned to look at her and she knew it was him.

"Michael kick you out?" she asked, sitting down. Melior smiled. He was wearing black sweatpants, ill-fitting canvas Chinese slippers, and a heavy wool sweater that Ruth recalled being a favorite of Michael's. Its oatmeal color made Melior's skin and hair seem even paler and it could have accommodated an additional person without any particular strain.

"No." Melior smiled. "But I am not so fond of being perched in such a hot and sealed height. The door locks of itself if you pull it shut. I came out here to think."

"About what?" Ruth asked.

Melior hesitated, then sighed, leaning forward to rest his

hands on his knees. His long hair spilled forward, hiding his face.

"He speaks, does this Michael who means me no harm in all the world, of what money my small goods will fetch, of purchasing for me suitable raiment at some gap. He speaks of what use I may be, and of what employment my hand may be turned to—in short, Ruth, he speaks of how I may fit myself to this world! And I cannot stay here! I *will* not!"

Melior took both of Ruth's hands in his, holding them strongly as if her belief could make some difference to him.

"I must find the sword—I must! And once I have—"

"You'll go home?" Ruth said.

"I will try. It is not as easy as that—if it were, I would leave now and return with an army to help me in my search. It is—" he stopped and shook his head, amused at himself. "And here I sit, trapped perhaps forever in the Last World, arguing magical geography with a mortal maid who is quite certain that I am plain and simply mad."

"You're not mad," Ruth said resolutely. She was conscious of his hands on hers, strong and warm and firm. "Maybe you aren't an elf, but I don't think you're mad."

"And your companions? Michael and Naomi and Philip and Jane? Do they grant any truth to the full-moon tale I have told them? It does not matter—they will have proof soon enough."

"Proof?" said Ruth, suddenly wary.

"Ruth, do they think I prate of cursed swords for simple pride alone? The Sword of Maiden's Tears is *cursed*. The human who wields it will become *grendel*—losing all humanity, he will become a monster that lives to slay, and subsists upon the flesh of what once were his fellow men."

"So all we have to do is wait for the bodies to start turning up—and follow them back to your sword?" Ruth said.

Melior stared at her as if she were suddenly mad. "I had not thought to find in you such a stony heart, Ruth. Do we but wait, it is true, the monster's predations will lead us to our prize—but what of the innocents who must die for such convenience?"

"These are the nineties. No one's innocent anymore. And people die all the time," Ruth said, nettled.

"Then I will be glad to leave here," Melior said flatly. "Even if I ride only to join my bloodline in disgrace and exile."

Ruth pulled her hands free abruptly.

" 'Welcome to New York—now go home,' " Ruth quoted harshly. Unreasonably, Melior's words hurt—and why should she value Melior's good opinion so much, only having known him half a day? "I'm sorry this place doesn't fit your fairy tale notions of good behavior—but then, you're a prince anyway; what would *you* know about real life?"

"I know about war, for I have seen it," Melior said somberly. "And I know that when war is over, and peace comes once more, then even soldiers put away the arts of war and live as peacefully as they may."

"Then you don't know very much." Ruth thought of the horrors she could rattle off without a pause, the catalog of poisoning, abuse, random shootings, bombings and mutilations, greed and madness.

And that without leaving the United States; worldwide she could add civil wars and famines, plague, treachery, and cruelty beyond the imagination of ancient tyrants. So much badness everywhere, and no one allowed to believe, even for a moment's respite, that things were better than they were or ever had been.

I have abandoned my search for truth and am now looking for a good fantasy.

"No," said Melior, breaking into her thoughts, "perhaps I do not. But I know that I do not want to stay here, and I know that every life the *grendel* ends is a life *I* have ended. If not for me, those who may die—and may already have died—would not have done so."

"Wrong," said Ruth. "They'd just be killed by something else."

Melior laughed. "What an odd way you have of cheering me, Ruth! Come, before you have heartened me into a black melancholy, let us waken Michael and persuade him to feed us—and disclose to me what gap holds my future garb. The day is well advanced, and I am persuaded it will be a busy one."

Michael answered the door on the first knock, his worried look vanishing at once when he saw Melior and Ruth. Though not as skilled as Naomi, Michael was a better cook than Ruth—who wasn't?—and over scrambled eggs and toasted bagels he explained the mysterious "gap" in Melior's conversation.

"Since you're here, I figure you could take Mel here down to The Gap and get him some stuff. Shirts, toothbrushes, that kind of thing."

"They don't sell toothbrushes at The Gap," Ruth said, just to be difficult.

"Use your imagination. Just get him a few things so he won't look like an escapee from the Christmas Revels," Michael explained, naming the large, Medievalist, and largely amateur production put on every December to raise money for charity. "Sneakers. Jeans."

"Using what for money?" Ruth asked patiently. "You're talking about a couple of hundred dollars, Michael, even if I only get one of everything."

Michael squirmed around in his chair until he had freed his wallet. He pulled out a sheaf of twenties and handed them to Ruth.

"Oh, Michael, I can't!" she said.

"It's a loan. I'll get it back. Mel says it's okay to sell his other stuff; I'll get it back easy."

"Not his clothes," Ruth said dangerously.

"Well, sure," Michael said.

"Ruth," Melior began, "they are only clothes, and—"

"Fine. If you don't want them, *I'll* buy them. Shirt and tunic, two hundred dollars, fair price." She shoved the money back at Michael, who had the baffled look common to men when the subject of clothes was raised. "We can hit up a cash machine on the way down to Macy's," she added, looking fiercely at both of them as if they contemplated disputing her.

Neither one did.

"You can pick them up when you get back," Michael said meekly.

And so it was that, at ten of the clock on a bright sunny morning that was the first Saturday in May, Ruth, a list of Melior's probable sizes in one hand and Melior's wrist in the other, was leading her charge down the slippery narrow steps on the IND and into the New York Subway.

She had decided on Macy's 34th Street for this expedition partly because she could put Melior's clothes on her charge card (and pay on the never-never, as they said in England), and partly for the fun of showing Melior a bit of New York. Melior's existence was impossible to deny, but Ruth found the magic and the cursed sword he feared equally impossible to credit. Magic swords were for Saturday morning TV, not real life—and Melior had said himself that magic worked poorly here, if at all.

So the sword wouldn't work, and he wouldn't find it, and so he'd have to stay. It was such an unworthy selfish thought that it didn't even make its way entirely into Ruth's consciousness, but it was there just the same.

Melior didn't balk at the stairs, though he did wrinkle his nose eloquently once they had descended far enough to smell the ambient perfume of the subway system, composed in equal parts of urine, rotting garbage, and unwashed bodies. Ruth handed over money and received tokens, and carefully guided her charge through the turnstiles and onto the platform.

Melior's face was bland and expressionless. His hair was neatly bound back at the base of his neck, covering those ridiculous, impossible ears. He stood near the edge of the platform, head down and body relaxed, lost in his own thoughts, and if Ruth had seen him all unknowing she would have thought him a student perhaps, a dancer, something lithe and graceful and focused on his art.

The train came before she knew it. Melior heard it first; head up, face turning toward her to gauge her reaction to this new experience. Then he stepped prudently back from the platform as the train came rushing in to fill the entire platform space with battered silver cars that rocked and wheezed.

It was late morning on a Saturday and Ruth was not quick enough to gain them seats; all the way down to the 34th Street Station she and Melior stood, clutching the centerpole facing each other, Ruth's nose occasionally buried in the oatmeal wool of Melior's sweater as the rocking ride jammed them together.

She'd expected him to be irritated or upset; frightened, haughty, any of these were proper reactions if—as he said he was—Melior was an elf-lord from some feudal fantasyland who had never seen a Manhattan subway before. In intermittent glimpses of his face, Ruth saw nothing of that sort; Melior turned a countenance smooth and bland to all assaults and sensations.

And so Ruth had no clue to how angry he actually was becoming, until it was much too late.

The 34th Street Station was located in what the announcers liked to call "Lower Midtown" and realtors swore was the heart of the business district. Penn Station was a block away on Seventh Avenue, Macy's occupied an entire city block, and most of the letters and numbers of the New York subway system crossed below, in a sprawling multilevel madhouse of arcade shops and misleading signs and people, people, people.

Ruth, clutching Melior's wrist tightly, plunged into that chaos with the ease of long practice, towing Melior behind her because needs must and dodging creeps, panhandlers, and incense salesmen with the obliviousness of the habituated New Yorker.

Melior was not so habituated. He did not ignore any of these myriad new sensations—each was brand new, any might be a threat, and so all required investigation. Dazzled and exhausted and cross, he followed Ruth as best he could, but something was bound to happen, and it did.

Ruth automatically veered left to avoid the annoying and semidangerous gaggle of loitering teenagers with their bizarre hairdos and equally peculiar shoes. Never get involved was still Ruth's motto, and the kids—impossible to guess ages when she was working so hard at not making eye contact—were looking for trouble. Anyone could see that.

Melior couldn't. She felt the sharp yank on her arm as he jerked back, tripped by one of the kids; heard all of them start yelling at once, jabbering in a *patois* she couldn't make out over the echoes and the noise. Heart starting to hammer, she pulled harder on Melior's wrist, and found herself yanked sharply back, forced to confront the situation.

Melior was facing the leader, gazing challengingly into his eyes. The boy was poised on the balls of his feet, bouncing back and forth, poking at Melior's chest and talking very fast. Out of the corner of her eye Ruth saw hurrying pedestrians glance over and then look away, unwilling to be involved.

"You godda pro'lem? You godda pro'lem wit me? Hey? Hey? Hey, geek, you godda—" the leader of the Lost Boys said.

Melior moved, capturing the wrist of the trespassing hand and twitching it. Ruth heard the pop of dislocated bone as if there were no other sound in the world, then Melior tore his other hand free of her hold and shoved the leader in the chest, hard enough to send him sprawling into his fellows.

The boy's wail of pain was high, supernaturally falsetto. No one stopped, or even looked his way.

"My problems are no concern of yours," Melior said clearly. "Is that understood?"

If they had been professional thugs, they would have finished him—rash defiance cows the hardened criminal only in bad fiction. Knuckling under was the only defense; the daily papers were full of the obituaries of those who tried to fight.

But probably they were, indeed, only schoolkids, and Melior terrified them as much as they frightened Ruth. They looked away, unwilling to face him, an animal submission as abject as a dog's. She could see tears running down the face of the boy whose wrist he'd broken; the flesh was already swollen and shiny.

"Good," said Melior, as if they had answered. He took Ruth's hand and allowed her to lead him away, but he never stopped looking back.

"What did you think you were doing?" Ruth demanded as soon as they reached the street. "You could have been killed!"

"They were not armed," Melior said dismissively.

Ruth grabbed a double handful of his sweater, and shook him, spent fear transmuted to anger. "And how do you know, Mister Elf-prince? Do you know what a gun is? Have you ever seen one? How about a switchblade? How about being arrested for assault and sent to Bellevue for observation and never getting out?"

"I will not be handled by rabble," Melior said flatly. He looked down at Ruth, leaf-green eyes bright and sparkling now with fury. "Do you think I do not understand violence and imprisonment? Yet I will not truckle cowardly to gutterspawn such as they. The laws of your world are not mine and I will not grovel before them."

"I don't understand you!" Ruth wailed.

"No," said Melior, "you don't. But that is of no moment—come, we will—" he broke off suddenly and stepped backward, staggering as if his balance had deserted him.

"*The Sword*—" Melior whispered.

Ruth looked around wildly, but nowhere in the busy street and bright sunshine did she see the sword that Melior had described to them the night before.

"It is gone," Melior finally said, sighing. "Perhaps it was never here." Gently he unknotted her clutching hands from Michael's sweater.

"What do you mean? Did you see it?" Ruth demanded.

"I— Perhaps to say I *felt* it would be best. I have held it, remember, and all Great Magic has its own unmistakable aura." Melior shook his head, dispelling the last of his preoccupation. "But I don't know where. And it has passed out of range."

CHAPTER 4

In the Hall of the Mountain King

He'd never been anyone worth being, and he wasn't now. His name was Kevin, and yesterday—April 30th—had been his birthday.

Yesterday was the day things had gotten bad—bad the way you read about in books, and always thought you could face better when it happened to you.

Last night, an hour after sundown, Kevin Shelby found he couldn't face it very well at all.

Be a man, Kevin. His mother's remembered voice echoed through his head. _Be a man, Kevin,_ she'd always said, just as if there were alternatives.

He wished there were. He really did.

When he was just a kid—yesterday he'd turned thirty— his teachers always used to tell him that he was bright enough to go far. The higher education didn't matter if you were smart—or maybe higher education would somehow magically appear if you had brains and manners.

But it hadn't. People talked about scholarships, when what they meant was that you'd get some money, a little money, not even enough for a whole year's tuition and there might be other ways, better ways, full scholarship ways, but on his own he could no more locate them and unravel their mysteries than he could fly to the moon. And so all of a sudden he was out of high school, just another bright boy with good grades and potential and a shiny new diploma that didn't matter, and all of a sudden the higher education mattered very much and there was no hope of getting it.

Kevin was a bright boy. He knew what "slipping through the cracks" was, and that it happened in the educational system all the time, and the _he_ had "slipped through the cracks" but there were ways around that.

There had to be.

From eighteen to twenty-five there were jobs—small jobs

at first but getting better, only there wasn't any way to save much with the bills always mounting at home and his mother and his brothers always needing something.

But he had five thousand dollars in the bank and a catalog from Pace University in his underwear drawer on the day his mother decided his space was more valuable than his company, and it was time a big boy like him—*be a man, Kevin*—got a place of his own.

So he did. Somehow he thought it'd help. But the money melted away and then so did the nice clean upscale job; he scrabbled for work—*any* work—and took in roommates just so he could pay the rent. It had seemed such a low rent, such a manageable rent, when he moved in.

He thought his luck had turned when he went to work for the TA as a track worker. A job with the city was secure, the risks of working on the underground railroad didn't bother him, and the money could be good. Only now he was twenty-five, then -six, then -seven, and the money went . . . he wasn't exactly sure *where* the money went anymore. Beer and weekend movies, bets on sure horses, fine clothes to impress women he didn't see twice, and once even on a motorcycle, stolen before it was insured, and leaving nothing behind but eighteen months of payments.

And slowly Kevin Shelby came to realize that some vital turning point had been bypassed; the signpost to that deserved future of respect and higher learning had been changed from "soon" to "never" some night while he slept. "Got any college?" the interviewers always asked, and now, forever, the answer would be no.

And he was still smart: a reader of newspapers and magazines, of history and fiction. Smart enough to see now that he would never do anything lasting, anything important; never do something that no one else could do, or, even, touch the lives of those around him in any way that he could be proud of. And some day he would die, and he might as well never have been born.

And much as if it had been party to his inner deliberations and wished him to know it endorsed them, the TA in its fickle wisdom laid off a good ten percent of its loyal work force—which included him—and at thirty, when he searched for jobs, Kevin did not possess that aura of youth and possibility that he now knew he once had worn like a cloak; that potential for success that had gotten him hired.

It was one thing to contemplate the inevitable fall into welfare and the gutter at three in the morning, safe and warm and well-fed in your own bedroom. And it was quite another, Kevin learned as the weeks went by and the unemployment benefits trickled down to nothing, it was indeed quite another thing to face a cold and hungry future on the streets without money or food or even a place to sleep when a young and healthy body and pampered sensibility insisted there *must* be another way.

There was. Kevin met Roy.

As the old joke goes, Roy was living with him at the time. Roy Turpin was the latest in the series of roommates who seemed constantly to come and go, one taking half the bedroom, one sleeping on the couch and with rent and utilities split three ways the apartment was possible—just.

But that was before the lost job and the tiny fractional unemployment checks and the scant savings dwindling. The stereo, the VCR, the television itself, all the luxurious toys of past prosperity trickled away, sold for too little cash, each sale shredding a little further the cloth of hope.

And then there was Roy. Roy who never had any difficulty coming up with his two bills for the monthly rent, Roy who worked various odd jobs and odder hours, Roy who when the last roommate left had picked up the slack without either comment or complaint, Roy who one day asked Kevin if he wanted to pick up some money—not a lot, just a little—for a few hours spent loading a truck up in Queens.

Roy offered a hundred dollars. If it had been more, Kevin probably would not have taken it, would have done the right thing—

Be a man, Kevin.

—would have continued riding the downward economic spiral until he fetched up against something, anything, that would give him salutary shock enough to make him *look*, make him see and feel and *do* something.

But it was not to be. In a lifetime of luck just faintly sour, never good enough to be heroic or bad enough to be romantic, Kevin took one more fractional step down the wrong road entirely.

The truck's cargo was stolen, of course, and even when he believed that absolutely, Kevin went on loading boxes, because if he didn't, if he made a fuss, Roy was sure to get mad, and move out, and Kevin needed the money desperately and besides, he didn't really know for sure. . . .

But that night, after the truck drove off and Roy clapped him on the shoulder and steered him to the nearest bar, Kevin felt as if he had lost something worth keeping, some talisman that, retained, would have shielded him from all the dark he saw ahead.

Be a man, Kevin.

That was only the beginning. There was more loading and unloading, daytime pickups and deliveries, all compensated in cash, and Kevin spent half his time worrying about how far he was in—dreaming fantastic Mafia dreams swagged in bloody tinsel—and the other half swearing he was in no trouble at all. Roy had never said they were breaking the law, had he? Well, then, they weren't.

And slowly the hope of an orderly real life dwindled. Kevin stopped looking for work at all. Roy always had some project he needed a little help on, and Roy became the center of Kevin's universe, replacing all other gods and ethics and futures, until Kevin Shelby (*be a man, Kevin*) measured every act not by legal and illegal, good and evil, but by whether Roy would like it, and whether he would be caught.

And then, in the end, it all came down to violence.

Yesterday had been Kevin's birthday. Thirty, the age you didn't trust anyone over. He would have liked to celebrate it—or mourn—but instead he and Roy had spent the evening with some of Roy's friends uptown.

Kevin didn't like them much, but what could you do? And besides, the casual talk was of dark knights and illegal acts, vicarious romance and self-determination, the refuge of the road. And a thousand dollars' worth of counterfeit subway tokens to take away, to package up and sell fifteen for ten dollars to a grateful public tired of fare increases.

They were almost heroes, Kevin told himself.

But then, on the way out, walking down Broadway, hungry for Chinese and beer and trying to think of nothing at all, it happened.

"Hey, Kev, wouldja lookit that?"

Kevin followed Roy's gaze without difficulty and saw a big blond in a red dress and a cape, holding something long and thin that glittered as if caught in a spotlight shining for it alone. Then the figure turned, rotating slowly as though determined to see everything at once, and Kevin realized it

was a man, not a woman—a man with long silvery hair
streaming over his shoulders, wearing strange clothes that
had the insistent familiarity of something seen in a dream.

"Damned faggot," said Roy. "Hey, Kev, let's have some
fun. Let's have some fun here, boy, whaddya say?" He put
an arm around Kevin's shoulders and hurried him toward the
man.

Accompanied by the staccato tocsin of outraged car horns,
the man in the red dress and cape crossed Broadway. That
the motorists stopped at all was perhaps a tribute to what he
held in his hands—five feet of dangerous glittering metal
and gem-studded hilt.

Less reckless, Kevin and Roy had to wait for the light.
Roy bounced up and down, jittering as he waited.

"Oh, boy—oh, boy! Now there's a sword just like in that
Conan movie. I know somebody'd give me a thousand bucks
for a sword like that, custom-made and everything."

And Kevin knew suddenly just what Roy planned, and
crossed the street with him anyway.

Possibly if Roy had been alone, he would have changed
his mind; as they followed their dreamwalking quarry down
the slope of 116th Street, it became clear that he was one of
the body-building kinds of faggot and not the wimpy kind of
faggot. But Kevin was there as witness, and so Roy went
ahead.

"Hey—you! Girlieboy!" Roy said, and the faggot turned
around and his eyes shone red and green and he looked like
something you'd see in a nightmare of a movie but never in
real life. And then Roy swung at him with one of the
sweatsocks full of bootleg tokens—aiming not for the head,
but for the wrist of the hand holding the sword. And the
sword fell to the ground in a brassy tintinnabulation because
the sock had burst and scattered bootleg largess everywhere
and the faggot, girlieboy—

Be a man, Kevin.

—was reaching for the sword when Roy hit him again,
knocking him to his knees.

"Get it, Kev!"

And Kevin grabbed the sword.

There in his hand was everything he'd ever wanted. The
chance to make it right, to make amends, to take back the
life he was supposed to have had. And the nightmare thing
lying in the street reached for it, grabbed at Kevin's leg, and

filled with revulsion and terror he struck out, bringing the sword down, the flat of the blade hitting the white-blond head with the sound of an ax on wood.

The man tried to get up one last time, and Roy kicked him down and went on kicking as if he wanted to be sure he'd done it right.

"Gimme that, Kev."

"I don't want—"

"You put him in with those trash cans—come on, hurry up." And Roy pulled the glorious renascent sword out of Kevin's shocked fingers and shoved him toward the body.

Kevin was strong. The health and strength that had first commended him to Roy's attention served now—he hauled their prey upright and slung it carelessly into an alleyway. The sound the body made when it fell made him smile. Some sort of balance had been regained, some eternal adjustment made.

The silken-swift/The gloriously fair . . . He'd read that in a book once and that guy/thing/creature/girlieboy they'd mugged made Kevin think of it now: beautiful in a dangerous inhuman way, but what right did that thing have to be beautiful when Kevin's world had all gone wrong? He turned back to his partner, and the sight of the sword in Roy's hands was jarring, unwelcome.

"Hey, Roy, give that here, okay?" Kevin said. Roy's face twisted in an ugly knowing grin.

"The hell, Kev. This's mine—I saw him first, didn't I? You wouldn't 'a hit on him without me. You want something, you go back and see what else he's got." Roy pulled off his jacket, began to wrap the naked blade. "Hey, Kev, you gimme your jacket, okay? Gotta get this covered up."

And Kevin, thinking and planning for the real world for the first time in his life, eyes and mind and heart fixed on a goal that was for the first time in his life something he could not bear even to think of not achieving, ready, willing to be-a-man and intent now with a will of a passionate intensity, that Kevin shrugged off his jacket and handed it to Roy.

To his good buddy, Roy.

For the sword.

For Being A Man.

They got out of there then, walking quickly up the sidestreet through the light April rain that had begun to fall, heading for home.

* * *

Kevin had always hoped for better things; each time
he saw his apartment he winced a little inside, knowing he
could have, ought to have had, better.

Be a man, Kevin.

But tonight he didn't waste a moment's mourning on the
worn, the shabby, the walls overdue for painting and the
ubiquitous roaches. Tonight he followed Roy in meekly,
locking the three locks, the deadbolt, and the chain, and
went off to his room to see if what he thought was there was
still there.

It was. And when he came out, Roy had unwrapped the
sword, had laid it out upon the once cheap and new and now
worn and shabby couch.

It did not contrast with its surroundings, shaming them by
its perfection. It simply dismissed them, as if in its presence
nothing else could be important. It was a little over five feet
long, with a yard of blade that tapered gradually from the
hilt to the point, as if it had been drawn out so, taffy-soft in
the child-time of its forging. The blade had a soft rich sheen,
promising sharpness; not mirror-bright like the daggers in
the Hoffritz window, rhodium-plated against tarnish, but
softer somehow, soft and sharp at the same time, like gold.
Precious as gold, with its soft white sheen.

Later Kevin would come to know the rest of it well: the
crosspiece, an undulating wave of the same white metal,
seeming to change form each time he looked at it, now serpent, now woman; the hilt, long enough for him to put both
hands around, ornamented with tiny gold beads later revealed to be the pulls of drawers he could never open, set
against a dark swirling richness that seemed now wood, now
stone, now goldsmith's lacquer. And then the pommel, the
counterweight that moved the center of gravity up the blade
so that a man holding it as it was meant to be held would
feel only its lightness, the pommel was a globe the size of
an orange, an opal or a diamond or perhaps a sphere filled
with swirling summer smoke, always changing.

"Hey, lookit this, huh, Kev? Lookit this—sure is something," Roy said prayerfully. His hands hovered above the
blade, making might-be mystic passes, unwilling to touch it.

Wild for to hold. Other scraps of poetry came to the surface of Kevin's mind, relics of a time when he believed in
the power of intellect. Now he had abandoned intellect, and

all he had left to voice his feelings and his fears were borrowed words, clumsy of fit. *Wild for to hold. Wild for to hold.* Was the wildness in the sword, or in him—or in some New Wave mixture of objects and life history?

"You got to give me that, Roy," Kevin said, sweet reason forcing the words out through the expanding lightness in his chest. "You got to give me that sword right now, Roy," he said, as his lips pulled back in a smile that made his jaws ache.

Roy turned away from the sword.

"Right now, Roy!" Kevin shouted on an upskirl of laughter, of a fine joke, the best joke ever, or certainty and rightness like champagne bubbles in his blood as he brought the bat, his Louisville Slugger from childhood days, down, and down, and down again.

And then he laughed until the tears came, kneeling there on the floor beside Roy, waiting for the labored, concussed breathing to stop as if its silence were his permission to go on. And he thought that all his life had led him to this moment, that it had given him as little choice as it gave the bullet fired from the gun's barrel, and as he waited for the breathing to stop he filled his eyes with the sword, with the sight and fire and tainted certainty of it.

"Be a man, Roy. Be a man," Kevin said to his dying friend.

He was afraid, and he was alone. He had no choice, and he knew it. And worse. He knew what he was going to do next.

CHAPTER 5

Pard-Spirit on 34th Street

Ruth finally convinced Melior to go on into Macy's as, even if he had sensed its presence (Ruth was inclined to doubt this), Melior's magic sword was nowhere he could get at it just now.

Once she'd succeeded in getting him into the store she wished she hadn't.

Ruth had lived in New York for three years, and had long since forgotten the dazzling rush of sensory overload brought on by her first exposure to The Big Apple. And even so, Ruth had come from another city; a smaller city, but still a city, Urban America at its best, the twentieth century.

Melior hadn't.

For a moment she saw it through his eyes: the golden marble, the sixty-foot ceilings, the space filled with people all rushing at top speed to no discernible place. The glittering piles of *Things*, all displayed to catch the eye, and over all the roar of conversation, the pong-pong-pong of the callbells, and the Muzak of some alien and unconsidered civilization.

Melior took a step back, pushing her into the influx of shoppers from the street, dazzled and blinded and completely helpless.

Ruth clutched at him, too. She took a deep breath, forced the sense of vertigo and helplessness away from her, and pulled him aside into a quiet backwater of the eddying onward torrent of trade.

And this isn't even Christmas Rush, Ruth thought to herself. Macy's was a little crowded, sure, but not impossible to navigate this early on a Saturday.

But what must it look like to someone who came from a realm of knights and castles, forests and quiet green fields?

If he did. If this weren't all some long elaborate hoax. But how, otherwise, to explain those eyes, those ears, except by the tale that Melior himself told, of war, treachery, and elfin magic?

Beware, beware/His flashing eyes, his floating hair, Ruth thought sourly. But if he froze up like hell's own autism poster child at the sight of a department store, how in heaven's name was Melior of the Silver Silences going to be able to get enough of a grip to search for a demon-infested magic sword in New York City?

But it was less than five minutes later that Melior released his death grip upon Ruth's arm and sighed.

"This is a marketplace?" he asked, in even, if faintly disbelieving, tones.

"It's Macy's. The world's largest department store," Ruth added apologetically. "I know it's a zoo, but we can get everything we need here."

"Except the Sword," Melior said with a ghost of a smile. "Except that."

Without Michael's checklist it would have been harder, since neither Ruth nor Melior had any idea of Melior's sizes. But socks and underwear were achieved without difficulty, and they went on to the next thing on Ruth's list.

"Shoes. You'll feel better once you've got proper shoes that fit." Ruth said hopefully. She consulted the store directory and headed them in the direction of the shoe department.

Melior's head was constantly in motion, turning to look at this and that, watchful, all of him moving with a kind of frantically-achieved stillness, a suppressed kinesthesia that made Ruth's jaw ache in sympathetic tension. He restricted himself to brief questions, all his will directed toward learning the parameters of this world he was trapped in. In the shoe department Melior was discouraged from his first choice—

"Not those."

"Why not, Ruth?"

"They're rain boots. For women."

—and became the proud owner of a pair of black leather high-tops (for which Ruth paid, wincing at the price, but this had been her idea, dammit). Michael's Chinese boxing slippers went into the bag; Melior wore the sneakers, looking somehow even less normal the closer he came to being properly clothed.

Next they recrossed the store to the men's clothing department. Ruth had been thinking of something casual, yet conservative: clothes, she vaguely thought, like Michael wore, bland and inoffensive. She headed for the display of blue jeans. *This won't take long,* she thought hopefully. Melior followed her.

"Here we are: Levis for It. We'd better try a few different sizes; Michael wasn't sure, but he thought a thirty-four inseam. . . ."

"No."

Ruth looked up. Melior ran his hand over the mound of folded clothing. He held up one pair—heavy folded cotton *de Nimes,* as it was once called, denim indigo-dyed, stiff and harsh—and shook his head.

"I cannot wear this, Ruth," Melior said.

"What's wrong with them?" she burst out, "They're *jeans,* dammit. I wear them, Michael wears them, everybody wears them!"

"Michael's are not like this." Melior reached out and stroked the fabric of her wool plaid skirt. "And you are not wearing them now." Melior tossed the jeans back in their pile, not appearing to notice Ruth's flustered retreat. The jeans hit with a thump like a book being tossed down— heavy and unyielding.

"They'll get like Michael's with time," Ruth said, half-stammering.

"I do not have time," Melior said flatly. He reached out and put a hand on Ruth's shoulder, pulling her toward him. "You say I must have clothing of this world so that I may move freely in it. I understand that—and believe me, Ruth, I am grateful for the time and silver you expend in my service."

"Plastic," muttered Ruth. The corner of Melior's mouth quirked upward.

"But I do not dress this way for my own joy, but to serve an end. And I cannot serve that end rasped bloody by peasants' canvas trousers."

"Well what do you want—silk?" Ruth snapped. It was true that jeans had begun as work clothes, cheap and long-wearing for ranchers and farmers, but they had long since become (with all inconvenience retained) the universal dress of the twentieth century. She knew Melior wasn't from here, but when faced with Levis, empathy faltered. If he would not wear jeans, what would he wear?

"I want suitable clothing for this time and place," Melior corrected her softly. "Everyone does not wear these—and there are so many things for sale here. Let us but search a little farther, my friend, and try if we may not find something that suits both our needs."

Melior gave her his most dazzling smile, and in the dim strange neon light of the "Young Actives" department Ruth saw for the first time that his teeth were pointed; curved canines a little longer than the rest, slanting down to meet the upward thrust of pointed teeth in the lower jaw.

Great. Just what I need. A vampire elf.

"Okay. We'll keep looking."

Now it was Ruth who followed Melior as he prowled the aisles of the "World's Largest Department Store." Suddenly he stopped, fairly quivering, taut as a bowstring. Ruth followed his gaze.

"Oh, no. Not that. Anything but that."

This particular department swore that it sold clothes for men 18-25. Ruth imagined that those numbers must refer to their IQs, as she couldn't imagine any sensible person shopping in a department lit primarily by red, green, and amber key lights and the glare from a dozen monitors all tuned to different music videos.

The mannequins were flat silvery cutouts, headless and ostentatiously jointed and wearing clothing that Ruth had never seen on any living body that wasn't on television. Melior went up to one mannequin and felt the fabric of the baggy batik-printed rayon pants.

"Yes, Ruth, here. If you please," Melior said.

In the end it was jeans they settled on—but jeans as soft and pliant as Melior's own buckskins; acid washed, frayed, and artistically patched. Melior ran his fingers over them and then held them up to his narrow hips, looking questioningly at Ruth.

"After all this you want jeans anyway?" Ruth gibed. The light made her eyes hurt and the music made her teeth hurt; she wondered why the management didn't just set off smoke pots if their aim was to drive customers out of the store.

"These are different," Melior said inarguably. "And I have seen many here wearing garments such as these."

"Well, you'd better try them on," Ruth said grudgingly.

Armed with a range of sizes—as Michael's list contained approximations, nothing more—Melior vanished into the dressing room. Ruth took advantage of his absence to collect for his future use a red snakeskin belt with a *faux*-silver buckle. Thank God she'd talked him out of the pink-and-turquoise baggies. Or the red, acid-washed, overdyed jumpsuit. Or the tie-dyed spandex jodhpurs. Or—

Honestly, Ruth, get a life. You're going on like you're dressing up a doll. Buying clothes like this—spending all this money—and it isn't even for yourself. You'll be paying this off until the Last Trump, and for what?

"It's worth it," Ruth muttered back at herself. "And he's worth it. And I don't want clothes like this for me, I want—" She ran the sinuous length of the supple leather through her hands, ran the ball of her thumb over the cold hard sculpture of the buckle. *I want someone who dresses like this for me.*

"Is this suitable, Ruth?" Melior had come out of the dressing room while she daydreamed; he stood before her—*a ghost of rags and patches*—in artistically-frayed and very tight jeans that molded the entire swell and sweep of calves and thighs and anchored Melior firmly in the twentieth-century world. His hair had come loose of its tie and flowed over his shoulders. He looked like a particularly delectable rock star; silvery and shining and insulated from mortal touch.

"Ruth?" Melior said again.

"It's good, it's fine, let's go pay for it, okay?"

Melior regarded her closely. "What is wrong, Ruth? Is this so unsuitable? I admit that I find this *department store* very strange, but surely you should not?"

"Go on. Take them off so we can go pay for them, okay? After all, they don't matter—they're just part of your equipment for this impossible mission, right?" She looked away in frustration, and when she looked back, Melior had retreated to the dressing rooms again.

"I do not withdraw my question," Melior said, once this new purchase had been added to their growing store and he and Ruth were out in one of the main aisles again.

"I'm so glad to hear it. Why don't we go get lunch—my feet hurt."

"I will not be toyed with," Melior said, stopping dead. Shoppers detoured around him, giving him wary and resentful looks. A small child, towed away by its uninterested parent, cried: "Ears, Mommy!" pointing up at Melior.

Ruth stopped, too, and looked back at him.

"Fine. Nobody's toying with you. God knows I'm not stupid enough to do something like that, great big dangerous interdimensional vampire elf as you are, and there's nobody else here. Whatever the problem is, it isn't you, and you wouldn't be able to understand the explanation anyway, so why don't you get off my case and let's go get some lunch?"

Melior took the time to think this through, giving her entire speech his active consideration for possibly two minutes while Ruth stood, glaring and irritated all out of proportion to the offense, and waited.

"We have not finished our shopping yet," Melior offered.

Ruth took a deep breath. Other shoppers swirled around them, oblivious.

"Fine. We will finish our shopping. And then we will go get lunch. And so we can go get lunch before the next glacial age is·on us, we are going to buy what *I* pick out and what *I* think you ought to be wearing and you are not going to argue with me. Is that clear?"

"Perfectly clear, Ruth," Melior said, with the corner of his mouth quirked in that maddening half-smile.

And that, of course, was how they wound up in possession of the black leather motorcycle jacket (on sale).

Ruth swept back through the menswear department like an avenging angel with a mission to shop and a tight deadline. She picked out a black turtleneck sweater, a white "river diver's" shirt with twelve tiny silvery buttons down the placket, and an orange-cotton T-shirt that said *"It's not my planet, monkey-boy"* in raised black paint-spatter letters. Along the way she collected a pair of Ray-Ban aviator sunglasses with a beetle wing mirrored finish, in the hope that they'd help to make him more *normal* looking. She thrust them at him as soon as they were paid for.

"Here! Put these on!"

Melior did, and was instantly transformed into an F.B.I. agent from Betelgeuse. But at least his eyes were hidden.

His flashing eyes, his floating hair—oh, stop it, Ruth!

And having filled out Michael's list and gotten Melior as much in the way of clothing as your average (male) freshman brings to college, she saw the jacket.

There were three of them left, hanging on one of those

movable stands that retailers use to tempt the unwary. Ruth
went closer and looked. "Sale," the sign said. "End of Season." Ruth ran her hand over the sleeve. Hard and slick, ac-
rid with the chemicals of its tanning. Lined in a slick acrylic
satin, almost as black. A thing of studs and buckles, zippers,
flanges, pulls, and straps. Twentieth century armor for a
real-world dark knight.

He'll need a jacket, Ruth argued to herself with insane
practicality. *It'll be useful.* But that wasn't why she wanted
to buy it and she knew it.

"Melior? Come over here; I want you to try something
on."

He wore it so she wouldn't have to carry it. It meshed
with the mirrorshades and clashed oddly with the dobby
sweater. They were almost out of the store when Ruth remembered one last thing.

"Hat."

"I beg your pardon, Mistress?"

"Hat," said Ruth. "We'll get you a hat. Covers a multitude
of sins—and ears," she added, remembering the little boy.
They'd been lucky so far.

They retraced their steps. Macy's was always changing its
ground-floor layout. All the impulse purchases were there—
and the luxuries. Jewels and perfume, silk scarves . . . and in
this day and age, hats. Ruth led him toward the haberdashery
display.

"It doesn't have to be much," she said. "This?" Ruth held
up a watch cap, silky black cashmere, and looked at Melior
hopefully. "No. That." Melior turned away and reached for
the hat: black, fur-felt with a low crown and a wide, sweeping, oval brim. He picked it up.

"That's a woman's hat," Ruth pointed out.

"I don't care. I like it." He put it on, settled it on his head
and looked in the mirror, gazing at his reflection, face half-
hidden by the sweep of brim; a cipher in mirrorshades and
leather. And he didn't look silly at all—he looked fine, better than fine, like a fey horseman riding out from the other
world to claim—

What?

Not me, Ruth thought, firmly bundling her imaginings
away. *I already know what he wants.*

"Okay. Fine. You want to look like Doctor Who? We'll take it."

"Do not bother to pack it," Melior said with his new command of idiom, "I shall wear it out of the store."

"Don't you think you'd better take the tag off first?"

And so they emerged, blinking and ravenous, from the underworld of the consumer-driven marketplace at about 2:30 of a fine Saturday afternoon. Ruth led them down Broadway until she found what she was looking for: a Blimpie's, chosen on this occasion because it had both seating and table service. She led Melior to a table in the back and handed him the menu. Melior stared at it for a moment, then handed it back.

"I cannot read this, Ruth."

She stared at him in surprise. She had just naturally assumed Melior could read—he seemed so *civilized*, that it was just ridiculous to think of him as illiterate.

"There was little time for scholarship during the War, but I can write a passable hand in Court and Common, read those and half-a-dozen more, and spell a passable *dweomer* in the alphabet of high sorcery," Melior offered in response to her blank look.

"But?" Ruth prompted, knowing there must be more.

"But here in the World of Iron I cannot read your sigils. Any of them."

"But you speak English!" Ruth protested.

"Do I? I imagine I would speak the common tongue of whatever land I found myself in. It is the way of things when one goes Gatewalking."

"Well this land hasn't *got* a common tongue! And everyone here can read. Mostly."

"So I gather. And so can I read, though not here. Perhaps you will teach me, if there is time." Melior took her hand across the table.

World enough and time. Had we but world enough, and time/Thy coyness, Lady, were no crime. . . .

"Hey, uh, excuse me. I saw you come in, and—could I have your autograph?"

Ruth jerked her hand away from Melior and looked up. The boy was standing in front of Melior, looking at him hopefully. He had on jeans and scuffed white sneakers and a sleeveless denim jacket open over an indeterminate heavy metal T-shirt. He thrust a copy of the restaurant's take-out menu at Melior.

"I really love you, man. I love you a lot," the boy said.

"Ah." Melior looked from the boy to Ruth and back. "Certainly. A pen, please, Ruth."

Ruth took the precaution of uncapping the pen before she handed it to him—no matter how sophisticated he was, Melior could never have seen a pen like her 89-cent Flair. But he took it without a bobble, and signed the menu in swooping curlicues of florid purple that matched no alphabet Ruth had ever seen.

"Hey, man, thanks—I saw you in concert last year. Got all your albums." The boy departed, still talking over his shoulder, and hit only one table and the trash can on the way out.

Ruth held out as long as she could and then burst out laughing.

"And what," asked Melior when she had subsided somewhat, "was that about?"

"Oh, wait till I tell Nai! He thought you were a *rock star*, Melior—it must be the jacket. And he— And you—" The thought was too much for her; the previous tension too great; Ruth began to laugh again. "What did you write?" she finally managed.

"My name. It was what he wanted, was it not? And now, will you read this ordinary to me so that we may be at meat?"

It was fortunate for Ruth that, lifelong anachronist that she was, she was aware that an ordinary was the bill of fare at an inn. After some consultation Melior chose a chicken sandwich and herb tea. Ruth had a tuna salad and coffee. The waiter who brought them smiled as if they were all in a conspiracy together.

Now that she was habituated to it she could see it: Melior acted like a rock star, a celebrity, and people treated him as one. Or perhaps it was the other way around, but now that she was looking it was impossible to miss the aura of anticipation, of charisma, of grand seigneur expectation that even New York roused itself to meet. Melior was famous, Melior was news—whoever they thought he was.

They dawdled over lunch. Ruth took the time to organize all the purchases into two large shopping bags; Melior removed Michael's borrowed wet-sheepdog sweater and put on the new orange T-shirt. Ruth saw herself reflected in his sunglasses as she read its printed slogan once more. *"It's not my planet." Right. And what if it isn't?*

If this were happening in a book or a movie, Ruth would have had her expectations ready. Whoever had tripped over this wonder should take it directly to the authorities. Fictional people rarely did, of course, and Ruth, reading or watching, was always vastly indignant with whoever allowed the strangeness to simply slip away unrecorded; to keep it selfishly and not add it to the universe's store of marvels.

But it wasn't as easy as that. *It never is. . . .* If she believed Melior was a lord out of Faery—*and I do*, Ruth promised herself fiercely—who could she tell? The Mayor? The President?

Faced with the personal task of making someone notice the unlikely truth about reality, Ruth realized she wasn't up to it.

And Melior was not some abstract cultural phenomenon; not an Elvis sighting in a 34th Street deli. Melior was a person, with things that he needed.

And she would rather give Melior what he needed than pay homage to some ideal of civic-mindedness that was as much a dead issue as the White Man's Burden.

In the end, what Melior was didn't matter. His existence made Ruth's world no wider.

"Come on. Let's go find a subway."

Melior held his tongue until they reached the street. Heads turned to look at him; Melior looked back.

"Subway's this way," Ruth said. "Come on. We've got to get back."

"I know. I will not go in those ways again. I will walk," Melior said. He looked up—taking his bearings from the sun, Ruth realized—and set off.

By the time they reached 42nd Street Ruth realized he was completely serious. He strode down the sidewalk perfectly possessed of both himself and it—*nobody would ever guess he'd been mugged flat last night,* Ruth thought admiringly—gazing openly around himself in a fashion no New Yorker would be caught dead doing, with the cold May sunlight glinting on the silvery spill of his unbound hair; flashing off the oil-slick surfaces of his sunglasses' lenses, and glinting upon the innumerable chrome widgets of his black leather jacket.

Jaded New York crowds parted for him as if they were the Red Sea. Ruth, soldiering on behind with two shopping bags full of underwear, was less fortunate.

She put up with this as far as 79th Street—Museum Row, and lovely and dangerous Central Park on her right hand. The pedestrian traffic was thinner here, and Melior had slowed down enough about an hour before for her to keep up with him.

"It's only a couple of stops on the subway to Michael's from here," she offered, having finally called a rest. She dumped the bags on one of the green wooden park benches that lined the sidewalk here and collapsed beside them, throwing a wary protective arm over them. Melior showed no sign of flagging.

"No. You may take the subterranean way, if you will. I shall walk."

"Walk? How are you going to walk? You can't find Michael's by yourself—you can't read the street signs!"

"I know the way lies north, and that the river is to the west of us. If I follow the river I will find it—and that I will do gladly, rather than venture into your underworld again."

Underworld is a good name for it, Ruth thought wryly. She did her best to remember that, no matter how frazzled she felt, she was at least in her right world, with no particular sins of omission hanging over her. Melior was not.

"All right. Okay." She rummaged in her purse and dragged out her wallet, scrabbling through it until she located the remains of her cash machine advance. She counted it carefully. "Fine. Let's take a taxi, then—I'm not going to walk another forty blocks carrying your underwear."

Hailing a cab was a difficult process—at least until Melior properly understood what a taxi was and why it was wanted. Then he simply stepped out into the traffic in front of one, bringing it to a horn-blaring stop.

"You could have gotten killed!" Ruth said once they were both inside.

"Yeah—you tell 'im, lady. Crazy foreigners. Where to?" the cabdriver agreed.

"One-sixteenth and Riverside, please." They might as well go all the way up to her and Naomi's place, so long as they were taking a taxi.

"But I was not killed, Ruth. And one can be killed in so

many ways. Every exercise of skill is a risk," Melior pointed out as the taxi began to roll.

"You don't know how things work here—you can't just take it for granted—"

"That the hired car will stop?" Melior smiled. "Ruth, I do not. And though this is a ghastly place, it is not entirely different from some places I have seen. It is only more so."

Only more so. What a convenient and time-saving way of putting things.

The ride uptown was brisk and uneventful. They stopped right in front of Ruth's apartment; the fare was seven-fifty, and Ruth, unwilling to argue, gave the cabby a ten. This left precious little in her wallet, and she hesitated even to total the Macy's charge slips lying like a nest of vipers at the bottom of her purse. But it was worth it. By dressing Melior in earthly raiment she made him hers, sort of. Or maybe it was a way of giving him all the help she could in regaining his sword.

The Sword of Maiden's Tears. Every time she tried to think about it sensibly, her mind skittered away, as from something too God-knows-what to take seriously. But the Sword—and its absence—was the central problem that had to be faced.

He'll never find it. Never. This is New York. It's gone. And it would be a minor life triumph if Ruth could figure out whether that made her happy or sad—and why.

CHAPTER 6

My Dinner with Melior

Ruth could smell the powerful fragrance of baking bread and Something-with-Burgundy the moment she arrived on the seventh floor. Melior's nose twitched, too; he looked at her, eyebrows raised questioningly.

"Oh, God, I forgot. Saturday dinner," Ruth said. "Everybody will be here."

"With such an ornamental puzzle presented for their delectation, how could they not be?" Melior said.

"Don't flatter yourself. Naomi's cooking. Everybody'd be here anyway," Ruth said.

Saturday—or sometimes Sunday—dinner at Ruth and Naomi's (Naomi's, really) had become something of an institution. Even splitting the cost of the raw materials four ways (Naomi provided the kitchen and skill) it wasn't as expensive as a no-holds-barred dinner out, and it was light-years above the *cuisine de scholastique* available in the Columbia dining hall.

More important even than that, Naomi's dinners took hours to prepare, and anyone who wished could profitably spend the day in the apartment, mincing garlic and the reputation of absent friends in an atmosphere of togetherness.

And that, thought Ruth with a cool dispassionate intelligence, was something none of them could get anywhere else, wasn't it? The thing that drew them all together was that all of them, each of them, was alone. Alone, but not loners. Just people who didn't fit in anywhere, which by some merciful alchemy made them more tolerant of others who somehow didn't fit. *How unlike life*, Ruth thought cynically.

When she opened the front door, the first thing she saw was Jane—surrounded by books, of course. Jane's guitar in its case sat propped primly against the wall under the window. Jane looked up as Ruth entered—and looked wholly disapproving as she saw Melior.

I wonder what that's about, Ruth thought.

"They're ba-a-a-ack," Jane called toward the kitchen. She made one more entry in her notebook, closed it with a slam, and began stacking the books in a neat pile to one side of the table. Ruth glanced at the spine-labels: 398 and 291—Folklore and Mythology.

"Ruth? Is that you?" Naomi called from the kitchen.

"No, it's Jack the Ripper," Ruth called back. She thrust the bags at Melior. "Why don't you go put on your jeans so everyone can get the full effect?" Ruth said, and headed for the kitchen without looking back.

Naomi was there, bending over and peering into the oven, which gave forth its lovely scent. She looked up when Ruth entered.

"Beef with Burgundy. It's cheap, it's stupid, it'll feed fifty. And how was *your* day?"

"Vertical?" Philip added sweetly.

"You're not tall enough for that gesture, Mrs. Siddons." Ruth shot back. Philip was crouched gnomelike on the step stool shoved under the window. One of Naomi's mixing bowls was on his lap; he stirred the contents intermittently with a long wooden spoon. She wondered how Naomi had ever gotten him to help.

"Melior thinks he saw his sword."

Although, looking back on those crowded few minutes outside Macy's, she wasn't sure that "saw" was the word she wanted. Sensed?

"Fine," said Naomi. She peeled up the foil on the pan in the oven and prodded mystically beneath it. Satisfied, she closed the oven. "We can talk about that after dinner. Michael's going to be a little late; he called."

"Off hocking Elfie's stuff," Philip added, surprisingly helpful (for Philip). His glasses flashed as he looked down at the bowl and started stirring again.

"Faery gold vanishes in the light of the sun." Jane edged into the kitchen beside Ruth. Jane herself looked as though she might vanish in the light of the sun, assuming she ever saw it. For one still cursed with the puppyish roundness of unshed baby fat, Jane gave a surprising air of insubstantiality. Her mouse-blonde hair (indifferently long), straggled down over the shoulders of the "pretty in pink" shetland sweater she wore. She shoved her glasses up on her nose again.

"It's just a good thing that the sunlight never reaches street level, or Michael'd be in trouble. I wish he'd go away," she added under her breath. Ruth knew it wasn't Michael she meant, but Jane had barely met Melior. What could he possibly have done to tick off Jane?

"Okay, you guys, get out of my kitchen. Ruth, why don't you go see if Mel would like a cup of tea, or something? Dinner won't be ready for an hour or so. Michael said you went clothes shopping, so I dug out an old suitcase to donate to the cause; it's on my bed."

"What's that?" Ruth pointed to the bowl Philip was stirring.

"Wouldn't you like to know?" Philip said.

"Out," Naomi insisted.

Jane preceded Ruth into the living room. Ruth, blissfully unwary in the comfort of her own home, looked up to see Jane's back stiffen into silent, long-suffering disapproval.

Melior had taken Jane's guitar out of its case.

One would not necessarily think of Jane in connection with the guitar. Guitars seemed so frivolous, somehow. Jane's whole nature cried out for nothing less than a grand piano, funereal in black lacquer, but as Real Life is conducted without an art director, Jane had come among them with an entirely ordinary acoustic guitar that reposed, when not in use, in a black fiberboard case innocent of paint or decals.

In Melior's hands, the guitar became a different thing entirely.

He had slung the strap over his back, but held the instrument almost vertically, his long pale fingers wrapped about the neck. His free hand stroked the strings and the sound box as if the guitar's whole shape were faintly unfamiliar but one that he was learning fast. His head was lowered, his face turned toward the guitar. In jeans and T-shirt, sneakers and sunglasses and long silver hair, he could be taken for any normal student at Columbia—and that made him just as much an outsider in this room as being an elf-king did.

"You shouldn't take things that don't belong to you," Jane said in a tight voice.

Melior looked up and focused on her. "I beg your pardon, Mistress." He dipped his head to slip the strap over it and held out the guitar. "My reckless curiosity has ever been my sin." He looked at Ruth. "And does this habiliment meet with your approval?" He held out the guitar.

"You look just like all the other kids," Ruth said.

"But you don't wear sunglasses indoors unless you want people to think you're a junkie," Jane added. "Are there guitars in Elfland?"

The question could have been either offensive or ingenuous, but Jane's perfectly-controlled tone gave no clue as to which it should be.

"Things similar," said Melior, still holding the guitar toward Jane. "And do you play?"

"No," said Jane, "I just carry it around for fun." She plucked it out of his hands, giving the impression of a small field mouse skittering around a large lion, and went to replace it in its case.

Children, thought Ruth, from the vantage of a decade's seniority. "Naomi says that dinner won't be for at least an hour. Do you want some tea?"

"Yes, I thank you," Melior said. "And is there perhaps a map of this city?"

"I've got maps," Jane said surprisingly. "I'll get the tea." She flipped the locks of the guitar case shut and went off to the kitchen again. Ruth looked at Melior.

"I am strange here, as well as a stranger," he observed. "Is it true, Ruth, that of all the Five Races only humans abide in the World of Iron? I had heard that was true, but it is always desirable to have firsthand information." He removed the sunglasses carefully and set them on the table. The silvery lenses reflected back at Ruth like a second set of eyes.

Ruth sat down on the couch, and got the benefit of the westering sun full in the face. "And what are the Five Races?—by which you may understand that, yes, as far as I know nothing but humans live here. There are rumors, of course," she added darkly, "but they're only fairy tales—myths."

"I am put in my place," Melior observed. "The Five Races are those peoples able to use magic. They live in the World That Is, though not all live together in one Land. In my own, humans and my kind live—and perhaps the Sea People, although they are wild and canny and dislike to meddle in the affairs of landsmen unless they can do so to their own advantage."

"How like life," Ruth muttered. "So there are mermaids? With tails?"

Melior raised his eyebrows and looked amused. "I have not enquired. But to summarize," he went on, his tone of voice putting Ruth forcibly in mind of some of her duller professors, "the Five Races which abide in the lands of the World That Is are these: the Earth Born, which are called humans; the Sea Born, called merfolk and *ceildhe;* Night's Children, who have as many names and forms as the stars cast shadows; and my own kind."

"The elves," Ruth supplied. "And that's only four."

"Ah," said Melior, "but you are not a scholar of the mysteries, and I will not burden you with gossip you will never have a use for. And "elves" is only what the Earth Born call us."

"Elf. In German, *Erl.* From the Old Teutonic *Eorl,* meaning 'Lord,' which passed into English from Saxon as 'Earl,' " Jane said. She set down the tiny tray with the brown Rockingham teapot and the sugar and creamer.

"So you do remember," Melior said.

"Not personally," Jane said. "And that has to steep."

Melior withdrew his hand from the teapot.

"So what do you call yourselves?" Ruth asked. She half-suspected she was being made the butt of an elaborate joke, with all this highfalutin taxonomy of races and titles. Modern anthropology had proven that every society called itself Us, and everyone else it met, Them.

"The Folk of the Air," Melior said quietly. "The Sons of the Morning and the Daughters of Twilight. The Star-Begotten."

"Twinkle, twinkle," said Philip mockingly from the safety of the doorway.

If Melior had done what Ruth half expected—flayed Philip where he stood with a backlash of hauteur and pride—it would have been possible for Ruth to successfully dislike him (even though she, herself, frequently felt that Philip would have been a good deal better company if he had been drowned at birth). But instead, unexpectedly, he laughed.

"Perhaps all peoples—if they were honest—have too high an opinion of themselves! But I think it must be far stranger to think there are no other peoples in all the wide world—although this world is not so very wide," Melior said.

"What do you know about it?" Philip said aggressively. "You guys are still fighting with cavalry and swords—what do you know about guns and bombs—and airplanes? Or computers? Or spaceships?"

"Nothing," said Melior, in tones that suggested he did not grieve for his lack. "And what do you know, my fine mannikin, of horsemanship, or sorcery, or Gatewalking; of the treaties that bind the Five Races—"

"Of which there are four," Ruth muttered.

"Or cars—" said Philip, adding to his list.

" 'In the time twixt the dark and the twilight/When the night is beginning to lower/Comes a pause in the day's occupations/That is known as For God's Sake, Shut Up, Philip,' " Jane misquoted strenuously. "We agreed; we could discuss this when Michael gets here."

Ruth realized that some agreement had been reached by the others while she and Melior were out; through a childish pang of hurt feelings at being excluded she wondered what exactly the agreement was.

The talk turned quickly and briefly to school; Ruth and Michael would graduate this June, but Philip and Jane both had another year to go. Ruth thought guiltily about her master's thesis, still unbegun. *"The Role of the Librarian in the Illiterate Society."* She wondered if there were elf-librarians, and what sort of books they guarded.

Having settled that he and Jane were both behind in their coursework and that it was a waste of time anyway, Philip flipped on the TV. The late-afternoon sunlight bleached the picture to oblivion, but the sound worked fine.

"A Bronx man is being sought in connection with the death of Roy Turpin, 36, of North Queens Avenue." The body was discovered early this morning by—" Ruth tuned out the sound and the pastel image of a shrouded body being bundled into a waiting ambulance. Just another beautiful day in Fun City.

"Your tea, Ruth." Melior sat down beside her, pushing a teacup gently into her hand.

She took it, but when she looked up to thank him he was not looking toward her. Melior was staring out toward the setting sun, his mouth set in a grim line.

Michael arrived at a quarter of eight, when the brownies that Philip had been mixing were long since baked and only perilously preserved from the depredations of starving students (or persons purporting to be starving students), an entire loaf of French bread had been anointed with garlic butter, toasted, and devoured, Ruth had removed the tags and staples from every one of the day's clothing purchases and stowed the clothing itself in a green vinyl suitcase of surpassing hideousness (she did not, even now, total her charge slips), and Naomi had finally said "the hell with it" and set the table.

"Hello, all," said Michael.

"It's about time you got here," Philip said.

"Oh, honestly, Philip, don't you ever think about anything but food? Don't answer that," Jane added.

"Hi," said Ruth and Naomi in ragged chorus.

Michael flung his windbreaker through the bedroom door and advanced on Ruth. "Okay, how much did you spend?" he asked.

"Why?" Ruth demanded suspiciously. Melior made a sound that could be taken (by the suspicious nature that even such a *sensible* person might be supposed to have) as amusement.

"You may understand that it must be a very great deal, my friend, or else she would tell you," Melior suggested.

"It couldn't be," Michael said. "Ruth doesn't *have* a very great deal of money."

"Oh, thank you so much, Michael Peacock. *For* your information, I followed your list exactly—"

"Almost exactly," said Melior.

"She got him a leather jacket," said Jane.

"It was on sale!" Ruth pointed out. "And he'll need it. He'll be cold."

"No he won't," said Philip with a smirk.

"Philip, dear, if you ever do find out what the facts of life are—" Ruth began.

"A leather jacket?" Michael said in tones of pained disbelief. "What's he going to do with a leather jacket? It's *May*."

"Join the road show of Shakespeare's Punk Elves in Bondage Revue," Jane said, looking as if it were nothing to do with her. "You can wear a leather jacket in the summer."

"I beg you will all stop discussing me as if I weren't here," Melior said. He did not raise his voice, but it cut efficiently through the cross-chatter. "I now possess a leather jacket, which was purchased at my insistence. It remains for Ruth to be reimbursed for this and for the other items."

"Right." Michael's face assumed an expression of studied disinterest, which would have been believable if not for the quirk in his mouth and the slant of his eyebrows. He pulled his wallet out of his hip pocket and pulled out a sheaf of bills bound together with a paper tape. It was not a terribly impressive sheaf until you realized that the "one" on each of the bills was followed by two zeroes.

"Five thousand dollars," Michael said. "Cold, hard, legal tender."

"Who'd you mug?" Philip asked with interest.

"Sold the earrings and all the sterling. Except this—" Michael dug deep into a pocket and flipped Melior's signet ring at him. Melior plucked it deftly out of the air and slipped it onto his finger.

Michael dropped the sheaf of bills into Ruth's hands. She stared at it as if it were a book she didn't want to read.

"I took the spurs down to the Met," said Michael, referring to the Metropolitan Museum of Art. "I've got a friend down there. Stephen Mallison. He's Arms and Armor, but he knows something about forgeries."

"Like the Cellini salt cellar," Jane said.

"I don't see why they had to take it off display just because it was fake," Ruth said. "It was an *old* fake—and besides, it was pretty."

"Beauty our only criterion," Naomi said.

"Pretty is Truth and Truth is Pretty—" Jane began.

"But anyway," Michael said, heaving the conversation back on track by dint of main force, "I showed him the spurs and told him *I'd* been told they came from Ancient Atlantis."

"And he believed you?" said Naomi with interest.

"Patience, my child. *I* didn't believe me; I made that clear. What I asked him was what they were really; I hinted I thought they were stolen."

"As a deception only," Melior clarified firmly.

(Philip: "What do you care, Elfie?" Naomi: "Philip—")

"I had to give him some reason why I'd come to ask him about them. Museums know what's old, expensive, and stolen—they have to in order to keep from buying it and then losing what they paid when they turn it over to the rightful owner. Anyway—"

"Dinner's getting cold," Naomi said. There was a brief interruption as food was brought from the kitchen and distributed. Ruth offered the money to Melior; he shook his head. She set it on top of the television set as a last resort and hoped nobody would forget about it, although how you could forget about fifty one hundred dollar bills was something beyond her capacity. When plates were full and most of his audience occupied with beef burgundy instead of airy badinage, Michael resumed.

"So he told me they were no more Atlantean than my grandmother and didn't look offhand to be very old. The workmanship was top drawer and they'd cost somebody a brick to make—solid gold rowels and all that—but Ancient Atlantean or ancient anything else they were not. He begged me to remind whoever I'd gotten them from that only mounted cultures which had invented the stirrup would have any use for spurs."

"I had a horse," Melior said. "It died. And the spurs?"

"I left them there; he said he'd show them around. You said sell them, so I didn't think you'd mind."

"Indeed not. You may keep them for all of me."

"So leaving aside however much Ruth spent on clothes—"

"Six hundred and eighteen dollars and thirty-five cents," Melior said.

Everyone at the table stared at him. Ruth's cheeks flamed, as if she'd been caught in secret sin.

"You told me it was a decimal currency, Ruth. One hundred cents to the dollar. The lackey recited the total each time you paid. I added it up," Melior explained. "Part of that is tax," he added.

"And the jacket was necessary," Naomi said, poker-faced.

"It was only—" Melior began.

"It was on sale!" Ruth interrupted.

"And that leaves," said Michael, who intended to become a children's librarian when he graduated and so had a great deal of practice in being heard over other conversations, "about four thousand dollars and change."

"Is this a great deal of money?" Melior asked.

Michael shrugged. "Depends on what you try to do with it." He applied himself to his dinner.

Four thousand dollars. Ruth was old enough to know that this wasn't the enormous amount of money it seemed—not when her and Naomi's joint rent and household expenses were nearly a thousand a month—but surely it was enough to last Melior until he found his sword.

And if he doesn't find it? He doesn't have a birth certificate, or a high school diploma, or a Social Security card. Or a passport—and where could they deport him to, anyway?

Dinner, having been so long delayed, was a swift, brutal business, accomplished mostly in silence. Finally Naomi cleared the plates away.

"And now, for dessert," she said.

"Damn! I forgot the ice cream!" Michael burst out. "It's in the freezer at my place. Look, Mel, I'll give you the keys—could you go down and pick it up for me?"

"That was the most unconvincing con job I've ever seen in my life." Ruth said, once the door had shut and the sound of Melior's footsteps on the stairs had been heard. "Why didn't you just say, 'Melior, why don't you get out of here so we can talk about you behind your back'?"

"Because doing it this way is what is called manners, Ruth dear," Naomi said. She sat down at the table. "I hereby declare the first meeting of the New York Council on Elvish Affairs in session."

"Right," said Michael. "And the first question is, who is this guy Ruth rescued last night really?"

"What's the second question?" Jane asked helpfully.

"Do we believe his story?" Naomi said.

"But if he's an elf—" Ruth began, and stopped.

"Very good," Michael said to her. "He could be a real elf with a fake story,"

"Or a fake elf with a fake story," said Philip, who was, in his own small way, a completest.

"Or a fake elf with a real story," said Jane, "although that means we still have to believe in *some* elves, just not *this* elf."

"Okay," said Naomi. "Reasons for believing he's an elf. Anyone? Ruth? You've spent the most time with him."

"Well," said Ruth. "He's got pointed ears."

"Plastic surgery," said Philip. "Makeup SFX."

"You'd see the line," Jane pointed out.

"Shut up, guys," said Michael. "Let Ruth think."

"And slit pupils, like a cat's," Ruth went on. "They reflect, too, like a cat's, and I've seen them change shape. People don't have eyes that green, and while that could be contact lenses, they don't reflect or make you pupil change shape like that. And his teeth are pointed," she rushed on, "like a—a wolf's. And it *could* be dental bonding, but *why?*"

" 'Why' comes later," Michael said. "Okay, he's got pointed ears and fangs and his eyes glow in the dark. And probably that isn't makeup; SFX makeup is meant to fool a camera, not a human eye; it just isn't that good. And something that isn't makeup is that beating he got last night. I looked him over then—it was pretty raw. But today his bruises are almost healed—and another thing. I looked him over pretty carefully twice. He's got a good set of muscles on him—and scars like you wouldn't believe. If you showed me that and told me this guy'd been off to a war where they fought with swords, I'd believe you."

"There's one other thing that isn't on your list," Jane said. "He could be a not-a-human-being and still not be an elf."

"Occam's razor," Naomi said.

"Or in English, cut to the chase," Philip added. "If he was a space alien, why say he's an elf?"

"Why not?" Jane shot back. "If he's a space alien, he doesn't think like an Earth person—and aliens are a lot more likely than *elves.*"

"Would you listen to yourself?" Philip said. "Space aliens are *likely?*"

"What reason do we have to *not* think Melior is an elf, after he's said he was one?" Naomi said pacifically. "Jane, you were looking through folklore today—what does it say about elves?"

Solicited in the area of her competence, Jane subsided.

"First, there are no reports of elves in America, only some unproven sixteenth century reports of 'weird black dwarves,' which lets our guy right out. Most of the folklore lumps elves right in with fairies, and it sort of boils down to: 'No force, there I was, out after dark and I saw this Real Weird Guy who took me home with him and we got to drinking and that's why I've been gone a week.' "

Jane shrugged. "Elves and UFO stories have a lot in common: time distortion, missing days, memory loss, and strange ailments suffered by those who've met them. In fact the descriptions of elves and of space aliens are almost identical, allowing for there being about seven hundred years between them, and this guy doesn't match any of them. What he really is, is a prime specimen of *genus Tolkienus*, the fictional elf. You know: tall, glowing, noble—"

"With a palantir strapped to his forehead and a long gray cape," supplied Naomi.

"He didn't say he was an elf. He said humans called his kind elves," Ruth pointed out, with a scrupulous regard for the facts.

"So we have a certain amount of physical evidence that Mel is Not From Around Here," Naomi summarized. "Anything else? Or opinions to the contrary?"

"The clothes and jewelry," Michael said. "It cost a lot to put that outfit together. If this were a con job that would net him a couple million, I could see a few thousand going to prime the pump. But it's *us* he's working this on—if it's a sting. There's no way he could get back his initial investment. So there's no reason to waste the money. And he was really thumped. Don't forget that."

"It's more than a few thousand. All those clothes were hand-sewn. Every stitch. They don't even do that for movie costumes anymore," Ruth said. She flung out her hands helplessly. "I can't even imagine what it would cost to make them."

"And don't forget the ring," Michael said. "It glowed. We all saw it. No lights, no wires."

"Not a dream, not a hoax, not an imaginary tale," Ruth said.

"And besides, I was looking around in cyberspace today. He wasn't there," Philip added. He dug around in the pack at his feet and laid something out on the table.

Photographs. Four Polaroid shots of Melior, looking pale and interesting, his eyes glowing like red moons in the flash.

"Just in case we want to fake him up some ID," Philip said. Naomi decided not to have heard him.

"Okay, show of hands: does everybody agree that Melior, who and whatever he really is, all semantics aside, doesn't come from here?" Naomi asked.

Ruth raised her hand, feeling a little ridiculous. Slowly, so did everyone else. Michael winked at her.

"Great. That subject's closed and isn't going to be debated any more. Saves time. Now, what about his story?"

"Which story?" said Jane. "The one about the elf-war?"

"I don't think we need to worry about that," Ruth said, after a pause. "I think the only thing we have to worry about is whether or not we believe that he lost a sword that he has to get back."

"Never mind that he's got a hope in hell," Philip said sweetly.

"Yeah, right, never mind that," Michael said.

"I think the question is, what would he want us to do to go looking for the sword?" Jane said. She fiddled with the hem of her sweater, staring off into space. "And what would happen if he didn't get it back? Really, I mean, and not just in elf-space. Here."

"He said," Ruth said, cudgeling her mind for scraps of a conversation that had seemed less important at the time than her own feelings, "I think he said that if a human had the sword, it was cursed—I mean, the sword was cursed whether a human had it or not, but its curse was, if a human had it, it—the human—would turn into some kind of monster."

"Tolkien again," Jane sighed. "Gollum, gollum, what has it got in its pocketses—can't these people ever be original?"

"Tolkien did it because it was an archetypal theme," Michael said. "The cursed thingummy that turns its owner into a beast. They're pretty thick on the ground in folklore and mythology."

"We'll just have to wait and ask Melior about it," Ruth said.

"You will not have to wait," said Melior.

CHAPTER 7

Fractured Fairy Tales: Hansel and Grendel

None of them had heard the door open. Melior stood there, with the bag containing the ice cream in one hand, and Ruth's keys on their brass ring keychain in the other.

He took those out of my purse! Ruth thought on a rising flare of indignation.

"You know," Naomi said with commendable calm, "you really shouldn't be back yet."

Melior smiled, wolf-teeth gleaming. "I ran," he said. "Both ways."

Ruth stared, with guilty complicity, at Melior's black high-topped leather sneakers.

"You spied on us," Jane said, as uninvolved as if she were reporting the weather.

"How did you get the door open without us hearing you?" Philip asked.

"Guile has its uses," said Melior, "and you were greatly involved. But since your councils were bound to affect me, I wished to know what their result was."

"You got back too soon," said Ruth. "We were just trying to figure out how you could possibly benefit by lying about the sword."

"We'd already decided you were an elf," said Naomi.

"I do not lie," Melior said. "Catch." He threw the bag, with fastball accuracy, straight at Michael.

He caught it with a thump. "I guess this means dessert."

"And then you can tell us all about your magic sword," Jane said. Philip sniggered. Ruth kicked at him but only succeeded in dislodging her precarious perch. She slid backward off the arm of the couch, but Melior was there to support her.

"You stole my keys!" she whispered to him in an accusing undertone.

Melior shrugged and released her. "I brought them back. I do not steal."

"Just like you don't lie?" Ruth shot back. Melior's eyebrows rose, a Mr. Spock gesture he could have no way of knowing was associationally hilarious.

"Exactly the way I do not lie, Ruth. I borrowed the keys."

"And would you borrow the truth?" Ruth shot back.

Something made her look sideways then, to meet Philip's china-blue gaze.

"Oh, go on," Philip said. "This is fascinating."

"Shut up, Philip," said Ruth and Melior in unwitting chorus. Philip made an obscure handsign and slithered off his chair to follow Michael and Naomi. Melior watched him go.

"Privacy," he said, "is a state devoutly to be wished for, and, like all wishes, unlikely to materialize."

"Look," Ruth began uneasily, "no one meant—"

Melior waved her to silence. "Of course you did. Who would not? Is that not true, Jane?"

"Sure." Jane was gazing aimlessly out the window, her lank mouse-blonde hair falling in snake-locks against the pink shetland sweater. To all intents and purposes she was paying no attention to Ruth and Melior. "We all voted you're an elf, so that's settled. But it doesn't mean you're a *nice* elf," she added, turning around.

"If he was nice, would he be hanging out with us?" Naomi said, coming back with brownies. "But seriously, Melior, none of us has any experience with sword-quests, or magic—"

"Or elves," interrupted Michael helpfully. He was carrying four dishes of ice cream, balanced perilously. Philip had the other two. Jane jumped up and went to unload Michael. "So naturally we're a bit curious," Michael went on.

Melior favored Michael with a crooked smile. "And you wonder how I twist my nets to lure you in. I cannot deny that I do, friend Michael. The stakes are too high; I need allies."

"Yes," said Michael carefully. "And we were sort of all wondering just what the high stakes are, you see."

"For myself, I lose all if I cannot present the sword when Baligant summons it. Myself, my kinfolk, all that I am or wish to be—gone." There was a pause, then Melior added, "I cannot imagine this tugs on human heartstrings greatly, and your charity in aiding me in this cause alone is rightly limited. Yet there is a matter that I would have—at least yesterday—held to be of your deepest self-interest."

"Why yesterday and not today?" Michael asked, getting his question in before Naomi elbowed him for interrupting.

"Because yesterday I believed you valued the life of your fellows—and today I see that this is simply not true. If hundreds, if thousands, if tens of thousands of your kind were to die, you are so many here you would not even notice."

"Way to go," breathed Philip.

"Why don't we just go back to pretending it's yesterday, then?" Ruth asked. She took a brownie and bit into it, distracted for a moment by pure chocolate ecstasy.

"Very well," said Melior. He prodded delicately at the mound of vanilla melting in the dish before him and obviously decided to leave well enough alone.

"If you don't want that, I'll eat it," Philip offered.

"Pig," said Jane.

"Slug."

"Louse."

"Maggot."

"*Children,*" said Naomi.

"Wormhole," Jane said, getting in the last word. Philip took Melior's dish and dug in, oblivious.

"About the end of life as we know it?" Naomi prompted helpfully.

Melior looked around at them all—wondering, Ruth suspected, why a group of mere humans took so little interest in a real live elf and his enchanted passions. Little did he know how wondrously the real world concentrated the mind—after a go at page one of the *Times* no one had much emotional energy left for any one else's problems, no matter how exotic the anyone. Other people's problems were distractions. And distractions made you lose your place on the ladder—not even of success, that would be too venal, but of simple garden variety survival.

Of course, after an eon or two of being, well, *sensible,* you got the reckless urge to gamble. To trade on other people's good natures, as they had so long traded on yours.

In short, thought Ruth crossly and personally, *one day you decide to chuck it all and get stupid.*

"The end of life as you know it," Melior repeated. "Perhaps. Perhaps only the ending of a great many lives. You did

not, either of you, find word of the Sword in your travels?"
He looked hopefully at Michael and Philip.

"That's another reason I went down to the Museum with
your spurs today. I'm guessing that if the sword is hocked,
sold, restolen, or just sent off to be appraised, Stainless
Steve'll get a hold of it at some point, or hear about it. As
of today, he hadn't."

"Nothing on the boards," said Philip. "I posted the reward. Maybe something will turn up."

"No," Melior said sadly. "If this—" he gestured with his
signet ring, "—has even a little magic, the Sword's wards
will be in full effect. At least for a while, and this while is
far too long for whoever has it."

"You keep saying that," Jane said, from the corner into
which she was barricaded. The Coke-bottle lenses of her
horn-rims turned to silver coins in the light as she tilted her
head. "You keep saying that, but could you be a little more
specific?"

"Very well, Mistress Jane, since you most particularly ask
it. The Sword of Maiden's Tears is, from a human's point of
view, cursed. One of the oldest and simplest spells—and
most powerful. Powerful enough, I fear, to work even here.

"Once a human seizes upon the Sword, he will begin a
transformation. A metamorphosis into a monster whose only
food is the flesh of the humans who were once his own kind,
and whose only desire is to retain possession of the Sword.
A reasonable desire, that, as once the transformation takes
place, the Sword is the only thing that can kill him."

"What about an atomic grenade?" asked Philip.

"Have you *got* an atomic grenade, Philip?" asked Jane.

"The only thing," Melior repeated. "Not fire, not sorcery,
not boiling lead nor cold iron. The Sword alone will slay the
grendel."

There was a pause. "Beowulf," said Jane.

"By the shore of Gitche Gumee/By the shining Big-Sea-
Water?" quoted Michael inquiringly.

"Wrong poem," said Ruth. "That's Longfellow."

"Grendel is a proper name," said Jane. "The name of the
monster who slew—and ate—King Hrothgar's warriors every night until Beowulf slew him. By ripping his arm off,"
Jane added, with gloomy relish. "It's an epic Olde English
poem from around 1000."

"*Grendels* are bespelled humans," Melior said. "They are

often used as guards. The transformation cannot be reversed, as it feeds upon a human's inmost heart to find the fuel for its work."

"Real scientific, Elfie," breathed Philip.

"Never mind the details," said Naomi just a little sharply. "So you're saying that whoever has that sword of yours will turn into a cannibal monster?"

"No. Only any human who seizes it. Against the Morning Lords this magic will have no effect. It was thought, at the time, to be a security measure," Melior said disgustedly.

"Okay, one monster. Height, weight, distinguishing marks? Last known address?" asked Michael.

Melior looked at him as if he suspected, for a moment, that Michael might be joking. Then he relaxed with a visible effort. "If I knew where it was, Friend Michael, I would go there and take the Sword back. Each hour it possesses the Sword renders it more powerful. And each kill. As it kills— and feeds—this hapless human will begin to grow, and change. A *grendel* never ceases to grow; some I have seen are enormous. The larger they are, the less human their form; they begin to go about on all fours. . . ."

Melior roused himself from what appeared to be a private memory. "You will know the *grendel* because it will not look elvish or human. And because it will be trying to kill you."

"Terrific," said Michael.

"Could you be a little more specific?" said Jane. "Like, how stupid is it? And if it walks around in broad daylight munching people, somebody's going to notice."

"The *grendel* is cunning, but is said to lack human reason. They shun the light; the older ones can stand it for short periods, but a man when he is first made *grendel* will instinctively retreat to a cave or other cover of darkness. As for the kills—" again Melior shrugged, and an expression of helpless frustration made a mask of his features, "—I had hoped they would be noticed, and reported to the magistrate or mayor of this town—"

Philip snorted.

"—but now I know they will not be." Melior put his head in his hands. After a moment's hesitation, Ruth put an arm about his shoulders.

"That isn't true." Everyone looked at Naomi. There was a frown line between her eyes, as if she were trying to reason

something out. She ticked off the points on her fingers as
she spoke. "We have a mugger who has your sword. Having
it—you say—will turn him into a monster, a *grendel* that
will murder—"

"And eat," said Philip helpfully.

"And eat people, hide during the day, and can't be killed
by anything but your sword. What does that suggest to everybody? Come on: the category is Fairy Tales and Folklore."

"I'd like to buy a vowel, Vanna," Michael said. Naomi
made a face at him.

"Werewolves?" said Ruth finally.

"Got it in one. And do you think werewolves won't make
the six o'clock news? He'll turn up," Naomi said grimly.

Melior looked at her, suddenly hopeful. "One could
wish," he said carefully, "that it did not require so many
deaths to reveal his presence."

"It's okay," Jane said comfortingly. "If your werewolf
didn't kill them, they'd probably die anyway."

"Almost certainly, given enough time," Ruth said editori-
ally.

"But it would be nice to catch our elvish Godzilla before
he started racking up a body count," Michael said, "if only
for neatness' sake."

"How?" said Philip, in his best "imitation of someone being helpful" voice.

"Consider his airs and his graces/And the way he kicks
over the traces/The shape of his head/And the width of his
bed/And be sure that you cover all bases," singsonged Jane
from some lost mine of doggerel.

"For the Snark *was* a boojum, so you see," added Naomi.

Melior looked from one to the next, baffled.

"Don't worry about it." Ruth squeezed his shoulder. "We're
like this all the time."

"Except when we're worse," Philip said, grinning evilly.

"But we'll help," said Michael firmly. "Right, guys?"

There was a pause, during which no one disagreed.

"What else have we got to do with our time," said Philip.
"Pursue higher learning?"

"Okay," said Naomi. "I declare the first official meeting
of the New York Council on Elvish Affairs closed. We help
Melior find his sword."

* * *

And what then? Ruth wondered, almost twenty-four hours later. The party the night before had broken up late; Melior departing with Michael and the maps of New York City that Jane had brought. Ten miles by two and home to eleven million people—how were they going to find one enchanted werewolf in all that?

Especially since it's so full of neighborhoods that I don't think even a werewolf would enter alone, Ruth thought. She stared at her textbook. She'd been staring at the same page for half an hour and had yet to make sense of it.

She had no real reason for believing that Melior would come to the apartment today. He'd gone home with Michael. Ruth fingered the bundle of currency on the table before her. And forgotten his money.

Why should Melior think anything more of her than he did of any of the others? So she'd taken him shopping, for God's sake. It wasn't as if it were the equivalent of a formal proposal. Just because he was the most exciting, exotic thing to happen to her ever. . . .

Didn't mean that the reverse was true.

The phone rang.

"Hello?"

"I wish to speak to Ruth." Melior's voice, sounding small and uncertain.

"Melior? It's me. Ruth. How are you?"

"I am arrested. They have said I may make one telephone call. I did not know who else to call, Ruth."

Ruth had never been any closer to a police station than an episode of *Hill Street Blues* and she didn't want to be here now. She had the wholly unfair superstitious feeling that she would be arrested, too; not for anything she had done or not done, but simply at some draconian whim. Ruth had been under the grindstone of the system; it was not an experience she cared to repeat.

"Excuse me," Ruth said carefully to the receptionist, "I'm here to pick up somebody." *I hope.*

And there civilized converse ended, because she had no idea what sort of name Melior might have given—if any— and she knew he didn't have any ID on him. But the receptionist, if not exactly gracious, was patient with Ruth's patent bewilderment, and soon Ruth found herself talking to a uniformed sergeant who was equally disinterested, and equally patient. What was her relation to the individual? When had he been arrested? Did she know the charge?

"I don't know," Ruth repeated helplessly, beginning to want to cry. She wished that she'd waited for Naomi, or called Michael, or even asked Jane to go with her. She'd never felt so helpless. "I don't know; he called me maybe an hour ago. Do I need a lawyer? Can I see him?"

There were none of the comfortable courtesies of Televisionland available here; when she saw Melior again, it was in the middle of a crowded hallway, and his hands were cuffed in front of him and he was sitting on a crowded bench with a number of other people, all under the watchful eye of a policeman. The black leather jacket that had made him look so trendy yesterday was scuffed now and only made him look hoodish; the mirrorshades lent his face an alien reptilian coldness.

"Ruth!" he exclaimed, and, to the uniformed patrolman, "There! I have sent for my hostage—now release me." He jumped to his feet and the handcuff chain jangled as Melior pulled on it. Ruth had a sudden snapshot vision of the links breaking outright. The cop put a hand on his baton—and who could blame him?, Ruth thought with a dash of desperate empathy.

"Nice to see you, too," she said, her voice shaking only slightly. "Good thing you remembered my number."

"Are you his sister, ma'am?" the policeman asked.

"Yes. Yes, I am. Please, what has he done?"

"Tried to beat the fare. Refused to take his summons. If you want to pay his fine now, you can both go home."

Ruth felt her knees go weak; the giddy relief was like half a bottle of Scotch. "Yes. Yes, thank you. I'll pay the fine."

The officer took a clipboard off the wall and sorted through the papers on it. He removed a sheet and handed it to Ruth. "Room 202, ma'am. The clerk will give you a receipt to bring back here."

Ruth took the paper. The policeman pointed off down the hall. Melior started to follow, and the policeman put a hand on his shoulder, warningly. Melior looked ready to explode.

"Sit down," snapped Ruth, as to an erring collie. "Wait here and mind your manners. I'll be back as soon as I can."

Luck; oh, blessed luck. Oh, don't let the fine be more than I've got on me, Ruth prayed to herself, but surely it couldn't be more than five thousand dollars if they were willing to let him go without booking him. She looked at the page in her hands, but all she could make out in that handwritten hash were the typeset words at the top of the form. "Arresting Officer's Report" it said.

But he hasn't been arrested. He HASN'T. And I can get him out of here.

And then I'm going to kill him.

The fine, counting everything, came to seven hundred and sixty-eight dollars. Ruth received a computer-generated receipt that listed dollar amounts next to citations from the New York Civil Code. A few hours in the library tomorrow and she could find out everything that Melior had done.

She already knew the worst.

"Fare beating," the clerk said. She wasn't wearing any uniform, just a photo ID with a name Ruth couldn't make out; she looked freeze-dried into some eternal senescence, Ruth's own nightmare of what she herself would resemble in twenty years' time, brought to Madame Tussaud life. "Cheaper to pay the fare than the fine."

It's not his fault. He didn't know. He's from out-of-town, Ruth wanted to say and didn't. Even as she chose not to argue it, she wondered if there might be some mistake. Yesterday Melior had flatly refused to go back into the subway tunnels. Why, today, should he be trying to beat the fare?

Mutely Ruth handed over currency and received her change and receipt. She went back downstairs with her paperwork and handed it to the uniformed officer, who inspected it carefully before reaching for the key to Melior's cuffs.

"Tell him to behave himself—next time we might not be so backed up. This is in the computers, even if we didn't book him," the cop said in a weary voice.

"Thank you," Ruth repeated, her own words giving her a sense of inanity, as if she were some kind of celluloid puppet; one of those spring-loaded things with a head eternally nodding. "Thank you very much."

Finally they let her take Melior away.

It was Sunday, May second, a drizzly gray evening on 42nd Street—and probably the rest of Manhattan—when Ruth and Melior emerged from the Transit Police station. The sense of freedom was overpowering; even though Ruth had been in no danger, she was trembling with exhaustion and the aftereffects of stress.

And I've got a nine o'clock class tomorrow. Terrific.

"Would you like to tell me just what that was all about? It's a damn good thing you had my number—and just *how* did that happen, by the way?" Ruth asked.

"Michael told it to me. He said I might have need of it."

"He was right. And I'm still waiting for an explanation. If I hadn't had that cash from last night, you'd still be in there, you know—and if you had to go before a judge, I really don't think he'd be impressed with your More Tales From Elfland biography."

"I *saw* it, Ruth," Melior's voice vibrated with utter conviction. "I saw the *grendel*. I was this close." He measured a space in the air with his hands.

"So you jumped over the turnstile to follow him," Ruth said flatly. Melior nodded.

"There was shouting. There was a man on the platform—I know what your guardsmen's uniforms look like, now, but I did not then and he seized me. The *grendel* got into a subway car. And I did not," Melior said, rubbing the back of his head.

"And nobody noticed they were in the same car with a *grendel?*" Ruth asked.

"No. It does not look any different yet, but the stink of high sorcery is on it. It is a scent your human noses do not catch, I think, for no one else remarked him. Yet it was he. So close—I *sensed* it—!"

"I sense the presence of Bellevue if you're not more careful!" Ruth snapped. "What if I hadn't been home? What if you'd gotten hurt?"

"Hurt?" Melior cried, stopping to stare at her. "I am slain already! Don't you understand? I'm lost—thwarted at every turn by the World of Iron, by the thousands who choke the streets of your city! He hunts where I am helpless, thwarted by his kindred! I'll never catch him—never! This beast hasn't a single throat—" Melior was shouting, now, and even in Times Square people were stopping to look.

"The people—that great beast!" Ruth tried to remember who'd said that. Alexander Hamilton? It was like him—the elitist of his day. Maybe Alexander Hamilton would have understood Rohannan Melior; God knew, Ruth didn't.

"Oh, will you shut up? Things *can* get worse—trust me," Ruth said with weary anger.

"How?" Melior turned on her savagely. "How worse than my failure?"

"Well," said Ruth viciously, "you might have to live with it. Here." And it was unholy what a shameless pleasure that thought gave her.

"Ah. Yes." Melior struggled with his surging emotions and won through to a white-lipped calm. "Very well. Walk with me, Ruth."

Bridled by guilt, she walked up Broadway with him as the day darkened. A mingy rain began to fall again; both of them ignored it. It sparkled on Melior's hair like crystal beading, too light yet to soak in. Late afternoon on a Sunday, and raining besides—the streets were almost empty (for New York). They jagged sideways, onto Fifth Avenue, and after a while Melior began to speak.

"I began where I had sensed him once. I spent all night studying the maps—I was certain I could find him, no matter his resort. It is only a handful of days since he and his fellow shamefully defeated me; he is weak yet. As weak as he will ever be. Perhaps, even, he has not fed yet. And he escaped me." Melior's voice was flat, uninflected. "And so he will continue to do, in this bizarre land where everything is out of joint. Whereas he, though a beast out of nightmare, knows what I do not, and can thereby twist the unjust laws of this insane realm to thwart me at every turn."

"Now just a minute, Hamlet," Ruth began.

"Tell me wherein I am in error, Ruth," Melior purred silkily. "Tell me how *well* I manage myself in this place. I am taken into custody for an offense I do not recognize as I commit it, children stare at me upon the streets, I cannot even read the handbills that are posted." Melior gestured at a passing bank window, filled with posters advertising its services.

"Okay," said Ruth. "You've convinced me. You're a failure. Give up. Go home."

They walked on in silence. Ruth wondered if she'd hurt him, or offended him, or if he'd even noticed what she'd said. The sky continued to darken. Twilight. Evening. Night, in an hour or two. Sunset was at 6:48, if she remembered rightly. Ruth Marlowe, compulsive memorizer of vital statistics. Today, unencumbered by packages or places to be, she was willing to walk, yea, even unto 96th Street, where Michael lived. They were passing 50th Street now. Rockefeller Center, Saks, Saint Patrick's Cathedral.

"How?" Melior said at last.

"What?" Ruth said.

"How shall I give up—and go home? Sorcery sent me here, to this place where sorcery goes awry. Without the Sword I cannot begin to hope of returning."

"And with the Sword?" Ruth asked.

"With the Sword, I may *hope*," Melior said, choosing his words precisely. He sighed. "I play with words and try your patience, Mistress Ruth. I cannot give up. I shall blunder on, hopeless, until I die."

" 'There's just no word to describe your behavior at times, Don Quixote,' " Ruth said, quoting the caption from a long-ago *New Yorker* cartoon. Melior shrugged. "You do have local help," Ruth said, trying again. Silence.

Ruth grabbed his sleeve and hauled Melior to a stop. "Look, just what is it that you want me to say? 'Give up'? You've already—"

Melior seized her in turn. And kissed her.

Ruth was not a cloistered nun. In her lifetime she had certainly been kissed and more than kissed on enough occasions that the act itself did not come as total surprise. On the majority of those occasions, however, Ruth's consent and cooperation had at least been solicited.

Melior solicited neither. With expert efficiency he pulled her close, pressing her body against him as if he were trying to drown in it. And for one moment Ruth was willing to help him. But—

"Not here!" She pushed him furiously away—Melior let her go—and uttered the first words that came to her. "Are you out of your mind?" She looked quickly around, but no one seemed to have taken advantage of this momentary lapse to pickpocket, mug, or worse, either of them. Madness, to become so distracted on a city street.

"Yes," said Melior. "No. If not here, Ruth, then where?" His intensity had no leavening gleam of mockery now, and Ruth's mind steadfastly refused to make any sense of the situation. Suddenly she felt as if New York was as alien to her as it surely must be to Melior. Why had he done it and what should she do?

Her mouth felt bruised, sensitized, tingling and tender and

naked. That it was beyond silly—what would a lord of Faery want with Ruth Marlowe—did not, somehow, ameliorate the physical sensations one whit. It took nearly all of her fast-fading store of common sense to pull free from the remains of Melior's grip and start walking once more.

She ducked her head and strode as if her life's ambition were to outrace Melior. Unfortunately, he had no trouble at all keeping up.

"Do you reject me?" Melior asked, coming up beside her.

"You can't just go and kiss someone on a public street," Ruth countered. "Something could happen."

"I did not kiss 'someone.' I kissed you."

"Well, why don't we just forget about that, okay?" Ruth's cheeks burned; her heart rattled its ivory cage far faster than brisk walking could account for. Melior had added a fresh and unwelcome dimension to the puzzle he presented, and wide new vistas of ghastly humiliation opened before her.

"Why don't we not?" he said in her ear. "Hold yourself my guide and preceptress; do you not, who knows what harm I may get myself into? I might, perchance, kiss young Mistress Jane," he added lightly.

Despite everything, the mental image so conjured made Ruth giggle. "She'd kill you," Ruth said. And then, more soberly, "Don't. She wouldn't like it." Not quite against her will Ruth slowed to a normal walking pace. 59th Street. Columbus Circle. Central Park.

"Even I know that," Melior chided her. "The paladin for Mistress Jane has yet to win his spurs. While I—"

"You're just looking for a good time?" Ruth said. She'd meant it to be light, nonthreatening, but despite herself her voice skirled and flattened, exposing pain.

"No!" Melior protested. "I want—I meant—" he stopped. "I find you passing fair, Mistress Ruth."

The opening was too good to miss; without conscious volition her internal monologist took over. " 'Passing fair, passing strange—sorry, just passing through,' " Ruth quoted airily. " 'The same thing happened twice last week: O' heaven help the working elf.' "

"Do you reject me, Ruth?" Melior softly repeated.

Oh, heavens no; just what I need to round out my year; a one night stand with a passing elf-king. "I think," Ruth said carefully, "that we come from two different worlds—"

Melior was surprised into a bark of laughter; only then did

Ruth realize what she had said. She laughed, too, the sound a little strained with tension.

"Right," she said. "Literally true. But you may be taking things for granted that we don't—here; and just maybe this isn't such a good time to rush into things? Besides, shouldn't you be thinking about how to off this *grendel?* You can do it; of course you can." She chattered on, hating the sound of her own voice and the way she was talking so he wouldn't, because she was more afraid of what Melior might say than of what he would leave unsaid, because, because, because. . . .

You wanted an adventure, Ruth told herself brutally. *You wanted things to be different; a chance to be . . . senseless? Insensible? Well, whatever the opposite of sensible is. You wanted it. You got it. Now quit whining.*

"And with you beside me my fortune is assured," Melior agreed ambiguously into the silence. "Is there ever a good time to rush into things?" he added rhetorically. "But there is no time, Ruth. There is no time left at all."

Sheer moral cowardice and the passionate desire to end this discussion kept Ruth silent; but even through her confusion a faint traitorous voice insisted that she, that Melior, that all of them were overlooking something vitally important.

CHAPTER 8

Gather, Darkness

In scattered moments of lucidity Kevin Shelby labeled Friday night the Last Good Time. Friday night—before. Before he had done what he did not have the strength to avoid doing, before he had firmly and irrevocably overstepped the line that separates the Okay People from those who have Really Bagged It.

Without knowing it, Kevin had always valued his self-esteem; his own good opinion of himself, the certainty that he'd always been right; justifiable. Now that sweet self-content was gone. It was as if some warm covering had been stripped from his ego, and something raw and red stood snarling in the chill.

But he had the sword.

The sword, and nothing else. He'd held it in his arms all that horrible Friday night, clutching at the hilt and staring into its jewels in order not to see Roy's body lying on the floor.

He'd thought it would be bloodier, somehow. More blood, and redder. The way it was in the movies. It wasn't like that, but Roy was still dead. Did it matter? Did it maybe not count because it had happened all wrong? Would the ever-present all-seeing *They* forgive it and forget it because he hadn't meant it to come out quite that way and besides it was all Roy's fault to begin with?

Would someone, anyone, please give him a second chance?

No. Bright, educated, admonished all his life to—

Be a man, Kevin.

—accept responsibility, Kevin Shelby knew the truth. No excuses. No second chances. Roy was dead and it was Kevin's fault. He'd killed him, and the weight of self-loathing, self-contempt, slid like a stone curtain between his life before and life after, cutting him off from contentment and filling his vision of the world with poison.

But he still had the sword. And to make all of this, any of this matter, to ensure that Roy Turpin had not died for nothing at all, Kevin had to keep it.

He could not stay here. Toward dawn that simple fact of self-preservation penetrated Kevin's consciousness. He became aware of what he had been smelling for some time—the thick organic scent of Roy.

The body on the floor. Nothing to do with me. Nothing!

Roy who was dead as a doornail, as last year's elections, as history. Roy was dead, dead, dead and decomposing, the blood on the floor pooled and drying to black jelly, the shards and gobbets dried and starting to look like any meat you'd accidentally left out of the fridge overnight, the smell of piss and shit transforming *the body on the floor* into just another Bowery bum. A disposable wreck. Human garbage. And eventually even the super in this building would bang on the door and then use his key, wanting to find out just what trouble his tenant was making for him now. Then there would be police.

And police would almost certainly want to know how Roy, how *the body on the floor* had come to be here. They would find Kevin's sword, and take it away, and then everything that had happened to Roy, that had happened to Kevin, would all be for nothing.

So Kevin got up. He pulled down the window shades because the glaring pink light gave him a headache. He turned back, and without thought the sword flickered in his hand like summer lightning, carving through . . . *it* as if it were hot butter, and when it had struck, Roy Turpin's head rolled free, gathering motion from the canted floor until it banged gently into the television set.

Kevin carefully wiped the blade of the sword on the couch and went into the kitchen, already forgetting what he had just done. He drank a glass of water, holding the sword point down like a dangerous walking stick. He threw up the water and everything else left in his stomach all over the dirty dishes in the sink and the clean ones in the drainer, and felt a certain cheap exultation because he didn't have to clean it up—he never had to clean anything up again. Then he drank some orange juice right from the bottle, and dropped the bottle to shatter on the kitchen floor as the juice came right back up in a pang of cramping nausea, still orange, in a vaulting arc that spattered the opposite wall. Kevin choked and spat, gagging, until his mouth was free of the rotten-sweet taste. Enough of this.

He went into the bathroom—carefully not looking in the mirror—and turned on the shower. And when the hot water had come up and the roaches been put to flight, Kevin took off all his clothes, gleefully popping buttons, and stood under the hot water and scrubbed and scrubbed until no possible trace of Roy remained on his skin or in his hair.

Through all this the sword stood propped against the wall, glinting faint rainbows in the gelid dawn light.

Then Kevin stepped out of the tub—*not* bothering to mop up—toweled himself off, and went into his bedroom. He pulled the blinds in here, too, a faint pang of worry breaking thorough for the first time. It was so bright out there. He felt the pounding behind his eyes already, the foretaste of a really bad headache. What if going outside gave him so bad a headache that something happened to the sword?

But he wouldn't think about that now. He'd think about that when he was ready. He polished the sword clean on the bedsheets, but once that was done and the covers had been pulled straight to provide a suitable backdrop for it, only the sword's presence proved that anything strange had happened in Kevin's life at all.

That was when Kevin had his great idea.

Maybe it was the light, or the memory of the last hopeful point in his life before the slide down to the Last Good Time. Maybe it was that, down deep under it all, Kevin Shelby was no fool, and smart enough to know how much anonymity a uniform gives. And knew, too, a place where he could vanish, far away from the light of the sun.

Kevin took down his track worker's uniform; the steel-toed safety boots, the gray work pants, the long-sleeved gray shirt with its sewn-on patches. He found his photo-ID and clipped it to his pocket. The authorization was out-of-date, but he wouldn't be needing to show it. And when he finally stood and looked in the mirror, he looked—ordinary.

Kevin smiled. He picked up the sword and crossed the hall to Roy's room.

Probably if he'd known he wasn't coming back, he would have been neater.

The thought made Kevin smile; with a swift gesture he

stabbed the sword down, two-handed, at the center of Roy's
unmade bed. It slid smoothly through mattress and box
spring, stopping as its point touched the floor. Kevin released it, and it wobbled gently back and forth, held upright
in place by the mattress stuffing.

Kevin thought it looked just like Excalibur in all the movies. But this one was his. *He* was King Arthur.

"Awright. . . ." Kevin breathed to himself, momentarily
distracted. The he searched the room and the closet, and
when he was done he had Roy's blue nylon bomber jacket,
worn on those outings when Roy wanted to convince someone he was a police officer or at least a security guard. It had
an American flag patch sewn on one shoulder and a Seal of
New York patch sewn on the other, and neither of these
easily-obtainable things by itself conferred legitimacy, although they looked very convincing.

Then there was Roy's secret store of cash—five hundred
dollars, stuffed in an envelope taped to the back of the
dresser. But Kevin hadn't grown up with five brothers without learning about hiding places like that. He put Roy's
money into his wallet and looked for the last thing that must
be here, because he knew Roy had a pair and because Roy
hadn't been wearing them last night.

He found them at last, pushed to the back of a drawer
he'd already checked twice. Ray-Ban sunglasses, just like
the Terminator wore. Kevin put them on, and the light
dimmed to a much more acceptable level.

His mouth was dry and cottony, and his stomach growled
with unfulfilled hunger. But he was ready to leave.

Almost. With shaking hands, Kevin carefully withdrew
the sword from its mattress anvil. It glowed, whispering
promises to him alone.

If he carried it openly like this, they would take it from
him. Kevin frowned. He rested the point of the sword on the
floor. Upright, its length measured him to mid-chest; the
pulsing jewel of the pommel resting over his heart. He had
to disguise it somehow.

A guitar case might have concealed it—if there were guitar cases that were five foot long, and Kevin didn't think
there were. A rifle case, maybe, only the crosspiece
wouldn't fit inside and anyway, a rifle case was just as bad
a thing to try to carry through the streets of New York. He
thought about it very hard, and then sacrificed his record

collection to sheathe the entire sword, blade tip to pommel, in album covers. He wrapped that in newspaper, and the newspaper in garbage bags, and strapped the resulting package in every conceivable direction with heavy silver duct tape. A friend of Kevin's had once said that duct tape was the force that held the universe together. Well, maybe it was.

He hefted the final package experimentally. It was clumsy, but no one would suspect it contained a sword—*his* sword. No one would suspect it and no one would take it and it would be safe, he would be safe. . . .

If he could only get to the subway.

Dressed and ready to go, the bundled sword balanced precariously under one arm, Kevin lifted one corner of the living-room shade and peered out. The sunlight made him hiss—even through the sunglasses the light was a blue-white hammer of pain.

He dropped the shade. He couldn't go out in that. He was hurt, he was sick— Kevin rested the sword gently against the wall and used both hands to clutch his temples. He whimpered, deep in the back of his throat. He had killed Roy—and Roy was his friend—and in that one irrevocable act he had wiped out all future content.

But he'd *had* to. Roy'd been going to take the sword away. They'd see that. They'd have to. And it was only Roy, and Roy (let's be honest) was just a cheap hood, a mugger; and compared to all that Kevin could achieve, *would* have achieved already if he'd only had the luck, just a little luck, a little. . . .

It took him an hour to convince himself to leave the apartment, and in his pumped-up desperate haste to go and be gone before he lost his nerve, he left the door unlocked.

Encouraged by the uneven slant of wall and floor in the ancient apartment building, the door drifted slowly open. When the super came upstairs to mop the hallway at nine o'clock, he found it open. He called out. Then he looked inside. Then he called the police, but by then Kevin Shelby was already far away, riding the underground railroad, his own private newly-renovated carousel, round and round and round.

His train passed through the 34th Street station for the umpteenth time a few hours later, and Kevin had no inkling how close he'd come to last night's victim.

Last night's *first* victim.

Kevin had other problems of a more pressing nature. Problems of hunger and thirst and guilt. And fear.

That he was losing his mind.

Or that he wasn't.

CHAPTER 9

Through a Glass Menagerie, Darkly

It was pitch-dark and her feet were tired by the time they reached Michael's apartment, but even so Ruth hated to leave Melior here and begin her lonely walk farther north.

From her sidewalk vantage point she could look up and see that the lights were on in Michael's apartment. No fear of leaving Melior to a chill and empty room in an alien land, then. The window was surrounded by ornamental bands of molded concrete; old, gray, baroque, and prewar. The shades were raised, giving Ruth an unimpeded view of the living-room ceiling five stories away.

"He's in," Ruth announced.

"Come up," Melior urged. "Michael will have to know of this, and undoubtedly you can tell him of that which I will omit."

For one paralyzed moment Ruth though Melior meant the incident of the kiss; then her mind unstuck itself from that broken record track and she realized that he meant the arrest and what had preceded it. With a charisma that undoubtedly commanded troops in Elfland, Melior led Ruth through the front door and up the five flights of stairs to Michael's apartment.

Swept along by the force of his personality, Ruth did not even stop to wonder if Michael might not be alone. Fortunately Philip was in plain sight as Michael swung open the door in answer to Melior's knock. Like the bad fairy in the tale, one forgot about Philip LeStrange at one's peril.

"I am arrested," Melior announced, as one wanting to get the ill news out of the way at once.

Michael stood back to let them enter. Philip was lying at full length on the living-room rug and staring spellbound into the tiny screen of his laptop—or, tonight, carpet-top. Two wires led from it. One was a phone cord. In the back-

ground the television babbled self-referentially, volume
turned down low.

"Way to go," said Philip, removing one fist from his chin
to hammer one-fingered at the keyboard. It was impossible
to tell whether he was addressing Melior or the computer.

"Arrested? Hi, Ruth. What happened?" Michael closed
the door behind them. There was a rattle of locks.

"Hi. I'm dead. Melior was arrested." Ruth walked across
the room on legs that suddenly felt like lead to collapse on
Michael's couch. She carefully did not look at Philip's keyboard. Where Philip was concerned, total ignorance was the
better part of valor, in Ruth's educated opinion. "Pepsi. Diet
Pepsi, ere I die," she enunciated, closing her eyes dramati-
cally.

"You're already dead," Philip reminded the ambient air
punctiliously. Melior entered the room cautiously (Ruth
could see from beneath lowered lashes) and perched on the
edge of a chair, a hard-edged contemporary figure of black
leather and mirrorshades. Only the sensuous curve of a
pointed ear beneath the fall of platinum hair proclaimed him
something else entirely.

Michael went off to the kitchen, returning with those two
staples of modern life, Diet Pepsi and potato chips. He de-
posited both beside Ruth.

"Arrested, you said," Michael informed her inquiringly.
"As in, *police*-arrested?" He sat down on the arm of the
couch, which creaked but seemed resigned to such treatment.

"Fare-beating," Ruth said comprehensively. She grabbed
the nearest ice-cold recyclable aluminum five cents deposit
in the following states can, popped the top with expert fin-
gernails, and quaffed nonnutritive sweeteners to the full.
Thus refreshed, she was able to sit up. "The transit cops
nicked him."

"Good going, Elfie," Philip said. Melior removed himself
from his high seat to crouch beside Philip, watching whatever was going on in liquid-crystal cyberspace.

"It isn't as if he doesn't have the fare," Michael said offhandedly. "Plus about four thousand and several hundred
more dollars."

"Not any more," Ruth said. "And besides, he'd left it at
my house—which was lucky, since I was his one phone
call."

Quickly, then, Ruth explained the rest: her trip down to the station, the good luck that let her ransom Melior without his ever really being booked, the ruinous cost of that one heedless turnstile vault.

"And he doesn't even *like* the subway. So we walked back,"·Ruth finished, leaving out great gobs of the story and hoping Michael wouldn't notice.

"If you are quite through with inessentials," Melior said crossly, "prove your teeth on this truth: if not for that guardsman's interference, I might have captured the *grendel*. So close to me it was, and still in the form of mortal man— and the Sword with it, though I saw it not."

"Yeah," said Philip in a meant-to-be-overheard aside, "but you didn't. You got caught. Close only counts in horseshoes and hand grenades."

Something must be going less than well for Philip; Ruth registered the fact clinically without having the slightest interest in finding out what it was. But for Philip to pick on Melior, who had a good six inches and a number of pounds on him, argued a more than usually complex death wish on Philip's part.

Ruth opened the potato chips with a loud snap and crunched a handful furiously, following this with a second Diet Pepsi from the six-pack Michael had brought out into the living room.

"And what," asked Melior with icy punctilio, "do you suggest I do?"

In the corner some sitcom Ruth had never heard of revolved around its sacred couch in living color. Philip tapped some key that seemed to signal an end to the evening's computer activities. He looked up into Melior's face, oddly anachronistic bifocals gleaming.

"Learn the rules. *Then* break them."

"Which brings us to something I guess we should have covered earlier," Michael said on a deep breath. "Tactics."

"As in 'How We Do What We've Already Made Up Our Minds To is Strategic,'" Philip said in an "aching-to-be-slapped" voice. Melior rocked back on his haunches and rose to his feet.

"Correct. You know 'What' but not 'How,'" Michael said to Melior.

Suddenly Ruth was aware of a sudden upswing of tension in the room. Had she and Melior wandered into the middle of a fight between Michael and Philip? But Michael never fought with *anyone;* he was a great big infinitely tolerant teddy bear who practically bent over backward to avoid confrontation. That was why he and Naomi were so much alike.

"Not so," Melior said evenly. "You forget, Friend Michael—I know precisely 'How.' I must track the *grendel* to his lair, claim the Sword, and kill him with it."

"Which you cannot do from Sing-Sing," Michael said.

"Or Bellevue," Ruth added. She was completely exhausted and she hadn't studied and now there was going to be some kind of ugly scene—she could taste it. Which meant she was going to feel like death on toast in the morning. Good-bye, one third of the final grade.

"You see, Melior, the, uh, real world has rules," Michael was saying, still with that charged politeness. "If you don't follow them, you're going to attract a lot of attention. And that is something you can't beat, believe me. They'll catch you, and if you're lucky they'll just think you're crazy and lock you up."

"If I am lucky," Melior repeated in an inflectionless voice.

"And if you're not lucky," Michael said, "they'll believe you. And then, my friend, you'll disappear into some five-sided room down in Washington, while they try to find out who you really are and where you come from."

"And how they can get there," Philip said unexpectedly, while Ruth tried not to stare at Michael—or indeed, at anything at all. Was this Michael spouting Oliver Stone conspiracy theories? *Michael?*

Philip folded up his computer and unhooked it from the phone. He glanced at Ruth, then away, his shoulders hunched familiarly. "Just think of all those taxpayers," he added obliquely.

"Aren't you both being a little pessimistic?" Ruth said. "Whatever happened to *Klaatu barrada nicto?* Or *IDIC?*"

"*Star Trek,*" said Philip with the scorn of one who was born the year it was canceled. Michael had the grace to look at least a little embarrassed.

"Well, maybe that wouldn't happen," he admitted. "But whatever happens once you're discovered, you're here illegally, and you're not human, Melior, so you've just got to be real careful—"

"That the soulless drones you call your landsmen do not

know me for what I am, lest I suffer the same unwelcome fate as any other intruder into an ant's nest."

There was a brief silence.

"Yeah," said Philip, "something like that. So make up your mind, Elfie, whether you want to do it your way—or do it."

On that note, Philip got to his feet and reached for his jacket. He tucked his computer back into his knapsack and slung that over his shoulder. "This is going to be a stupid conversation. See you tomorrow, Michael. Coming, Ruth?"

Ruth was so surprised to be considered by Philip that she let the moment pass her completely by. Not getting an answer he shrugged, turned, and left, pulling the door shut with a jingle of hardware behind him. Michael went to lock it. Melior sat down at the opposite end of the couch from Ruth, taking Michael's place.

"What I like about Philip," observed Ruth after a moment, "is his unstudied naturalness; his total freedom from the toils of worn, outmoded, convention. For he is a child of Nature, and takes after his mother." It wasn't quite fair; but on the other hand, Philip wasn't here any more either.

"But is he right?" asked Melior.

"Yeah," said Michael, coming back. "He is. That's the problem." He pulled up the stool to make the point of an invisible triangle halfway between Melior and Ruth, and sat down on it.

"*Your* problem," Ruth added, with a mean-spiritedness that surprised her.

But Melior did not seem to be able to understand that, Ruth realized with a sinking feeling about half an hour later. This was what the strange "before-a-storm" feeling was all about; this particular argument must have been building since Michael took Melior home with him on Friday night. Over and over again Michael explained about how *big* the city was, how intolerant this particular civilization was of error or transgression, how different from a land with elves in shining armor where men made war on horseback. Melior was a stranger here; his only hope of moving freely about the city—of moving freely *at all*—was to not be noticed, not really.

Once he was seen for what he was, it would be all over, and the possibilities after that ranged the Gothic gamut from guest appearances on *Oprah* to being winkled down some

Alphabet Agency rabbit-hole and never being seen again. Along with all the rest of *them,* of course, just to make things interesting.

Ruth believed him. Why not? Michael made perfect sense—and besides, he was right.

And over and over Melior patiently explained that these things did not interest him—that all he wanted was the sword, and given that, he would give them also his solemn word to trouble them no more.

"Look," Michael said finally, long after the time when Ruth would have been reduced to interrogative screaming. "You've said you want our help. That you need it. And, frankly, you owe Ruth here a helluva lot. So. Bottom line. How reasonable are you going to be?"

"I *am* being reasonable, Friend Michael," Melior began once more.

"You are not being reasonable!"

Michael's full-throated bellow sent the adrenaline of shock rinsing through Ruth's overtaxed veins. She stared at him in horror. He was on his feet, and, as she watched, Melior got to his feet also. The two of them faced one another like mirror images.

"You—are *not*—being reasonable!" Michael shouted. "You are saying we're all going to do it *your* way—and I am here to tell you, my pointy-eared elf-boyo, as you seem to be a little hard of hearing, that your way Will—! Not—! Work—!"

Sheer volume flattened Ruth in her seat. She heard him, Melior heard him, probably everyone else in the building heard him.

"Now the question you have got to ask yourself is whether you believe me. Are you saying to yourself 'this mere human has an agenda of his own'? You're right. I don't want to be arrested or any other thing for having anything to do with you when you run right smack up against a system that's just too *alien* for you to understand. Because you do that and you're going down, my friend, and it just might be that you don't know how far down Down can be."

Michael was breathing very hard and talking very fast, low now and intense with his face flushed and his breathing ragged. Ruth watched him with the spellbound intensity of one who has seen a teddy bear turn into a wolverine right before her eyes. In the spaces between his words the television, unregarded, whispered its gibberish below the level of the senses.

"But there's another way. Our way. My way. You do it that way and it just might work. You might get what you want. But there's no more going off alone. There's no more plans that you try without clearing it with one of us. This is going to have to be a team effort, and if the way we do things looks silly to you, it's just going to have to look silly and you're just going to have to do it anyway, because our way—*my* way—is the only way things are going to get done."

Ruth continued to stare at Michael as if she'd never seen him before—and in some sense of the word, she hadn't. Not this Michael.

"And if I do not do things your way?" Melior asked.

"Then walk right out that door and keep on walking, elf-lord. None of us wants anything to do with you."

Ruth would have opened her mouth to protest, but some pang of self-preservation kept her silent. With clinical detachment she noted unconnected things. The beads of sweat rolling down Michael's face. The tightness of his clenched fists. The brilliant green of Melior's eyes, open very wide and fixed unblinkingly upon Michael, as if Melior were some strange cockatrice that could slay with a gaze. The moment stretched, until Ruth thought the tension of waiting to see how it would end would make her scream.

"Then, it seems, I must accede to your terms, Michael of the World of Iron. And I wish you joy of them."

Melior's voice was so even Ruth nearly missed the capitulation. When Michael turned away, she actually twitched; a jump dying stillborn.

"That's okay, then," Michael said in a voice that only shook slightly. He ran a hand over his forehead. Ruth handed him a Diet Pepsi. He popped the top and poured the entire contents of the can down his throat; a masculine gesture Ruth envied even while wondering how it was that men could do things like that and she couldn't.

"The first thing you've got to do is, always pay your fare in the subway. And the second thing is, when you go out looking, you've always got to take a native guide."

"And the third thing is, when I see my lawful prey, I should turn away again and pretend I do not." Melior's voice was flat.

"Maybe." Michael's voice was equally uncompromising. "Because it might just be that if you jumped him just then, he'd get away. Or a bunch of people'd get killed. Or you'd get dead. *You don't know the rules, man,* and if anything you've said is true, you don't have time to learn them."

"It is you who do not have time, Michael. The *grendel* preys on manflesh. His appetite is as endless as the ocean, and as he feeds he grows. With so many tempting morsels for his plate, soon he will be immense. But his appetite will be greater."

It was too much tension; Ruth had to focus on anything other than them. And so she was staring at the television when the ten o'clock news came on, and the screen flashed red with the display graphic for the lead news story.

"Shut up!" Ruth hissed.

Michael looked where she was looking and lunged for the volume control. The newscaster's accentless midlantic diction filled the room.

"—arrant case of *cannibalism* in the New York Subway, Spokesman Dale Werther of the Transit Authority explained."

The screen jumped to the image of an anonymous bureaucrat in a suit standing on a vaguely familiar subway platform. He was the sort, Ruth thought, that you would automatically decide was lying, no matter what he said. Thirty years of selective nonstop disinformation in the form of high-pressure advertising had produced an American consumer so savvy that he wouldn't even believe the truth.

"Every year over two hundred riders expire while in the subway, for reasons having nothing to do with the subway services."

"Like being mugged," Ruth said.

"The tunnels are also home to a number of animals, one of which may have had access to the body before it was found. We are investigating—"

"But the witnesses who found the body tell a different story," the news reader intercut smoothly. The news clip this time was of an older woman, indignant tears streaming down her face. The images were bleached and grainy, not the careful PR lighting of the spokesman.

"I don't care what nobody says—somebody *ate* on him, and I don't think it's no rats, and he didn't just die there in the car!"

"This footage was taken by one of the witnesses," the

news reader said. "Transit officials could not be reached for further comment."

Last image of all, and the strongest saved for last: the inside of the subway car, jiggly with a hand-held Minicam, the color grayed almost to black with poor light and bad film. The unaccustomed eye took a moment to adjust, then enhanced the images to lucidity: the black streaks on the walls were spattered blood. The horribly altered bundle on the floor of the car was a body.

"Authorities are continuing their investigation."

The screen went bright with the network logo.

"And in Queens, a dyslexic woman teaches her daughter to read, back after this."

Michael flipped off the television. Silently, he began to pace the length of the apartment, reminding Ruth of a caged leopard and making her wish she were somewhere else. The televised images—more vivid in retrospect—made Ruth's stomach churn in helpless fury. This was the dark side of the fairy tale: the monsters to match the princes.

"And now he has gone to ground, in the trackless caves that lie beneath your city, and you say I may not hunt him?" Melior said bitterly. "The World of Iron is only a fable for sorcerers, but even so I did not think its men were mad."

"Yeah, right," said Michael, who wasn't really listening.

"But it isn't trackless," Ruth said in the over-reasonable tones of shock. Both men stared at her. "It's got plenty of tracks. Michael, Melior's talking about the *subway*. The monster's in the subway. And the subways are *mapped*."

But strangely now it was Melior who held back.

"The *grendel* has fed, and will be more dangerous with each passing hour. I must know its territory before I seek it out. I am no coward, but much rides upon my life: if I am slain, then the chance of the *grendel*'s death dies with me."

"I thought you said the sword was what would kill it?" Ruth said.

"Aye, sweet Ruth, and who will wield it if I do not? For any mortal who takes it up will change as well, and another *grendel* will take the place of the first."

"You have a point," Michael said. "Do you have a plan?"

"I must go once more into the subterranean *way*," Melior said seriously, "and travel its byways and turnings. Perhaps I will sense the Sword's nearness again. In any event, I shall gain an understanding of the ground over which I must fight."

Michael thought about this. "Okay. Tomorrow you ride the subway. But one of us goes with you. Ruth?"

Ruth hesitated. It seemed vastly mean-spirited to protest that she had her final exam in Cataloging tomorrow—except that she *did,* and if she missed it she might as well blow off graduating in June. And that meant the summer to get through without a job—maybe more if the course weren't being repeated until spring—and all of that meant money, time, trouble. . . .

"No; I forgot; we've got the Cat final tomorrow. And Naomi's rehearsing for her orals. That leaves Philip or Jane to go with you," Michael said inarguably.

Just about then the phone rang. While Ruth was still looking around to try to find where it was *this* week, Michael grabbed it.

"Hello? . . . yeah, she's here." ("Naomi," he mouthed at Ruth.) ". . . yeah, we saw the news. Mel thinks it's his *grendel;* he wants to go check it out . . . of course not. I'm going to send Jane with him." After this last statement there was an extended pause, through which Michael listened with patient good humor.

Which had been the only emotion Ruth had thought him capable of, before tonight. What was happening to all of them—was it *Melior* who was making them all unravel like badly-rolled string?

"She can skip that," Michael said at last. More pausing, then: "Yeah, I know that, Nai, but do you think I ought to send Phil with him?"

Ruth grinned to herself, and in truth that seemed to be a clinching argument, because soon after that he hung up.

"Naomi says I'd better call you a cab. So okay; you're a cab," Michael said agreeably.

"Gee, thanks," said Ruth. She stood up; looked around for coat and purse. The day had been full of too many strong emotions for her to feel anything at all now. The thought of the additional distance she had to cover was daunting, but Ruth had that vague distrust of taxis which a certain class of New Yorker feels, as if traveling by some means other than the preordained paths of buses and trains is somehow fraudulent and dishonest.

"But seriously, folks," Michael said. He dialed another

number and gave instructions to the dispatcher. "Be here in about fifteen minutes," he told Ruth.

"Which gives us more than enough time to call up Jane and tell her she's cutting classes tomorrow—and why."

Michael began again to dial.

Ruth and Melior stood on the sidewalk in front of Michael's apartment, waiting for the cab. The spring darkness had closed in entirely, but here it did not frighten, instead lending the riverside the charm of unclarity.

"Michael thinks my quest in vain; it angers him," Melior said.

"Something did," Ruth pointed out. Her figurative ears still rang; who would ever have thought *Michael* could lose his temper?

"He fears to know himself a coward, and twice fears to test the knowledge," Melior said simply.

Michael a coward? Ruth shook her head in bafflement. She didn't think he was, but then she didn't think he was especially brave, either. Cowardice and bravery, like honor, were not concepts that came up very often in daily conversation.

"And do you, Ruth, also think I ought not seek the Sword?"

Yes, thought Ruth before she could censor herself. "New York is an awfully big place," she began, hesitantly.

"And I should content myself with securing my own happiness," Melior suggested, looking sideways at her. "Though I admit I had never thought to find it here. But what use is happiness when one is dead?"

"Dead?" Ruth echoed. She stared at Melior.

"If I remain here in this World of Iron I will die, Ruth, whether I face this *grendel* or not."

"*When?* I mean—"

"In fifteen years. Perhaps twenty." Ruth's shoulders sagged as relief replaced tension, and Melior smiled bitterly. "You think it a sufficient time, but even you, Ruth, would outlast it. And it is not so very long a time to one who was not born to die."

Furious with her own transparency, Ruth turned away. She still had her back to Melior, staring at the river with every evidence of fixed interest, when the taxi arrived.

"Ruth, I want—" Melior began, but Ruth didn't wait to

hear it. She leaped into the taxi as if pursued by devils. It pulled away, leaving Melior standing alone on the street.

"Where to, lady?" the question came, and numbly, automatically, Ruth told him.

Coward, coward, coward, Ruth thought bitterly. *Always afraid of what people will think. Always. Still. After everything.*

She didn't remember her last night on earth, but she'd seen pictures. Her prom dress had been pink: pale satin spaghetti-strapped bodice, the skirt yards and yards of pale-pink tulle tinted darker pink at the edge of each asymmetric layer. Mom had snapped her picture just before she and Jimmy'd left the house.

But she didn't remember that. She didn't remember buying the dress, or why she would have bought something that, in retrospect, made her look so much like a flamingo. She didn't remember going to the Senior Prom, nor Jimmy Ramirez getting drunk, and most of all she didn't remember *why* she'd gotten into the car with him again. He had to have been very drunk, drunk enough so anyone could tell. The coroner's report said so. So her father said.

June 7th, 1981. And early on the morning of June 8th Ruth Marlowe's world ended, as she and three other kids hit a tree at something in the vicinity of eighty miles per hour.

Ruth graduated in absentia while on total life-support in the County Hospital. She'd been thrown clear; broken arms, broken legs, broken collarbone, but nothing that wouldn't heal.

Except that Ruth wouldn't wake up. *Coma,* they said, and, as time passed, *irreversible.* They unhooked the respirator. Ruth slept on.

Time passed and the world went on. And then, eight years later, Ruth woke up.

Woke up five years ago to find her mother dead, her father dying, the house she'd grown up in sold long since to pay the medical bills and all the world changed. Not beyond recognition. That would have been kinder. But changed just enough that everything seemed like a reflection in some cruel looking glass. Her father died about the time Ruth learned to walk again; it was almost a release from those painful interviews, each of them in their respective wheel-chairs, when he tried not to blame her too openly for destroying his life and Ruth searched vainly for her father in this ailing, bitter, widower.

Seventeen going on thirty, and the only thing left for her to do was cobble together some kind of adulthood and pretend she agreed when the nurses called her lucky. Lucky, with what people called "the best years of your life" vanished in a night. She hadn't even had to go into Elf Hill to lose them. All she'd had to do was ... whatever she'd done, that night. Something stupid, something cowardly, something that cared more for what people—Jimmy—would think than for life itself.

No wonder she'd been ready, ripe, and reckless for the first stray elf-lord who came along. Who didn't treat her like the thirty-year-old she wasn't, or like a raree show, or a science project, or like someone who should be *grateful*—!

Oh, yes, Rohannan Melior was something worth having. But what did something that wonderful want with *her?*

CHAPTER 10

Bread and Roses

He was hungry. Hungry, and thirsty, and he knew the only thing that would ease him. Kevin Shelby rode the subway, a magic sword from Elfland concealed in the awkward bundle at his side, and planned.

The run through the sunlight had been bad, very bad. Bad enough that Kevin did not wish to contemplate a repetition of it. By the time he had reached the subway entrance three blocks away, tears of pain were streaming down his face beneath the Terminator sunglasses.

He'd retained enough presence of mind not to vault the turnstile into the subway: Transit cops lay in wait for fare-beaters and if they caught him they would take him back toward the sun.

No, even in his pain and hunger, Kevin made himself worthy of the sword. He flashed his out-of-date ID at the token booth clerk and was buzzed through the "Employees Only" gate. The gate clicked shut behind him and he moved down the platform. Then Kevin was free—free in the system.

Even though the subway system itself was lit up bright as night indoors, the light wasn't nearly as bad. The blue-white pain behind his eyes receded and the sense of impending doom left him. He was in the New York Subway System, with hundreds of miles of track. It ran twenty-four hours a day, and all he had to do was avoid the parts of the Brooklyn and Queens lines that ran above ground and he'd be fine. He could transfer across platforms from Uptown to Downtown lines; he could even buy food, hot dogs and stuff, without ever leaving the system.

At the thought of a hot dog, Kevin's stomach lurched. His mouth was dry and cottony, a torment of an entirely different order than the pain behind his eyes, and his midsection was occupied with a sick numb cramping that testified to a too-long emptiness. But a hot dog was not the answer.

The train came and he got on—a car near the middle; safest place to ride the train. The doors shut with their familiar two-note chime, and the train started to move. Kevin braced himself against the rocking with the ease of a lifelong New Yorker and headed for a seat.

This early in the morning he had his choice; he chose one of the corner side seats at the front of the car, near both the doors to the platform and the doors that led between cars. Carefully he propped the sword, sheathed in record jackets, against the fake woodgrain veneer of the car's bulkhead and leaned back on the gaudy orange plastic seat.

Safe.

But immediate physical safety only left Kevin with the leisure to think of all the ways in which he was not safe, and of all the things he lacked. He rode the subway hour after hour, up and down and around, while the thought of food came to obsess him even more than it nauseated him.

He had to eat. And that understanding became the anvil upon which his fear was hammered, because that which he desperately must do was that which he could not do.

He tried. He bought sodas, candy bars, potato chips, mustard pretzels, soft-serve ice cream, candied popcorn, gyros, falafel, and hot dogs.

He threw all of them away before taking even a bite.

He couldn't even drink *water.*

The hours passed. The cars filled up with weekend ridership, a seething mass of assorted humanity that remained constant throughout the day. The car filled, but somehow there was always an empty seat beside Kevin, huddled in his peculiar misery, guarding the sword and riding the subway.

He was there when Roy Turpin's body was discovered, though he didn't know it. The story broke in time for the evening editions; he could have picked up a copy of the *Post* or its sister papers at any number of newsstands on platforms serving the IND and the IRT lines. But his head hurt too much to read, and television and radio did not penetrate the layers of concrete, stone, and steel that separated Kevin Shelby from the light of the sun.

By eleven-thirty Saturday night the cars were empty once more. By that time all of Kevin's fear and guilt were distilled into the particular horror of *need.* His mouth watered constantly, though that did nothing to alleviate his thirst, and for the first time he began to understand how it was possible to go mad with hunger.

The worst part was, he didn't have to be hungry.

He didn't know when the knowledge came to him. Sometime during that long dim suffering day he had roused into brighter awareness and knew the solution. He knew what he could eat, what would soothe him and nourish him and not fill him with sickness, nausea, and pain. He *knew*.

In some dying corner of his mind the part of Kevin Shelby that had tried to be good rebelled. Frantically it built barriers of impossibility against the sweet seductive reasonableness of that inner knowledge.

It would be dangerous. It would be messy. He might get caught, or hurt, or it *might not work*. The only defense he did not use was that it was wrong, for Kevin had forfeited the right to that defense sometime late Friday night.

And eventually sheer privation wore him down.

It was very late. He didn't quite remember how long he'd been here, or what he'd done before that, but he knew it was late. The car he was riding in was empty. His entire body vibrated with an unwholesome dishonest energy imposed from without, as much destroying his body as enlivening it. His hands shook. The vivid images of his intention painted themselves against his eyes, offering heat but no warmth.

And then The Other One boarded the car.

The Other One was a person of the sort that Kevin, in better days, would have avoided out of an instinctive sense of self-preservation. For one thing, anybody riding the trains at this hour *had* to be crazy. For another thing, he looked like the sort of person that somebody riding the trains at this hour would naturally run into, which was why nobody who wanted to keep their wallet and their neck rode the trains at this hour.

The Other One wore a long green raincoat and high-topped sneakers and hummed to himself as he selected a seat at the opposite end of the train. Kevin watched with hungry fascination.

The train began to move, pulling out into the tunnels and the relative darkness. The Other One got up and moved to a seat in the middle of the car. Kevin was on the "A" Line now, and the Uptown stations were several minutes apart. He clutched at the Sword in its clumsy wrappings. Sometime during the day he had picked through the plastic and tape and newspaper sealing one end. If he reached inside he could touch the cool curve of the jewel in the Sword's pommel.

He had to be strong. That was the important thing, the most important thing. If he failed, if he died here, it would all have been for nothing. His *life* would have been for nothing—all the things he might be, all the things he could have been . . . gone.

His mind hurt in a muddled, painful way. There was something wrong with his reasoning, somewhere—but he felt so bad. The thirst was the worst, worse even than the hunger.

And there was only one food that would appease the hunger and thirst.

"Hey, man, you got any spare change?"

Kevin said nothing. Now The Other was close, very close; Kevin could see him, smell stale breath and stale sweat and beneath it all the living aroma of *food.*

"Hey, man, I'm talking to you. What's the matter with you?"

The Other was his chance for life. If he didn't take it, he would die. It was that simple. And so Kevin Shelby took the final step that made his own life more important than right or wrong.

He stood up, forcing The Other back, and thrust his fist through the hole he had made in the cardboard record cover. His hand closed over the roundness of the pommel and slid further to the ridged hardness of the haft.

"Hey, man, you got a problem with me?"

"No problem," said Kevin, and yanked to pull the sword free.

But it slid out only a little way, and then tangled in the tape and newspapers that Kevin had so carefully wrapped around it. And The Other laughed, and pulled out something small and shiny.

A knife.

Roy had always said—when there was Roy—that a knife would scare people more than a gun up close. Because a gun really didn't look like much, if it wasn't one of the ones too big to hide, but a knife always looked like exactly what it was.

Something to cut.

"Give me that," Kevin said reasonably, and The Other laughed. His eyes were on the jeweled pommel and Kevin knew he had made a mistake.

"Give what you got there and I let you keep your money."
The Other reached for the Sword.

Kevin grabbed the knife.

The blade slid along the palm of his hand. It bit deep into his wrist. Kevin didn't care. He knew what he wanted. He clawed The Other's fingers open, getting at the knife, and now The Other was trying to get away, but that didn't matter; Kevin was pushing him back, and back; The Other's body hit one of the poles in the center of the car and he tripped with Kevin on top of him trying to get the knife right way round in his hand.

The train pulled into a station. After a moment the doors opened onto the empty station platform.

"Help! Help me! Help! I being mugged!"

Then Kevin found the right way around with the knife.

It slid in so easily at first it didn't seem that it could have worked, but The Other was suddenly silent, and lay quietly beneath Kevin as the doors shut and the train began to move again.

And then there was the cutting, which was good, and the eating, which was sweet relief. But even the eating wasn't enough somehow, so there was cutting and cutting and cutting. And when it was over, Kevin's skin felt stiff and hard, and with the new bright energy he felt he ripped the coverings from the Sword.

It was simple, then, to jam the switchbox so the doors of the car wouldn't open. And around five o'clock in the morning, when the train was on standby in a tunnel, it was simple to use the Sword to lever open the doors again, so that Kevin could step out of the train and into the tunnel.

CHAPTER 11

The Looking-Glass War

As an elf he was a total washout. And as a way to spend Monday, it was comprehensively stupid.

Jane Greyson had few illusions about Life and was willing to get by with fewer. She had no idea why people insisted on making the best of things, as transformation was a concept unknown to her philosophy. Hers was a policy of Things As They Are, and if something wasn't best there was no point in trying to pretend that it was.

In that context, whether or not the person called Melior was an elf as defined in the Oxford Unabridged Dictionary New Revised Edition was of much less importance (as less subject to logical proof) than the fact that Ruth and Michael and Naomi had all agreed to treat him as an elf and to do what they could to help him. Once that was settled, Jane had something to work with, secure in the knowledge that her opinions would not be consulted.

Thus it was that Michael and Ruth had not really had to explain that Melior couldn't be trusted to run around loose. In Jane's opinion nobody could be. The world was too endlessly inventive; if your number was up, it would get you, and that was that.

But Ruth especially had insisted that Melior had to have somebody with him who knew the ways of the world, and though Jane knew that the others regarded her as an unworldly little incompetent whose sole recommendation lay in that she was *not* Philip Leslie LeStrange, she supposed they felt she had at least enough sophistication to guide a pointy-eared whatever-he-was around the subway system.

He wasn't an elf. Jane clutched that cockle-warming knowledge to herself with all the surety of one who has read several very good translations of several very elderly Eddas. The *Aelfvar* were a race of Norse demigods who lived in Aelfheim and stayed out of the affairs of Men. Furthermore they were dark-skinned and short, and probably didn't have pointed ears at all. And most of all, they didn't exist.

But nobody would have believed him if he'd said he was a Vulcan.

Jane considered this carefully and decided that probably Ruth would have believed him, but would never have admitted it to the others. And possibly it would have mortified her so much that she would even have tried to conceal *him* from them, too, so all in all it was just as well that he'd said he was an elf.

Even if he wasn't one.

But they'd all voted to let him be an elf, so Jane abandoned the ultimately fruitless question of what Melior *really* was, and concentrated on what they were doing.

Which, on this fine Monday morning in May, was almost precisely nothing.

The record time for traversing every last inch of the transit system is somewhere just under twenty hours; every year an impromptu "subway rally" is held to try to better that time. Today she and Melior weren't even trying to come close to it; they'd ride as much of the subway as they could cover until around three—when Michael and Ruth would be done with their exams—and then go back and try to figure out what to do about the creature that Melior said was down in the subway.

Personally, Jane couldn't see what the fuss was about. She understood that Melior wanted his sword back—Jane understood about wanting to retain ownership of one's own possessions—but she really couldn't see that one more crazed cannibal roaming New York could make a difference one way or the other. So what if he ate people? *Stone cold dead hath no fellow,* Jane quoted to herself. If they were dead, who cared what happened afterward? They didn't.

Still, taken all in all, the day was a wash.

After the phone call last night, Jane had spent some time planning out a suitable route. Fortunately, the book on subways that mentioned the subway rally also mentioned enough about the paths taken for her to reconstruct it. This morning, bright and early, at the ghastly hour of 7:00 a.m. she had presented herself at Michael's apartment and prepared to be bored.

Melior was living up to her expectations in that respect.

At least he hadn't tried to talk to her. And she *had* brought a book.

Ruth chewed on the end of her regulation Number 2 lead pencil and wished she were somewhere else. Anywhere would do, but specifically she wished she were the one with Melior on the subway instead of Jane.

The room where she had thirty-five other bored and nearly-graduated student librarians were being tested to destruction did nothing to improve her mood. Vast, chalk-scented, dusty, scrupulously silent, and seemingly devoid of all human life, it seemed to be a dress rehearsal for the buildings in which she would spend the rest of her working life.

Ruth noticed the test proctor looking her way and quickly bent her head to the test paper again. She hated library school. She hated her *life*. No, worse, she was *bored* with her life, and being bored with your life before you'd really even started it led to chilling speculations on the whichness of what you would do for the rest of it.

No, not even bored. Dissatisfied.

The right word at last. Ruth stared at her paper and tried to summon up some interest. Cataloging: Dewey or don't we?

Back to work.

The questions were multiple choice, but that didn't make them any easier. All the answers were *almost* right, but in the eyes of God and Columbia there was only one really right answer.

Melior.

Not an answer, no, not even a question, and not a problem she could avoid, after last night. The defiant fact of his existence was an assault upon the fabric of her world, was a wound she would carry with her forever, and in all honesty and good conscience she still had to deal with his problem: the missing sword, and the monster that had been caused by it.

What if it was a coincidence? Ruth's logical mind insisted. *Murders are horrible, but they happen. None of us had inside information about that killing. What if it's just an ordinary lunatic and not a GRENDEL?*

Melior thought it was a *grendel*. But Melior, Ruth realized with a chill, standoffish clarity, wanted magic to work in this world. If magic didn't work here, he would remain here until he died.

But would that be so bad? He said his world was at war; here he'd have years of peace. WE'D have years—

Which was the root of the matter, really. She loved Melior—how could she not? And she thought, maybe, that he loved her, but if he found his sword, he was going back to Elfland.

If he could.

And Ruth, who wanted his happiness more than she wanted her own, suddenly wished he couldn't.

The Computer Department of Columbia University had, until quite recently, occupied the basements of several scattered buildings. Only last year, in a series of shuffles reminiscent of Three-Card Monte, had the Powers That Were consolidated their mainframes, their LAN-servers, their freestanding PCs in one location.

The students called it Hacker Heaven.

But, of course, nothing like that went on there. The Age of the Hacker was past: penalties were too high if you were caught, safeguards were too stringent. Cyberpunks existed only in the imagination of the media.

Right?

Michael knew better. And so, while Ruth, who was no morning person, slogged slowly through her Cat Final, Michael checked answers with the reckless abandon of one who only needs to graduate to become employed, and finished the three-hour exam in forty minutes flat.

And went looking for Philip, knowing where he'd be. Where they'd both, unknown to the others, agreed that Philip would be.

"You know that this is illegal?" Michael Peacock said, mostly because he knew it would give Philip such pleasure to hear it. And it had been his own personal wonderful idea, too.

"I know, I know," Philip muttered, not really listening. "Isn't it wonderful?"

His laptop reposed on the table beside the computer reserved for student database searching, connected to the bigger computer—and its modem—by arcane means. The big screen was currently welcoming them to Columbia's Electronic University Services. At intervals Philip hit a key on his laptop, to no apparent effect.

Suddenly the database computer screen went blank and the laptop emitted a small, self-satisfied beep. Philip sat back and looked at Michael.

"It's showtime," he said.

"Okay, kemo sabe, where do we go from here?" Michael asked.

"Anywhere," Philip said. "Okay," he added, in his voice for lecturing the mentally deficient. "What goes in here—" he indicated the laptop, "—goes up there—" the computer, "—but we can use the programs stored in here to modify there." He sat back, smug.

Michael had long since given up wondering what Philip was doing in library school. There was no point in asking, because Philip didn't seem to know either. There was going to be trouble there, ten-fifteen-twenty years down the line, sure as taxes. And there was more hope of avoiding taxes than of derailing the trouble for his friend.

Michael Peacock knew something about human nature and inevitability.

"Okay, Phil. The first one should be easy. Get us into the Department of Motor Vehicles database."

After five hours on the subway, Jane felt that lunch was in order. She mentioned this to her companion.

"How do you live like this?" Melior responded. He had been staring out the window almost the entire time—except when they changed trains—watching the interplay of light and shadow and the alternation of station and tunnel that were familiar-bordering-on-invisible for Jane.

"Consider the alternative," Jane said. "Do you want to stop for lunch? Because I do, and this *grendel*-thing is as likely to be in a McDonald's as anywhere else."

Now Melior looked at her. He'd taken off the mirror-shades that Ruth had bought him, and Jane stared into eyes of a green found only in coloring books, with slit pupils that waxed and waned in the light. Jane felt her stomach lurch with more than hunger; with an instinctive rejection of the unnatural. Of Melior.

"Come on," she said. Once she'd gotten him moving, they could find some place to eat. First things first.

"You do not believe, do you?" Melior said, showing no

inclination to shift himself. He smiled, showing pointed teeth. "Were I in my proper place, I could show you magic to freeze your young blood; wonders to lift the heart. Then you would believe."

"You really don't get it, do you?" Jane said. "*It doesn't matter.* Magic or not—who cares?"

" 'Who cares'?" Melior echoed blankly. "But, child, it is *magic.*"

"I don't care. Nobody cares. And I'm hungry," Jane said flatly.

"Then we shall eat, of course." Melior rose to his feet in a perfect motion that made Jane sharply aware of her own clumsiness. The comparison did not make her like him any better.

Since Melior had the window seat, she got up and moved to the center of the car. They were just coming in to a station now—someplace in Brooklyn she'd never heard of. But there had to be McDonald's even in Brooklyn, didn't there?

"But tell me, Mistress Jane," Melior said to her back. Jane stopped but didn't turn around. She knew what came next. Now he was going to say something witty and obscure that was supposed to make her feel like a jerk.

"If you do not believe in me, why are you helping me?"

There it came. Jane's view of the universe was reconfirmed.

"Because Ruth asked me to."

"And would you do anything for Ruth?" Melior asked, still in the tone of one who hopes to play verbal trumps.

"I'd do this," Jane said, conceding nothing.

The doors opened on yet another unfamiliar platform. Jane walked out through them without looking back to see if he followed.

In the computer room, the screen was filled with endlessly scrolling lines.

"Don't worry about it," Philip said. "I'm downloading everything to the capture buffer."

"Great," said Michael, who wasn't absolutely sure what all this meant but it *sounded* good.

From the DMV computer they had progressed by easy stages into the Coroner's Office computer for New York County (which is to say, for Manhattan and Brooklyn). If there were a *grendel,* and if it were killing, the resulting bodies would be entered here.

It hadn't been that hard to get in. Michael had been surprised.

"The thing is," Philip had said, "people lock up the information they think is valuable. Too bad they don't know what it is. How do they know what I'm going to want to know? Or they leave it unprotected but scattered, which really isn't going to slow anybody down. You can always put it back together. A librarian is a synthesist, isn't that what they're always saying in class? A specialist in general knowledge? People are such dorks," Philip added, on a sigh of pure disgust.

The screen scrolled up into darkness, leaving only a flashing square of cursor.

"What's wrong?" Michael asked.

"We're done. All the homicides since April thirtieth. Of course, we've only got Elfie's word for it that that's when he showed up—" Philip pointed out sneeringly.

"If this is a scam, it's a scam like I've never seen," Michael said. Philip looked at him curiously and shrugged. His bifocals went flash-flash in the light.

"Look, Michael—I don't care. Elfie's a moron and he's going to get us all killed. But who wants to live forever, especially at these prices?"

It was better away from the train. The train was too bright. Too . . . dry. It was better here, in the lay-bys and access tunnels of the underground railroad. There was rest. And there was food.

If only his skin didn't itch.

When he had been human, Kevin Shelby had been a track worker in his underworld kingdom, and perhaps some of the knowledge he had gained then remained to him, but it was more a matter of instinct now that led him to the deeper and less traveled sections of the line; to the storage cupboards, the equipment depots, the niches for a man to stand in as a train passed by.

The prey.

Only hours after that first, well-publicized kill, Kevin—who still, for a while longer, remembered that he had once had a name—found his second subterranean victim.

It was dark in the tunnel. The air they pushed ahead of

them in their headlong flight warned him well in advance
each time a train was due. There was plenty of time to find
safety; to crouch in a niche designed for the purpose until
the heedless glass-and-metal worm was gone. Eventually he
reached a place in the system where the tunnels opened up:
four, five, six sets of tracks running parallel for a few yards
before diverging to their separate lines once more. And in
the vaulting darkness on that quiet Sunday, Kevin could
sense movement.

He could smell food.

He did to have to debate within himself for very long before killing; the maddening hunger that had left him so
briefly had returned again, stronger than before; the hunger
that was the Sword's true legacy to humankind: an unslakable and very specific appetite.

And about the time his last victim was discovered, Kevin
killed again.

Somewhere between the subway car and here he had un-
sheathed the Sword from its makeshift scabbard. There was
no need for concealment any longer; he carried the Sword
naked in his hand. He heard a voice call out to him, and
flinched momentarily away from the beam of a weak flashlight, but whether this new Other was track worker or fellow
interloper Kevin did not choose to care. Between recogniz-
ing the prey and lashing out with that killing engine was no
more than a heartbeat.

And then again there was food; warm glorious soft sweet
fulfilling food.

He gorged until he could eat no more, crouched there between the pillars. He was safe; such trains as passed in the
distance carried no one who would see him for what he was.
At last, satiated, he stopped groping toward unfamiliar del-
icacies in the intermittent darkness. What he left behind
would be finished by rats; it was unlikely that this body
would ever be found, no matter who it had been. Kevin wandered on, with a vague certainty that his journey now led to
some definite destination.

It was then that his skin began to itch.

The dark glasses had gone long since. Now the militaristic
nylon bomber jacket was discarded; its heat and weight
maddening to skin gone suddenly raw and sensitive. He
paused again and again to scratch everywhere his hands
could reach, until his nails drew fresh native blood to mingle

with the dried blood that caked his clothes, and found no relief. Eventually shirt and undershirt were abandoned in the
tunnels as well.

He folded them neatly and set them aside carefully, out of
the damp. Perhaps, at the time, he even meant to come back
for them. And some unreckonable time later, what was left
of Kevin Shelby found the cure for the itch, just as it had for
the hunger.

She'd known he wouldn't do something as sensible as go
to McDonald's.

Melior caught up to Jane just as she was about to go
through the antique yellow-painted wooden turnstile that led
to Darkest Brooklyn.

"Wait," he said, and like an idiot, a worldling, a mundane,
she did.

"Stay a moment," he said, just as if he thought he was
Shakespeare and she was PBS, "there is something I wish to
see."

And then he went back to the edge of the platform, to the
sheer drop-off that led only to the tracks below—and
jumped off.

"Hey," said Jane.

Her voice sounded weak and unconvincing, even to her. If
not for the fact that she felt completely unequal to the task
of explaining this to Ruth, she would have gone off and left
Melior-the-elf right then, and if she had held out any hope
that he would have stayed put she would at least have had
lunch before she dealt with him.

But since she knew perfectly well he would not, and
equally she knew that Ruth would not be satisfied by even
the best and most reasonable explanation of events, Jane
abandoned lunch and egress and went back to the edge of
the platform and looked down.

Melior was nowhere in sight. Jane was methodical; she
looked both ways. She even looked behind her, back toward
daylight and sanity. Nothing.

"Hey!" she cried, a good deal louder this time.

Two glowing green orbs of the cat-in-darkness sort appeared out of the blackness. They flashed and vanished as
Melior looked away.

"Mistress Jane?" Melior said. His voice, pitched low to
carry, sounded weirdly as though he were standing just be-

side her and not several yards away. "It is just as I thought. Come and see for yourself."

Jane looked all around, but this station was not one of the ones with a manned token booth (or any sort of token booth at all, to be brutally accurate), and apparently this quarter of Brooklyn was not particularly well-traveled at 12:45 Monday afternoon.

She looked up the tracks. She didn't see an oncoming train, but uppermost in her mind was the fact that if Melior here was to get himself creamed by a train, she didn't even have to bother to go back to Ruth and the others. She could just jump in front of the next one.

"Where are you?" Jane called, trying very hard not to feel ridiculous.

Melior came out into the light of the platform, looking like a fifteen-second clip from the next thing in horror films. He'd taken off his mirrorshades, and in the shadows his eyes flared green-yellow and silver, reflecting all the light there was. His pale skin seemed to pluck up shadows from the surrounding air, making him look not only unearthly pale, but white in the way of mushrooms and fishbellies and things far better left unexamined. His leather jacket hung open, his shirt was smudged with tunnel grime—a thousand innocent things conspired bizarrely to form one snapshot image of horror.

Jane jumped backward, emitting a mouselike and inelegant squeak. She gritted her teeth. He'd done that on purpose, she was almost certain.

But either Melior was a very good actor (granted) or innocent of such subtle plottings as Jane assigned him. He walked up the railbed to the edge of the platform and heaved himself up.

"I could not be certain from inside the *cars*—" Melior's distaste gave the word a foreign and unfamiliar flavor, "—but now I am certain. This is such a place as a *grendel* would lair."

" '*Just the place for a Snark/I have said it thrice: /What I tell you three times is true.*' Lewis Carroll. Charles Dodgson, if you prefer. *He* saw fairies at the bottom of the garden," Jane added expansively. "Which doesn't mean there were any."

"But there is a *grendel*—and it has been here, at least recently," Melior said.

What did it do, leave graffiti? Jane thought, but did not say it. Offensively smartass remarks were Philip's speciality. All Jane did was state the obvious. They couldn't get you for reporting the facts.

"Or so I think," said Melior, with sudden suspicious humility, "but, as I have been told far too many times for my liking that I do not understand this World of Iron, I wish you to see what I have seen as well, and tell me, if you may, wherein lies my error."

"You mean I'm supposed to tell you if you've made a mistake. And I have to go down there to do it." *I can hardly contain my rapture.*

It was spring, so it had been raining recently, and, as after every rain, pools of water had collected at the bottom of the faintly-curving floor of the railbed. The tunnel was littered with garbage tossed from the windows of passing trains or flung from the platform itself, and from where Jane stood she could see the busy and entirely unworried—and large, and well-fed, and nothing-at-all like Stuart Little—rats saunter to and fro.

Melior vaulted down off the platform again and held up his hands, obviously ready to assist her.

"We're all gonna die," Jane muttered. Hissing curses between her clenched teeth, she sat down on the edge of the platform—wincing at the filth—and slid off into the unknown. Without help.

The drop was farther than she had expected, and jarring. The first sensation she registered was the soft but not treacherously moist squish of compacted litter beneath her sneakers.

The second was the wind that heralded an oncoming train.

She flattened herself against the platform, but without Melior's help she had no hope of climbing up it again. Jane was not particularly tall; the lip of the platform was a foot and more above her head. It was streaked with grease and soot and probably the entrails of a thousand rush-hour suicides.

And Melior stood there, oblivious.

"It's a *train*," Jane said, in a voice that refused to be either steady or audible. She knew she had to do something, but terror held her still. Movement was a surrender to fear.

And now Melior reacted, but slowly, slowly: where every

instinct screamed at Jane to run, he had to reason out the danger with instincts honed to something entirely other.

The light was a faint spark in the distance now. The train-man had seen them, or seen something; the despairing wail of the seldom-used whistle echoed through the tunnel.

And Melior caught her by the arm and began to run.

They ran. Wet garbage slid beneath Jane's feet. They ran away from the lights of the platform and into the darkened tunnel where there was no light to see by, and despite this Jane's greatest fear was that she would lose her glasses and be blind in truth. They passed the end of the platform and ran on. The smooth close walls of the tunnel mocked their efforts, providing them no place to hide.

And even if there were a place for one, there would not be a place for two.

The train's klaxon was constant now, and with some unoc-cupied portion of her mind Jane recognized that it was not slowing as it neared the station: an express, or some other line running on the Double-L's tracks. The roadbed beneath her feet pitched sharply downward; she would have fallen if not for Melior's inflexible grip on her arm.

And then, miraculous—though also what Melior was run-ning toward, having seen it in his previous explorations—the tunnel intersected with another, and in the safe hollow where the rails crossed, Melior dragged Jane to her knees and threw his arms around her.

The train thundered by instants later.

Sparks sprayed up from its wheels; there was a teeth-setting scream of metal on metal. The wind of its passage stank of burning oil and liquid rot. And it was *loud,* a rhyth-mic thunder that terrified by sheer disorienting volume, even while the reasonable mind insisted that the sound came from a machine that was bound by Man's laws, incapable of trans-gression.

It seemed to go on forever.

At last the train, with one last wailing tocsin, fishtailed its way to its next destination, and left them behind.

Slowly Jane became aware that Melior was holding her in an embrace so tight it hurt. His face was buried against her neck; the upraised collar of his leather jacket tickled her nose. He was shaking. She wondered if he was crying and desperately hoped not.

But of more immediate interest was the knowledge that

she, Jane Treasure Greyson, had survived a genuine urban myth folk legendary experience and was now invested with bragging rights.

Melior raised his head. Jane saw with sincere relief that he was not crying. Maybe elves just didn't, but Jane was thankful for small favors, whatever the genesis.

"Have you taken hurt, Mistress Jane?" Melior said.

"No, I'm fine." Which, whether it was true or not, was one of those automatic dumb things people always said to prevent true communication from taking place.

Although on this occasion it was more true than not. Jane was more than fine. She was exalted.

She had won. She wasn't quite sure what game they were playing, but she knew she had won. She'd done it. She'd been competent. She *hadn't fucked up*.

Melior seemed a bit taken aback by her matter-of-factness. Slowly, stiffly, he unwound his arms from about her and got to his feet. Jane scrambled after, inelegant but unwilling to be assisted. She realized with dismay that she had been kneeling in something not only gross but *wet*, and the palms of her hands were greasily black from their contact with the tunnel walls. She wiped them defiantly on her powder-blue corduroy slacks.

"So," she said, with a dawning delight at how cool she sounded, "what was it you wanted to show me, before we were interrupted?"

"Forgiving me for my foolishness; it seems that Friend Michael was right, and I do in very truth need a keeper. I did not wish to place you in such mortal jeopardy, Mistress Jane, I did not realize—" Melior broke off in the manner of someone who realizes they're about to be less than politic. "I did not precisely understand the nature of these conveyances," he finished instead.

I wonder what he was going to say before he stopped? Jane thought with less than urgent curiosity.

"Well, now you know," she said equitably. Self-confidence swelled like a golden balloon in her chest. *She had done it.*

"Yes," said Melior, "now I know. And I fear that when Mistress Ruth discovers how I have used you, she will be less than kind." Melior sounded more upset by that than by his recent brush with trainicide.

*And Philip will be sure to say something disgusting. At
regular intervals. For years.*

"I wouldn't, you know, *mind* if you didn't mention it,"
Jane suggested carefully. She looked up the tracks the way
they had come. The platform was a surprising ways distant.
There was no train in sight.

She looked back at Melior. He was smiling.

"Then we shall not trouble the mind of Mistress Ruth
with inessentials, by your leave. And for this day's grace,
Mistress Jane, know that you have some claim upon
Rohannan Melior of the House of the Silver Silences, who
has incurred a debt that he shall repay."

*Yeah, right. That and a dollar-fifty'll get me a ride on the
subway.*

But Jane smiled back. "So what was it you wanted me to
see?"

What Melior had wanted her to see lay some distance farther down the tunnel, where the light from the platform
dwindled to inconsequence and only the red-and-green of
the lights in the tunnel gave any illumination to see by. Now
that she was habituated to them, the subway tunnels took on
a weird beauty, almost as if they were caves instead of human creations. Every surface was covered with the furry flat
blackness of greasy soot, and the signal lights did little to il-
luminate the space.

Once they had to pause for the passage of another train,
but there was plenty of warning, and plenty of space to slide
into. Jane estimated that they had walked the equivalent of
about two city blocks when Melior stopped.

"Here," he said.

"Where?"

They were standing almost beneath one of the signal-
lights. It was green, indicating that a train might pass with
impunity, but even in its ghastly viridian light the interior of
the tunnel was only shadow-shapes.

"Here," Melior said again, and now Jane could see that he
was pointing downward, at something wedged between two
of the girders that held up the roof and divided the sets of
tracks from each other.

"I can't see in the dark, you know," Jane pointed out.

"I do not want to touch it. The *grendel* has been here, and
left this behind."

Jane took a step forward and poked at the bundle experimentally, then pulled it out before Melior could stop her. It wasn't that much of a gamble; the thing looked dry, and if it turned out to be stuffed full of human hearts she was already braced not to squeak.

But it wasn't, and she didn't.

"Mistress Jane!" Melior protested, but Jane was already holding it up. She felt cold zippers, nylon, and acrylic fur. A bomber jacket like the police wore.

"Get a life, will you?" she muttered under her breath. Something on the jacket flaked off as she ran her hands over it, but the darkness was too deep to see.

"Don't touch that. Put it from you; it reeks of evil."

"I don't smell anything."

But who could, down here? The mingled smells of urine and rotting garbage had long since put her nose on overload. Jane could no longer smell them, and *l'air du subway* was only a burnt-rubber taste in the back of her throat.

Or maybe Melior was feeling metaphorical?

"I said leave it!" To Jane's surprise, Melior grabbed the jacket and flung it away into the outer darkness. There was a squeaking and a scuttling that would have played havoc with Jane's delicate nerves if she'd happened to have any.

"If that was your proof, you've just thrown it away," Jane said after a pause.

" *'If'?"* Melior demanded. "The creature sheds its varied skins; I show you proof and you mock at it."

"Oh." Understanding came with a jolt, the way it often does when a companion's bizarre actions suddenly make luminous sense.

"But it wasn't proof, Melior. Not of anything. Not to me. Not even to Ruth." *It was only somebody's jacket.*

And there never would be proof, Jane realized suddenly, and there probably wasn't a *grendel,* either. Because whether Melior was an elf or not, he was also crazy.

"How can I make you see, before it is too late?" Melior groaned, and Jane, galvanized to honesty, answered.

"I don't know."

CHAPTER 12

When the Magic's Real

Alone in the apartment after Ruth's hasty departure, Naomi pulled the notebook she was keeping out of its storage place and glanced through it. A cup of tea stood at her elbow, spiraling steam into the air.

Nothing had changed. Everything was just as it had been the last time she'd looked: what he'd told her, what they'd done. She'd even sketched pictures of his clothes and jewelry—the clothes and jewelry of a self-proclaimed Prince of Elfland. And hadn't Michael said there was just too much of it to fake? Those eyes, those ears, those *teeth*—

My, what big pointy teeth you've got, Grandma.

None of it helped. She'd seen the same news broadcast Ruth had. The murder in the subway.

Melior thought it was his *grendel.* And what else, after all, could it be? *Almost anything.*

Too real for me. Naomi shook her head in sad self-rebuke and closed the book again. In the children's books she loved things like this never happened. She believed Melior (with reservations) but what she'd really been expecting was for his sword to turn up in the window of Sotheby's. Or something, anything, just so long as it wasn't this cross between *The Taking Of Pelham One Two Three* and *Silence Of The Lambs.*

Naomi shuddered. Did the murder make this more real, or more fantastic? She didn't know. She only knew that she resented it deeply. *"A real toad in an imaginary garden."*

And she was worried about Ruth.

"Sensei, I have a problem."

Master Paul Robillard was Naomi's sensei, or teacher, in the gentle art of kendo. His dojo was located on Broadway a few blocks south of her apartment, in a bright corner space two flights up from a greengrocer's. There, three evenings a

week, Naomi and seven others took master classes in the
Way of the Sword.

"If you'd stop dropping your wrist when you attack,
you'd be fine."

Mornings, no one was here, except Sensei.

"It's not that sort of a problem," Naomi said.

"Well, why don't you get dressed and we'll talk about it?"

There were windows in three walls of the dojo; the huge
square space with its white-painted walls and bare wood
floor, was drenched in light. The back wall was still mirrored, and a barre ran around all four walls, legacy of its
one-time use as a dance studio.

Naomi padded out onto the floor in her *hakama* and slippers, and bowed to the altar with its photos, oranges, and lit
candles. Then she turned and regarded herself in the mirror.

She'd come to Sensei Paul for help, but what could she
say? Ruth was the one with the problem, not her.

Since the fall semester, with graduation suddenly on everybody's mind, Ruth had been, well, looking for a way out.
Advanced coursework wasn't the answer—as it had been in
her case, Naomi thought wryly—since Ruth had to get out
there and earn a living before the Student Loan Officer decided to take the debt out in white slavery.

But if Ruth were using Melior as a form of escapism, it
was going to backfire, badly.

Sensei Paul came out onto the floor, holding two masks in
one hand and a pair of *bokken* in the other. Paul was tall and
handsome, with skin like polished teak. He looked like a
poster boy for street crime and was the gentlest soul Naomi
knew. He even made Michael look aggressive. He crossed
the floor and handed her the mask. Like most of the senior
students, Naomi kept the bulkier items of her kendo costume
here. She put the mask on, settling its familiar contours
against her face, then took her sword. It was shaped like a
rough sketch for a *katana;* light brown wood and a plastic
sword-guard. Almost harmless.

But even a toy sword could kill.

Paul Robillard put on his mask, and Naomi's friend vanished. All that was left was Sensei, who would whack her
severely if she made a mistake.

It settled the mind wonderfully.

Naomi bowed. Sensei bowed. And then she let the sword-mind flow into her as Sensei slipped easily into position and began circling her. Part of her mind watched, waiting for her own opening, but, flying high above the room, the other part considered Ruth.

Things could be worse than they were, of course. Ruth could have fallen for some guy and gotten married as an escape from reality. Only Ruth never dated. Naomi had known her for almost three years and would have been happy to make suitable introductions. For a while she'd thought Ruth and Michael might pair up, but Ruth had made friends with him instead.

But if Naomi were any judge of human nature, Ruth was falling for Melior. And that would not be a good thing at all.

Whack!

"You're not paying attention," Sensei said. Naomi wanted to rub the stinging welt on her hip where the blow had landed, but didn't dare. She raised her sword again, but Sensei did not raise his. After a moment he straightened, and pulled off his mask.

"It must be a very bad problem, to make you so stupid," he observed mildly.

Naomi sighed. She'd deserved that.

"It is a bad problem. It's not mine, you see, and that makes it worse."

"Ah. A friend?"

"Yes." And the only thing Naomi couldn't decide was whether it would be worse for Ruth to fall for Melior—or for her to be the sort of person who never fell in love at all.

"You cannot solve the problems of others. Each person is his own problem, and his own solution."

"Thank you, Master Po. If I want Zen, I can go to the library."

Sensei Paul smiled. "Well, if "no-mind" won't work, why don't we see if we can beat it out of you with a good workout? And after that, you can tell me what's wrong."

"I have this friend," Naomi said. She was wrapped in a terrycloth robe, hair still damp from her shower, sitting on a stool in Paul's tiny New York kitchen while he whisked a bowl of green tea into an opaque froth. "She's getting really attached to this guy, and I think he's going to be a lot of trouble."

"That isn't a very detailed outline of the problem," Paul observed.

"I think details would get in the way of the facts," Naomi said.

"And how much trouble can this guy be for your friend?" Paul said after a moment. He set a bowl of tea in front of her. Naomi sipped and thought about it.

"I suppose he's what you could call the "attractive nuisance" type. No job. No money. In fact, he's sleeping on Michael's couch at the moment. He's got a ... problem he wants help with. The help could turn out to be pretty costly, in the long run, but he's so gosh-darned cute it's hard to remember that when he's asking for just one little thing. It's like chasing a dream. She could pour her whole life into him and it wouldn't be enough."

And wouldn't Melior's dream be preferable to anyone's reality? Who wouldn't rather live in a world of evil emperors and magic swords, of monsters and heroes? Everything clear-cut and obvious. The perfect escape, with a side order of moral rectitude.

"And how does this come to be your problem? You aren't your brother's keeper, as a great Zen master once said." Paul regarded her steadily, his hazel eyes allowing for no evasions.

Naomi studied her tea a while longer. "I think it's my problem because I'm not objecting to what he's doing," she said at last. "If I see something that I don't like, and I say nothing, then it's the same as endorsing the thing I don't like. Isn't it?"

"That could be a hard philosophical position to live with," Paul said, as if addressing the bonsai in the window.

Naomi sighed. "It could be a hard position to live without."

CHAPTER 13

The Dream You Never Found

Ruth finished her exam, handed it in, and went off to check her mail. She stood in front of her mailbox in the Student Union with its contents in her hand.

A letter from Carol in Idaho. A Macy's bill. Her student discount rate copy of *Library Journal*. Five crisp, bland, and forbidding envelopes—the fruits of her most recent spasm of job searches. Pray that they were all at least invitations to interview. One of them would be her future.

Suddenly the sight of them revolted her utterly; she crumpled them in her hand and stuffed them into her purse, seeking for the bottom, knowing that her defiant gesture was only empty theatrics, that later she would open them and read them out.

But she *did* throw the *Library Journal* in the trash.

Safe, sensible, prudent Ruth. Who never did anything drastic. Who never made a gesture that mattered.

With the crumpled letters still at the bottom of her purse, Ruth walked out of the Student Union.

She was contemplating wildness—or at least another pint of Häagen-Dazs Double Chocolate—and blinking in the unexpected May sunlight when she was hailed from below. Squinting down the steps, she peered until she made out Michael and Philip.

Philip's backpack was crammed to even more overstuffed proportions, and his laptop was balanced (with an accompanying sheaf of papers) upon his hip. Michael stood beside him, towering over Philip as usual and looking faintly uneasy. He was not the one who'd shouted.

"Hey, yourself," Ruth said, descending the steps.

"Looking for another line of work, yet?" Philip asked.

"I'll leave that to you," she said which, if feeble, was at least something. "I understand that there are positions in license-plate technology opening up every day." And where was—

"Seen Jane?" Michael asked, and Ruth's nagging disquiet kindled into six-cylinder life, even though she had a close concept of where Jane must be; she'd gone off to the subway to be Melior's Keeper-For-A-Day at an hour when Ruth was still doing her best to prop her eyes open. They'd been supposed to be back by one or two, but it was only the *subway*, for heaven's sake, and if she wasn't here she had every reason to be late. Ruth looked at her watch. Two-thirty.

Not so very late, but the unfocused fear still cut through her like a knife. "No," she began.

"Lucky you," Philip said, but Michael quelled him with a glance.

"She's probably with Nai," Michael said. But if she was, Ruth worried on, then why had he asked?

"If she didn't get arrested," Philip said.

"That social refinement we leave to you," Ruth said with gracious poison.

"Would you guys cut it out? I want to talk to Melior," Michael said.

Philip produced an eloquent subvocal rumble but said nothing. Michael headed across the street and the other two followed.

"How did the exam go?" Michael asked her when he had them both in motion.

"How does any exam go? And yours? I hate cataloging, I hate cataloging exams; everybody buys LC cataloging nowadays which means that some gnome in the basement of the Library of Congress or probably his computer is making us all file *Outlaws of Sherwood* under Folklore and books on the Miss America pageant under Beauty Aids and what's the *point?*" Ruth finished in a rush.

"Take it easy," Michael said.

"The point is, there is no point." Philip spoke up surprisingly. "No one here gets out alive. And over a sufficient period of time, all choices tend to normalize on a curve of random distribution."

"You mean if you wait long enough, nothing happens?" Ruth said.

"In a hundred years, who will care?" Philip smiled a lopsided and not terribly happy smile.

But I don't even care now, Ruth thought forlornly, and

wondered what evil she had committed in the lost hours of that long-gone summer's night that was enough to poison all the rest of her years.

Naomi turned out not to be home either, though in her case a scribbled note proclaimed her out of eggs for the cake and back in ten. Ruth, putting on the kettle for tea, saw the cramped utilitarian student housing as if for the first time; a clarity of sight she was unable to ameliorate. Vinyl couch patched with plastic tape and draped with a length of tattered fabric. Threadbare sage-green carpet. Age-yellowed, obscurely-stained shades; each object a blatant letter of an alphabet in an unfamiliar tongue. Shabby, threadbare, rock-bottom, bone-weary. . . .

Ruth stared blindly at the spotted paint behind the stove and realized, with horrified clarity, that she was going to cry. Over the *couch*, for God's sake? She must be losing her *mind*. . . .

And there was no one here but Michael and Philip.

Snuffling only a little, Ruth lit the stove, and in the soft bloom of blue gas flame set the kettle on the stove and turned around to the sink. She splashed water on her face, but the sense of despairing dread still hung over her, like foreshadowing in a bad novel.

Heavens. How perfectly Celtic, Ruth thought mockingly. *The next thing I'll do is sit down and howl at the moon.*

But that wouldn't be sensible, some ghostly interior counterpoint inserted. Ruth sighed sadly over her inability to carry off a really good dramatic interior monologue and turned away from the sink.

Michael was standing in the doorway. Things always tended to look too small around Michael; he was large enough to make even Ruth—were she so inclined—feel small and kittenish, which was no mean feat when you stood five foot eight in your stocking feet.

"Feel better?" Michael asked.

"No," said Ruth honestly. She waved the unspoken words—hers and his—away. "I don't know. Melior. What if—"

"What if there isn't a sword?" Michael finished. "Or what if we just don't find it? What if he's stuck here forever? What if he dies?"

Ruth stared, struck reasonably speechless.

"Why is it you women always think that guys don't ever talk about anything but sex and fast cars?" Michael smiled, to take the edge off it. It did, even if only a little. "He's been sleeping on my couch for—what?"

"Three days," Ruth supplied automatically. "Friday, Saturday, and Sunday."

"And if he stays here, he's dead. He said he told you."

"He did."

Michael shrugged, uncomfortable.

"What is it, Michael-mine, that you found out between breakfast and lunch and aren't telling?" Ruth, goaded, pounced.

Michael met her gaze squarely. Michael always looked everyone in the eye, no matter what he had to say.

"The people who're supposed to be being killed, aren't being killed," he said simply.

It took Ruth a moment to shift mental gears from interior monologues to homicide and figure this one out.

"Which means his *grendel* doesn't exist," she said flatly.

"If," said Michael, leaning back against the wall and blowing out a breath of pure exasperation, "*if* his *grendel* is a magical creature, and *if* this world is the World of Iron his mythology talks about, and *if* elf-magic works as badly here as Mel seems to think it does, then he might not be right about his sword working better than that."

Ruth took a moment to puzzle all that out.

"No *grendel*, no way to find the sword."

"The real question is," Philip said, pushing his way past Michael to enter the kitchen and the conversation, "how *long* are we going to look for it before we give up?"

Philip's hair was pulled back into the thin queue that always reminded Ruth of a white rat's tail. His steel-rimmed bifocals made his eyes alternately distant and flat featureless coin-mirrors in his narrow mustelid face. He stood with shoulders hunched and both hands jammed into the pockets of his red windbreaker and seemed to be addressing his remarks to the refrigerator. But for once he wasn't trying to score verbally off anybody.

"How long?" Philip repeated. "He's sleeping on your couch" —to Michael— "and you've spun major plastic on him" —to Ruth— "and ya-ta-da ya-ta-da and ill-met by moonlight proud Titania—"

Ruth stared in shock. She hadn't known Philip ever read anything but software manuals.

"But the bottom line is: how long?"

Silence.

"After a certain point, finding the sword is like finding the kidnap victim: impossible. At least with what we've got to work with," Michael observed.

"Six hundred bucks and a leather jacket," Philip footnoted. "So the question is, 'can he type?' "

"What?" Had Philip been out in the sun too long? (In *May?*) Was he trying a new designer drug? (He didn't even drink *coffee.*) Was he all there? (But in his own sweet sociopathic way, Philip LeStrange was always all there.)

Philip turned away and hunched his shoulders even higher, as if denying the existence of his ears. "After the ball is over, Cinderella. And we pack it in. You and Michael are graduating this year, y'know. After that."

"I don't think," Michael said slowly, "that he's going to give up."

Philip shrugged angrily and stalked back to the living room. After a moment Ruth heard the tap-tap-tap of his keyboard.

But the obvious last line remained, as clearly as if he'd said it.

So when are YOU giving up, Ruth?

It was a morose and disaffected party which greeted Naomi's return.

A brown Rockingham pot of infused but undrunk tea sat in the middle of the living room table. Michael was sprawled on the couch. Philip was sprawled on the floor. Ruth was curled, feet up, in a chair almost too small for the gesture, paging through an old exhibition catalog and pretending neither of the others was there.

Naomi put down one of the sacks and shifted the other one to her hip.

"Who died?" she asked. "Or is that remark not in the best of taste?"

"No one died," said Michael, "and *that* was the curious incident."

"I see," said Naomi. "Do I take it, then, that the customary trappings of the wake are in order?" She lifted the lid off the teapot and pulled out the tea ball. The liquid running from it was almost black.

"I think it's done," she commented, heading for the kitchen. She returned a moment later with four mugs strung on her fingers like useful rings and the remaining necessities for tea gripped precariously among remaining fingers. She extracted the tea ball and poured tea.

"We were trying to think of what kind of job Melior could get," Ruth volunteered, at last, into the silence.

"Male model?" Naomi suggested at last, which at least drew a snicker from Philip. "But seriously, folks—is Jane all right?"

Ruth kept herself from snarling with an effort, and as a result Naomi's question stood unanswered when the buzzer rang.

Michael uncoiled from the couch with surprising violence and lunged for the buzzer. "Yes?" he barked, and the hash of street noise he got back seemed to satisfy him, because he hit the unlock button and held it down for a long minute.

"They're back," he announced, looking at Naomi's startled expression.

"You kids lead such interesting lives," she commented, and went on into the kitchen with the bag.

It was Michael who held the door open, allowing the sounds of sneakers on stair treads to fill the apartment. Ruth stared at her hands, as if she were being paid good money not to look. And eventually they got there.

Jane came through the door first, and for a moment Ruth didn't recognize her. The white turtleneck with the blue flowers, the matching blue cardigan, the pale blue corduroy slacks which were the closest Jane ever got to jeans were streaked and barred with black grime. The knees of her pants were literally black, with a polished-cotton sheen of ground-in dirt. There were even smudges on her face, painting on a faint *faux* glamorie of *trompe l'oeil* cheekbones.

"What the *hell* happened to you?" Ruth demanded in a voice she hardly recognized as hers.

Melior entered behind Jane. The black leather jacket, the artistically-distressed jeans, showed the dirt far less than Jane's once painfully-neat ensemble, but when you looked for it, it was there. Ruth got up. Jane ducked past Michael and fled to the bathroom.

Melior ran a hand through his hair. "We have been in the

subterranean ways, Ruth. And as I foretold you, the *grendel* is there. I have found proof." He set down the bag he'd been carrying; Ruth saw a familiar fast-food logo.

Michael shut the door behind him. "And did you, ah, bring this "proof" with you?"

Melior regarded him with schooled blandness, and once again Ruth felt that ghostly echo of clashing wills between the two men.

"And how does one bring the scent from the earth, or the track from the mud? Yet they are no less real for that. The *grendel* casts off its human seeming, and becomes more powerful with each passing hour." Melior advanced into the room, wrapping the leather jacket around himself as if he were cold. "And we are here."

"Everybody's gotta be someplace," Philip commented. He sat up and leaned back against the couch.

"And I and thou are here," Melior said. "And yet I am forced to wonder, Master Philip, why should this be so?"

"Come again?" Naomi said from the kitchen doorway.

Melior turned toward her and favored her with a smile of dazzling charm. "I would not forgo your company easily, Mistress Naomi, nor yet the table you set. But I have learned, as you wished me to, that this world is wide. And so I wonder: when I fell prey to the traps which bespelled the Sword of Maiden's Tears, why should my place in it be here, and not some other place?"

"Well," said Naomi slowly, "there's no place like this place anywhere around the place, so this must be the place."

"Why?" said Melior.

"Why not?" said Philip to his shoes.

"Because things do not happen save for reasons," Melior said patiently.

Naomi laughed. "Brother, are *you* a long way from home."

"Yes," said Melior seriously, and smiled. He walked across the room to Ruth, and looked down at her. "But as you see, I have gone and come back again, unimpeded by the city guard."

"On Earth we call them policemen," said Philip.

Jane came out of the bathroom, damp and hostile. Her face was scrubbed pink and her cotton cardigan buttoned up demurely over the worst of the grime. She glanced at Melior; Ruth saw her do it and felt a flash of reasonless jealousy. Melior's hand closed reassuringly over Ruth's shoulder and squeezed warmly.

"So exactly where in the subway were you?" Ruth asked.

Again Melior and Jane exchanged glanced. "Somewhere in Brooklyn," Jane said finally.

"And that's where the *grendel* is?" Michael said, working very hard to keep his voice neutral. From the kitchen there was a momentary whine of an electric mixer and a clatter of pans.

"No," said Melior patiently. "That is where the *grendel* was. But, so I am told, the tunnels are all linked, and it will not venture forth into the light willingly again."

"So it's in the subway?" Michael repeated again, as if it were very important that this question be answered. There was a rattle and bang of the oven door, and Naomi came back into the living room.

"Forty minutes," she said cryptically. She sat down on the arm of a chair and swept the room with a glance, very much as if they were all books and she were about to catalog them. "So. Why don't we all tell each other what kind of a day we all had?"

There was a moment's silence. Ruth felt again that strong sense of *peril;* as if the words spoken here would serve as choices; would set paths that all of them here would have to follow.

She was almost spooked enough to warn the others; to suggest it, making it a joke, when Philip spoke.

"Well, Michael and me hacked into the Coroner's Office and found out that whatever else this *grendel*'s doing, it isn't leaving a bunch of bodies lying around. Guess it isn't very hungry, huh?" Philip shoved his glasses back up on the bridge of his nose.

Ruth felt Melior go very still behind her.

"This is Monday afternoon," Jane said, getting all of her facts straight. "We heard about the last kill Sunday night, but it had to have been killed Saturday night at the latest, because it was found Sunday afternoon. But this *grendel*'s supposed to be hungry," she added, looking half-challengingly toward Melior.

"It starves from what it battens upon," Melior agreed. "The hunger that was a man's in life for glory or fame is transmuted by the curse into unslakable appetite."

"Betcha can't eat just one," Philip muttered.

"So if there is a *grendel,* as you believe," Michael said, "there should be more victims."

"Should there?" said Melior. He stepped away from Ruth now, and all five of them watched him. "How do you know there are not?"

"We didn't find any," Michael said. He sounded as if he'd looked personally, but Ruth knew he meant that it hadn't turned up in Philip's, um, *hacking.*

Philip's hacking. Was Michael really taking Philip's word over Melior's?

Was she willing to take Melior's word over Philip's?

When was she going to "call it quits"?

Was she going to?

"With your machines," said Melior, as if it were a personal insult. "The machines see nothing, so you say there *is* nothing. But these machines know only what men have told them."

"In the nonexclusive sense of the word 'men,'" Naomi added.

"So you're telling us there's something we've missed," Michael said, carefully neutral.

"I am saying I beg your trust, Friend Michael. For a time—a *short* time—more. You say there is no magic—" Melior raised his voice and spread his arms. The sweeping gesture was meant for a cape but somehow did not look silly when performed in a leather jacket. "*I* say there is. And I say that the creature I seek is there. In the subterranean. It hardly matters if you believe, you know. You are not worldlings for me to beguile with tales of sorcery, nobility, and gold. I ask you now for one simple thing—"

"This is something more substantial than buying a ticket, isn't it?" Naomi said, cutting through the spell of Melior's words.

"Yes," said Melior. "I do not need the cars. I need to get into the tunnels. On foot. I need your aid for that."

Jane shifted where she sat, but only Ruth noticed. She thought Melior might have tried to go down into the tunnels today, but probably Jane had stopped him.

"Into the tunnels," said Naomi. "Just jump over the side of the platform. Sounds easy."

"And get creamed by an oncoming train," said Philip.

"I would need provisions. Lights. And weapons; a good club; a sword or a boar-spear."

Philip made a noise. "In the first place you can't do it. In the second place, they'll arrest you. And in the third place, there isn't anything down there to chase. Period."

Now it was out and all of them had to face it. Not disbelief in Melior-as-he-was; only disbelief in his goal.

"If there is nothing there, then no harm can come, can it?" Melior said.

"We could be arrested," said sensible Ruth. Sensible *traitorous* Ruth. "We could get killed—by the third rail, by rats, by passing muggers. And if we got caught down there they'd fine us to death. I mean—"

"Bye-bye Columbia," Michael finished.

"You got a better idea?" said Jane, surprisingly defensive of Melior.

"*Not* getting creamed by an oncoming train leaps instantly to mind," Philip said helpfully.

"I do not propose that you do," Melior said. "This is not your battle. Only provision me, and I shall go alone."

"That'd look great on the six o'clock news. *'Dead Elf Found In Subway, Pictures At Eleven.'* "

"If you can't say something helpful, Philip, would you please go home?" Jane asked long-sufferingly.

"I know that you do not believe," said Melior, "and this makes no difference—not to me, and certainly not to the creature I hunt. And I must hunt it—with your help or alone."

Melior looked beseechingly toward Naomi. She ran a hand through her short black hair. "With us or without us," she said. "But, Melior, you just don't understand—"

"I think you should let him do what he wants, even if it is stupid," Jane said flatly.

"It isn't that it's stupid," Ruth began.

"Although it is," Philip said.

"But there's the little matter of unlawful trespass, breaking and entering, little things like that. It's illegal," Michael said, a hint of truculence in his voice.

"Illegal?" Philip said. "I sure hope so." He laughed, then frowned. "Get down on the tracks. There's got to be ways. The subway guys do it all the time."

"The 'subway guys' are trained to do it," Naomi said. "They know all the nooks and crannies of the system. And the train schedules. And everything."

"The trains—and the schedules—are on computer," Philip said sweetly.

"No," said Naomi flatly. "Not without proof—*real* proof."

Everyone looked at her. "This is not a game. This is not 'for-fun.' And it sure isn't the steam tunnels at Michigan State University," Naomi said. Her face was set, determined, and her voice vibrated with conviction as she spoke. "Everything Ruth's said about the third rail and the trains and everything *is true*. And it isn't just a matter of Melior not getting hurt—what if he caused a train wreck? Hundreds of people killed or injured—and our fault?"

"You'd have to do it at night," Philip said. "There aren't as many trains then."

Ruth had always suspected Naomi of being soft on Philip, for some unbelievable reason, but the look she riveted him with now was filled with such contempt that even Philip noticed. He ducked his head quickly, ears red, and didn't say anything else.

"I'm sorry, Melior," Naomi said. "We can't just go off and play in the subway on your word that there's something down there. This is real life, and this is dangerous. There isn't enough proof. I'm sorry."

That was that, and they all knew it. Even Melior didn't bother to argue. "I thank you, then, for all the patience you have shown me, Mistress Naomi. In my own place, I do not think that such kindness would have been shown to strangers." He inclined his head, acknowledging his defeat.

And then he turned and walked out the door.

"Hey!" In the moment Ruth realized he was really gone she lunged up out of her chair and flung—she'd never realized the description could be correct before—herself out the door. She thought someone tried to stop her, but if that was so, they didn't try as hard to keep her as she did to go.

Melior was waiting for her just outside the street door—or, if not waiting, then at least not leaving very fast.

"Wait," Ruth gasped, clutching at the edge of the door for support.

"Isn't it amusing, in a quiet way, that a Prince of the House of the Silver Silences, whose blood is filled with silver and starlight, who has commanded men in the field, and broken the Successor Lords on the Field of Glass, cannot entreat a moment's fealty from humans? *Humans,* Ruth. Can you credit it?"

"I'm human," Ruth said.

"Then perhaps you can explain it to me." He took her arm and drew her onto the sidewalk. He put an arm around her shoulders, and she leaned into him. The late-afternoon sun was just warm enough, and no one looked at either of them as they walked south on Riverside Drive, with the glassy swell of the Hudson beside them.

"I'm right," Melior said softly after a while.

"So what?" said Ruth mournfully. "It doesn't matter. It's a big thing to ask, you know. It's dangerous down there."

"I asked no one to accompany me," Melior reminded her.

"That wouldn't stop them," Ruth said darkly. "But it's—I know it's important to you, Melior, but it— It's just another *chanson geste* to you, and for us it's real. It's our *lives*."

"And when I am dead, and you are *grendel*-ridden; when the House of the Silver Silences is cast into the Outer Darkness forever and the balance of power in the Morning Lands slides inevitably toward Night, then, *then* you will say that you had no inkling of its import." His voice was quietly bitter.

"That isn't fair."

"I'm not in a mind to be fair."

"You want us to throw over everything—on your word alone—for something that probably isn't even there! *What's in it for us?*"

"Ah." They walked on for a few moments in silence, past skateboarders and a hot-dog stand, past frisbee-throwing kids and joggers. "But what if it is there?" Melior said.

Once again it was Ruth's turn to be silent. Because much as she wanted to believe in the *grendel,* even with Melior's technicolor presence to bolster her faith, she couldn't. Not when it was so much more likely to be the forlorn delusion of a dying exile. Not when cynical twentieth century probability said that was the way to bet—against monsters and heroes, bright promises and valorous deeds.

"If it is," Ruth said, coward compromise in her voice, "there'll be proof, won't there? More killings? Michael said there weren't any, and. . . ."

"He said the machines had recorded none, not that there were none. This city of yours is vast beyond imagining, and rich beyond the dreams of madmen, but it holds its poor who sleep in doorways. I have seen them. And I think, were I such a poor man and did I have the coin, I would choose to sleep in the subterranean where the rain and wind come not. If such a man dies, who mourns him? Tell me that, Ruth."

"Well, maybe," Ruth said irritably. "But it isn't *proof*, Melior. It's just another fairy tale."

"And you, Ruth? Will you do for love what they will not do for reason?" Melior stopped and pulled her gently around to face him.

Conflicting emotions spun through her panic-stricken brain, but topmost of all was the sick certainty that there was no *grendel*, and that if Melior went down into the tunnels the inevitable They would catch him and trap him and put him in a cage, and then even frustrated hope would be dead.

"Love?" said Ruth, through a choking throat. "Who said anything about love?"

Melior stared at her for a long moment, his pupils dark vertical flicks against the light of the setting sun.

"I did. But it seems that I misspoke myself."

He let her go and turned away, and left her with a long loping stride that she could not have matched, even if she'd cared to. She sat on a bench, and eventually the unwelcome and low-comic certainty came to her that she was going to have to go back home and tell them all *something,* and that undoubtedly by then there wouldn't be any chocolate cake left, either.

CHAPTER 14

Darkness at Noon

The land he passed through had neither sun nor moon. Its voice was the roaring of the distant ocean, and the water through which he walked was as warm and fecund as blood. Kevin Shelby had come into his kingdom at last.

Only he didn't know it—or to be perfectly precise, the one who possessed all these fastnesses did not precisely remember that once he had been a man who dreamed of glory. The One who was now would have thought Kevin Shelby's ambitions laughable if it had been confronted with them. The One who was now wanted only two things: food and the continued safety of The Object.

It was always hungry. There was still plentiful food available here in its realm, but with the focused facility of extreme paranoia The One knew that this soft sweet comfortable food was—still and also—a source of danger to it. A time would come when to hunt would be to imperil the safety of The Object, and The One did not want that. It was making arrangements against that day. Provident arrangements.

And there was one other source of danger. An Other, unlike either The One or The Object, an Other who wanted The Object for himself.

But The One was making arrangements for that, too.

Determined to pretend that nothing had happened, Ruth went back up the hill, away from Melior, toward Broadway and the Columbia campus. There she spent most of the afternoon, until twilight and a rumbling stomach made her admit that what she was really doing was trying to avoid her friends.

And feeling as if she wanted to avoid them wasn't *fair,* dammit, it wasn't *Ruth* who'd done anything to blush for. It was Melior who'd been so unreasonable; in fact, all of this was All Melior's Fault.

She wished she believed that.

She wished she knew what to believe.

But Melior had asked them—all five of them, Ruth and Michael, Naomi and Jane and Philip—for something they couldn't give him. It was all of their futures on the line here, and this wasn't some convenient fairy tale where the price of their mistakes would be death. No, it was worse than that: any mistakes any of them made would be mistakes they'd have to live with, all down the gray cheerless years of quiet desperation that were shaped by those mistakes.

You're a bundle of cheer tonight, Ruth told herself.

But it was true. It was a lot easier to gamble when the stakes were Success or Death. Half a century of being an impoverished failure was a little harder to swallow cheerfully.

She didn't believe in the *grendel.* And she didn't believe Melior would ever stop looking for it. And sooner or later he was going to run splat into the power structure and they'd take him and lock him up and—

Her hands were shaking. And her mind was, as it always did when she was upset, trying to push into the gray space that lay between eighteen and twenty-six, trying to find reality in what was actually and always would be a long gray vast shapeless expanse of nothing.

And that was the real joke, if Melior only knew it. She had so little to lose that she would gladly have gone into the subway with Melior bearing only an arc lamp and a machine gun—if she'd been able to believe.

In anything. Anything at all.

Ruth swallowed hard and wondered what he was doing and where he'd gone. *Melior* believed; good God, he had enough belief for any three normal people; he'd believe in something at the drop of a hat; just watch him and you could get yourself convinced of anything from the Doctrine of Signatures to the Ninety-Five Theses of Luther to the importance of flossing after meals.

Melior had passion. *Passion.* And wasn't that what everyone thought was such a hands-down terrific lifestyle accessory? A sensibility that went for the gusto like a starved pit bull? Mind, it might not know enough to come in out of the rain, but. . . .

If it had hurt less, she might have cried.

Some time later she looked up, conscious that someone was watching her. Jane was standing about three feet away, wearing a pink denim jumper (she must have changed her clothes) and balancing a load of books on her hip.

"I thought you were probably here," Jane said, sitting down.

"Welcome to previews of my post-collegiate depression," Ruth said mockingly.

"There wasn't anything there," Jane said simply.

"In the subway?" Ruth guessed.

Jane nodded, and sighed. "And he's going to go look for it anyway." Their glances locked, in wry complicity over the utter predictability of none-too-bright Tyrant Man.

Ruth shrugged, weary to the bone. So much for reaching out to grasp at magic. All it left you with was a handful of ashes.

"So we've got to stop him," Jane said stubbornly.

"What do you suggest, a straitjacket?" Ruth shot back.

"The New York Subway System has twelve hundred and fifty-seven miles of track and over ten thousand units of rolling stock. And somewhere in there he thinks there's a *grendel* and a magic sword. The *grendel* guards the sword. The sword is the only thing that can slay the *grendel*," Jane said pedantically.

"Right so far," Ruth said.

Jane leaned both elbows on the table, her lank hair swinging forward over her cheeks.

"So the only thing the *grendel* (if it really did exist) has to do to not get killed is *hide* the sword, right?"

Ruth stared at Jane and tried to find some flaw in her reasoning. Unfortunately it was seamlessly logical, as Jane's reasoning always was. Ruth wondered if the (probably non-existent) *grendel* was as smart as Jane Greyson.

"Right," she said hesitantly.

"And even if it's too stupid to think of something like that, strategy requires that you act as if it *will* think of it, in case you get caught flat-footed. So whether the *grendel* thinks of hiding the sword or not, Melior has to."

"And?" Ruth prompted.

"So Melior," said Jane with a sour expression, "has to make an *enormous pounce*. He can't give the *grendel* time to know he's hunting it, because that would give it time to hide the sword. He has to move fast."

Light dawned. "So he has to know exactly where he's going," said Ruth. "Right?"

Jane nodded. "And if he has a chance of getting accurate tactical intelligence, he won't move without it," she finished matter-of-factly.

If Melior had enough information to know where the *grendel* was, wouldn't that mean that there'd be enough information to constitute *proof* of its reality?

"But he isn't going to believe we'll do it! Not after—"

"He'll believe Philip will do it. Because Philip will do anything for money. And you've still got Melior's money," Jane said.

Ruth made a guilty grab at her handbag, but Jane was right: there it was, a little over thirty-six hundred dollars, all that was left after the shopping expedition at Macy's and the run-in with the Transit Police.

"I couldn't. . . ." Ruth began.

"*He* doesn't care what you do with it. And I bet you can't get Philip to do it for free. And if you did, it wouldn't give you—" there was a pause while Jane hunted for *le mot juste,* "—plausible deniability."

Ruth made a face. Jane was undoubtedly right about that. Only Naomi—and sometimes Michael—could induce the spirit of cooperation to inhabit the breast of Philip Leslie LeStrange.

But it could work. It might work. Bribe Philip, and have him go to Melior, and—

"So it's a deal?" Jane prompted.

"Sure," said Ruth, recklessly promising. "But where are we going to find Philip?"

None of them had much interest in hanging around after Ruth and Melior had left, even with the promise of one of Naomi's cakes in the offing. Jane had left almost immediately, and Philip had lingered only long enough to repack his laptop and rucksack. He'd left the printouts behind, the printouts that proved that the killer that Melior said was loose, could not be loose.

So not very long after Philip left, Michael left, too.

Monday was one of his nights at Lundgren's Gym; he walked downtown a dozen blocks and spent a couple of hours that afternoon working out with the free weights. A healthy mind in a tired body.

But at last it was ten o'clock, the last of the customers gone and the last of the weights racked and machines reset and towels bagged and vacuum run and all the hundred and one little chores by which Michael paid for his gym time accomplished, and the only thing left to do was go home.

And hope he didn't dream.

"I could be bounded in a nutshell, and count myself a king of infinite space, were it not that I have bad dreams. . . ."

So he went home to his adequate apartment and opened the window for night air as fresh as New York's ever got, and he popped a beer and was flipping channels looking for something amusing on the public access channels when the door opened and Melior came in.

He wasn't wearing that stupid movie-star hat he and Ruth had been so pleased with, and the mirrorshade aviators dangled from one of the pockets of the S&M Biker Slut jacket. His hair stood out around his head like a movieland special effect, and he looked as if he and the clothes were only coincidentally in the same place.

"May I come in?" Melior said, although he was already in and the door shut.

Michael sat up and put both feet on the floor. He had four inches and at least thirty pounds on the elf-guy and ought not to feel this sense of *threat* every time he faced Melior. But most guys would back down from somebody Michael's size, or do their best to let him know they didn't have to. Melior just seemed to take it for granted that if there was a fight, he'd win it.

Except there'd been a fight today. And Melior had lost it. Badly.

"You're already in," Michael pointed out. "Two questions: Are there any hard feelings about today? And where's Ruth?"

"Mistress Ruth left me shortly after I left you. And as for your refusal of aid. . . ." Melior sighed and shook his head. "I do not understand, but I must accept it. You have sheltered, fed, and clothed me, even if only for Ruth's sake and the amusement of the thing. That alone is more generosity than I could rightfully lay claim to in these lands."

"Uh-huh." There were any number of half-insults in Melior's speech, if Michael wanted to take him up on them. Michael didn't. "So, what are you going to do now?"

Melior regarded him with an exasperation that was very

near the end of its patience. "I am going to take such of my possessions as I require, and bid you farewell, and go to hunt the *grendel,* which lairs in the *subterranean way* and has stolen the Sword of Maiden's Tears. If, upon discovering it, I took the Sword and slew it, then I would take the Sword and go to my own place, and pray I was in time. That is what I am going to do now, Michael Peacock."

"And, ah, what if it isn't there?" Michael said, very carefully, ignoring the fact that Melior seemed to have lost his grasp on the concept of present tense.

"It *is* there," Melior said flatly.

"Look," Michael said, getting up. "I didn't want to say this before, in front of the others, but whether it's down there or not really isn't the issue. What matters is that you can't just play Peter Pan in the subway tunnels without getting caught. If you go down there, they're going to catch you and lock you up somewhere the sun don't shine, if you take my meaning, and that isn't going to do you a whole lot of good."

"And doing nothing at all is?" Melior demanded. "Michael, try to understand. I swore an oath upon my father's head that I would find the Sword and bring it back. I *swore.*"

"I swore an oath once," Michael said. Melior's attention sharpened, focused on Michael as if the words Michael was about to say were the words Melior had been waiting for since the moment they'd met.

And because of that, Michael swallowed hard, forcing all the words that might have been back into silence. "I broke it. End of story."

"No. Not the end, Friend Michael. And this oath I have sworn I will die in attempting. *I want to go home, Michael.*" The words were uttered in a tone very like a wail, and Melior threw himself into the chair that stood beside the door. "When Baligant is vested, and the Sword is not among the Treasures, Line Rohannan of the House of the Silver Silences will be cast out, wolfshead. Doomed, and it will be my fault, who could not see the trap or, having sprung it, retain possession of that which it was death to relinquish."

"If you go down into those tunnels, you are going to hit the wall, Mel, and then it isn't going to be a case of won't. There won't be anything in God's Creation we *can* do for you." *And you're going to break Ruth's heart either way, my friend, and there's nothing to do about that but watch.*

"There is nothing else I *can* do now," Melior said bitterly. "I cannot compel your aid, and it is little consolation to me to know that the *grendel* will fatten itself upon the bones of my failure, growing in power until all this land is in despair, and no hero will come from the Morning Lands to succor you."

"That's a chance we're going to have to take." Thus spoke Michael Peacock, child of his times, growing up with A-Bomb drills in school and calluses on his neglected soul from living beneath the shadow of Armageddon.

"And you could have stopped it," Melior said. "That knowledge you will carry with you into the next life: you could have stopped it."

Suddenly something occurred to Michael. "Why are we talking about his as if it's already happened?"

Melior stood up. "Because I will not kill the *grendel*. This much I know for truth," Melior said, and walked into the kitchen.

Michael gave the remark about three beats' worth of thought and followed him. Melior was hanging over the open refrigerator, gazing into its electric depths. He'd had several rude things to say about New York America Earth beer when Michael had introduced him to the stuff, and passed it by now in favor of the two-liter bottle of unfiltered apple juice.

"You aren't going to kill the *grendel*," Michael said uninflectedly.

Melior removed the cap from the bottle with the innocent pride of a recently-learned skill and raised the bottle to his lips. "I am not going to kill the *grendel*," he agreed, and drank.

A powerful sensation of being the straight man in an old Abbot & Costello routine took strong possession of Michael. "Maybe you could explain why it was you decided not to share this little factoid with us this afternoon?"

"You already do not believe in the *grendel* when I have told you of it," Melior pointed out reasonably enough for an elf who was a few sandwiches shy of a picnic in the first place. He put the cap back on the apple juice. "Why should you give any more credence to any other facts I might relate?"

"In the first place they are *not* facts and in the second place would you mind explaining this new theory of yours?"

He was actually going to lose his temper, Michael realized with a distant amazement. Again.

Melior replaced the apple juice and closed the refrigerator door. He waved his hand; the gesture of an elf-prince who is at a loss for words.

"It is not a 'new theory,' Michael. It is a fact; an ability of my kind. I was not certain at first that it would work in this world, even though I had found my heart twin here, but now I know that it does. The future is not fixed," Melior went on, launching well and truly into his explanation, "it spreads like the fingers of a hand, of a hundred hands, each finger growing from all the choices that precede it. And when there are so many branchings—when any thing is as possible as any other—our kind is as blind as any human to what Will Be.

"But there are times when the choices do not matter, when the branchings of the future are few, and the road we must take is inevitable. Then the Sons of the Morning can see farther into What Will Be than those of mortal blood. The branches of my future are narrow and few. And I do not see the *grendel*'s death upon them."

Michael heard this speech out in a respectful silence, and then gave the silence a little more elbow-room while he thought about it.

"You aren't going to kill it."

"True."

"But you're going to go out and try to kill it anyway."

"Yes."

"That is the stupidest thing I've ever heard," Michael announced.

"Then you haven't heard much, Friend Michael," Melior told him.

A few hours earlier, but in much the same area, Ruth and Jane, soldiers of the same side, plotted their next move.

"First we've got to *find* him," Ruth said helplessly. She could not imagine where to begin. Michael might know, but Ruth did not feel like seeing Michael just now. Where *would* you go to hang out, if you were as strange as Philip LeStrange?

"Come on," said Jane, no indecision at all in her voice. She got up and strode off. Ruth shrugged and followed.

They drew cover first at Hacker Heaven and came up

empty; Monday night and the first week in May, and the only people in the computer center were harried students engaged in legitimate pursuits.

"Maybe he's at Michael's," Ruth said reluctantly, but a quick resort to the pay phone in the hall outside the computer lab revealed that *no one* was at Michael's, or if they were, they weren't answering the phone.

Jane hung up the phone and turned to Ruth. "Maybe he's at home."

For a moment Ruth thought Jane meant her dorm room, but that wasn't possible. Then she realized Jane had to mean *Philip's* home, and the dazzling possibility that Philip actually had an apartment somewhere struck her speechless. What sort of an apartment would Philip LeStrange have—and how did Jane know where it was, anyway, when none of the rest of them did?

Ruth said something to that effect.

"It's on his ID," Jane explained simply, which left only the question (better unasked) of what Jane had been doing with Philip's wallet.

In an orderly universe (or even at a college in the Midwest) Philip would have been in on-campus housing, subject to the laws of the Dean and the watchful scrutiny of his more stable peers. But Columbia was a campus in a city where space was at a premium and the students were encouraged to find any other place to live than the campus.

"Here?" said Ruth doubtfully. They were up above 120th Street, east of Columbia, and Ruth felt as if she were wearing a large sign with the words "Mugger Bait" blazoned on it. The street was dark, and dirty even by New York standards, and the doorway was one of those deep cubbyholes in the shadows of which anything might be hiding.

Jane didn't even hesitate. Up the steps, yank the handle (the outer and supposedly-locking door's lock was permanently sprung), and into the New York Urban Airlock. There was a round hole in the doorframe of the inner door where the electric lock was supposed to be, but at least the lobby lights worked.

Nobody had attended to basic daintiness in the lobby for quite some time.

"Sixth floor," said Jane.

The journey was accompanied by the distinctive grace

notes peculiar to an unloved New York apartment building: rotting garbage, urine, antique grease, cooking spices, disinfectant, multilingual quarreling, dogs barking, the insistent bass thump of an overcranked canned music source.

Poverty. Or as it was called these days, low-income housing. The economies of depleted resources. Ruth thought of coming home every night to a place like this and recoiled inwardly. But some people had no choice.

And for some it was only a way station.

"Here we are," said Jane. If she disliked this place as much as Ruth did, she didn't show it. Her face behind the heavy horn-rims was as stolid as a plaster saint's. She raised her hand, and banged on the door with a vigor that made Ruth jump.

The noises within that had been making their feeble reply to the backbeat ceased. Jane thumped again.

The door was finally opened—on the chain—by a black-haired boy with a haircut that couldn't make up its mind whether it was punk or unkempt. He had on a black-washed-to-gray T-shirt that seemed to be a homemade advertisement for necrophilia. He looked at Jane, then past her to Ruth, and his eyes widened in disbelief.

"Uh, you got the wrong address," he said finally, which made Ruth grin inwardly.

"Is Philip here?" she said, knowing that Jane would simply argue the question of was-this-or-was-this-not the right address for Jane's purposes.

"Uh," said the boy again. He slammed the door.

"Phil!" they heard him yell, "It's somebody's mother!"

"I resent that remark," Ruth muttered. If she were a character in a movie she'd spin around now and kick the door open. The chain would break, and—

The small peephole in the center of the door went dark as someone looked through it, then there was a rattle as the chain was taken off. Philip opened the door. He was, Ruth was relieved to see, not in the state of undress that the inhabitants of all-male housing usually were. Philip looked, as usual, clean, neat, composed, and nonnecrophilic.

"What do you guys want?" he asked.

"Ruth had an idea," Jane said.

"Would it be okay if I had this idea inside?" Ruth asked.

"Um," Philip seemed nonplussed by this suggestion. "Just a minute." The door closed again.

"I could have gone home," Ruth remarked to the ambient air. "I could have stared at my *own* front door in perfect comfort and safety."

"They're probably all naked," Jane said grimly.

Which was apparently pretty much the case, judging by the hurried retreats and slamming doors that followed once Philip came back and opened the door again. By then Ruth was interested enough in getting out of the hallway that her standards were appreciably lower than usual.

Which was just as well. This was a Never-Never Land without Wendy. *Sleep all day, party all night . . .* Ruth thought grimly, as Philip relocked a series of chains and deadbolts behind them. The (empty) living room seemed to be decorated in Early Cardboard Box. There was a mattress and a pile of drawers *sans* chest-of- over beneath the windows, which were obscured only by ancient roller blinds, some with posters taped to them. The floor was covered with a medley of newspapers, books, album covers, and rug scraps. Linoleum showed through in places.

The walls were their original color of utilitarian gray, except where someone had made the attempt to redecorate, apparently with a can of glitter-purple lacquer. There were the remains of a couch, without cushions, up against one wall, buttressed by two more stacks of boxes and an array of cognitively-dissonant high-end stereo equipment perched on a set of college-traditional books-and-bricks shelving.

Male student housing, as per the norm.

"What do you want?" asked Philip. He seemed nervous, and Ruth could imagine why. Personally, she expected troglodytes to come lurching out from behind the bundled heights of paper.

"It's about *him*," Jane said.

"Oh." There was a pause, while Philip reluctantly made the ultimate concession. "Come on."

When this had been a prestigious address, this had been a luxury apartment; left over from that halcyon era was the room that you got to by going through the kitchen and pantry: the maid's room, where once upon a time before color TV, some (Irish) cook or maid had wiled away her leisure hours.

There was a combination lock on the door. Philip worked it quickly, without explanation or apology, and opened the door.

The long-ago maid had made do with a room about six
feet by eight—and it had probably been spacious in those
days, Ruth thought, or at least seemed that way. She
squeezed in beside Jane to the eighteen-inch walkway which
was all the free space she could find. Philip slid in beside
her and shut the door.

The ululation-and-static of a police band scanner broke
the silence. Ruth looked upward at piles of junk on racks of
gray steel industrial shelving, and located the source, but
barely.

Some of the junk was lit and humming, and some of it
wasn't, and Ruth was certain of very little evidence that
Philip had every form of semi-licit listening device known to
Man jammed in here. There was another scanner, tuned to
the car-phone frequency, and a CB that seemed to be putting
out mostly static.

By then Jane had edged around the first redoubt of technology and into an open space fully three feet square. It contained half a door balanced on top of two buckling file
cabinets and supported a computer whose monitor was
scrolling lit lines of gibberish. In front of this *mesalliance*
was what seemed to be the room's only chair. Ruth sidled
into the open space and turned around. Jane moved down
next to a tidy bookcase completely crammed with imper-
sonal technology. Ruth glanced around from her new vantage point. There was no sign of a bed anywhere. She looked
back at Philip.

Philip looked as embarrassed as if they were reading his
personal love letters. "Well?" he said. "This had better be
good."

"How much would you charge," Ruth said, choosing her
words with care, "to track all the disturbances of the kind
Melior is looking for in the subway?" On her right, various
scanners warbled and blatted.

Philip looked suspicious and interested; which was to say,
his face went completely blank.

"Why?" he said.

"Why not?" said Jane.

"There aren't any," Philip said.

"Did that ever stop you before?" Jane shot back.

"What's he going to do?" Philip asked. Dear Philip, with
no sense of social responsiblity anywhere in sight; he'd been

one of the votes, Ruth remembered suddenly, in *favor* of the expedition to Downbelow Station.

"He's going to go get it." Jane shrugged. "But he'll wait until he knows where it is."

"If he thinks we're looking for it. If we *are* looking for it," Ruth amended.

"So you want me to look for smething that isn't there?" Philip asked, with a certain air of exasperated superiority. Beside Ruth the computer finished doing whatever it was doing, emitted a satisfied *queep,* and covered the blanked monitor with a rotating starfield.

"Which word didn't you understand?" said Jane.

"The part about how you want me to do an illegal hack for money," Philip said, smirking.

"Oh, come on, Philip, would you do it for free?" Ruth snapped exasperatedly.

Philip fixed his gaze on a point three feet above her head and an indefinite distance away. "You want to string him. Okay. I can do that. I won't even charge you for it, much, just expenses. Because it isn't going to work for very long. And then he isn't going to pay any attention to anything any of us says."

"You mean like he does now?" Ruth said.

"How much for expenses?" Jane said.

Philip bit his lip and figured. "Two hundred. That's just for the connect time. That's the truth."

Ruth took out her wallet and started counting twenties. Philip took them and stuffed them in his pocket. "Done deal. So why don't we go get some Chinese? I'm starved. Mel can pay."

"What makes you think we want to buy *you* dinner?" Jane said.

Philip smiled, his typical nasty smile; techie in the catbird seat. "Because you want me to explain to Elfie what he just bought."

Michael Peacock stared at Mel the Elf across the kitchen, and running on through his mind like an idiot refrain was the phrase: *this changes things, this changes things . . .*

Melior not only believed there was a nonexistent *grendel* haunting the subway system, he believed he was foredoomed *not* to kill it.

This changes things, this changes things . . .

Michael came from a large and aggressively Irish family, and, besides the usual collection of bluff, no-nonsense uncles, he had an accumulation of long-haired bookish aunts who, in addition to collecting advanced degrees at European universities, knew the folklore of their own particular ethnic group rather well indeed. Even if he didn't believe in them, Michael was more than familiar with doomed heroes who could see the future.

Having one of them in his own kitchen changed things, though.

This changes things, this changes things....

"Mel, that makes it even more stupid. If you *know* you can't kill the thing ..."

"I swore I would retrieve the Sword. I will fulfill my oath or die," Melior said simply.

Which might make YOU sleep well at night, boyo, but doesn't do much for the rest of us, Michael reflected.

"There are—" he began.

There was a knock at the door. Michael looked at his watch.

"Christ, it's after eleven." The knock came again.

Melior flowed out of the kitchen like cats and rivers and any number of other apposite similes. He placed himself behind the door and looked at Michael.

A cold hackle of foreboding whispered down Michael's spine. Angry with himself, he shook his head and went to the door.

"You going to open up or am I going to stand here all night?" came Philip's voice, only slightly muffled, from the other side of the door. And Michael, who *always* had to know how the story came out, opened the door.

Philip wandered in, looking, as always, like a cat checking out a new accommodation that he might not choose to approve. He looked around. "Where's...? Oh. Hi, Elfie. Slain any good orcs lately?"

Philip came the rest of the way in, gazing about himself like a visitor to the Prado, and only then did Michael realize that Ruth and Jane were with him.

"Hi," said Ruth uncomfortably.

"Oh, what the hell," said Michael, standing back to let them enter.

"I better call Nai," Ruth said as soon as she was in. Michael looked at Melior. The elf's face was scrupulously composed, as if he were a cat trying very hard not to laugh.

"I suppose you're wondering why I called you all here," Philip said.

"The suspense is nearly bearable," Jane commented. She glanced at Melior, then away. In the kitchen, Ruth's voice was a low expository mutter on the telephone.

"It's after eleven," Michael pointed out with a certain amount of sweet reasonability. "It's Monday."

"Yeah, well, first you weren't here and then if it waited until tomorrow *he* wouldn't be here and that's the whole point, isn't it?" Philip said.

"Is it?" Michael asked.

"Look," Philip continued, Sweet Reason at its most arch. "You don't believe in *grendels*. I don't believe in *grendels*. There *aren't* any *grendels*." ·

Ruth came out of the kitchen at the end of this speech and looked rather stunned at this intelligence. But what else had she expected Philip to say?

"There are," Melior said. He did not look at Ruth.

"But what we *all-l-l-l-l-l* agree on is that if there *were* a *grendel*, it'd leave *tracks*," Philip continued.

"Cut to the chase, wetbrain," Jane muttered.

"Thank you for sharing this with us," Michael said. "Phil, it's late, we all have things we'd like to do with our tomorrows, we *know* all this already."

"Fine. You can leave. Him I'm here to cut a deal with."

"It's his apartment," Melior explained to Philip.

"Everybody needs a straight man," Jane said in an aside.

Michael walked ostentatiously over to the couch—his *own* couch, if anyone was interested—and sat down. "Tea?" he said to Ruth.

"That would be lovely," Ruth said, and went to make it.

"You want to find that *grendel*, right?" Philip said to Melior.

"I *will* find the *grendel*," Melior corrected him.

"Right." Jane spoke up. "But you've got to find it without it knowing you're coming, otherwise it's got options and you don't."

Melior looked from Jane back to Philip, an expression of bland wariness settling over his face.

"So *you* say the *grendel*'s going to start killing people. So when it does, someone'll notice," Philip said.

"It has already begun, and no one has noticed," Melior reminded him.

"Maybe," admitted Philip. "Maybe not. But if there's a Creature from the Black Budget in the subway eating people, there's all kinds of ways it can get noticed. Not just corpses, which, hey, you already know I didn't find. But ways."

"Name them," Melior said sternly.

Philip smiled, all cherubic innocence. "Transit police overtime. Changed train schedules. Missing persons reports. Thefts, burglaries, love letters to the Animal Control Officer. Everybody always wants to cover his tracks. And most of those tracks get stuck in some computer or other. And I can find them. All it takes is time, money, and knowing what you're looking for."

The teakettle began to whistle; a hoarse, off-key note. Jane went off in that direction, following Ruth.

"And you would do this for me?" Melior said tonelessly. "Even though you do not believe?"

And you are going to stand there and let him, Michael thought, *even though you're convinced it won't do you or any one else a damn bit of good.*

"Hey," said Philip, doing his best to look like a used-car salesman. "I'm a believer in free enterprise. Rent my time and I'm yours to play with."

Ruth came out of the kitchen holding two mugs. She handed one to Michael and, bracing herself only a little, crossed to Melior to hand him the other. Melior took it without removing his attention from Philip.

"I am to pay you to discover the *grendel*'s lair?"

"Yeah, something like that," Philip said.

"With what?" Melior said.

One look at Ruth's face was enough to tell Michael whose idea this originally had been. And this was something she hadn't thought of, either.

"Well, that, for starters." Philip pointed at Melior's ring.

Jane came out of the kitchen and nudged Ruth hard, handing her a teacup. Michael watched her take it, and wondered if she was going to pour it over Philip.

Melior looked down at his hand. He spread the fingers wide, and the strange flat oval in its baroque silvery setting flashed in the living room lights. "This?" he said. Philip's grin widened.

There was an almost imperceptible pause, and then Melior drew it slowly off. "Done," he said, flipping the ring through the air to Philip. "Fair bargain, Child of Earth, and silver and gold to bind it."

"Philip LeStrange, how *could* you?"

Ruth advanced upon Philip where he stood upon the sidewalk in front of Michael's building. Twelve o'clock. Witching hour. And Ruth didn't intend to leave enough of Philip for a good broom to sweep up.

"I had to make it look convincing, didn't I?" Philip demanded. "I can always give it back later." He flipped Melior's ring up and caught it. Flash, went the stone in the streetlight.

All of the replies she wished to make were cut short by Melior's unexpected arrival. He turned a glowing basilisk gaze on Philip. "You will see Mistress Jane safely to her door. I will accompany Ruth."

Philip opened his mouth to comment but couldn't think of anything to say. He looked at Jane.

" 'Night," Jane said, and strode off dormward with an air that said Philip might follow if he liked. Philip shot one last look at Melior and scuttled after her. Melior looked at Ruth.

"And you will accompany Ruth," Ruth said.

"Yes," said Melior. They started north.

"It feels strange to go about unarmed," he commented after a while. "I cannot remember a time that I went unweaponed before."

"I'm sorry about today," Ruth said tightly. Even while she said it she hoped they weren't going to restart any conversation containing words that started with L and other discredited romantic notions.

"But you did not fail me, even though you do not trust me. Did you not bribe young Philip to discover the truth I require?"

It is a peculiar sensation to feel your jaw drop from shock; Ruth filed the sensation away for later cataloging. "You—!" she said. *You knew.*

"An idiot, perhaps, but not a fool. You have hired him— but *I* have sealed the bargain." Melior's mouth curved in a private amusement. "And while awaiting my vindication, I shall acquire those items which are most likely to amuse a *grendel*."

Ruth glanced sideways. Melior's mouth was grim again.

"If you knew I'd put him up to it, why did you let him chouse you out of your ring?" Ruth finally said.

"It is of less value to me than his cooperation. It is, after all, as easy to lie to me as to actually seek the truth. But he has made a bargain with me, and will give me that which he has said he would give. Philip is an honest creature."

"Philip?"

"A poor servant, but mine for this while." He stopped, and took Ruth's hand. "And it is of some value to me to have . . . more time, Ruth."

"Time?" Ruth was baffled; flustered by his nearness. "Time for what?"

"For everything; for nothing. For you, my Lady Bright, my heart twin—but fear not, Ruth; I recall your dislike of being courted in the open," Melior said. He walked on, not releasing her hand.

"I have a dislike of being made fun of, too, if anyone is at all interested," Ruth said in a tight voice. She yanked on her hand, but it was not relinquished. Perforce she matched her pace to his. After a moment Melior slowed to accommodate her shorter stride.

"And do I have an interest, even at the best of times, which this is not, in making sport of mortal girls?" Melior shot back.

"That's 'mortal *women*.' 'Girls' is politically incorrect, you know." *Stop, I'm from the Language Police. Surrender all your adjectives and come out parsing—*

"My Line has never taken overmuch interest in politics. But how, my lady, shall I court you, if I may not speak you fair, and costly gifts are beyond my power?"

"Cut it out," said Ruth. This time she pulled so hard she pulled him to a stop. Such a common sight of urban New York; a lovers' quarrel, but they weren't lovers nor were ever likely to be.

"I do not care if your heart is given to another," Melior went on, "though I do not think it is. I ask only the chance to incline your thoughts to me; why should I not hope?"

"Because you don't want me!" This time Ruth managed to get her hand loose; she would have slapped him if she felt she had either the coordination or the moral authority to carry through the gesture. "It's just a *game* to you—"

She stopped when she saw the look on his face.

"Game?" Melior repeated dangerously. "*Do not want you,
mortal girl? You mock me at peril—*" He lunged for her.
Ruth didn't wait to discover his intentions. She ran.

It was New York. No one noticed. And it took him less
than half a block to catch her. One moment she was running;
the next he simply lifted her off her feet and yanked her into
the shadows.

"Is everyone here blind and deaf as well as mad?" Melior
demanded crossly. Ruth felt the poky parts of a building
pressing against her back and hoped it looked as if she were
being mugged.

"This is no game, Lady Bright," Melior said. For one mad
instant she thought he was going to bite her, but no.

This time was not like the last time. For one thing, Melior
knew she was likely to object to being kissed. For another,
Ruth wasn't sure she wanted to object.

Melior kissed her.

She could feel the zipper on his jacket where it pressed
against the back of her hand. She could feel Melior's body,
warm beneath the T-shirt and every muscle tense. A faint
scent of cinnamon and bergamot clung to him, making ab-
surd cross-circuited ideas skitter across her preoccupied
brain. Finally she was able to work one arm free and put it
around him beneath the jacket. When he felt her touch, he
broke the kiss and stared down at her.

"Necking in doorways," Ruth said breathlessly, "how ju-
venile." Her heart was a jarring staccato in her chest and she
found it ridiculously hard to breathe.

"I no longer regard you as a reliable source of information," Melior informed her. He bent his head to kiss the side
of her neck, and Ruth closed her eyes to the sensation of being in a rapidly-falling elevator. Fortunately, he wasn't likely
to go any further than this in a doorway. She hoped. At least
she thought she did.

"Ah, Ruth, were it not for the Sword, even exile and death
at your side would be bearable," Melior groaned.

How sweet. I wish I believed it. Hesitantly, she raised her
hand to stroke his hair, just as she'd wanted to from the moment she'd first seen him. It was soft and fine, dandelion
silk beneath her fingers.

"You don't even know me," Ruth said, voice whisper-soft.

"I have always known you," Melior said quietly. "I saw

your face in my dreams and sought for you in the Morning Lands all my days. I did not know I would find you here."

Which was lovely to hear, but what they never told you in the books was that Capital-L Love didn't solve any problems, it just added more to a life that already seemed more than ordinarily overfull of them.

And what did he mean by it? Not a long white dress and orange blossoms, 2.5 kids, a Volvo, and a house in the suburbs—or, probably, anything else she could instantly imagine.

"Well, here I am. And it— It's cold, okay? I want to get home." But she wasn't cold. Not even a little.

He pulled her away from the wall, but only to put both arms around her and hold her as if someone were trying to take her away. When Ruth began to feel that he really might not be planning to let go, he released her and looked away.

"I forget my manners," Melior commented. Ruth let that remark sail by. "If only there were more time," he said wistfully. He put an arm around her shoulders. Ruth looked around to see if there was anyone to notice. There wasn't.

"But Naomi waits," Melior added, looking up the curving slope of street.

"Yeah," said Ruth, sighing. *No time? Waiting for me?* It was hard to think with her thoughts skittering through her brain like self-willed butterflies. But butterflies or not, she and Melior were going to have to have more than a little talk.

Because if he meant half of what he said, maybe she could use it to keep from being killed.

CHAPTER 15

The Ill-Made Knight

In adventures, Ruth reflected sourly, there were not *longeurs* during which everyone stood around waiting for something to happen.

Not that Ruth was standing around, by any stretch of the imagination. The Country of Mundanity wouldn't leave her alone long enough. It was the *adventure* that was standing still.

And the real world was strangling her. Last night it had been Naomi: was she okay, how was she feeling, did she want to talk? Ruth, distracted by Melior's avowals on the walk home, had been safe in bed and halfway to sleep before the similarity of those questions to the ones the psychiatrist she'd quit seeing used to ask made the penny drop.

Naomi thought there was something *wrong* with her. For which (Ruth admitted with scrupulous honesty) she had some grounds; Naomi was her best friend, and Ruth couldn't remember a single conversation they'd had since Melior had shown up.

Nonetheless, it was unreasonably annoying. And since Ruth knew the questions that Naomi would ask were all the ones Ruth knew were unanswerable, she was going to continue to avoid her.

Or would have, except for the fact that Naomi's first and last words to her at 8:30 this morning were:

"Don't you have a nine o'clock class on Tuesdays?"

Heroines of fiction would have laughed off nine o'clock classes and gone on mapping their rich emotional landscape. Ruth leaped up like a galvanized frog and made it to her class only ten minutes late.

And this afternoon, when heroines of fiction would go off for *tristesse* trysts with their lovers, Ruth was pretty sure she was going to keep the appointment she'd made three weeks ago with the Placement Office and answer those letters she'd shoved to the bottom of her purse.

Why, why couldn't she ever do something random and wild and burn all bridges behind her without looking back?

Because the one thoughtless act she'd committed—*must* have committed, although she had no memory of it—half a lifetime ago had cost her everything she had.

The bell rang, the class was over, and for all her punctilio in attending it, Ruth could not remember what had been discussed. She stood up, grabbed her books and purse, looked up.

Melior was standing in the doorway. Curious students eddied around him, leaving; Ruth was glad to see his hair was loose, carefully covering those fatal Spockian ears. He saw her and smiled.

"Michael knew your schedule, Ruth. He said he thought you would be here."

"Yes." Simple mortification turned her words to monosyllables. She walked out of the classroom with Melior beside her.

"So I will company you," Melior said, his speech making one of its strange slides into an archaism that was mere precision for a society not hers. "And lend to Philip the hours to spin his webs. And he will divulge to me where the beast bides."

Only even with the best will in the world, nothing Philip did would do that. And then what would Melior do? And what would *she* do?

They walked down the hall together. The sunlight blinded her momentarily as Melior pushed the door to the outside world open. Ruth started to speak, found her throat was suddenly dry, and tried again.

"What if— He might not find anything, you know. For reasons."

"Then I must search without the aid of his malicious engines, much though I would joy to have it. But I expect him to find things, Ruth. The *grendel*'s appetite grows with what it feeds upon. How can its murders continue undetected?"

"And if they do? If he doesn't?" There it was, the hard question, the one she needed the answer to.

"Three days, Ruth," Melior said, answering the question she'd asked and all the ones she hadn't. "Today and tomorrow and the day next, and when the next day's sun dawns, I shall go."

Into the subways, chasing monsters. A giddiness that ought to have been strong emotion but was probably actually a missed breakfast made her lurch into him. His arm was steady, a welcome pressure about her shoulders.

Who are you, Melior, and who have you been? What's your favorite color and who did you want to be when you grew up? Tell me all about Elfland and the girls back home and why just because you're the most beautiful thing that's ever walked into my life I should believe that you want me as much as I want you?

"Breakfast," said Melior firmly. "And then, perhaps, you will show me, Ruth, where in this city I may purchase a weapon."

It was late afternoon when Ruth (who had canceled her Job Placement Counseling interview) got back to the apartment. She'd left Melior with Michael, having exhausted all the (licit) avenues of weapon purchase in The Big Apple. And Melior didn't even want a gun.

He wanted a sword.

Or, failing that, a stout spear, or even a crossbow and a quiver full of bolts, as he had explained helpfully.

They had gone to sporting goods stores, antique stores, camping supply stores, and any store Ruth could think of that might hold something that could be adapted to Melior's needs. The results were less than encouraging.

And three days from tomorrow—win, lose, or draw— Melior was going off to the subway. And getting arrested, if he was very lucky.

She turned her key in her lock and went in—both actions overlaid with a touch of strange, now, because her mind kept imagining these acts as Melior would view them. She went through to the living room and found Naomi waiting for her.

"Did it ever occur to you, Ruth, that we could all have been wrong?" Naomi said.

Naomi was sitting in the comfy chair beside the window. She wore a white polo shirt and khaki pants and looked as though she'd been sitting there waiting to ask the question since Ruth had left that morning.

She hadn't been, of course. Ruth took comfort from that thought.

"Wrong about what?" Ruth asked. She heard the defensive edge in her voice and hated it, and covered her feelings by turning away and painstakingly making certain that all the locks on the door were, indeed, locked.

"About. . . . Where's Mel, by the way?"

"At Michael's gym. He— There's some stuff he wants that maybe Michael can get for him."

"Uh-hum." Naomi picked up a mug of tea and stared into as if it were some form of caffeinated teleprompter. "You remember we all agreed that Melior *had* to be an elf. Nobody could do makeup that good. . . ." Her voice trailed off.

Slowly, unwillingly, Ruth advanced into the middle of the room. She looked down at the top of Naomi's head, still bent over the tea.

"They can't. Seamless. Waterproof. Glows in the dark. And the stuff he came with: emeralds, rubies, fine hand-embroidering? Come on." Hesitantly Ruth pulled out a chair from the table and sat down next to Naomi. "He's *real*."

"Just how real is he?" Naomi looked up from her tea and turned to face Ruth. "Philip thinks he's a science project, Michael'll rescue any stray kitten that meows, I've never been able to figure out why Jane does anything, and I'm just waiting to see what happens. What about you?"

"Me?" The word was emitted as an inelegant squeak, and Ruth felt her cheeks go hot.

"Yesterday I told him we weren't going to play any more, and he took off—and you took off right after him. I suppose it isn't any of my business, but—"

"Oh, Naomi," Ruth said, half amused, half exasperated.

Naomi smiled. "Well, what if he turned out to be an escaped serial killer with plastic surgery? If I lost you, they'd make me buy a replacement before I could graduate, and after six years I'm just about out of money."

Ruth snorted. "And then you'd have to travel door-to-door, selling Chocolate Suicide Brownies and rum-orange butter cookies to make up the difference. For heaven's sake, it isn't like that, Naomi, it— It just isn't," Ruth finished lamely, and stared at her friend.

Naomi smiled sadly. "I know; one elf appears out of nowhere and I go all over Sigmund Freud on you. It's just that I've had too many friends who went and did the *damnedest* things when they should have been thinking."

"And you think I'm one?" Ruth said, striving for lightness.

"You're about to graduate. You've hit the Big Three-Oh. And you— Something happened to you before I met you, Ruth; I wish you'd tell me what it is. But don't let it push you into being in love with this guy just because you can't think of anything else to do with your time!" Naomi finished up in a burst. She looked away, cheeks flushed. "Now you tell me I'm a jealous, interfering jerk."

"You're a jealous, interfering jerk," Ruth said obligingly. Naomi swatted at her; Ruth laughed, then sobered. "No; you're right; I don't know what's been wrong with me lately; one birthday divisible by five and I go all to pieces. And I'll tell you about what happened someday, I promise— but that isn't it with Melior."

Ruth took Naomi's hand; for whose comfort, she wasn't certain. *Why is it so hard to say? "When I was eighteen I became a Movie of the Week." Simple. The word is "coma."*

It would be easier to confess to being Batman.

"With Melior, the thing is, he says he *loves* me, Naomi, and I'm not sure *what* I feel. He's like a book I'm reading; I don't know whether I like it or not, but I don't want to stop before the end." Even telling the bare truth made Ruth feel the blush-heat on her cheeks again.

The silence might have stretched if she had let it; but Ruth jumped up and fled to the kitchen. The teapot was still half full. She poured a cup and drizzled honey into it, and stood drinking the tepid brew while staring out the window at the twilight.

The Seven Houses of the Twilight, and if Melior doesn't bring the sword home there's going to be six, not seven, and it doesn't seem real at all. Of course, why should it. . . ?

"Have you considered, when you think about him like this, that the reason he's so fascinating is because he's crazy?" Naomi said from the kitchen doorway. She threw the rest of her cold tea into the sink, took Ruth's mug from her hands, made a face, and slid it into the tiny microwave perched precariously on top of the refrigerator.

"I'm a librarian, I know these things. 614.58: Mental Health, all you have to do is look it up. Melior's insisting that things are a particular way because he wants them to be that way, not because they are or aren't or are even *likely* to be or not. And leaving aside sanity, he's on a collision course with the real world and there isn't anything you can do . . . except decide whether to jump ship or crash with him."

The microwave pinged; Ruth eyes filled with tears.

"Oh, Naomi, why isn't it that simple?"

Forty blocks south of Columbia (give or take the odd block) lies a district variously called Museum Row or Museum Mile: the Museum of Natural History, assorted foundations and galleries, the Planetarium; an interlocking warren of high culture and the dregs of Old Money overlooking Central Park South. Old brownstones with new brass plaques. An embassy or two. *Haute*-class tea shoppes.

And the largest collection of people with obscure knowledge outside a college campus.

"And do you think your friend can help us?" Melior asked.

"If it was forged, Stainless Steve knows where. If you want a sword, go to an expert."

Michael Harrison Peacock and Rohannan Melior of the House of the Silver Silences walked up the steps of the Museum of Natural History.

His friend Michael walked over to a guardsman in uniform, seated at a podium which, Melior supposed, must indicate his purpose and allegiance. But if there were letters upon it, Melior could not read them. The sorcery that had given him command of the local tongue (a common enough magic, useful when one traveled between the Lands) had not taught him to read its letters. The others forgot that, often; as young scholars, their lives revolving around books, must.

Ruth was such a scholar. And if he brought her to his world and stripped her learning from her, would she hate him, or would she feel their love was worth that price?

Folly, to think of a future when his life ended here.

"Come on, Mel. Steve can see us."

Stephen Mallison's work area was behind and below and in back of any number of exhibits, and reaching it was made particularly difficult because half the floors of the museum were closed for reasons as various as setting up an exhibition and renovating all the dinosaurs. They had to go all the way up to the fourth floor before they could find an elevator that would take them down to the right side of the basement.

It was, Michael realized as the doors closed, the first elevator Melior had ever been in.

The doors shut. Melior, seeing nothing but a small empty room, turned to Michael for explanation. And the elevator began to descend.

Michael stared at him, mouth half open and several reasonable explanations jammed in his throat. Melior flung himself back against a wall, scrabbling for a dagger that wasn't there. His pupils dilated, flashing red; he snarled, and Michael could see the long canid teeth gleaming in the faint fluorescent elevator lights.

"Hey; it's just—" Michael began helplessly.

Melior saw him; saw Michael's ease and knew there was no danger; and worse, knew that he'd looked like a fool. His green gaze fixed on Michael, and for a moment Michael felt the fury that raged against the bars of Melior's will like a separate thing.

Then Melior looked away and pretended neither of them was there.

It was the longest four floors of Michael's life.

When the doors opened, it was on the unlovely subbasements of the Met, and before the doors were fully open Melior had reeled through them. He turned and faced Michael defiantly; a creature caught between two fables in a land undeniably mundane.

"It's an elevator," Michael said lamely. Melior said nothing. Michael sighed inwardly, knowing Melior would be especially difficult now. Well it only stood to reason, as the spaceman said of the alien computer. Michael didn't like looking like a fool, himself, and he guessed an elf-prince in exile didn't either. "Steve's this way."

Stephen Mallison's office was at the end of the narrow brown and yellow corridor. A tall narrow oak door marked "Properties" barred the way; Michael rapped on it twice and opened it.

The chamber the door opened onto was both vast and crowded. Smells of rust and iron, dust and paper and oil and myriad alien scents assailed Melior's nostrils. He followed Michael into the space.

There were glass cases filled with artifacts; standing armor, racks of long-unused weapons, wooden crates scribed with glyphs that Melior couldn't read. The space had the orderly disarray of an archivist's.

In the largest open space available was a broad white table. To one side was a glowing box of the type called *computer*. There was a man sitting at the table. His pale red hair was as long as Melior's own, held back with a scrap of leather. His back was to them.

On the table before him were Melior's spurs.

"Hi, Steve," Michael said. "Don't bother to get up."

The man addressed as Steve spun his chair around on its large shining wheels. Still seated, he wheeled his chair to where Michael stood.

"Took you long enough. This your friend from Ancient Atlantis who wants the sword? Hi, I'm Stephen Mallison. I'm a Cataloguer at the Met, which is to say I'm a glorified packrat and mostly with the computer." He held out his hand.

Melior knew this custom. He extended his hand for Stephen to grasp. Stephen's grip was warm and dry; a little rough and much stronger than Melior had expected.

"I am Rohannan Melior," he answered only, for to be so brief was not rudeness, not among humans and not here.

"And those are your spurs. Terrific. You know they've been driving me nuts for *days?* My real specialty is Restoration and Re-Creation of period weapons, and I've even got a degree to that effect stashed around here somewhere, but they don't look like anything I've ever seen. Where'd you get them?" He turned his chair on its wheels again and went back to the table. Apparently he was not going to get up.

"They were my father's," Melior began, but Michael interrupted him.

"Steve, do you know of anywhere around here we could lay hands on a sword?"

"Or a boar-spear?" Melior added helpfully.

Stephen gestured to the crates and cases in their serried ranks. "We got fifteenth, sixteen, seventeenth—*lots* of seventeenth; there was a war on practically everywhere in Europe—some eighteenth, mostly ceremonial. Take your pick. It's no trouble; it all belongs to the Museum, and they're never going to display *or* deaccession it. And if they were important pieces, they wouldn't be left down here to rot."

"You, uh, *are* joking, right? About giving away Museum property?" Michael said.

"Probably," Stephen said. "But on the other hand, if your friend's a collector, it is usually possible to pry something loose quasi-legally. I could kick it up to Doctor Bonner."

"No," said Melior. "These won't do." He touched the glass lid of a case and then wiped his fingers on his jeans, making a face.

"Well, what is it that you want them to do?" Stephen said obligingly.

"I wish to kill a *grendel*," Melior said seriously, before Michael could stop him. "These would break."

Stephen looked at Michael.

"A reproduction," Michael said hastily. "He wants a *new* sword."

"I take it we are not talking SCA-hit-them-with-rattan-wrapped-in-duct-tape type sword here?" Stephen said.

"Live steel," Melior said, and Stephen smiled.

"Now you're talking my language. Let me consult my files; we should have a list of the smiths we use to do our Re-Creation work."

Stephen Mallison turned in his chair and wheeled over to a bank of two-drawer file cabinets that supported shelving stuffed with long, paper-wrapped parcels.

"Why does he not rise?" Melior said to Michael, in puzzled tones.

The chair stopped and turned around. Melior saw the look that passed from Stephen to Michael and knew that somehow he had made another strange World-of-Iron error.

"Steve, it's just that he—"

"A horse fell on me, spinal nerves don't grow back, the miracle cures you see on television are the exclusive province of people with good health insurance and money to burn, and there isn't much call for a blacksmith who can't stand up. I go to Therapy three times a week and that takes all my spare cash. Now can we change the subject?"

"Ah," said Melior as understanding dawned. "You are crippled."

Michael groaned. But, Melior's strange charisma worked even here, and amazingly, Stephen smiled.

"That's right. I am not *challenged*. I am not *differently able*. I'm a cripple. But at least I've got my health." Stephen smiled a crooked smile.

"I think you are very able," said Melior, as if he had given the matter considerable thought, and as if his opinion mattered.

"Yeah. Thanks." Stephen turned back to his file cabinets.

"You've got a big mouth," Michael said under his breath.

"Michael, if you had told me he was a cripple, I would not have asked," Melior said reasonably. "But it is wonderful, that chair with the wheels. I wish—" He stopped. "I wish I could tell my sister that such things exist. I think we could make one."

Now it was Michael's turn to stare. He'd never thought of Melior having a sister, let alone a sister who would be grateful for a wheelchair.

A sister who was going to die because Melior wasn't going to be able to bring The Sword of Maiden's Tears home.

"Here we are," said Stephen. He bent sideways awkwardly, and straightened up with a thick manila file folder in his hands. "Two guys in California, one in South Carolina, one in Maine. They all do custom work. Two grand and two years, and you can have a sword that Conan the Barbarian would be glad to call his own." He spun his chair around and wheeled over to Melior. Melior took the folder, and gazed down at glossy colored pictures of swords laid on velvet as if they were jewels.

"But I cannot wait two years," he said helplessly. "I must have it by tomorrow's dawn."

"Then you're out of luck," Stephen said flatly.

"Steve," said Michael. "There's got to be something."

"Fine. Go down to Acme Rent-a-Sword and give them your credit card. Nobody uses swords any more, Mike—this is all custom work for collectors. And it takes time."

"Well, what about secondhand?" Michael heard himself say. "Or someone willing to *loan* one?"

Stephen looked from Melior to Michael for a long moment. He wheeled backward until he reached the table. He reached around behind it and came up with a canvas-wrapped bundle about a yard long, bound in three places with twine. He picked up a knife and began sawing through the twine.

"Do you know what a *gladius* is?" he asked Melior.

"No."

"Roman short sword. Sword of the legions. They conquered half the world with an oversized pocket knife *cast* out of a metal so soft that iron can chop it right in half: bronze." The twine was gone. Stephen flipped the canvas open.

He'd called it an oversized pocket-knife. Michael estimated it at about thirty inches long. It had a wide straight blade that came to a spade-shaped point. The quillons were narrow. The haft seemed to be wrapped in braided horsehair.

Melior stepped forward and picked it up. Hefted it, testing its balance.

"It's the last thing I ever made. Beryllium in the bronze instead of tin—ain't *nothing* going to chop that baby in half. You take that. I'll keep the spurs. Deal?"

Melior looked down at Stephen, saying nothing. Michael, standing behind him, suddenly realized that Melior's pupils would have narrowed as he walked into the light.

"I will return this if I can. The spurs are yours."

"No biggie. And now why don't you guys get out of here, and leave me alone so I can get some work done before this place shuts up shop for the night, okay?" Stephen said.

Melior rewrapped the *gladius* in the canvas and tucked the bundle under one arm. He walked past Michael toward the door. Michael waved good-bye to Stephen and followed him.

Stephen's last words reached them at the open door.

"And I hope you get home safe, Rohannan Melior."

CHAPTER 16

Love Among the Ruins

Tuesday and Wednesday were replays of Monday, with Ruth getting edgier by the hour. Melior's plans for Thursday morning hung between them like the Sword he was looking for, keeping them from talking about any of the things that really mattered. He bought a canteen and a flashlight to go with the sword he and Michael had come back from the Museum with, and now in a few short hours he would be gone, and Ruth would have to try to make sense of a world in which the book that was Melior would go forever unfinished.

And the two of them had no privacy at all.

Melior slept on Michael's couch. Ruth shared a one-bedroom apartment with Naomi. And the moments and half-hours of privacy they'd snatched had been enough to make Ruth heartily regret that fact and not enough for her to be able to do anything about it, even if she could manage to find the nerve.

And he said he loved her. Said that she, Ruth, was the woman he had searched for, to woo and win, all through the Morning Lands—whatever they were (but, thought Ruth wistfully, they sounded pretty).

"If," said Melior, drawing the word out lazily. They sat in perfect propriety and chaperonage in a forgotten inglenook of the big main library down on 42nd Street. Melior sat across the table from her; mirrorshades and leather jacket and an expression of faintly rueful longing that made Ruth want to. . . .

"If," Melior began again, reaching across the table and taking her hand, "If the Sword were mine, and you and I were set upon the high road to Chandrakar—"

" 'You and I'?" Ruth quoted back to him.

"Did I go, I would take you with me, would you come,"

Melior parsed carefully. "They say the lower world holds the memory of the higher; did you never dream of Chandrakar the fair?"

"And if I did?" Ruth bandied back.

"Then you would go, did you hold me in fond affection or not. But if you have never dreamed her green hills and silver rivers, I must assume that it is I alone who am the attraction."

"If I went," Ruth pointed out prosaically.

"Oh, Ruth, do!" Melior leaned across the table. "Say you would come to Chandrakar for Rohannan Melior's asking. He would do you all honor, and set you at his right hand. It is not true that no human blood runs in the Houses of the Twilight; such alliance is a thing done, aye, and done before; you will see—"

"If I come," Ruth said. "And when did you develop a twin brother?"

Melior smiled instead of answering, and Ruth felt her innards go custard-pudding weak. Go to Elfland, like the man was asking—it would sure as hell get her out of finals week, wouldn't it?

And Melior's Chandrakar could be no more strange to her than the modern world was now.

Eight years. Not quite a decade. But in that time there'd been another Star Wars movie, almost half a dozen Star Trek movies, something called AIDS, two terms of President Reagan. . . .

And somehow, as if Life were an exceptionally boring book, Ruth had lost her place. Lost her place and all desire to regain it. *I try to take things one day at a time, but lately several days have attacked me at once.* Eight years of days, served up in one moment of awakening that Ruth, honest now, realized she would never recover from.

Melior said he loved her. And Ruth knew she wanted him. And if both of them turned out later to have been mistaken, well, lots of people were.

"Okay, Rohannan Melior. Take me to Chandrakar." *If you can, if you go, if and if and if and IF. . . .*

Wednesday evening. Ruth supposed she'd missed classes. She didn't care. She'd spent the day with Melior at New York Public again, consulting all the maps her skill could find for him. Maps of New York, to be laboriously compared against the subway maps. Geo-survey maps of the island Manhattan, its stone and water-table, marl, schist, and aquifer. Maps of such terrain as the place had left to it after four centuries of building.

But most of all, the subway. Where Melior was going to go. And die, in all probability, even if it was only through being hit by a train.

A proper heroine, Ruth supposed glumly, would have spent the time begging him not to go. But she'd known it wouldn't do the least bit of good, and so she'd—*sensibly!*— done what she could to help him and let the rest go unsaid.

Everyone knew he was going after the (unproven) *grendel* Thursday morning. Michael was particularly upset—twice she had caught him and Melior arguing in corners—and Ruth had cherished a traitorous hope that Michael would stop him; do something splendidly male and physical and knock Melior over the head, tie him up in the closet, do *something* until the fit passed and sweet reason prevailed.

But when they'd left the library and gone back to Michael's, all Michael had done was propose Chinese at Naomi's, and Melior had volunteered to pick up the order Michael had already phoned in.

And all her idiotic purchase of Philip's cyberstealth had gained her was these three days.

Ruth wasn't quite sure how she'd ended up going with Michael, but she had, and now she was back at her own apartment, and he and Naomi were watching her with close fond anxiety; her dear friends watching over her to make sure she didn't do something stupid.

Like go with Melior. Into the subway, if not to Elfland as he'd asked. She hadn't told anybody about that.

Only there wouldn't be much point to following him into the subway, now, would there? They probably wouldn't let them have connecting rooms at Bellevue.

Ruth fiddled with the glass in her hand. Red wine; a good bottling, a special treat; or was it just cheap and sleazy nepenthe? She swirled the liquid around in her glass and stared down into it. Red as blood. The language of fairy tales.

Naomi fidgeted. Michael fidgeted.

"What in God's name is taking him so long?" Ruth snarled as, with perfect timing, the downstairs buzzer buzzed.

"He was going to stop by Philip's tonight," Michael said. "Probably on the way."

He didn't tell me, Ruth thought, unreasonably jealous. Of their last hours together, even if spent in company. And maybe tonight. . .

"Then he's lucky he isn't stuffed and on display in an antique shop on East 57th by now. Michael, have you ever *been* to Philip's apartment?" Naomi said.

"I have denied myself that pleasure," Michael said gravely.

"*I* haven't," Ruth said sadly, her mind elsewhere. "It's probably cold," she added, meaning the Chinese food. She stood in the open doorway listening to the elevator rise, waiting to see Melior again.

And after tomorrow morning you won't see him any more. This is the way the world ends. . . .

You couldn't see the elevator from their corner apartment. Ruth heard the doors open, and waited.

They say it settles a man's mind wonderfully knowing he is to be hanged in the morning. If that's true, why am I so jittery?

Philip LeStrange came around the corner. He held a shopping bag from the Chinese take-away in each hand.

He wasn't Melior.

He saw Ruth and stopped, and some of the pleased expression vanished from his face. It probably hadn't occurred to him until that moment that he was going to have to face Ruth.

"Where is he?" Ruth said. Philip set down the bags and took a hesitant step backward.

"Philip?" Naomi brushed past Ruth and went out into the hall. Ruth felt a hand on her arm. Michael.

"Come and sit down," Michael said gently.

"But it's Philip," Ruth said with the bewilderment of someone who has taken a mortal wound and doesn't quite realize it yet.

"Come on, Ruth," Michael said.

It was at least five minutes before Philip and Naomi came into the apartment. Philip still hung back, glancing sideways at Ruth as if she were a houseplant unexpectedly turned carnivorous. For once he had neither backpack nor laptop with him.

"He's already gone, hasn't he?" Her voice was remarkably even, Ruth noted with a certain pleased vanity.

"That's right," Naomi said. "Come and have dinner, Ruth." Her voice had the careful tone one associated with speakers to the hysterical. Or the mad.

"No, thank you," Ruth said, equally carefully. With careful, measured steps she left the living room. She passed through the bedroom into the bathroom. There she shut the door tightly, and turned on the shower as, after all, the walls of even the best New York apartments are rather thin.

Ruth had been in there long enough to get over the worst of her tears and to begin to notice that the spray from the shower had soaked the left side of her skirt. The hammering on the door was enough to make her jump.

"Ruth!" Michael's voice, raised in a bellow to bring sinking ships to mind. "Get *out* here!"

She unlocked the door. He shoved it in on her. He grabbed her and yanked her out into the living room, without giving her the opportunity to make even the most elementary repairs to her tear-blotched complexion.

"—irst footage of the Subway Snatcher. The footage you saw was shot by a rush-hour passenger who had intended to tape his daughter's sixth birthday party. Transit officials still will not say whether this . . . amazing occurrence has any connection to the closing of six Lower Manhattan IND stops earlier this week."

The living room television was on. Half the screen was filled with a graphic of a red claw superimposed over a black silhouette of the front of a subway car. Beneath it in yellow, jagged letters screamed: "Subway Snatcher."

"Kelly Groen is standing by live at City Hall. Let's go to her now. Kelly?" the perky newsreader (male) said. He turned expectantly toward the graphic. Nothing.

"While we wait, Rob, why don't we run that clip again?" said the other perky newsreader (female).

"Ladies and gentlemen," said Rob, "we would like to remind you at this time that what you are about to see has not been authenticated. We prefer to let you judge for yourselves." He spoke in the hushed tones of a very expensive mortician.

The screen went dark and *cinema-verite* jiggly; the symptom of home movies through the ages. The watchers took it on faith that this was a subway station; it might as easily have been any of a dozen hundred other things.

Whatever was happening was already in progress. The people moved with frightened pointlessness. The image on the viewfinder of the invisible cameraman veered wildly; at one point the image bleached out as the camera pointed directly upward into a light.

Finally the picture stilled. The dark blobs resolved into bodies at the edge of the frame. At the center of the picture was a hand, grayish-black and far too large for any proper hand, splayed on the subway platform as it levered its possessor up onto the platform from the tracks.

Blackness, as someone got between the camera and the picture. A sharp discontinuity as the camera was dropped. The platform's surface filled most of the frame, but off at one edge a hominid figure could be seen, blurred as footage of Bigfoot, walking away holding an awkward pale burden.

Then the film stopped.

"The victim has been identified as twenty-six-year-old Theresa Scarlatti, a secretary for Burford, Foote, and Hoo. Relatives—"

"We're ready to go to Kelly now," said Perky Two, and the picture did another two-step dissolve to a windblown blonde against a late-afternoon backdrop of rescue equipment, holding a microphone beneath her chin and prepared to tell the world at great length that she knew nothing, nothing at all.

Ruth looked at Michael. His face was pale, stretched with shock; it seemed almost as if she could look down *into* his skin and see through it to the skull beneath.

"There's a monster in the subway," Naomi said.

She'd thought she was tired before, but now a weariness beyond bearing stole over Ruth. She leaned against Michael. He put his arms around her and held her.

"Yeah," Ruth said. "It's real. Too bad we didn't know when it would do any good."

Kelly-Groen-at-City-Hall spent two minutes explaining that nobody knew anything, including when subway service would be restored, before the inevitable cut to a commercial about Life on the Edge with your favorite soft drink.

Ruth pushed Michael away and walked over to a chair with lagging, ungraceful steps and dropped into it. The Chinese food still sat, virginal and untouched, in its bags. She reached in and extracted a fortune cookie. *"It is better to travel hopefully than to arrive,"* it said. Sure it was. *Welcome to the Outer Limits City Limits.*

"Philip," Naomi said in a voice of soft and dangerous gentleness, "what did you tell Melior when you saw him?"

Ruth looked up, curious-rapidly-becoming-appalled as inspiration struck. Philip was sitting in the big chair under the window with his arms wrapped around his knees. He looked like he'd been kicked in the stomach. He didn't look up.

"Philip." Naomi's voice, still soft, but demanding.

A mumbled response.

"Phil. You were checking the police reports to find the *grendel*," Michael prompted.

"'What did you tell him?'" Naomi repeated, and finally Philip raised his head.

He wasn't crying—that would be too much, even for Philip, Ruth observed with glassy detachment—but behind the silvery bifocals his eyes looked red and irritated. He pushed them up, rubbing his eyes, reminding Ruth once again of a white rat grooming.

"He paid me," Philip said, only slightly muffled this time. There was a hint of desperation in his voice; a trace of actual feeling that must be as stunning to Philip as it was unbelievable to his friends.

"Yeah," said Michael. "He paid you to find the *grendel*. Well, it was on the six o'clock news, so—"

"*I* paid you," Ruth's voice cut across Michael's; banked coals on the edge of flaming. "*I* paid you to find it out, so tell me what I paid for."

Philip stood up and dug in his pocket. After much digging he produced a crumpled wad of twenties and set them on the table. Melior's signet ring gleamed on his finger.

"He paid me," Philip said. His voice was rough, slightly hoarse. "He paid me to tell *him,* not anyone else." Philip's entire body vibrated with the tension of futile resistance. "He gets what he paid for."

Michael had a look on his face indicating he'd bitten into a peach, only to find it rotten inside. "You made a bargain to look for the information for him. But it isn't a secret, is it?" Michael said coaxingly.

Philip closed his eyes. Ruth had problems of her own;

only behavior as *out of character* as this of Philip's could draw her notice now.

"We made a bargain," Philip said, his voice strained.

"What sort of bargain exactly, Philip?" Naomi asked gently.

Philip rubbed his eyes again, and stared at the television as if the sports and weather could save him. When he spoke, he chose his words as if they were footsteps through an invisible minefield.

"He came and got . . . what there was to get. And he told me to pick up the stuff from Hunan Balcony and bring it here. And he told me not to tell you anything else until tomorrow," Philip sounded exhausted at having told them this much.

"But he doesn't think he's going to kill it," Michael said.

Michael's words didn't quite sink in. "If anyone else makes a stunning revelation," Ruth announced, "I shall burst my bud of calm—"

"And blossom into a copyrighted quotation," Naomi agreed. "If Philip feels honor-bound to do what Melior said we can talk him out of it later. After Michael explains *who* isn't going to kill *what*."

Michael didn't bother to tell them what he suspected; that it was magic, not honor, that motivated Philip's reticence. If they had doomed heroes, why not a *geas* as well? And speaking of which—

"Melior isn't going to kill the *grendel*," Michael said. "He said so."

He hadn't been here before, but the passersby were glad enough to furnish the information. And he had memorized the workings of the telephone.

"I know where I must go now," he said when she arrived. "Will you accompany me, Mistress Jane?"

It took Michael a while to explain elvish precognition to the others—especially as, he suspected, he hadn't understood Melior's explanation very well himself. But what he did manage to make very clear was that Melior believed that he could see into the future, and that Melior couldn't see himself killing the *grendel* anywhere in the future he saw.

"But why would he go if he knew he wasn't going to kill it?" Philip said in frustration.

"Because nobody else would go with him," Ruth said bitterly. "None of us believed in him, none of us trusted him enough to—"

"Hold on, Ruth," Naomi said. "Just how detailed is this vision of Melior's, Michael? Does he see the *grendel* at all? Does he see someone else kill it? We *know* it's there."

"Now," Philip added.

"When I get my hands on him," Ruth said in a low voice of promise, "*I* am going to kill him. The *grendel* isn't going to have anything to worry about."

"I don't know," said Michael. "He just kept saying we'd all be sorry later that we'd missed this chance."

"But anybody who has Melior's sword can kill the *grendel*," Ruth protested. Her head hurt, and thinking was an effort. Her *brain* hurt.

But underneath the exhaustion and pain was hope, because if Melior's *grendel* was real after all that meant there was a way for the hero to win.

"Not quite," Naomi said. "The Sword of—what was it?"

"Maiden's Tears," supplied Michael.

"—is what kills it, but any mere human who touches the sword is going to turn into another *grendel*. You might kill that one, but there it'll be to do all over again."

"A woman's work is never done," Ruth said, with a faint attempt at humor.

"So where is it?" Michael said. "The sword, the *grendel*, the whole tamale?"

All eyes turned to Philip.

"No." Philip's voice was quite determined. "And I wiped the disks and tapes and shredded the papers." He looked grimly unhappy, as anyone might who was in the process of alienating his only friends.

"But, Philip," Naomi said coaxingly, "You've got to tell us. We can't help him if we don't know where he's gone."

"We had a bargain," Philip said wearily.

"Leaving aside how we could help him if we knew where he'd gone," Michael said.

"Well, this has got to be the first time you ever did something because somebody asked you to," Ruth snapped Philip-ward. "It's just a stupid promise—he won't ever know and I don't care if he does. *Where is he?*"

"If promising is stupid, then so is going down there when he knows he won't kill it,' Philip said with desperate logic.

"Granted," said Naomi. "It *was* stupid."

"No," said Philip. "It was a covenant. If you don't do what you say you're going to do, nobody can ever trust anybody."

The words were obviously Melior's, and Philip's look of anguish was proof of the indigestibility of the concept. Ruth would have been less surprised if he'd started spouting Classical Greek.

"You ought to know better than to make promises to elves," Michael said sternly to Philip. "Leave him alone, Nai. I don't think he *can* say. I hope Melior had a good reason for making him promise."

"To get himself killed," Ruth said miserably.

Naomi bounced to her feet. "We've got to do something."

"We are doing something," Michael said. "We're waiting for midnight. Twelve-oh-one. Tomorrow. So why don't we have dinner while we wait?"

Their train was stopped at 34th Street.

"What are we supposed to do now?' Jane said. The station was jammed with angry commuters, jammed as if it were peak rush hour. The PA system was repeating helpful information over and over again with its speakers turned to "High Distort". Useless.

"I must get to the Down Town," Melior said. "The *grendel* is there."

Stephen Mallison's sword was carefully wrapped in brown paper with a red-and-white mailing label on the front. Melior carried it, hoping it would be as inconspicuous as Jane thought. He wore a *nylon backpack* slung over one shoulder; it was heavy with trailbread and chocolate and a two-quart canteen filled with brandied water. He carried a small lantern, and in the *backpack* were a dozen candles to power it.

And behind him stood his squire.

It might have been Ruth. It ought to have been Ruth. But Ruth loved him and Jane did not. Jane could bear to watch him die.

In fact, thought Melior, she might even enjoy it. He looked at Jane.

Jane's head swiveled as she regarded stalled commuters, backed up trains, and the indefinable air of Great Events in the wind.

"The *grendel* is downtown," she said, wanting to be clear on this one point.

"Philip's scrying has told me so. There have been vanishments and tales of prowling beasts, and now I will seek it at the center of its web of destruction."

That was the information Philip had given Melior, the information that made this work. The pattern of the kills. Jane did not waste time wondering if the information was true or false; it didn't really matter to her. This was the data they were using, and the rules of the game were that it didn't matter if the data were true or not. It simply *was,* and on its basis Melior would go to a certain place and begin his hunt.

She had already been prepared when he called her—not hoping she would be asked, because hope was not a word in Jane's personal lexicon, but, rather, being ready if he did.

No one else had to know, after all.

And so Jane, always so neat and ladylike, had real denim jeans and waterproof boots, a military surplus pullover, and a black watchcap pulled down over her hair to hide its telltale gleam. No one had seen her leave her room dressed that way; there was no one to ask her what she meant by it and no one to laugh; Melior had no clothes-sense anyway.

And everything she had could simply disappear once this adventure was over, even the backpack, with its freight of food and water, flashlight and map. Disposable. Deniable.

Assuming they ever went anywhere at all.

"The trains aren't going downtown," Jane pointed out.

She did wonder why the trains had been stopped, but not very much. How to get to where Melior wanted to go, following the laws of this world, that was Jane's puzzle.

"There is a way. There must be a way. Find it for me!" Melior pled urgently.

Jane thought hard for a moment. The trains weren't going downtown. Fine.

"Come on. Let's get out of here. We're going to the World Trade Center."

"She isn't there," Naomi said. She set the telephone receiver back in its cradle.

"Quarter to ten. They shut the phones into the dorm down at ten," Michael said. "I could run over there."

"No, leave it. Why shouldn't she get a good night's sleep?" Naomi said.

"Even if we don't," Ruth said. "Twelve-oh-one," she said to Philip's hunched shoulders.

Philip shook his head and said nothing. He'd already told them that "tomorrow" meant dawn at the earliest—the start of day in a society with no clock but the sun. Ruth thought he was probably right, but had no intention of letting that stop her.

"And what then?" Naomi said. "*Think*, guys—Melior's in the subway chasing a monster. The monster's real. What do we do?"

"Call CNN," suggested Philip, but his heart wasn't in it.

"Where do we start?" said Michael to the air. "Even when we know where to start," he added. Philip winced, very slightly.

"I think you're making this too complicated," Ruth said slowly. "You're looking for a *grendel* in the subway. Okay. It's grabbing people in Lower Manhattan, fine. But where is it *living*? Not on the tracks. This *grendel*'s supposed to be not-too-bright, right? But it's managed not to get hit by a train—and even if a head-on collision didn't kill it, it'd still do a number on the train, right?"

"And make the six o'clock news. And the pages of all the newspapers," said Michael. "And this hasn't happened."

"So the *grendel*," said Ruth logically, "hasn't been hit by a train. Or seen by one, because that'd be on the news now, you'd better believe."

"Right," Naomi said. "But it hasn't been. And the first thing anybody's heard was the news tonight," Naomi said. "The first thing *most* people heard," she emended.

"Not quite," said Philip, and clammed up suddenly.

"So where in the subway system do the trains *not* run?" Ruth asked. "We can start looking there. Simple."

"Break into the New York Subway System and she calls it simple," Naomi said.

"It beats working for a living," said Michael.

"New information on the Subway Snatcher. Details after this," said the television.

* * *

He found he did not like the subterranean way any more this time than he had the last time he had been here. Rohannan Melior of the House of the Silver Silences stepped, with painstaking caution, onto the subway tracks.

Mistress Jane had been correct. Far south, in the World of the Trade Center, was the terminus for the Double-E line. Commuters, forewarned, had made other arrangements. They had reached that place by surface means. Once there, the unguarded platform there had been empty.

And he and Jane had descended.

Jane shone the light down along the tracks, careful not to blind Melior's dark-adapted eyes. And as she walked she thought, trying out Melior's plan for practicability. Walk down to Wall Street. Track the *grendel* to its lair. Grab the sword, which Melior was sure would be there. Cut the *grendel* into collops. Leave.

The difference between a plan like that and wishful thinking was small, if even extant. And it required luck of a staggering order of improbability to work.

But Melior wasn't asking for Jane's opinion. Only for her help. She could give that.

"If someone sees you, they're going to stop you," she offered at last.

Melior stopped and turned back to her. Jane flicked the beam of the flashlight away as he moved, shining it away from him. In the darkness his eyes were metallic changeant moons; the light flashing from dilated pupils. Melior waited.

"The platforms. You can't get near them without being seen. There could be someone up there. Subway cops," Jane said.

A map both accurate and representational of the subway system was hard to find, but Jane had one. She peered at it. Down here the intervals between the stations were shorter. The flashlight's beam turned her map into a paper lantern; lighting the paper and turning the lines to gray scrimshaw.

"Or commuters. If there are any. If they see you, you'll be in trouble," she added.

Melior saw no reason to doubt her. Jane was not lying, and he knew it. "These commuters," he said after a pause, "there is one time more than another when they are likely to be here?"

"Sure." Jane looked at her watch. "Gone by ten, maybe,

especially this far downtown. But you still can't get *past* the platforms without being seen."

"When the time comes," Melior said, "you may leave that to me. For now, we must find a place to occupy the time until we may proceed."

It was twelve o'clock, and Philip hadn't told. He was neither triumphant nor defiant about it, and even through her anger Ruth sensed that Philip was as frustrated by his refusal as they were.

"We've gone about this all wrong," Naomi said. She cradled a large earthenware teacup in her hands. She wasn't looking at Philip.

"Red hot needles, maybe?" Michael said. It was hard to tell if he was making a joke. Maybe Michael wasn't sure himself.

"About Melior," Naomi said. "he came to us for help. We shouldn't have just said 'no.' "

"He wanted to go hunting space-alligators in the subway," Michael pointed out. "*Grendels.* Whatever. But—" he sighed and rubbed the back of his neck. "Too bad we didn't know then what we know now."

"We don't *know* anything," Ruth pointed out wearily.

"But that isn't the point," Naomi said. "Going down into the subway is a stupid idea, take it all in all. It doesn't matter whether what's there is fictional or real. And we should have found another way for him."

"But you didn't." It was Philip who spoke. For the last several hours he had been all but silent, as the strange game he had played with Melior went from being a joke, to a business proposition, to a tragedy, and on to a contest of wills.

"No," said Naomi. "We didn't."

"And what are you going to do now?" Philip asked her.

"What are *you* going to do, Phil?" Michael said.

Philip's mouth twisted mockingly. "Me? When did I ever do anything that mattered, Michael?" He shrugged angrily. "All you've got left to do is take up a collection for the funeral."

"It's May 5th. Sunrise is at five-oh-five a.m." Ruth blurted out. She put the newspaper down. "And at five-oh-six a.m. . . ." She paused.

"We have to figure out what to do," Naomi said. She regarded her companions. "*Think* about it, guys. There *really is* a monster in the subway. It's killing people. Melior's gone after it, but he doesn't think he's going to do very well. It's up to us. What do we do?"

Anything was better than thinking about where Melior might be and what *he* was doing. "He asked for a sword," Ruth began.

"But only *The* sword will kill it. So he says. But since we don't have anything better to go on, we might as well take Melinor's word for it," Michael said.

"So we get *The* sword," Ruth said slowly. The rules. All magic had rules. A story where the magic didn't have rules was no fun for the reader. There were rules to everything if you could only find out what they were. "But the *grendel*'s guarding it—isn't it?"

"Well," said Naomi consideringly, "*I* would be. It sounds like first we've got to get the *grendel*."

The One no longer slept. The One guarded The Object; guarded and fed and waited the day that The Other foretold to it would come and be destroyed.

Insofar as it could be, in the grip of its monstrous and eternal hunger, The One was content. It had purpose; the thing which its human chrysalis had always lacked. It had a function to perform, and, as far as its truncated intellect could perceive those abstractions, a sense of achievement, of honor, of glory and struggle.

And triumph.

The Other could come as he chose. The Other could come down into The One's kingdom and search as he chose. The Object was secure. And The One could disappear at will.

But The One did not choose to. At this moment there were Men in The One's domain, and The One remembered Men.

Men meant *food*.

Jane had explained the third rail and its lethal properties to Melior very carefully twice—the second time once she realized that he didn't have the faintest idea what electricity was. She was pretty sure now that he knew that if he touched it he would die. She had not bothered to enumerate the scant exceptions to that rule; they were unlikely enough to occur, and since he probably thought the whole thing ran by magic anyway, there was no point in confusing him.

The tunnels weren't so bad once you got used to them.

They spent the waiting time sitting against the wall of the tunnel, near a cubbyhole they could retreat into if a train came. Jane had brought extra batteries for her flashlight; she spent the waiting time reading a book.

And no trains did come. It was strangely silent here in the tunnels beneath the bottom tip of Manhattan; only a faint suck and sough of wind from a place miles away where the tunnels broke out into moonlight. Even the ventilation grates which marked some of the older tunnels were absent here. A separate world, an underground dominion where there was neither sun nor moon—

Abruptly Jane sat up straighter. Neither sun nor moon. Sun nor moon. . . .

And there was neither sun nor moon/And all the roaring of the sea—*"* Suddenly Jane wished for her guitar, the words of the old ballad mocking her. Neither sun nor moon. A sound like the sea roaring, or what you heard when you put a seashell to your ear, or wind. Rivers of blood, or something at least as disgusting.

Fairyland. By all the laws of ballad-land, the New York subway tunnels were Fairyland.

Was this the actual answer, the unriddle that would solve Melior's quest? The knowledge that the Real World— Melior's World of Iron, possessed all the landmarks and appurtenances of Faery, if only you looked at it just right?

"Ill met by moonlight, proud Titania." "How many miles to Babylon?/Threescore miles and ten." "Oh, where are you bound?/Said the false knight on the road" "The sedge is wither'd from the lake/And no birds sing."

A faery knight, a ravished sword, a monster monstrous through its own cupidity. What was there in that baggage of twice-told plain tales from the hollow hills that could help now?

"It is past midnight," Melior said suddenly, "and those who travel are safe within doors. It is time for us to travel, Mistress Jane."

She looked at her watch. Almost one o'clock in the morning, and a couple of miles of tunnels to cover before they got to the place where Melior wanted to be.

"Whassamatter you guys? Ya wanna live forever?" Jane quoted, getting to her feet.

Now that she had made the connection, new evidence kept presenting itself; images from the ballads Jane loved to play without reposing the least belief in them. For Jane, normally unfanciful, these associations clothed the prosaic ugliness of the subway tunnels in faery. Once, in a place where A and C crossed 4-5-6 and several sets of tracks ran parallel, there was a faint mournful wail in the distance, and Jane and Melior retreated into concealment to watch the passage of a yellow-and-black flatcar. It did not rely on the third rail to power it; the watchers in their hiding place heard and smelled the workings of a gasoline engine.

Three men stood on its open surface, peering out into the dark. One carried a rifle. A Border Patrol for the line between fact and fantasy. When it was gone, Jane and Melior went on.

They reached the first platform. Harsh blue incandescence like a special effect spilled out along the tracks. The pools in the center of the trackbed were silver footprints, and every soda can and discarded wrapper was an elphen horde.

It was at this point that the first faint disquieting sensation came upon Jane that things weren't precisely right. *The time is out of joint.* She had the sneaking suspicion of the teetotaler that there might have been whiskey in the whiskey, a feeling that the description "self-controlled" was no longer Truth in Advertising.

Melior stopped just short of the point where anyone standing behind the yellow line which passengers are urged not to cross when a train is not in the station could see him. He held two fingers to his lips in an almost-familiar gesture and motioned Jane closer. She put out her flashlight and came over. The soot on the wall was the black matte softness of velvet and the slick untrustworthiness of grease.

"First I will go, and mark you well how I do it. Then follow, and haply no one will reckon us," Melior said. He looked over his shoulder at the platform. "And should the alarm be raised, do you draw them off and I will make my way as best I might."

And leave me to take the rap. But from Melior's point of view it was reasonable. He was best equipped to kill the *grendel.* She was just the spear carrier. If Melior'd happened to have a spear.

And Jane was very well equipped to deal with any question that began with "why". *Why did you, why don't you, why will you, why won't you, why do you. . . .*

Tolerated everywhere she'd ever been. As opposed, perhaps, to being wanted, welcomed, valued. Not noticed enough to be disliked; in a world where isolation kills and science has shown that any attention is preferred to none, Jane Treasure Greyson was tolerated; not even noticed enough to get rejected. Tolerated. And what is there in that to connect with enough to fight it? Tolerated. Blandly unseen, glossed over, endured. Until any one who dared communicate was forced to pay the teind for all those who never tried to. And driven away, so that she could keep the one thing she had.

She knew exactly what she did. Pitiless insight isn't called that for no reason. Pity makes allowance and turns its face away. Intellect does not. And so the same thing that let her see their neglect, that caused their neglect, made certain that they would never simply leave her alone, because such a clever little thing, such an earnest, forever hopeful of being loved little thing, such a biddable little thing must surely be useful, somehow—

But Melior valued her, without ever trying to know her. Without using her, except in such a blatant and obvious fashion that it was almost as if she gave her help freely. And for that Jane would provide the one gift in her ken. Loyalty.

"You'll need the map," she whispered back, and transferred it, carefully folded, to his waiting black-gloved hand.

But all was anticlimax, as after that Melior crossed the open space, crouched low and moving swiftly, crossing directly beneath the platform, hugging it closely to minimize the time when he would be visible. To discover whether there were watchers in truth would have revealed them; they could only go on as if there were and hope that there weren't. His silver hair was a bright flag in the darkness; the sword a golden sparkle at his hip.

And Magic was afoot in the world.

Melior crossed, safely, making his way into the other darkness, hidden again. It would not have surprised Jane if he had gone on and left her there; after all, he had almost warned her. But instead he stopped, turned back, and waited.

And now it was her turn. She hesitated. It had looked easy when he did it. There probably wasn't anyone up there anyway. All she had to do was walk, very fast and crouching optional, across the space that was the open front of the platform.

And still she wavered. What if she slipped, what if she

fell, what if there was someone up there after all? *What if she looked stupid?*

Go. The demand was almost a spoken word; clear enough to have been heard. Jane let it galvanize her; push her forward without thought.

Her shoulder slid along the soot, a featherwhisper scraping that told her she was going rightly. She watched her feet, chary of the bottles, the wrappers, the noisy treacherous footing beneath.

A subway platform is at least the width of the street above, sometimes the length of a city block and more. A distance hardly thought of when choosing which car to enter or stairs to exit by. A tiny eternity to cross through the gloom of the railbed below. Her heart hammered; consciousness was suspended in the throbbing silver of the Eternal Now and for once Jane Greyson lived in the moment.

Melior faded back into the darkness as she advanced, preserving the distance between them until she was safely past the point where she might be seen. Then he allowed her to catch up to him.

They went on. After a few yards the darkness closed in again and Jane flicked on her flashlight. A few blocks to the next platform, and then a little beyond that the crossing of tracks where they changed from uptown to crosstown lines as they navigated this web of angles toward their goal.

"Can I get there by candlelight?
Yes, and back again."

CHAPTER 17

Judgment Day

Dawn was a white sheen over Fort Lee, New Jersey.

No one had slept. Not Michael, not Ruth, not Philip looking red-eyed and stubborn like a mutant Spartacus of laboratory rats. The excitement of plotting how best to go after Melior's *grendel* had foundered on the complete lack of information and—on Ruth's part—a worry for Melior that was literally, surprisingly, paralyzing. He was facing the *grendel*. The *grendel* was real. Melior was foredoomed to die and he'd cut out on her without giving her a chance to make a real nuisance of herself, just like a paperback hero.

And she knew, with sharp and annoyed certainty, that her life was in suspension and would hang fire forever if she could not see Melior again and ask him—

What?

"Wall Street," said Philip in a flat, tired voice. "The attacks all center around the City Hall Station, down by Wall Street."

"Attacks?" Michael seized on the word. The morning sun was shining on his face, lighting his eyes to a brilliant green. But not the impossible green of Melior's.

"Attacks," Philip said. "Six or seven people that they know of are missing-presumed-history and about a dozen more are incommunicado, a small town in New Jersey. Trackworkers, and like that. And the street people are avoiding the Lower Manhattan stations for sleeping and panhandling."

"How did you find all this out?" Naomi asked, honestly curious.

Philip pushed up his bifocals. "Stats. Missing person reports. I cracked BlueNet, the cop BBS, and pulled the local gossip for the last week or so. Everybody's jumpy, but it could look like just a lot of coincidence, you know?"

"Until last night," Ruth said bleakly.

"Which brings us back to Topic A: what do we do?" Naomi said.

"We could, of course, let the trained professionals handle it," Michael said. "That *is* what they're there for. They've got manpower, resources, access to tools. They can get an animal control officer in there with a net and drag the thing out."

"You're no fun," Philip said under his breath.

"Before it kills how many more people?" Naomi asked.

"That's a cheap shot, Nai," Michael said. "They're doing what they can right now, and telling them what we know isn't going to change that. Every whack in New York and the five boroughs is already calling up and confessing to being the Subway Snatcher. We'll sound like just one more nutcase."

"So we just say "What is Truth?" and wash our hands of it?" Ruth said. "What about Melior?"

"Well, what do you think we could do to help him—walk up to the *grendel* and refuse to let it graduate?" Michael asked.

"If he isn't going to kill it, and if all your damned trained professionals are so hotshot, why don't we get him out of there?" Ruth snapped back.

"Getting Melior Down and Not Hurting Anybody," Naomi said, gazing at the ceiling. "Does it matter whether the *grendel*'s dead if it's captured and Melior has his sword back?" she asked.

"Not to me," Ruth said. Suddenly the gears were turning in her head again. "I think we've been going at this inside-out. We've been concentrating on the *grendel,* because that's what Melior thinks is important. But the *grendel* isn't as important as the sword—"

"So forget the *grendel,*" Naomi finished for her. "Find Melior, hold him off until the police catch the *grendel*—"

"And then find the sword," Michael finished.

"Which will be one of two places," Naomi said.

"Either where the *grendel* hid it," Ruth added.

"Or somewhere in Washington crated up next to the Lost Ark from *Raiders,*" Naomi finished, "which may be difficult to get to but not impossible—"

"And burglarizing the CIA or searching the MTA will be a lot easier without playing Bullets and Bracelets with the

Thing from Forty-thousand Plotlines," Michael said. "So all we have to do is get our hands on Melior and convince *him*."

"That's Ruth's job," Naomi said.

Everybody looked at Ruth, and Ruth had the panicked feeling of having been asked to speak in public.

"He'll listen to her," Naomi added inexorably.

"He won't do it," Philip said, not about Ruth.

"He wants the sword, not the *grendel*," Michael pointed out. "This is a way to the sword. If he doesn't get picked up. We didn't turn Melior over to the cops in the first place because if we did, he'd disappear into a little underground room somewhere. Which he still could, if we can't get him out in time."

" 'The mistake was in not forbidding the serpent,' " Ruth quoted. " 'Then he would have eaten the serpent.' Mark Twain."

"So how do we find him?" Naomi said.

"Come home, Elfie, all is forgiven," Philip muttered.

"Go where he's gone," Michael said. "And there's no good time for that."

"Right," said Naomi. "Come on, Ruth, let's get dressed for a little nightcrawling. Michael, we'll meet you at your place in about forty minutes. Check the radio to see if they've started running the Lower Manhattan lines again. We'll have to figure out how to get onto the tracks somehow."

"Jane was," Ruth said suddenly. "Down on the tracks, I mean. The day she went on the subway trip with Melior and came back all over soot. They were down in the tunnels somewhere. They have to have been."

"Fine," said Naomi. "They turn on the dorm phones at six." She looked at her watch. "It's almost that now. We can call her. Get going," she added, as Michael stood up. "And you," she said to Philip, "had better get back to your computers. I think this time you're going to work for free."

It took them four hours of painstaking subway crawling, backtracking, and waiting, to reach the stalking ground. In the pauses Melior told Jane as much as he knew about the nature of *grendels*.

"Their food is the flesh of their kind, and their whole nature is to hoard beyond their use and spoil what they cannot take away. And their appetite grows with what it feeds upon, until at last their hunger lays waste to all that is near."

Jane had pondered this as a lifestyle choice and then asked: "Well, just how much area can they lay waste to?"

Melior had smiled. "Anything within their reach, and their reach grows with time. If they could ever bear to abandon their hoard, they would be even more dangerous. But it takes much to dislodge a *grendel* from its place, and then the creature only lairs again as soon as it may."

"If it can stand the sun," Jane had added, and Melior had agreed.

"But this one may be strong enough to do that even now. And if it is not, there is so much darkness in your city that its choices are many."

But Melior had not spoken for the last half hour or so. At their last stop he had made Jane put away her flashlight, and handed her, in exchange, one of those small camping lanterns that is simply a candle enclosed by glass. *How many miles to Babylon?* Now she followed him by the light of the candle *Threescore miles and ten* and tried to ignore the words that circled round in her head *Can I get there by candlelight?*

Yes, and back again.

"Hist," said Melior, and Jane was so keyed up that it was only much later that she registered that the archaism should have been funny. "It is very near."

The scent of evil that these Ironworlders refused to ken hung in the tunnel like sickly marsh mist. The beast was near, and Melior hoped without knowledge that Mistress Jane would run when he bid her, when the *grendel* turned first to him, ancient enemy, and he made his futile assault upon it. Twisted product of magic gone wrong—elphen magic—it was his responsibility as March-Lord of the Silver Silences to undo what his kind had wrought.

Perhaps the little magic he hoarded against this moment could harm it; cripple it so that those who came after would find the *grendel* easier prey. Stephen's sword hung naked at his hip; there had been no time or chance to contrive furniture for it, but the weight was welcome—oh, to hold a sword again; to die a clean death with it in his hand—!

But he was so very far from home.

And his failure loomed dark and tangled across all the leys of the future, strangling his Foresight in its single asseveration: that the *grendel* would not die by his hand.

So it must be that he would die, and when he died the Sword would be lost here forever, and Baligant who had plotted his Line's downfall would reign triumphant.

He could see no way to escape that. Ruth and her friends would accept no proof he could offer that this danger existed. And even when Philip spread out all his truths to them as he had to Melior, would they say any different?

He did not know. He had not dared wait to find out. Each time he had brought them proofs they had thought him mad. Perhaps this greatest proof would have seemed to them only the greatest madness, and then they, lovingly and with kindness, would imprison him to keep him from doing what he must.

Perhaps he *was* mad. But as the humans of this land said: even though you were paranoid, it did not mean you had no enemies.

Jane wasn't there. Naomi put down the phone and looked at Ruth, who was just pulling on her jacket of choice. Merrie Month of May or not, it was going to be cold down there.

Ruth had scoured her wardrobe, as Naomi had, for clothing she wouldn't mind throwing out as soon as she got back. She wore a sloppy long-sleeved singlet that was already the shade of gray it would otherwise turn, gray-green cargo pants, and an Army Surplus windcheater that had seemed like a much better idea in the store than it had when she'd got it home. The black canvas hi-tops on her feet were another such purchase; impulsive and impossible and too much like the ones Philip wore. She'd pinned and braided her hair up into a hard knot on the back of her head and covered it with a crocheted black bun-doily that Naomi had dug up from somewhere. When she looked in the mirror Ruth decided she looked like the Terminator's fashion-victim sister.

Naomi, of course, looked as if she'd been shopping for months with the aim of schlepping through subway tunnels. She had on tightly-laced green rubber duckblind halfboots into which were tucked crisp poplin suntans (*ironed. . . .*) over which was a no-nonsense bush jacket. She was even wearing gloves, and Ruth, thinking of what she'd have to touch down there, wished she weren't the sort who regularly lost her winter gloves every March.

"You look like an outtake from *King Solomon's Sewers,*" she'd said, as Naomi was dialing Jane.

"Just trying to bring a fashion sense to urban fantasy," Naomi had answered as she listened to the phone ring on unanswered. Now she looked at Ruth, hand still over the receiver.

"We can worry about her or about Melior," Naomi said to Ruth, as if she were offering her a choice between chocolate and vanilla. "And personally I think Jane could be lots of places in no trouble while we know exactly how much trouble Melior is in."

"Right." Ruth drew in a deep breath, which did her exactly as much good as the last one had; none.

"Come on," Naomi said. "Let's get Michael."

A long time afterward Jane decided that what the problem had been was that it was too easy.

It was true that Melior behaved as if the situation was dangerous, but then, Melior behaved as if walking the streets of New York was High Adventure. And it had been hour on hour, and all they had done was walk, through an environment that lost all of its terror and much of its charm through long acquaintance.

Now that changed.

It was after four o'clock in the morning, an hour in which Jane's body was asleep even if she wasn't. The first candle had burnt down and she had changed it by flashlight. Melior had given her his pack and canteen to carry as well as her own and panthered forward on flexed joints like a dark and dangerous balletomane. And she wasn't paying attention to much of anything beyond following him and wondering if they could stop soon.

There was a hiss. A clang as the *gladius* rang off the subway wall. Melior sprang sideways, landing directly in the center of the railbed. The sword flashed in the light of Jane's lantern and Melior's every gesture spoke of fearful threat.

She backed away, icy with the uprush of fight-or-flight chemistry, and in that instant there was a "tok" sound like the Babe hitting one over the fence and the scunnering ring of the sword sliding away into the dark, both combined with the snapshot image of Melior flung boneless to the ground.

It had happened so fast.

Facts. Jane dealt with them, the momentary chemical alarm pushed back to unimportance. New information reached another of her senses. Jane looked up, beyond the silver flame of Melior's hair being slowly extinguished by blood and black water.

She raised the lantern higher, but even so the light barely reached what stood in the shadows, that had struck Melior down so casually.

Jane looked at the *grendel*. The *grendel* looked at Jane. Melior's body lay between them; vulnerable.

It was so much taller than she was that there was no point in assigning it a height. It smelled of excrement and rotting meat, thickly and insistently; as she stared, she saw it more clearly.

Its skin was the livid purple-gray of gangrene, wrinkled like a raisin and beginning to scale. Patches of what might have been mold spotted the skin here and there; exotic fauna known only to pathologists. The *grendel*'s eyes were small white globes set in an angry weeping expanse of scarlet flesh; abraded sockets swollen and peeling.

If she had screamed, if she had run, if she had shown any reaction to it at all, things might have gone differently. If it had not eaten, recently and well, it might have taken more interest. But she was not The Other, and she was not The Object, and soon The Other would not be able to hurt it at all.

Jane stared at the *grendel*. Her heartbeat did not race; it was possible she was not thinking of danger at all. She simply looked, and recorded what she saw, and waited for what she saw to change.

There was a blast of sound; an eerie, flatulent howl. Startled, she dropped the candle and could still see; Jane looked behind her. Far but not far enough she saw the flatcar they had seen earlier; but this time it was on the tracks behind her, sweeping the tunnel with its spotlight. The over-amplified yowp of an electronic bullhorn stunned her with pure noise, its message lost to distortion.

She looked back. The *grendel* was gone as if it had never been there. Melior raised one hand; a feeble gesture.

"Run," he whispered.

There was only one direction possible. Melior on the tracks would delay the flatcar, moving at its stately 35 mph. She could get away.

This time Jane did not pause to think. She threw away everything she carried and ran.

The bullhorn squawked. The spotlight drilled into her back, but it had not cost her much of her night vision. Down here the lines converged again, and in the underground cathedral vastness warning lights burned like the stars of an earthbound constellation. On her left, across a no-man's-land of third rails, she saw the pale gleaming refuge of a station platform.

She heard the change in engine pitch as the flatcar stopped at Melior's body. If she was quick, she could reach the platform and a state of plausible deniability.

She didn't think the *grendel* would follow her to the light; more precisely, she didn't think of the *grendel* at all; that was something for later, after she had performed the function for which she now knew Melior had chosen her, and brought back the truth of her own eyes to the only people left on earth who might be able to act upon it.

There was a monster loose in the New York Subway.

It was on a May morning, and just like in any ballad the day was determined to be beautiful enough to make Pollyanna suspicious. Ruth had the edged feeling of too much tea and too little sleep, and the air like wild silk and the light like raw honey did nothing to anchor her in reality.

Michael was waiting for them on the corner. Philip was nowhere in sight. Conversation was superfluous. They walked over and caught the A Train downtown.

New Yorkers are a blasé lot. Once, many years ago, for a bet, to prove a point, or on some esoteric scientific *raison* a man undertook to walk stark naked (except for shoes) the length of Fifth Avenue. Extant photos (snapped from behind) show him passing among New Yorkers who are neither looking nor not-looking, strenuously proving themselves sangfroidian even at the cost of common sense.

This, combined with Warhol's heart-held dictum that there is a fifteen-minute time limit on fame, assured that no matter who had been dragged by what off a subway platform at the height of the rush hour the night before, today the trains were running and nobody would be so *gauche* as to wonder whether making the morning commute was worth the personal hazard.

The only trouble the three of them had was finding standing room on the rush-hour trains.

It took them more than an hour to reach West Fourth Street from 116th, in between the profit and the loss, in the T.S. Eliot where the dreams cross. When they reached it, Michael gestured and they were borne onto the platform in a tide of Thursday morning lemming ballet.

"Now I know why I don't work for a living," Naomi panted as they fought their way to freedom. "Where now?"

"Phone call," said Michael. "Coffee. And maybe one of you professional geniuses can figure out how we're going to get down onto the tracks in the middle of all this without being either seen or creamed."

"Easy enough if Lower Manhattan's still stopped," Naomi said.

"There's only six or seven ways to find out," Ruth pointed out.

"Come on. Let's find a phone that's working."

On the way out, Ruth glanced at the clock overhead. The time was seven-twenty-eight.

It was eight-thirty-five when Jane let herself into Ruth and Naomi's apartment with her spare key. It had been a little before five wen she finally reached the surface of New York, at a station and line she'd never seen, somewhere in the depths of Wall Street.

She'd struck out first for Broadway, and had seen the red warning flashes of emergency lights before she'd seen anything more.

Paranoid as a lifestyle choice, Jane had not had to think twice about heading south, toward Battery Park and away from police vans, emergency vehicles, firetrucks, minicams, and anything else containing someone who might ask her questions. She had a pretty good idea that the *grendel* wasn't Melior's little secret any more—which would account for the fact that there'd been no subway traffic until the flatcar full of fuzz showed up—but she didn't know how much of what version anybody knew, and she didn't intend to be the one to lighten the load of their ignorance. Jane had other plans for her Thursday.

Having gone south as far as was safe she headed east, having no desire to be mugged, either at any time or before she'd delivered the news to the others. Melior'd been right all along, and that should just about fry Philip to the ultimate max.

Earliest morning broke about twenty minutes after Jane came above ground; bright and clear, one of those mornings that seem almost to be safety-sealed for your protection; too good to be true. Vintage season, and like the C.L. Moore story, only the overture to the most select form of apocalypse.

But up-and-coming Gotterdammerungs weren't Jane's affair, and frying Philip LeStrange was. Philip *Leslie* LeStrange.

At the hour and in the area she had chosen, Jane's tatterdemalion appearance was not too much noticed. Just another strange street person, this one young enough to be a runaway.

She knew what her few observers thought and it suited her fine; Manhattanites weren't a charitable people. It took her until about six a.m. to hoof it clear of the media circus pitch and find a phone that worked.

It did not occur to her that she was already missed, that there was already videotaped proof of the *grendel*'s existence and that the others were already trying to figure out how best to save Melior from himself. She thought there was all the time in the world, and that Ruth would hardly relish being awakened so soon after dawn.

And so, hesitating, trying to decide not only what Melior wanted her to do but what a reasonable person *would* do, Jane waited until six-thirty to phone Ruth and Naomi.

The phone rang. And rang, and rang, until Jane was quite certain no one would answer.

She phoned Philip's number. Whoever answered hung up the phone without speaking, and after the third time, Jane gave up. Served Philip right for not giving them any of his *private* phone numbers.

Michael was out, too. But that was reasonable; Michael liked jogging, and morning classes, and other masochistic pursuits.

She found a McDonald's and ordered breakfast, simply because it was the sort of thing that normal people did and

Jane, perhaps, had new doubts about her ability to fake normalcy. She ate it walking back up the street, wondering whether she was going to have an attack of nerves about going down into the subway again. She decided she wouldn't, and caught the "A" Uptown at Canal.

She tried Ruth and Naomi once more, while waiting for the train. No one answered. Jane did not speculate; she went home.

It is entirely possible that Jane passed Ruth and the others at some fulcrum point on the A Line. It is certain that when she reached their apartment (a better place to go than the dorm, where there would be more of that tiresome tribe, nosy people with awkward questions) and buzzed for admittance, there was no answer.

There was nobody home. Without any particular sense of guilt, Jane investigated the apartment thoroughly, but the scribbled notes and lists in Ruth's and Naomi's handwriting conveyed very little.

Except that they were both gone, at a time when they ought not to be gone. She phoned Michael again, but after fifteen unanswered rings she gave it up. After much thought, she even phoned Philip again, but all she got for that was a shouted "Not here!" and the receiver slammed down.

Curiouser and curiouser.

The television only had late-morning happytalk news to offer, and Doubleyew-ten-ten-Wins News Radio was spending its time on things with "East" in the title, like the Near East and Eastern Europe.

She could, of course, dash off and try to rescue Melior. Only she had no idea how badly he'd been hurt, or whether he'd been arrested, and whether anyone claiming to be his friend might just be arrested in turn. She was pretty sure that rescuing Melior would require extensive and creative lying, a skill she knew she lacked, and if she were detained in any fashion Melior's message might not get delivered. Besides, people might call her parents, and then there'd *really* be trouble.

And she knew that Michael or Naomi would be much more efficient at dealing with the mundanes. And success was to be preferred over speed, if you had to choose just one.

Jane gave up and took a shower, scrubbing until the water

ran clear. She borrowed a skirt and sweater of Ruth's and a
garbage bag for her subway-crawling clothes. Then she
headed back for her own dorm room, trying to form a criterion for deciding when she'd have to do what she could
without the others.

And then, having walked nearly twelve miles and been up
for more than twenty-four hours, she fell asleep on her
dorm-room bed before she began to wonder precisely how
trustworthy Philip's roommates were in the matter of phone
messages at eight-forty-five in the morning.

"Nothing." Michael hung up the phone.

"What *kind* of nothing?" Ruth wanted to know.

"No police reports. Philip says Downtown subway lines
are on a half-hour delay, but they're running. No sign of
Jane," Michael elaborated.

"Is he sure?" Naomi said.

"He called her again while I was on his other line, and
he's got the computer scanning continuously in several
places I don't even want to think about. No Jane."

"Dear Philip," Ruth said. "Three phone lines, no waiting.
I don't even want to think about how he does that."

"Illegally," Naomi said. "And if he weren't feeling so
guilty right now, you still wouldn't have the phone numbers."

"Well I do have them," Michael pointed out unnecessarily,
"so come on. I think I know a way to get to where Melior
is."

"And then we can play Dodge 'Em cars with real subways. Cute," Naomi said.

"Especially when you pause to consider that there's no
place to dodge to," Michael answered cheerfully.

Rohannan Melior of the House of the Silver Silences,
firstborn of his Line, of the line of the sons of the Morning
Stars, Marchlord and Swordwarden, had had better days.

Much better days.

As it was, he had luck of a sort on his side. The Guardsmen had not seized him armed, and much as he grieved over
the loss of Stephen's sword, things that Ruth had said had
convinced him it was a better thing in this land to be found
unweaponed.

The second point in his favor was that he was injured. In fact, his captors had used him with much solicitous concern upon finding him hurt, and Melior had let them, knowing that every moment spent on him was one more in which his squire might win her freedom.

They asked a number of odd questions about his name and their fingers, about who took precedence and what state he was in. "Utter confusion," Melior had answered honestly to that last, and after that they left him alone with the throbbing pain and sickness in his head until a litter could be brought. Until it came they would not move him, Melior had discovered, and as he lay across the tracks their machine could not proceed.

He realized, listening to them speak among themselves, that some felt he might be a mere thrill-seeker, whatever that might be, but others that he might be victim to the creature that they hunted, which had taken human prey in sight of many only the previous day. Melior closed his eyes against the pain in his head. Now Ruth and the others would have their proof, but Melior was no longer certain it would do any good. These humans who seemed to place too much emphasis upon maintaining the surface illusion at any cost did not seem to have the knack of hunting *grendel*.

He did not think their race would survive.

But at the moment it was Melior who wanted to survive, and not to be taken away to rooms without windows by tribes with meaningless barbarian names like Seaheyah or Efbeyah and tortured there to give up the secrets of his Line.

It was not hard to seem hurt and wearied when the lackeys came to carry him off. When they shifted him onto the litter they had brought, a bright light seemed to dawn behind his eyes and he lay only faintly aware until the cool morning air washed over him. Straps held his body to the pallet; it steadied and jarred as its handlers shifted it, and then began to roll forward on wheels.

Melior opened his eyes once and closed them again. Lights in a spectrum of colors, some flashing, some not. Barking voices, men's and women's both, and a constant howling as of war-horns. So much strangeness, and no Ruth beside him to show by her example that things were proceeding in the normal fashion for the world.

They lifted him into a small hut of the sort that moved and he did not fight them. He did not think he could stand, much less break the straps and run, and innocence was his only defense now that he had fallen into the toils of those his young friends feared more than *grendel*.

A Guardsman got in behind him, and the hut began to roll forward. It increased the sickness in his head, and he only hoped he'd made the right choice and not once more done something that Ruth would think was foolish.

The Guardsman spoke to Melior, his voice hard and barking. A woman's voice interrupted his, telling Melior that this wouldn't hurt, and asked again the meaningless questions about names and fingers and precedence while she shone a light in his eyes.

His eyes. Ruth said they betrayed him. He stared at the white-clothed woman in alarm.

"Reflexes normal," the woman said. "Hi, my name is Holly Kendal, and I'm your EMT for the morning." She brushed his hair back, very carefully, regarding the ears which his lady Ruth had been pleased to call beautiful but entirely wrong. He watched Holly Kendal, who was his EMT, as she sank white teeth into her lower lip and hesitated the briefest instant, and it came to him that she would not betray him.

"How are you feeling?" she asked carefully. "Do you speak English?"

"Dizzy," Melior said, closing his eyes in relief. Holly pressed cool fingers to his wrist. She said she was taking his vitals, that he was being admitted to Bellevue, and a number of other things that Melior simply did not find worth the trouble of remaining conscious to hear.

Michael took them downtown. It was after nine by now; the great commuter crunch had eased, and they had the weekday morning subways almost (comparatively speaking) to themselves.

Ruth hadn't counted on the rubberneckers and licensed gawkers. The station that Therese Scarlatti had been taken from yesterday was locked, iron gates and all, and removed temporarily from the roster of subway stops. The train might be running, but half the Lower Manhattan IRT stops were closed.

"Worry not," Michael said, and proceeded to take them around a number of crisscrosses and shortcuts that made Ruth exceedingly glad that she was doing this in the company of a six-foot-two weightlifting student librarian.

"Here we are," said Michael finally.

It was a passageway of the sort that let you transfer between uptown, downtown, alphabets, and numbers without paying another fare—assuming, always, that you thought being mugged was worth the trouble. The walls were white tile, the ceiling was claustrophobicly low, and Ruth wouldn't have touched the paving beneath her feet with her bare hands for anything short of life-threatening incentive. The corridor smelled strongly of unpoliced bodily functions.

Interrupting the white tile was a green metal door with a padlock and hasp.

Michael pulled out something that was not quite a key and jiggled it in the lock. After a moment the padlock popped open.

"If anyone is going to break any more laws, I don't want to know about it," Ruth said faintly.

"This is next to last," Michael said reassuringly. "Ladies and, um, ladies, allow me to present to you the jewel in the TA's crown; a little-known access corridor to take you directly—do not pass 'Go', do not collect two hundred dollars—to IRT track-level. If we're caught in here or on the tracks, it's B&E—that's Breaking and Entering to you civilians—but we'll probably get off with a fine providing nobody mentions elves, which will get us a complementary seventy-two-hour commitment for observation in the nearest loony bin. Just keep your mouths shut, okay?"

"I love it when you go all macho," Naomi said. "But how did you know that was here?"

"A friend of mine in Transit told me about it," Michael said, which made Ruth wonder until his opening the door made her forget. He hustled them inside quickly, which made her think this might be even more illegal than it looked.

There was a deadbolt on the inside of the door, and Michael dead-bolted it. He hung the outside padlock on the inside lock and gestured theatrically.

This corridor was smaller than the last, marginally

cleaner, and lit by 40-watt light bulbs placed at the longest possible intervals.

"After you," Michael said.

"Idiocy before beauty," Naomi answered, and Michael started down the corridor, ducking.

CHAPTER 18

One Flew Over the Basilisk's Nest

That place which mortals named *Bellevue Emergency* caused Melior to revise his opinions about this world's humans. If they maintained such places as this for their sport, surely the *grendel* could not seem so evil to them.

The sliding doors of the ambulance entryway opened for the lackeys who bore Melior's wheeled cot. Holly Kendal walked beside him, carrying the board and papers upon which she had written.

Within the citadel the light was uncharitably bright, and harsh mechanical stinks burned Melior's nose while doing but little to conceal the odors of pain, fear, sickness, and blood which lay beneath. There was a harsh wailing and the polyphony of voice raised in a fashion which he had never heard outside of a battlefield.

Holly-his-EMT placed a clipboard carefully on his chest and patted his shoulder. "You'll be all right," she said, but Melior could hear the unsureness in her voice.

She stared at him a moment longer and then walked away. The last Melior saw of her was her waist-length russet braid bouncing as she strode.

Then he was brought to another place, with no more interest shown him than if he had been as inanimate as the bed he was bound to. The Guardsman stayed with him, and there was much incomprehensible talk of preserving his simple rights and of someone named Miranda, who seemed to be the matriarch whose name must be invoked to solemnize his detention. Lackeys in white lifted him onto a metal table and off again, his chest was prodded with cold instruments, and through it all he forced himself to wait, muscles limp and face impassive, lest they put him back into the iron cage from which Ruth might not rescue him twice.

They kept him bound upon the pallet, called *gurney* among them, lest he damage himself before they could see the damage done him, and asked him many questions. His name. His age. His address. His occupation. To all of these except his name he gave answers that were true for Michael. They asked about his assurance, which puzzled him, and when they asked for his assurance card he said he had lost it.

The Guardsman asked him again and again what he had been doing in the subterranean way and how he had gotten there, and Melior answered as Michael had coached him for some other long-ago occasion:

"I do not know. I do not remember."

The white-robed ones came and went for an hour's time, though the Guardsman never left his side. They spoke, when they were present, much to one another of pictures coming back, and though this made no sense Melior did not question it. To expose his ignorance would be fatal.

At last a minion came, waving blackened sheets of flexible glass, and said things like "mild concussion" and "absence of subdural hematoma" and called him lucky.

Melior did not feel lucky.

But they unstrapped him from the moving bed after that and let him stand for a moment, and though he thanked them for their help and said that he would go he was told that he might not. They gave him pills to swallow from a tiny cup of paper, and gave him water in a larger cup of the same material. The Guardsman stood by, watching.

And so Melior submitted tamely to the removal of his clothes, to their replacement with a smock he would have blushed to see the meanest of his servants wear, and permitted them to bind up the wounds which the *grendel* had made. One minion laved the blue-black place on his cheek where the *grendel* had struck with burning evil-odored lotions. Another came and bound the edges of the wound together with painful sorcery, and then covered his work with pads and ointments and a swathing of pale cloth.

His hearing was very keen, and he did not miss the whispering in corners about his physical differences. His ears, his eyes, the beat of his heart; they had sampled all of these and liked none of them.

At last Melior was let to stand, but only so long as it took for them to bring a wheeled chair such as Michael's friend Stephen possessed. To the mean smock they had granted him they added a tattered blue robe of the material called *terrycloth,* which served to cover him more acceptably. It was probable, Melior thought, that they meant to keep his own clothes as payment for their services, and he was sorry for Ruth's sake, but there was little there he valued. His backpack and Stephen's sword were still in the tunnel, and the sword he did miss, but just as well to lose it there if he were to keep it only to lose it to jackals such as these.

He wondered if they would loose him now, but thought there must be more, and in this much he was right. Frank wanted to talk to him, it was said, and so once more Melior marshaled all his patience and waited for Frank, though his head still ached.

But Frank was not to come to him. He was to go to Frank.

They would not let him walk, but pushed him in the wheeled chair and brought him to a room that smelled of bitter smoke and poisons. In it was a couch, much like Naomi's couch, and there they bid him wait for Frank.

Part of The Object was missing. The One had reasoned this out slowly, taking painful hours to reach that conclusion. Part of The Object was missing—some essence, some informing spark. At first The One had wailed its rage, hot and blinding, but The Object had not kindled. Then The One had mourned over Its loss, knowing It could never venture out into the hot bright Destruction to seek the missing part.

Even striking down The Enemy had not cheered it, for The Enemy was not Food and was not dead.

But surely The Enemy must have died soon thereafter, else why had such a great benison been granted? The One did not have to find a way to survive the great Destruction to seek the part of The Object which had been lost. It was coming here. The missing piece of The Object was coming to The One.

Coming here. Seeking its other self.

Coming within his reach.

"Yeuch." Ruth slid gingerly along the tunnel wall and wished with all her might that she possessed the transcendent nobility of spirit that would allow her to ignore the fact that it was absolutely *filthy.*

She had never held an ambition to schlep around in the subway tunnels. Vincent of *Beauty and the Beast* held no fascination for her. If sensibility was an aversion to cheap theatrics, well, then, let it be so; Ruth was sensible.

But her heart was a sick weight in her chest and she desperately wanted to find Melior. *All* of Melior—and soon.

"We're inside the target area," Michael said softly, ticking off their blessings. "*Grendel* country. The disappearances—allowing for the layout of the tunnels—form a rough circle. We're inside it."

"Wonderful," said Naomi. "But where exactly is the "target area"?"

"Somewhere near City Hall," Michael said. He pulled a flashlight out of his jacket and shone it around.

"What do we do if a train comes?" Ruth looked around nervously.

"See these?" Michael shone his flashlight into a nook built into the wall, a door-shaped alcove that Ruth had seen but thought just for decoration. "Duck into one."

"Oh, thanks," Ruth breathed.

"If the trains were running half an hour apart during rush hour, they may not be running at all now," Naomi pointed out. "Half an hour! Usually it's five minutes."

"Come on," said Michael. "And keep your voices down. Sound carries. We're looking for Melior, not trouble."

"Who writes your dialogue?" Ruth muttered under her breath. But she followed.

Naomi was the one who found the sword.

It was fifteen minutes later, long enough for Ruth, who brought up the rear, to become inured to walking through a cylindrical garbage heap filled with rats which might at any moment chose *not* to scurry the other way and not long enough for her to stop flinching every time she heard a sound that *might* be the herald of an oncoming train. The three of them walked in single-file along the rail-bed, spread out far enough that only two of them would have to crowd into any one-person niche.

Ruth was desperately trying to keep from asking Naomi, who might actually know, just how much wider the tunnels were than the trains that ran through them.

If at all, Ruth emended mentally.

For some reason her hands were shaking badly, making the beam of her flashlight jump in ragged Morse along the ground ahead. It was that, more than anything else, which her mind had chosen to fix on, insisting that it meant she would probably faint, fall down in the muck, contract hepatitis, and die. Melior might be dead already.

And everything he'd told them about the *grendel* was true.

She was concentrating on that bleak prospect so hard that Naomi's sharp indrawn breath of surprise hit Ruth with the violence of a shout.

"Michael—Ruth—LOOK!"

Ruth saw it then: the gold gleam of the *gladius,* lying neglected and unlooked-for directly beneath the third rail.

Melior's sword. Ruth felt sick.

Michael started across the tracks toward it.

For God's sake, Michael! Ruth thought but didn't say aloud.

Michael knelt on the tracks, shining his flashlight on the blade, carefully making certain the sword nowhere touched the rail that carried its multi-thousand-volt freight of raw power. Then, still kneeling, holding the flashlight in his left hand because there must be, could be, no mistake, Michael began, very slowly, reaching out for the sword.

Ruth felt the gentle puff of breeze on the back of her neck. Like the breath of time.

Like the wind from an oncoming train.

How trite, Ruth thought. She saw the white oval of Naomi's face as Nai turned toward her; knew that Naomi had felt it, too.

Michael went on reaching for the sword. Ruth had to force herself to see what was there, not the bright arc-welding halations that imagination conjured so vividly.

Oh, God, Michael, RUN.

But Michael didn't run, and Ruth herself stood paralyzed, sick with fear or him, and wondering with giddy self-contempt if a little thing like breaking into a subway tunnel to chase a cannibal theriomorph at the word of an elf-prince—now almost certainly dead—from Otherwhere and finding herself caught in the path of a subway train was enough to induce a nervous breakdown in her, frail vessel that she was.

Naomi reached her and grabbed her arm, pulling her toward one of the niches. Behind Naomi, Ruth could still see Michael. He had his hand around the sword-hilt and was carefully, painstakingly, pulling it free.

*It's Melior's sword, the one that Stephen Mallison gave
him. He wouldn't just go off and leave it.*

The train's headlights were a glow around the curve of the
tunnel. Its horn sounded, not that it could have seen them,
and the sound boomed off the tunnel walls like a peal of
thunder.

"Ruth!" Naomi shook her, pushed her, dug sharp nails
into her arm, and finally Ruth broke free of the paralysis
enough to move.

They reached the alcove with an eternity—ninety seconds
at least—to wait before the train reached them, time enough
for Ruth to invent and discard a dozen better plans for
safety. Then the train began to pass.

Ruth stood with her face pressed into Naomi's shoulder,
both of them huddled tightly into this technological priest's
hole as the train thundered by, and for all her terrorized anticipation, all Ruth felt as its passage hammered her with
sound was annoyance that it would not leave and let her deal
with whatever new horror awaited. But when the train had
gone, rocking and wailing as it retreated down the tunnel,
what Ruth saw was Michael.

He was holding the replica Roman short-sword as if he
didn't want to be anywhere near it.

"Steve'd want this back," he said simply.

"What about Melior?" For a moment Ruth was surprised
that her voice sounded so steady, then realized it was Naomi
who'd spoken.

"This doesn't prove he's dead," Michael said quickly,
watching Ruth. "All it proves is that Melior dropped it and
couldn't pick it up. There could be a lot of explanations for
that. He could be back in jail."

"How do we find out?" Naomi asked calmly. Once more
Ruth envied her friend that. Oh, to be one of those self-
possessed people.

"Get out of here and call Philip. Call the police."

" 'Excuse me, have you arrested any elves lately?' " Naomi suggested, and Ruth, stifling a hoot of laughter, felt the
tightness in her chest ease.

"Or something," Michael said. "Or he could still be down
here with a busted ankle. I want to finish looking around."

And so they went on, faster now, knowing that their target
must be blatantly obvious or absent altogether. Through the
still-damp-from-last-week's-rains-but-drying tunnels Naomi,

Ruth, and Michael hurried; interlopers by need but well-aware of their precarious legal position; flashlights flickering off things that gleamed, scurrying crouched past the empty prosceniums of deserted stations at a New Yorker's walking pace.

There was suddenly a curious absence of rats. And Ruth was about to mention this; was tormented afterward by the certainty that had she only mentioned it things would have been different, different altogether.

"I don't think—" Michael began, and his words overlaid the *slithering* sound Ruth heard behind her. She turned toward the sound.

Shock; her body understanding terror and filling her blood with nightmare cocktails long before her blinkered modern mind could react. Then realization, and—oh, God—the *smell!*

"Muh—*uh!*" Ruth stammered, skittering backward, flashlight falling from fingers numb, nerveless with an extremity of terror never felt before, not even in nightmares. And the *grendel*, it had to be the *grendel—oh, God, so that's what it looks like*—reached out for her; slack-jawed drool and yellow twisted teeth.

Ruth, pedaling backward, fell. The sudden unexpected slap of the ground at her back was baffling more than anything else; her eyes teared with the unfairness of it all as the *grendel* shambled toward her.

She saw Naomi vault over her as she lay on the ground; saw the upraised golden flash of Stephen's sword and heard Naomi grunt as she shoved it into the *grendel*'s unaffected flesh. The *grendel* shrugged Naomi off and Ruth heard her fall and roll; heard the low *hu!* of expended air and knew Naomi was attacking again. She saw the lights of the tunnel walls blotted out as the horror stooped over her, ignoring the attack. She felt the *grendel*'s hand upon the side of her face and then Ruth, with some relief, recorded nothing more.

Michael had turned back when he'd heard the noise. Still talking, he turned the flashlight automatically to follow his sight and saw Ruth. And saw the *grendel*.

It was nearly eight feet tall, and seeing it Michael knew that Melior must be dead. He could not believe that this was something that had ever been human. Its arms were ape-long, and wicked horn-colored claws gleamed at the end of short fingers on blunt pawlike hands. Its skin was blackish green and toxic, cracked and scaled and shredding, its head an insignificant neckless bump between shoulders broad to the point of parody. Nose was lost in the swelling thrust of muzzle, giving its blunt-featured earless face a vaguely saurian look; cartoon dinosaur until it opened its mouth, then frightening impossible extension and jutting yellow fangs. The stink wafted from it like a frog; morgue and mass burial, blood and murder.

How could anyone hope to kill it?

Michael wished—desperately, unreasonably—for a flamethrower, knowing that if he had it in his hands this instant he could not use it, because the *thing* was close to Ruth and coming closer, reaching out one moist unclean hand like all the parodies of Frankenstein that ever were, unfunny at last.

It seemed an eternity before Ruth began to move, backing away slowly when Michael knew that what she should do was turn and run.

And then she fell.

He started forward, slow underwater-seeming motion with every muscle protesting at the movement, knowing he would not be in time and could do nothing if he were. They'd come down here unarmed, knowing what they knew, and Michael hated himself suddenly for that stupidity.

Naomi moved faster.

She'd been standing a little behind Michael, now she ran to him, pulling Stephen's sword out of his hand while Ruth was still falling. Michael grabbed vainly at empty air where the sword had been and ran at last, but not as fast as Naomi.

She sprang over Ruth's body, sword in her right hand and her shouted *kiai* echoing in the tunnel like a sea-bird's cry. His last sight of her was of Naomi poised in midair, golden sword gleaming in the light of the flashlight that Michael had somehow managed not to drop. The *grendel* raised its head and looked at him, its eyes like cankers of burning phosphor.

And then, without transition, Michael was standing, not running, standing staring and wide-eyed off into space, as still and dazed as if he had just awakened from a deep sleep, and all three of them were gone.

"No—!"

He ran forward, waving his flashlight, but there was nothing there. Not Ruth. Not Naomi. Only Stephen's sword lying on the tracks, and Ruth's flashlight, and the broad wet footprints of something that never should have existed at all.

What had happened? One moment he'd been running toward it, the next—

I want to die. Oh, God, please let me die. Not again. NOT AGAIN.

There was silence in the tunnel. After a long hesitation, Michael picked up the sword, then turned away and slowly began to leave.

"How are you feeling?"

That inane question humans liked to ask each other, this time from the mouth of a man dressed as no man Melior had seen yet: gray his strange garb was, gray as all the colors of smoke and morning mist.

"I'm Detective Lieutenant Frank Catalpano, N.Y.P.D. I'd like to ask you a few questions about what you were doing down there on the tracks, if you don't mind."

Melior knew that tone. The courtesy of princes; empty words, as no one would dare to refuse their orders. And this man was a prince of a sort, Melior guessed; only a ruler would dare show such arrogance, even to a wounded foe.

The gray man sat down upon the cheap couch and brought out a notebook and stylus from his pocket.

"Am I arrested?" Melior asked.

The detective lieutenant regarded him gravely. "Let's say we aren't making any charges at this point. The subway's a dangerous place to go, you know."

"So I have been told." Melior's first instinct was to lie, and he would have followed it without compunction, save that a lie must always be convincing, and Melior did not know what words were plausible and what words would betray.

"Just how *did* you get down there?" The gray man asked.

Ah, this was simple enough. "I do not remember," Melior said. He touched his bandaged head and winced. "I was going home," he added, which was truth of a sort.

"And you don't remember anything other than that?" The gray man patently did not believe him.

Melior shook his head and winced; and that at least was

no act. "I fell," he suggested, putting uncertainty and guessing into his voice.

"And where is home, exactly?" the gray man asked. No prince, this, Melior realized now, but a prince's man; brutal with the trust his sovereign reposed in him; elegant with a simplicity that disdained courts. Not even a warrior, this, but that which was much more fearsome. A *manhunter*.

Melior gave him Michael's address once more.

"Lived there long?" was the next question.

"Only a short time. I am staying with a friend." Half-truths and simple statements. Melior began to hope they might let him go.

"We didn't find your wallet." Prompting, helpful and encouraging. Looking for him to reveal something—but what? Melior wondered.

The silence stretched, achingly. Melior thought of a hundred ways to fill it and spoke none of them.

"Your friend got a name?" the grey manhunter asked.

"He is Michael Peacock," Melior said. "And surely he will wonder at my absence. If you do not arrest me, you must let me go to him."

"Hold on just a minute," the manhunter said. "With a knock like the one you got, you shouldn't be wandering around alone. What were you doing riding the subway at that hour, anyway?"

"It was rush hour," Melior suggested. "It is later now."

"What were you doing for the last twelve hours?" Questions again and again, and now Melior knew they were merely a veil for a certainty he could not guess at.

"May I call Michael now?" Melior asked.

The manhunter to princes pushed the stylus and a sheet of paper over to Melior. "Write it down here and we can have one of the nurses notify him," he said. "I've got just a couple more questions."

Melior stared at the blank sheet of paper. The gate to this land had given him knowledge of its spoken tongue, but nothing more. He could neither read nor write.

But a good commander—and Melior had been one—must be able to draw a map, however crude. Carefully Melior rendered the twisting angular symbols that were on the buttons one must push to activate the spell that would reach Michael.

Detective Lieutenant Frank Catalpano looked at the paper, folded it carefully, and put it in his pocket.

"I'll be sure to have one of the nurses call your friend for you, but before that, maybe you could tell me what you were doing in the subway," he said with polite insistence.

CHAPTER 19

A Candle in the Wind

"Have you heard from Melior?" Michael's voice on the phone was harsh and abrupt.

"No." Philip did not bother to glance up at the endlessly-searching computer. He already knew the answer. No elf. And it wasn't his fault, but the girls weren't going to see it that way.

"I've seen the *grendel*. It's got Ruth and Naomi. Stay there till I get there."

The phone went dead in Philip's ear before he could think of a reply. Above his head the police scanner continued to broadcast its cryptic shorthand of 10-codes and civil citations.

The *grendel* had Naomi and Ruth?

Philip had thought things were already as bad as they could be.

He'd been wrong.

They'd just gotten worse.

His name, as it happened, really *was* Frank (For Francis Marion) Catalpano, although he was not with the N.Y.P.D. He was, however, on the side of the angels, if you defined the side of the angels as the side of the law.

Laws, it must be noted, can be rewritten, from time to time, for expediency's sake.

Frank worked for a mostly-unknown agency with the curious distinction of being the only private-sector service provider in a field usually reserved for governments friendly and un-. This agency (which had a fine, vague-but-impressive-sounding name) leased its services to the United States Government, which paid very well indeed for an exclusive lien on the agency's time. This was not to say that Frank's employers did not have other clients, only that they did not do for these other clients what they did for the United States Government.

At least in theory.

And, being an exclusive private-sector subcontractor to the biggest employer there was, it was easy for Frank's bosses to move mammal-fast around the ankles of the Federal dinosaurs, so that almost before the first report had come in, Frank had been on the scene, complete with convincing ID and plausible cover-story, appropriate warnings-off to appropriate bureaus, and people in every New York City department who would say that Frank Catalpano was exactly what he appeared to be.

And as for the man in the room Frank had just left. . . .

The flashing eyes, the floating hair (as Frank's former wife Denise, a space cadet who'd held a liberal arts degree from Vassar, would surely have characterized them), and even the pointed ears of his prisoner did not faze Frank. He had seen them before.

This was another one. And as soon as the right people and the right equipment arrived, this one would vanish, too. Maybe the killings in the subway would stop, then, but Frank Catalpano neither knew nor cared. His agency was paid well by its biggest account to remain very focused.

"Detective?"

Frank turned to face the doctor. He looked at the name-badge on the rumpled white coat. Jenkins. The admitting physician.

"Yes?" He pulled his *persona* around himself like a cloak; world-weary New York 'tec who'd seen it all, done a lot of it, and could never on any account be forced to explain.

"Are you going to charge him? This—" Jenkins squinted at his clipboard, "—Ronald Melon?"

Rohannan Melior, Frank corrected him silently. *Of one of the Seven Houses of the Twilight. I'll bet my quarterly bonus on it. He's got the look.*

"No," said Frank, as soft and heavy as a fall of graveyard dust. "We're not going to charge him. Yet. But your patient, Doctor, is very upset. He needs rest. He needs to stay here for the seventy-two-hour observation period permitted by law so we can see what it is he's going to do."

Jenkins opened and closed his mouth. Frank plucked the clipboard out of his hand. He glanced over the crabbed hieroglyphics, and then took a pen from his inside pocket and wrote "Violent. Delusional. Do Not Approach." diagonally across the page.

"You got that, Doctor?" Frank said.

"The man's got civil rights," Jenkins muttered. "We have to notify the family, let him telephone—"

"You're real busy here, Doctor Jenkins." Frank gave the name full weight. It was wonderful what you could do with a name. Say somebody's name in the right way, and all of a sudden they got nervous, just as if you might take their name away from them as a prelude to other horrors.

Frank smiled. "I'm sure you're too busy to pay too much attention to one violent whack. Just give us a break, Doctor. Let us do our job for once, okay? Seventy-two hours. Okay?"

Frank watched Jenkins, as he'd watched so many others, looking for the moment that Jenkins would choose the easy way over the right way. They almost always did, and Frank was waiting for them on the other side.

It would be incorrect to say that Frank Catalpano didn't know right from wrong. In fact, Frank had a highly-developed sensitivity to right and wrong, and could always tell them apart. What he was doing was wrong. What he was asking Jenkins to do was wrong.

But for Jenkins it was the easier way.

And for Frank, it was legal.

"I don't suppose it could do any real harm," Dr. Jenkins said.

Frank Catalpano smiled.

Jane awoke with the sudden start of one who has overslept, forgetting important business. Recent memory slammed into place with a nearly audible thud. Melior. The tunnels. The police. The *grendel*.

The police had Melior now, and Ruth and the others didn't know about the *grendel*. And even if they did, they could look forever and not find it.

But Jane knew where it was hiding. She threw on the first clothes that came to hand and ran across the campus and down the hill to Ruth and Naomi's apartment. She let herself in, panting only slightly with the exertion of her run. Late afternoon sunlight streamed through the window. Two p.m.

And Ruth wasn't here, nor Naomi, though by all the laws of all the odd gods at least one of them should be.

If they weren't here, where were they?

Jane sat down on the couch, an unaccustomed feeling of

let-down washing over her. They weren't here. She'd been counting on them being here. Someone to tell. Someone to save Melior.

But there was no one.

They did not mean to let him go. Melior accepted this with a resignation he did not extend to his confinement; he had not expected his luck to change.

He was in a small room with a bed and an unopenable window. "Held for observation," the white-robed monk-physicians had said when he had asked, and "seventy-two hours."

But he would not wait seventy-two hours until they discovered more pretexts upon which to detain a lord of the House of the Silver Silences. He would escape this place and warn his companions, if Jane had not already done so.

Melior did wish he knew if Jane had escaped in truth and not merely in his hopes. He wished he knew how far news of the *grendel*'s existence had spread.

He wished his head did not hurt, and that he had his clothes, and that he did not feel so helpless in the face of an evil that the humans of the World of Iron would scoff at until the last of them had been hunted down and made food for its endless appetite. This city held more humans than Melior had ever seen; soon, feeding upon them, the *grendel* would be strong enough to burgeon until in all the land there was nothing more to eat.

The *grendel* must be slain. The *grendel* could be slain only by The Sword of Maiden's Tears. Which could only be wielded by one of the Sons of the Morning, lest some human paladin's attempt make him *grendel* in his turn. And the only Morning Lord in all this world, to the best of Melior's knowledge, stood here in this room.

Ruth and Naomi were gone. Dead, probably, but Michael could not make himself believe it. People died in a thousand ways every day, but they did not die at the hands of monsters created by magic swords.

Melior must be dead, too. Michael could think of no other reason, now, for him to have dropped Stephen's sword. Melior dead, and Ruth and Naomi, too.

And he hadn't done a single thing to save them.

Failure and coward, and *safe,* now, which somehow hurt

the worst. That, and the thought of having to explain to Jane
and Philip how it was that he'd just stood there and watched
Melior's *grendel* do . . . whatever it had done.

Michael had learned long since in the roughest school of
all that true life was nothing like fiction. He'd believed it,
and asked nothing more of life than never to be reminded of
the truth again. But he hadn't gotten his wish.

He could think of nothing he could do, no course of action
he could pursue, and retained enough presence of mind to
know that he was shocky; his judgment was gone. All he'd
do now was mess things up further—if that were possible.

He called Philip and took a taxi home.

He could hear the phone ringing from the floor below, and
when he got to his own front door he could still hear it, only
faintly muffled. *How like life,* Michael thought as he
dropped his keys. The phone went on ringing. Michael
swore, and fumbled with his key ring.

On the fourteenth ring the phone went silent. Michael,
who had just gotten the door open, snarled and kicked the
door shut. It slammed with the sound of a gunshot, flat and
final.

Jane put down the phone. No Ruth, no Naomi, and now
no Michael. And it was almost four, too, on a Thursday;
someone should be home.

Philip. Her hand hovered over the receiver for a moment,
then she drew back. It occurred to her that Philip, having
double-crossed Ruth in the matter of finding out about the
grendel, might be lying extremely low. *Maybe later,* she
temporized, and went to see if there was any news.

The Subway Snatcher was the lead story on the four
o'clock news broadcast. Jane listened with interest to the
story of the "alleged" disappearance of Therese Scarlatti
from the platform of the City Hall Station yesterday evening.

But if that had been yesterday, Michael and Ruth and Naomi already knew about it. They'd known there was a real
live *grendel* since yesterday night.

Jane puzzled over what to do with this new information,
trying to decide what they would have done with the knowledge. Then, resolutely, she picked up the phone and began to
dial Philip.

* * *

Philip LeStrange was in a quandary—which, as he would be happy to tell you, was a small wheeled cart used to transport lepers. He'd even phoned the dorm, but no one had answered; which would be reasonable enough if people hadn't been trying to reach Jane-the-Pain since seven-thirty yesterday night. Philip's nature was paranoid, not suspicious. It did not occur to him that Melior had confided in Jane instead of, say, him.

And now Michael said that the *grendel*, which had been only intellectual exercise even while Philip had been gathering the positive proof of its existence, had taken Ruth and Naomi. Taken them how? Taken them where?

And how were they going to get them back?

They had to get them back. Of course they did. Naomi was tough; she could beat up just about anyone Philip could think of. Of course they'd get them back.

It would be an adventure.

But he'd feel a lot better, he really would, if he was absolutely *sure* of where they were now and that they were safe.

Someone hammered on his door.

"Phone!" Alex shouted.

Not Michael if he was calling on the communal line.

"Tell them I'm not here," Philip shouted back.

There was a pause while Alex retreated. And returned.

"She says you got her pregnant," Alex shouted through the door.

This was peculiar enough to investigate. Philip went and opened the door.

"Hello?" Philip said into the communal phone.

"Where are Michael and the guys?"

Jane.

"Michael's home. Probably by now. Where've you been?"

"Michael didn't answer his phone. Has Melior called?" Jane asked again, very cautious.

"Why would Melior call?" Carefully; there were people listening.

"He's been arrested, probably," Jane said with the lugubrious satisfaction of being right.

"Where *are* you?" Philip, defeated, asked.

"I'm at Ruth's. Where is *she?*"

Even if the watchers had not been there, Philip couldn't

say, despite what Michael had told him. Some fastidious revulsion to saying the words, or perhaps merely simple self-
preservation, to refrain from speaking the sentence that must
come out either callous or maudlin.

And perhaps, after all, he'd only misheard what Michael'd
said over the phone.

"I'll be over there in a few minutes. We've got to talk,"
Philip said instead.

He met Michael on his front steps.

"Where did you think you were going?" Michael demanded dangerously.

This was a new sensation for Philip, and he didn't like it.
He annoyed people, he revolted them, he made them envi-
ous. He did not make them angry. Michael was angry, now,
just as if this weren't an *adventure*.

He didn't think, though, that Michael would appreciate
enlightenment just now. Philip chose diplomacy as the wiser
course.

"Jane's at Ruth and Naomi's place. She just phoned. She
knows something about Melior."

"Come on," Michael said.

There was nothing he could do to gain his freedom, save
wait until that unbroachable door should open. Melior accepted this, just as he had accepted the foreknowing of his
own helplessness to stop the *grendel,* and let his mind turn
on the only thing left that mattered besides escape.

Why *here?* In the Art Magic there were no coincidences;
if the spell-trapped Sword had delivered him to this spot,
such delivery had been purposed. To kill him and put the
Sword beyond his kindred's reach forever would have been
a simple thing, did he only appear at the bottom of a lake or
the bottom of the ocean or the furnace-maw of a volcano.

It had been the new York city that he came to for a reason.
Find the reason, and find perhaps the knowledge that would
arm his human friends in their fight.

What did he know of magic? Not so very much; the
swords that Melior fought with were physical things. But he
was a prince of the House of the Silver Silences and the Heir
of Line Rohannan, and he knew more than nothing.

He had assumed all along that it was mere accident that

landed him here in the World of Iron, but what if the spell-trap laid upon the Sword was the trap of pulling it *here?*

He had not fallen through all the other worlds on his way to the Last World. He had been brought here, as the spell-bound Sword snapped back along its invisible tether, cleaving tightly to its other part.

The part that was native to this place.

But what was it, invisible and yet so tightly-binding, native to the World of Iron and yet capable of being drawn into the higher realms where magic worked?

Melior knew. A child's riddle, that, and in turn a child's answer, so simple that he was filled with momentary fury at having been blind so long. When fury gave way to hope, he crushed the dawning emotion savagely. To hope would only make him careless; he must set forth his theory as painstakingly as a rhetor his argument, and solve it for his truth as any alchemist. The mad logic of his enemy—vindictive, and clever merely—seemed to mock at him, and Melior knew now there were no puzzles left, only answers that he prayed he would be able to prove in time.

Souls.

Souls wander in sleep as every wizard knows; wander and return to their source, having gone only a little way in their own world. And death is the longest journey of all, to a land so distant the soul does not retrace its way.

But there are states between sleep and death, when the transmigrant soul of even a mortal from the World of Iron could journey outside its native land; could even, if the time were long enough, journey to be trapped in a soul-cage and used, by an evil and bloody-handed wizard, as an ingredient in a spell-trap.

A spell-trap to bring the Sword of Maiden's Tears to the World of Iron.

The mortal thus riven would be bound to seek his other part, the part that was bound up in the Sword. The mortal whose soul had been wizard-thieved would be *linked* to the Sword. Would be able to find it, as a compass needle finds True North.

One of his human friends must be the key; all Melior's knowledge of the rules of magic said it. The Law of Contagion, of Consanguinity, the Doctrine of Signatures . . . each in its own way assured him that he had already met the mortal whose life had been Sword-touched by some rogue artificer of Lord Baligant's. All Melior need do was find the one among them who had journeyed in the twilight land between Sleep and Death and set that one to following the faint soul-call of The Sword of Maiden's Tears.

And to do that, Melior must be free.

Something was exceptionally wrong. That much was perfectly clear. Because Ruth and Naomi were not here, and Philip wouldn't say where they were. Because Melior wasn't here either, and because Melior knew enough to make the one phone call they always had to give you, and would call Ruth or Michael. Because everybody in New York seemed to know about the *grendel* now, and that complicated the equation of its slaying in ways Jane had not yet had time to reason out.

Because Melior had faced the *grendel* armed only with a bronze sword, after telling them all time and again that only the Sword of Maiden's Tears could slay it.

That was stupid.

And Melior was not stupid.

The downstairs door buzzed.

"Who is it?" Jane demanded, punctilious no matter what temporal blandishments beguiled.

"Oh, come on," Philip said, at the same time Michael said, "Knock it off, Philip."

Jane buzzed them in.

She knew beyond question that something bad had happened as soon as she saw Michael's face, and, Janelike, demanded the worst at once.

"Where are they?"

"They're down in the tunnels with the *grendel*," Michael said.

Jane sat down, thinking about the creature she'd seen. She refused to think past that vision and on to the brutal horror Melior had dressed so grandly in iambic pentameter. Down there. *La bas.* But not dead. Michael had not said they were dead and Michael was generally reliable about telling you the whole truth.

"Melior's been arrested," she offered.

"How do you know?" Philip shot back.

"I was there." That was a little better. At least Michael was looking at her now.

"Melior and I went down in the tunnels last night and found *it*. It hit him. The cops showed up and he stalled them, so I came back here. *It* took off. I don't think they saw it."

"He's alive." Michael's voice wavered, its owner unable to settle on an emotion.

"He hasn't been arrested," Philip said positively. "You think I wasn't looking?"

"That isn't very useful information just now," Michael snarled, rounding on him.

Philip took a step backward.

"This is your fault," Michael went on. "If you'd told us what you knew, *when you knew it*—"

"It wouldn't have made any difference," Jane interrupted. She might dislike Philip, but the satisfaction of seeing Michael slam Philip was not worth the sight of Michael losing his temper.

Michael rounded on her, red-eyed and numb with a dangerous grief.

"It wouldn't," Jane insisted stubbornly. "The only thing that can kill it is Melior's magic sword. It wouldn't have mattered if Philip had told you. You wouldn't have had the sword. But I know where the *grendel* lives, Michael. And the sword has to be there, doesn't it?"

CHAPTER 20

The October Subway

The Alfred Ely Beach Tunnel (most recently immortalized, after a fashion, in *Ghostbusters II*) was constructed—no surprises here—by Alfred Ely, who built it in 1870 in strictest secrecy (having rented the basement of a nearby department store for his project headquarters), tunneling clandestinely beneath Broadway to prove so far beyond a shadow of a doubt that a subway was feasible, lucrative, and safe, that the violent and semi-legal opposition of Boss Tweed and the Tammany Tiger (one of the first and greatest of the political machines in the days when politics was a sport but not a regulated one) would have its interfering fangs pulled forever.

Mr. Ely tunneled nearly 360 feet beneath and along Broadway, and, since the idea of an Underground Railway was still new and frightening, did everything that Victorian sensibilities could to ease the public's mind about its safety. The waiting area of his tunnel—which led from nowhere to nowhere, being only a pilot project—was adorned with crystal chandeliers, fountains, and murals. There was even—for reasons known only to the post-Federalist mind—a tank full of fish. The single subway car was a miracle of plush velvet and rare woods, and everyone who rode the subway spoke admiringly of its comfort, pleasure, and safety.

It is almost unnecessary to add that Alfred died in obscure poverty: so obscure that when the tunnel was rediscovered in 1912 during excavations for the Broadway BMT line—New York having finally got its subway system a mere thirtysomething years later—no one remembered who had built the tunnel or how it had gotten there. When next you stand at the City Hall Station on the BMT line, spare a thought for Alfred, one of history's most organized, dynamic, visionary failures.

Ruth wished she could. But at the moment her mind was on other things.

She had come back to reality lying on the ground; or, rather, in a nest of Snapple bottles and Pepsi cans that scattered noisily when she moved.

It wasn't dark, not entirely; a faint reddish glow came from somewhere and convinced her, for some seconds, that she was still dreaming. Then everything came back; Melior dead and the *grendel*—

Ruth sat up with a jerk, gasping as one does out of nightmare. Chilled stiff muscles protested, but Ruth didn't care. She stared around wildly.

The *grendel*.

And no merciful providence had chosen to intervene during the scene change, whisking her back safely to her own warm, dry, clean apartment to have the *denouement* explained to her by Michael and Naomi who would have seen everything but be, nevertheless, safe.

Ruth got stiffly to her feet and looked around. Scrapes and abrasions she didn't remember getting protested; her jacket was torn and her hair had long since come down out of its tight careful knot. It clung around her face, stiff and damp and foul as though it had been dipped in ink.

Ink would be a godsend.

Then she saw the sword.

It stood a few feet from her head, propped against the wall, point-down in a pile of bizarre winnowings from some punk-twisted Borrower. Hazard lamps—the source of the light—pop cans; liquor bottles; lunch boxes; curled bits of subway posters; anything that was even slightly shiny. A magpie's midden.

The sword towered over all this, pristine and gleaming and fake-looking as a special effect. It had a jewel in its pommel the size of a baseball and seemed itself to shine with a faint light. And if it wasn't Melior's magic sword, Ruth had been grossly misled about magic swords in general and the Sword of Maiden's Tears in particular.

She wondered what it would be like to hold it. She reached for it—

"Don't touch that." Naomi's voice, behind her. Ruth squeaked, startled, and shot a confirming glance over her shoulder. But she withdrew her hand.

"Hi, stranger, how's tricks?" Naomi said.

Ruth stepped gingerly out of the trash. Naomi smiled, a little crookedly.

"Long time no see, and all that."

"Naomi!" Ruth flung her arms around her, glad to see her even if she wouldn't wish her worst enemy in this mess, hugged and was hugged hard in return. "Oh, God, you're still alive!"

"Yeah," Naomi said.

Reluctantly Ruth released her and took a good look. Naomi was now nobody's idea of a fashion plate. Her short dark hair was matted, her face was bruised, and her clothes looked as if she'd been dragged through a canebrake backward.

"Welcome—in the words of the popular broadsheet ballad—to my nightmare," Naomi said. But she was still alive. They were both still alive.

For now.

The room they were in was big—*huge*—at least a hundred feet by sixty, maybe more. The floor still gleamed dully in patches, and the light was just enough to show Ruth the shadowy pattern of marble parquetry beneath her feet. The wall against which the sword rested was lavishly ornamented, a bewilderment of niches, coffering, and crumbling plaster medallions still faintly gilded.

"I know what you're going to say. It looks like an outtake from *Phantom*. But it gets better," Naomi said.

Ruth completed her survey of the room and looked back at Naomi. Naomi's eyes were feverishly bright; her mouth was set.

"I read the book. So why don't we leave this party and go home?" And despite all her best intentions, Ruth felt hot tears prickle as past and present injustice mingled. Not fair, oh God, nothing at all fair, and if she'd been marked down to die why couldn't it have been a dozen years ago instead of now, in the dark, where being eaten alive wasn't just a sick joke but a probability?

"Good idea," Naomi said. "How?"

Ruth just stared at her.

"I've been looking around here. It's the damnedest place; looks like Miss Havisham's subway station. But the tracks don't go anywhere. They just stop. Solid rock."

Ruth took a second and more careful look, and this time she saw what her eye had missed before; the carving in the shadows there was not carving but a tiny antique railway carriage; and ahead of it were curiously narrow and delicate railroad tracks.

"I've already walked them. The tunnel goes about a hundred yards and stops. I don't think it ever went through. But there's no way out that way," Naomi said.

"We got in here somehow." She was calmer now, but now that instant panic was past, Ruth was feeling other things. Like cold, and hungry, and tired, and scared, and pretty beat up when you came right down to it.

"Yeah." Naomi looked back toward the delicate half-scale car. In the sword's glow Ruth could see her mouth set hard. "You were out a long time, Ruth; I was worried about you."

Oversleeping our specialty. But even that macabre joke couldn't raise Ruth's spirits in the face of the horror of reality. "How long?"

"About six hours. It's about seven o'clock Thursday night, if you're keeping track. Assuming my watch hasn't gone wonky after what it's been through." Naomi brandished her wristwatch, guaranteed waterproof, shockproof, and, now, *grendel*-resistant. Ruth wondered if the manufacturers would care.

"And. . .?"

"Our host isn't back yet," Naomi added dryly. "But he-she-or-it will be."

Ruth's stomach lurched involuntarily; she looked toward the sword.

"And whoever picks that up is going to be just like him, her, or it," Naomi finished fair-mindedly.

"We don't know that," Ruth said desperately. She'd feel safe with the sword in her hands—she was sure of it.

"Ruth." The tremor of fear in Naomi's voice riveted Ruth's attention as nothing else could have. "Everything else Melior's told us has come out true, so why don't we go ahead and believe this one? Touch that sword and you'll be the new *grendel* on the block. And I don't think the other one wants to share."

I don't care! Ruth wanted to scream. Instead she drew a deep breath. "Okay. We'll leave it for Melior. If he— If he's—"

"I haven't seen him," Naomi said, and something in her voice cut Ruth's incipient crying jag off sharp. "He wasn't with the others," Naomi added flatly.

It wasn't very hard to figure out where Melior was, once Michael put his mind to it. He'd been injured in Lower Manhattan, he was in police custody, and even at his best Melior was a few sandwiches shy of a picnic by Earth-plane standards.

Where else would they take him?

It was seven o'clock Thursday night when Michael, Philip, and Jane walked into Bellevue Hospital. Carefully-phrased questions got them directed to where, by mutual unspoken consent, they all felt they ought to start: the Psychiatric Wing. There, as on other floors, there was an information desk or something that looked like one.

"May I help you?" asked a nurse, in tones that plainly translated the question into: "Oh, for Christ's sake what do you want *now?*"

"Well, you see, ma'am, we're looking for a friend of ours. We hoped he might be here."

Michael Peacock, wearing a suit jacket for the occasion, did his best to sound and look friendly, honest, and sincere, just like they taught you in Library Public Relations Courses, even though, beginning his second twenty-four hours of uninterrupted consciousness, he felt none of these things.

"Why don't you check with Information, downstairs?" the nurse said, but more kindly this time. She had never met Frank Catalpano and did not know that one of her observation patients was supposed to be held incommunicado, nor would she have cooperated with the notion if she did.

"Well, you see—" Michael began.

"No, Michael, it's okay." Philip pushed past him to stand in front of the desk and the nurse. "He's my brother, okay? Mom and Dad left him with me when they went to visit Grandma. I was sure it'd be okay," Philip said plaintively.

"He's your brother. . .?"

"Melvil. Melvil LeStrange. But he might not have said so, especially if he got excited. He's just a little different," Philip added, putting just the right note of defensiveness into his voice. "He's got a card he usually carries, but I guess he left it behind this time." To Michael's amazement Philip dug around in a pocket and produced a battered wallet, one that Michael was pretty sure had once been his. Philip offered it to the nurse. Over Philip's shoulder Michael could see a battered and carefully-typed card containing his name and address. It even had Melior's picture, clipped from one of the Polaroids Philip had taken that first night.

"Sometimes he says his name if Rohannan Melior. I think he got it out of a comic book. Is he here? Please, could you just let me take him home?" Philip said. "He didn't do anything wrong, did he?"

The charge nurse wavered visibly.

"Just let me see him, then," Philip pleaded. "He'll be so scared," he added, as if the confession had been dragged from him with hot irons.

"Well, all right," she said, "but just for a minute."

So Philip was borne away, and Jane and Michael remained behind. Fifteen minutes later Philip was back, looking properly chastened.

"They won't let him go," he announced in the tones of a forlorn oboe. "They think he's messed up in some kind of police thing. Mom is going to kill me," Philip added, sotto-voce but playing to the gallery.

"Why don't you come back tomorrow during the day and talk to the supervisor?" the charge nurse suggested.

Philip nodded and shrugged, obviously biting back tears of manly emotion. "Yeah," he said. "Yeah. You'll take care of him, won't you?"

Jane wanted to kick him. Philip was overplaying as usual. Subtlety was better, and then people could read into it anything they liked.

But the nurse didn't seem to notice. "Of course we will," she said, and even patted Philip on the arm. Philip didn't try to duck away as he usually would; he just gave her a brave little smile and then turned away.

"C'mon, guys," he said.

So Michael and Jane followed him back out to the elevators. Once inside, and safe from inopportune viewing, Philip once more became his old self. He rocked up on his toes and whistled tonelessly.

"Helpful so far," Jane said. Philip smirked, still enchanted by his own cleverness.

"Look, what exactly did you do back there?" Michael demanded. Philip turned to him, bifocals flashing.

"He's up there, he's locked in, they aren't going to let him go while they're waiting for him to turn into a two-car garage. But the doors up there are all spring-locked, so I slipped him a credit card and told him we'd meet him in the parking lot."

It was half an hour before Melior joined them. He was wearing a long white coat, tattered slippers, baggy green pants, and a baseball cap that seemed to be advertising the roman numeral "ten." He carried a clipboard and looked like the White Rabbit (medical division) on his way to being terribly, horribly, late.

When he saw them, he burst into a run, stripping off the jacket as he ran. He bundled it together with the clipboard and slung both beneath a car. He kept the cap. Michael could see bandages beneath.

"Are you all right?" Michael said.

"No," Melior answered. "But I think I have the answer, and the answer finds the Sword."

"It better," Michael said grimly, "because the *grendel*'s got Ruth and Naomi."

Their stories were exchanged on the run, heading north and west from the hospital. Ruth and Naomi, gone in an eyeblink. The *grendel,* real beyond controversy.

"You must not think hardly of yourself, Friend Michael. The *grendel* has the power to spellbind its foe if it chooses, holding him dreaming, yet awake. Thus it kept you harmless while it made its escape."

"Hypnosis," Jane said.

"Do you know the art?" Melior asked. "It will make the next task easier, can we but command a few of the *grendel*'s arts."

"I did not ask the question I ought to have sought the answer to most of all," Melior told them, once they were forgathered (for safety's sake, as Melior had given the police and the hospital Michael's address) in Ruth and Naomi's apartment.

"Melior, we really don't have time for another one of your stories," Michael said with ragged patience.

"Peace, Friend Michael, this is the last of my stories and it will be brief. It was not chance that brought me here, or caused you to befriend me. The Sword was *compelled* here, by a magic which entrapped some part of the *soul* of an

Ironworlder within the Sword. Falling through the worlds it sought its other part, and so came to you."

"Or to the muggers," Jane said. Melior's face twisted in pain.

"I pray not, but it could be so. I hope, rather, that it is one of you."

"Friends, are you feeling pale and listless? Write now for our free brochure describing the seven warning signs of your soul being stolen by a magic sword. Get a continuum, Elfie," Philip said.

"What is it you mean, exactly?" Michael asked.

Melior hesitated. "One among you, by accident or design, will have fallen, some time agone, into a state between sleep and death. There, helpless, with your soul caught between making and unmaking, you—"

But Melior did not get to finish this sentence. Philip sat down on the couch at the other end. He leaned back, staring at the ceiling. "Ruth," he said. "It's Ruth."

The other three stared at him. Melior's eyes were wide with horror, as if a number of things were suddenly clear.

"Ruth," he said. "My lady Ruth."

"Ruth was in a coma for eight years," Philip elaborated. Michael looked disbelieving; Jane looked blank.

"She never told me," Jane said.

"Well, she didn't tell me, either," Philip shot back waspishly, "but it made the news in a lot of papers when she woke up. I searched her name through a database," he added.

"Fine," said Michael. "This gets us absolutely no-more-where at all."

"But now we know she is alive—oh, yes, Michael, the *grendel* will not kill such as she, who shares the nature of his treasure. Ruth is still alive, and will continue if we are in time."

"The place you want to go is the City Hall Station," Jane said.

Everyone looked at her, and Jane wished, for a faint moment, that she'd said nothing. But if she didn't, Ruth would die.

"The subway there crosses an old tunnel. The *grendel*'s got to have somewhere to *be*, doesn't it; somewhere it can sleep and not worry about getting hit by a train? Somewhere it can—put things?" Even Jane's voice wavered a little on that last phrase, knowing too well what those things were. "Look there. You remember the map," she said to Melior, "I showed you."

"Yes," Melior's voice held a faint hiss; a blood-hunger kin to the *grendel*'s. "We will seek it there. And though I will not kill it, you, Michael, will be my sword-hand."

"I can't." Michael's voice was low. Definite. Melior watched him, cat-eyes green in the darkness.

Philip's face twisted; he held a hand up as if to ward off the words, and Jane, watching him, was suddenly certain he knew what Michael was going to say.

Of course.

If he'd searched *Ruth's* name through a database, he'd searched all of them. Philip did nothing by halves.

"I killed somebody," Michael said. "I killed a kid."

Then, again, as if he needed to convince even himself, "I killed a child."

The words were ugly, heavy, clinched and waiting for their frame: their explanation and their meaning.

"I was a cop." This explanation, like the other, bereft of meaning, pregnant with emotion. "I was almost a cop."

Another pause, longer than the last.

"I was going to be a cop. My dad, my uncle—Irish, you know? Hereditary cop families, right? I knew it like I knew I was going to grow up and shave, get married and have kids. Grow up and be a cop. I did the whole thing— scholarship to John Jay, the two-year course, the Police Academy on Long Island, the works.

"So I get out, and I get a job. My first. Rookie cop. Police Academy pin-up boy. I was twenty-four. Six years ago.

"Did I ever tell you my family came from Newark? A lot you care, Mel; you wouldn't know Newark if you were standing in the middle of it. Which you wouldn't be long. Visit beautiful downtown Newark, New Jersey; a city half-way between a joke and a war zone. You talk about twenty minutes into the future. Okay. That's Newark. I've seen the future and it sucks. And my folks being from there, it meant I was a rookie cop on the Newark PD. For two weeks. In the ghetto.

"The ghetto kids, they've got a sport you might not have heard of. It's hitting the news now. They had it then. Doughnutting, they call it. What it is, a kid steals a car, goes joy-riding. Looks for a cop car to ram, maybe run down a couple officers. Fun. And they'll be back on the street again in twenty-four hours, because they're *kids*. Eight, ten, twelve."

Michael stopped, staring off into a specific place and time that was not here. His voice was even, patient, testifying for the thousandth time to an indifferent truth that was incapable of causing him either pleasure or pain.

"What they do most copshops—what they did there—is pair up a rookie with a veteran. Let some practical knowledge rub off. My partner's name was Sam DeHorst. Of course by the time I met him everyone called him Hoss. So every night for two weeks I spent eight hours in a unit with Hoss, hearing about life, cops, and Newark. The other guys called us Animal Farm—as in, Horse and Peacock. It was one of those things that was meant to be.

"And one night— And one night—" Michael took a breath and went on. "It was late. End of shift, end of tour. Quiet, clear, hot, summer. And we pull a vehicular D&D— Drunk and Disorderly, DWI—Driving While under the Influence, Reckless Endangerment, every little thing that makes life a joy. So we head off to the area where the report's from. Bad neighborhood. And all there is are these two cars piled on each other. Recent. Gasoline all over the street. So Hoss gets out to take a look.

"I should have gotten out, too. I should have. But it was late, I was tired. He told me to stay in the car. Didn't look like there was anyone around.

"I should have remembered that doughnutters travel in pairs. It came out of nowhere, and hit him, and then I did *all* the right things, make on the car, partial on the plates, "Officer Down" code. And while I'm doing that it goes right into a bunch of parked cars—having too much fun to drive, I guess.

"I can see Hoss. He's down, and he's hurting bad—broken hip, broken pelvis—but he's stable. The crash car could blow any second. So I do some more right things. I head off to the end of the block to try to get them out. By the time I get there the heap's clean. Six of them in it, probably. Swarmed out like rats out of a flooded sewer. Kids. No way I'm going to chase them. So I turn back.

"Hoss was lying in the street. He couldn't move. I could smell the gas from where I was. He was *lying* in it. In the gutter. And out of nowhere this little black kid shows up.

Six—eight—with malnutrition who can tell? He was wearing a red and white striped T-shirt and tan shorts. Black
high-topped sneakers. He was holding his hand out funny.
And then I saw why.

"He was holding a cigarette lighter. He flicked it on. And
then he threw it on my partner. Hoss went up like a torch.
And I shot that baby in the chest.

"That's all. And that is why I'm not going down there
with you. I won't do you a damn bit of good. That's life.
That's the way it is." Michael stared off into the distance at
nothing at all.

Jane risked a glance at Philip; to move meant the possibility of being noticed, but she had to know. There were high
spots of color in Philip LeStrange's cheeks; he looked like a
china doll that had been rouged with a lavish hand. Up-
staged, and in no possible way the baddest dude in the Val-
ley. Jane looked at Melior, but all his attention was on
Michael.

"And your partner?" Melior said.

"He died after four weeks in the Burn Unit. Hero's funeral. Wife and three kids. I got a whitewash job and a
psych discharge. And that's all," Michael's voice was flat,
telling over the ancient maiming as if it had happened to
somebody else.

"No," said Melior. "That is never all."

"Why did you have to *tell* him?" Philip cried. "Don't you
see, Michael—he's going to use it, now, just the way he uses
everyone to get what he wants!"

Philip gestured. The ring on his finger flashed.

"And did I not keep my side of the bargain, Child of
Earth?" Melior asked. "Silver and gold."

"Shut *up*," Philip said.

Philip, Jane noted analytically, was about as flustered as
she'd ever seen him get. He glared furiously at Melior
through bifocal lenses.

"I was going to leave you there. I should have. You
aren't worth the grief you're handing Ruth. You aren't worth
Nai taking the trouble over you. But you've got them in
trouble now, so I guess you'd better get them out. I hope it
kills you," Philip said viciously

"It may well," Melior said. "And as I believe so well in
your hopes, Michael must come with me."

Michael stared at his feet.

"Michael, my friend," Melior said softly, "you must come with me. Who will wield the Sword, do you not? I do not think that Master Philip would prevail; the blade is not his weapon. The man who seizes it must be able to slay with it. Who will slay the *grendel*, if you do not? I ask much of you, I know, but rest assured: once you have slain the *grendel* I myself will slay you in turn."

"*What?*" Philip said.

Melior turned to him. "The enchantment is yet death, Philip LeStrange. Any of humankind which touch the Sword will yet become *grendel*. And since I ask Michael's help to wield the Sword, I promise him release also."

"Well, why can't *you* do it?" Philip demanded, even though he knew the answer as well as any there.

"I will try," said Melior. He spread his hands. "And perhaps I will die. I know no longer; the future I can see is dim, and perhaps only my fancy. I am no longer sure."

"What a great time for your elf superpowers to wimp out," Philip said, falling back into superiority as an only refuge.

Jane sighed. "*Leslie,*" she drawled, in bored, long-suffering tones.

Philip's head whipped around toward her. His ears turned red, and his eyes narrowed furiously.

"Michael, will you aid me?" Melior asked again, ignoring both of them. "There is little I can promise you—"

" 'But blood, toil, tears, and sweat,' " said Jane, from some oft-dredged store of quotations, " 'and gentlemen in England now a-bed/Shall think themselves accurs'd they were not here/And hold their manhoods cheap while any speaks.' " "And if the British Empire and its Commonwealth last for a thousand years men will still say, 'This was their finest hour.' *Henry the Fifth.* And Churchill."

"Don't you understand? *I can't do it.*" Michael said.

"If you're going to be a failure, Michael, you might as well be one underground where nobody can see you," Philip said brutally. "He won't leave you alone until you do."

Philip's face was set; for a moment he almost looked majestic. "And if nobody wants me for anything else, I'm going to see if I can shut the system down so maybe Elfie can get himself killed in peace. See you around."

The sound of the door closing was not particularly loud, but Michael still flinched.

"I blew that one, didn't I?" he asked of no one in particular. "What about you, Jane?"

Jane considered the matter. "If you give me your keys, I can get your stuff from your apartment, because the police are probably looking for you or Melior. And I've got another copy of the map I had in my room. I'll bring that, too. And I guess Naomi wouldn't mind if you make yourself dinner or something."

Michael ran a hand through his hair and looked at Melior. "I'll go with you," he said, and stopped. He made a gesture that somehow encompassed the whole bleak quixotic situation. "Like Philip said. I might as well."

CHAPTER 21

The Bloody Chamber

Naomi hadn't wanted her to look, but Ruth had, of course. There were flashlights in the magpie midden, and the hazard-lights could be unshipped from their moorings. There was light enough to see by, to explore every byway of their prison, even those which Naomi had already explored.

To Ruth and Naomi, accustomed to modern New York subway platforms, this strange Victorian subway platform—as if *The Wild Wild West* had chosen to set an episode in New York City, and this were some construction of the evil dwarf Miguelito Quixote Loveless—was lavishly deep; the short trackspace leading from nowhere to nowhere almost an afterthought. The engrimed, damp-rotted walls had once been gay with frescoes—allegorical depictions of the marriage of science and hedonism.

Beneath the arched cathedral space of the groined vaulting, from which hung shattered and plundered chandeliers, an alabaster fountain, dry forevermore, placed Phaeton and his fiery team in eternal and improbable juxtaposition with naiads spouting water. Even the car that had made its brief pointless journey into the darkness and back remained; moored at one end of the platform like a time-rotted but still improbably baroque gondola. Ruth started toward it.

"Don't go in there," Naomi said, but, like Bluebeard's wife, Ruth had to see.

There were bodies.

Ruth stood in the open doorway. This was the source of the sick-sweet heavy smell that she had noticed-without-noticing. Her emotions seemed cut away from intellect by an impermeable shield. On one side there was measured gratitude: that the *grendel* had been in existence only a week; that the temperature here, so far underground, was cool. On the other, there was horror, and the power of something experienced with the eyes and mind to reach out and assault.

The photographs this scene resembled did not, by their existence and by her memory of them, dull the intimate edge of it. It was no more atrocious than those sights which the generation just preceding hers had imbibed with their dinners, nor than the images brought home from a declared war to *their* parents.

But it was here, in front of her, and what Ruth's heart cried out against was not its horror, nor the pain it represented, but the *reality* of it; as if the realness of this one experience might cause all the rest of the world to match it in intensity.

The interior of the car had long since been reduced, by time and damp and mice to the bare shell of what it had once been: Victorian underground railway car. Only the iron skeletons of the seats remained. But at one end of the car, piled up against the bare rock face in careful husbandly fashion, there were bodies. There were enough bodies that there were too many to count, stacked as they were, but not so many that the situation was distilled into its own *guignol* sort of farce; less than a dozen. Several of them had been neatly beheaded, and the heads jumbled to one side. Most of the bodies had been at least partially undressed, and the ones on the top of the pile were dismembered to some extent. Blood had leaked from the bodies at the top of the pile onto all the ones beneath, and the ones at the bottom of the pile had been pressed, by the weight of their fellows, quite empty of fluids. A blackish, shiny trail led from the pile across the floor of the car, and drained, through a hole in the side, onto the railbed.

And perhaps even that could have been contemplated in quietude, except for the fact that the rich and varied underlife of the city was not absent from this part of it. There were ants, and some kind of large black beetle, and rats made tunnels through what was, after all, when all was said and done, meat.

Ruth backed away, bumped into Naomi, and screamed. She turned away, staggered half-a-dozen steps, and retched with dry mouth and empty stomach, eyes and nose running. Naomi held her up, and offered her a handkerchief when she was done.

"*No,*" Ruth said.

"No," Naomi agreed. "But there's something else you ought to know."

Ruth looked at her, exhausted, numb.

"It brought us down here and left again. It left you in that pile of junk around the sword."

Ruth thought about that.

"It left me in the car," Naomi finished.

Ruth saw for the first time that Naomi's clothes were black and clotted with something other than subway grime, and began weakly, undramatically, to cry.

It took Jane about two hours to make her various rounds and return. She carried Michael's duffel bag, stuffed full, over one shoulder, and her guitar case in her hand. When she came back into the apartment, she turned the duffel upside down, and out tumbled a strange mix of Michael and Melior's possessions: gray cape and flak jacket; high-topped boots of stamped and gilded leather and battered combat boots; scarlet tunic and black T-shirt.

Abandoning this pile, Jane turned to her guitar case. She opened it carefully, and equally carefully removed the original of the ancient survey map, illegally removed from one of the New York Library's map files in a coup worthy of Philip LeStrange. She spread it out on the table and smoothed it carefully.

Melior had been in the kitchen, eating as Michael had been unable to. Now he came out and sorted through the clothes on the floor. He picked up what was his and walked past Jane and Michael into the bedroom. Jane continued straightening what was by any standard a very large map, never meant to be folded as Jane had folded it.

"Um, Jane . . . ?" Michael said hesitantly, wondering where to begin.

"I'm not going with you," Jane said, as if finishing his sentence. "Where you're going I can't follow, and what you're going to do I can't be any part of. And besides, I'd just get in the way," she recited with sarcasm so arid Michael wasn't entirely sure he was hearing it.

"Right," he settled for.

Melior returned, dressed once more as an elf-king out of Faery. The only thing that marred the illusion was the very real-world bandage in his forehead.

Michael bundled up the clothes he'd asked Jane to get and went off in turn.

Jane sat down on the couch and began tuning her guitar.

Her face was tilted to watch her hands; the pale fall of hair hid her face entirely.

"There's something you should know," she offered to Melior, "even if it's stupid."

"But you are not stupid, Mistress Jane," Melior said.

Jane regarded him, while, all unregarded, her right hand picked out, note by note, the first bars of "True Thomas."

"The way to Fair Elphame," said Jane Grayson, "is neither dark nor light, with neither sun nor moon, no wind but the roaring of the sea, and a river of blood to cross to get there. And so's the New York Subway System. You can get there by candlelight," she added, although she hadn't meant to.

"Ah," Melior inclined his head. "Fair word and fair warning, Mistress. I shall remember." He went back into the kitchen.

"I *said* it was stupid," Jane said under her breath. She pressed the fingers of her left hand down and began to weave the melody into slow mournful chords. " *'And there was neither sun nor moon/But all the roaring of the sea. . . .'* "

Michael came out, flak-jacketed and steel-toe booted, holding something in both hands as if he were afraid it would bite.

A gun.

Naomi's gun.

It was a long-barreled .38 revolver, looking like an Old West six-gun if you didn't know better. The six-inch barrel made it a good choice for target shooting, which was what Naomi used it for. Michael had helped her pick it out. When not in use, it lived in a steel box with a combination lock that Naomi kept in a drawer.

"It's loaded, but I couldn't find any spare ammo," Michael announced to no one in particular. He slipped the gun into the waistband of his jeans and pulled his shirt down over it.

Melior came out of the kitchen with a teacup into which had been poured the last of Ruth's birthday wine.

"That we three shall meet again," he said, offering it around.

"That's not the way to bet," Jane said, and drank.

It was ten o'clock Thursday night, six days from the day of Melior's arrival.

* * *

Suicidal disregard for consequence lent their actions a bitter elegance. Rohannan Melior and Michael Peacock moved directly, profligately, toward their goal. A taxi to Wall Street. A quick few blocks walk to the City Hall Station, closed still, but easy enough to force its iron gates if you simply didn't care if anyone noticed.

Down the steps. Into the station. And for Michael Peacock, into nightmare.

The gun felt *right* in his hand. *It's funny how it all comes back to you. The cop walk. The cop talk. The cop MIND.*

Michael watched as Melior leaped lightly from the edge of the platform—*covering his partner*—down into the tunnel and crouched, looking about himself. Michael followed more slowly, sitting on the edge first and then sliding over it. He held the .38 up, near his face, where it could not be knocked aside or fouled by something below eye-level. And when he saw the *grendel* again. . . .

He still didn't know if he could pull the trigger.

But the cop inside—never dead, never quite disavowed—assured him that he could pull the trigger if he had to.

It didn't say whether he could live with himself afterward. But then, he didn't have to, did he?

All he had to do was find the *grendel.*

Jane's maps were detailed but not precisely clear. The IRT line sliced through the Alfred Ely Beach Tunnel at this location, but how much of the tunnel—if any—was left after the construction, and where and how it connected with the tunnel they were in, Jane hadn't been sure.

And, in the end, they were only guessing that the *grendel* was here—and not, say, in the Second Avenue Subway, which had lain unfinished and awaiting habitation since 1975.

To *know,* apparently, they needed Ruth.

If she was still alive.

If Ruth and Naomi were still alive.

And there was just one other thing.

"There's something I've been meaning to talk to you about," Michael said, pitching the half-whisper to carry down the tunnel to Melior ahead.

Melior stopped and turned back, and Michael saw, with a certain bleak satisfaction, that Melior was *glowing,* a faint silvery aura that served to light the tunnel far better than Michael's flashlight.

"You aren't exactly as deficient in magic as you've been claiming, are you?" Michael asked, catching up to him. "I should have caught on sooner. The sword works here. And that precognition thing of yours, that works, too. And you did something to Philip."

"We had a bargain," Melior protested mildly. "With silver and gold to seal it, as one must with a Child of Earth. I did not lie to you, Friend Michael; in comparison to what I could call upon in my own place the magic I have is small, and weak, and once it is expended in this place I may not find more," Melior answered, a response that was oblique at best. "I use it now to draw the creature, if it can be drawn. You I leave to claim the Sword."

It was a sentence of death and Michael knew it, but it made him curiously happy.

"All we have to do now is find our way in," he said.

Ruth's tears did not last long; the time they had was precious. The *grendel* might come back. She hugged Naomi and said nothing, and they went on with their search.

Neither of them quite wished to try the narrow tunnel, to see if it was not as much a dead end as it looked. It was too easy to imagine being trapped in that narrow cut with nowhere to run.

They found the stairway to the surface from the days of this place's long-ago construction. The ornate brass rail and green marble steps—still bearing shreds of a carpet once red—disappeared after less than ten feet behind a pile of bricks and rubble; trash from the long-ago era of its construction.

"I wonder what this *was?*" Ruth said.

"Jane would know," Naomi answered.

"I wonder where she is?"

"I hope she's all right."

"I hope *somebody's* all right," Ruth said, with an attempt at bravery. It was hard to be brave when you were buried alive and your future looked like being eaten ditto.

Neither of them ventured nearer the sword than they had to. It glittered balefully amid its dragon hoard, promising any number of things.

"That thing gives me the creeps," Naomi said. Ruth

agreed, slowly, but she didn't really agree. Some inward imp
of perversity assured her that *she* could handle the sword
and take no harm; that in this one thing the magic would not
work as Melior had sworn it would.

They carefully explored their prison: the platform which,
if this were only a book, Ruth would demand be described
in all its perversely beautiful detail. The stairway to the surface (blocked). The car with its hideous contents. The sword
with its trash at that end of the platform.

No escape. The car blocked half the platform. The railbed
was sunk only eighteen or twenty inches below the edge of
the platform; easy enough to get down to the trackbed, walk
the hundred yards to the bare rock of the other end. No escape.

"There has to be a way out!" Ruth cried in a strangled
voice.

"We just haven't found it yet," Naomi said, sounding
calm where no calmness was possible. And so Ruth tried to
be brave, in a situation where no bravery was possible.

They even, in the end, went down to the far end of the
tunnel, to where the dressed stone gave way to the raw rock
face, and found nothing at all. It began to seem, to Ruth,
more and more possible that the *grendel* simply walked
through walls, but if that were so, how did he get all these
bodies here?

She had never felt so tired. All last night spent waiting up
for Philip to tell them where to look; Ruth couldn't really remember how many hours it had been since she last slept,
and thirst was a growing ache at the back of her throat.

Maybe they would die of thirst before the *grendel* had
them for dinner.

"Maybe," Naomi said, and Ruth realized she'd spoken
aloud. "There's something that looks like a canteen in that
pile of junk around the Sword. I didn't grab it before because I thought it might attract the *grendel* somehow, but
maybe it's worth the try."

Ruth hesitated. "I'll go," she finally said. "And don't argue with me. If—*it*—put me on that pile in the first place, it
can't have any objections to my going near it. And I'm
thirsty."

"There might be nothing in it," Naomi warned.

"Then I'll swipe a bottle and cut my wrists," Ruth said. "Just don't touch the sword."

The platform space seemed wider when you were crossing it waiting for a *grendel* to pounce at you. She'd made Naomi stay at the other end, back by the blocked staircase. Victorian decorator logic said that there should be one at this end, too, but there didn't seem to be. Perhaps they'd forgotten it.

The large round orange hazard light in her hand made an unwieldy lamp, but Ruth carried it doggedly. To be down here in the dark would be a thousand times worse.

She reached the trashheap. No *grendel,* and the sword still there like a brand plucked from the burning, infinitely alluring.

Ruth dragged her attention away from the sword and studied the trash. Yes, there was the canteen, and what looked like a sealed box of granola bars next to it, although you could never really trust those things to be what they seemed.

My mind is wandering, thought Ruth with an air of discovery, just as if it were an achievement. She'd better hurry.

She set the lamp carefully on the floor and was reaching for the canteen when she heard the sound. Metal on metal, and, impossibly, the subway car shifted a few feet.

And there it was; the *grendel;* spider-spread on the top of the subway car, squirming its way toward her, mad eyes gleaming. Ruth snatched the canteen—and the box—and ran.

Both were heavy in her hands, and a part of her mind must have registered that fact; why else had she not dropped them in her mad flight to simply get *away?* It was darker but not quite black without the light, and Ruth already knew the floor was clear. She ran.

Naomi grabbed Ruth as she caromed off the wall beside the stairwell. Terror modulated Ruth's shriek to a frightened whimper. It was only as Naomi grabbed her that Ruth realized the *grendel* was not behind her.

But if it had wanted to, it would have had her.

Naomi drew her up the stairwell.

"Wh— Wh— Wh—" Ruth demanded, still clutching her prizes.

"It didn't follow you. It went into the car," Naomi said. Ruth clung to her and shook

The canteen was full. Naomi tested it cautiously, emitted

a snort of disbelief and passed it to Ruth. Ruth sniffed at the opening.

"Brandy," she said.

"Brandy-and, I think," Naomi said. "Drink up." She tore the lid off the box of granola bars, trying to make as little noise as possible. The contents were both fresh and dry.

Ruth drank, and felt the bite of brandy, even though it was reassuredly diluted with a great deal of tap water.

She knew exactly how much. And she'd bought the little bottle of Courvoisier to spike it her very own self.

"This was Melior's," she told Naomi as she handed her the canteen.

"Yeah," the word came on a long exhalation of disgust. "I'm sorry, Ruth. You loved him."

"He never stood a chance," Ruth said in a small voice. Her eyes burned, but this time no tears would come. She leaned back against the smooth marble of the stairwell and wished, desperately, that she were anyplace but here.

"It explains why Philip never found anything about the bodies," Naomi said after a while.

"What?" Ruth felt groggy; exhausted beyond bearing.

"The *grendel*. It's been grabbing people all right; anyone it could find; maybe even homeless; and bringing them here—to its larder. No wonder there were never any clues." Naomi sounded more disgusted than anything else at her inability to have reasoned out this simple fact.

"So how come it left us alive?" Ruth asked unwillingly.

"Maybe it left them all alive at first," Naomi answered remorselessly. "They'd keep better that way. It'll probably leave us alone until it runs out of supplies."

"We'll be dead by then."

"And you're complaining?" Naomi asked.

They huddled together in the stairwell and tried not to think about the *grendel* and its dinner arrangements.

"Now we know where the way out is. Behind the car. Maybe. . . . When it's asleep," Ruth said hesitantly.

"I don't think it sleeps. And I don't think we could be quiet enough to not wake it up. And I don't think we could move the car enough, or climb over it, to get out."

"We have to try," said Ruth, who was trying to believe this.

"Maybe," said Naomi. She put the cap back on the canteen and tucked away the last of the granola bars. "C'mon.

I know it sounds idiotic, but why don't we try to get some sleep? I'll wake up if we hear it coming."

"And there isn't any place to run anyway," Ruth said. She snuggled up next to Naomi. Naomi put an arm around Ruth's waist, and Ruth put her head on her friend's shoulder. They settled themselves as best they could against the marble wall.

And Ruth, assuring herself that she'd give it about ten minutes before telling Naomi that sleep was impossible under these conditions, fell asleep.

Dark on dark; they would have missed it entirely except that Melior's fingers, skimming lightly along the subway wall, abruptly met thin air.

Too regular to be a crack, it was as if the subway wall simply stopped and started again; an eighteen-inch gap in the concrete. It seemed impossible that the hulking *grendel* body that Michael had seen could have forced its way through such a space, but Melior's expression, eloquent of loathing, seemed to say that it could.

"Is it. . . ?" Michael said.

"A way the *grendel* uses, if not the path to its lair," Melior said in answer. He reached his arm into the crevice as far as it would go. "Bare rock," he pronounced. "Were this a castle in my own world, I would call this perhaps a ventilation shaft to the lower levels."

"That would fit with Jane's map," Michael said, hesitating. He shone his flashlight directly into the cut. Rat-eyes flared red and vanished. The walls were rough rock, the passage narrow. Getting down it would be a long process, and all they might get for their pains was stuck.

But they had to check it out. Like an alleyway door hanging open.

Like a wrecked car that might blow.

"You want to walk point or drag?" Michael Peacock asked.

When Ruth woke up, it was dark. Naomi must have turned the flashlight off to save batteries. In the darkness the distant light from the sword was deceptively intense.

And Naomi was talking.

"When I was a kid," Naomi said, "growing up in Brooklyn, and that's another story, which I guess you're not going to get to hear, no loss; everybody had relatives—uncles, aunts. I used to ask my mom, 'so where're all my relatives?' because I didn't have any, and for a Jew not to have any family, well, that's really unusual. But we had nothing. And one day when she got tired of me asking she pulled out a family tree she'd put together when she was about the age I'd been then and showed me my family. She was the youngest of eleven—I'd had six aunts and four uncles, and they'd all had families. . . .

"She had the tattoo; she'd been in one of the camps for kids. Sponsored over here in '48. Her foster parents helped her look for her real family, but. . . . Anyway. You know.

"Two hundred generations of European Jews. All gone, just as if they'd never been. It was the first time it was really real for me—just as if I were standing at the top of a ladder and somebody yanked the ladder away—and I was still standing there, only now it was *possible* to fall, because all my connections had been cut away, and there I was looking down into empty space, thinking about how I'd come this close to just not existing at all."

Ruth sat up straighter and shifted away. Naomi must be certain she was awake now, but her tone never altered.

"I don't know if you can understand that, Ruth. Understanding it is not something I would wish on anyone. But in a weird way it made me realize that I was personally responsible for continuing my own existence—for not getting erased or swept under cover as if I'd never existed. And I vowed to myself that I'd be *real,* that I'd be big and important and *noticeable.* Because I wanted to live. Because it's not enough to remember. You have to make certain that *no one* forgets."

"Naomi?" Ruth said hesitantly. She reached for Naomi's hand, but now Naomi pulled away and stood up.

"And sometimes, Ruth, the only way to live . . . is to die."

Before Ruth could react, Naomi was on her feet, skipping down the half-flight of stairs as if they were brightly lit. Ruth, groggy and now personally terrified, followed her, but she was too late. In the silence the scuffing of Naomi's feet on the marble sounded like large hisses, and in the faint radiance of the larger room Ruth saw her, a darker shadow, dashing the length of the platform to where the sword stood upright in its nest of glittering trash.

And Ruth, who had never really forgotten it, remembered that Naomi's martial art was kendo. The *sword.*

There was an earsplitting roar from inside the remains of the subway car. The *grendel* stormed out, rearing up in a terrifying bearish gesture that made the sweat of terminal fear well up in Ruth's skin. Her mouth was so dry it hurt; when she opened her mouth, no sound came.

But Naomi reached the sword. Reached it, gripped it, and pulled it free in a clangor of rolling five cent deposit cans, holding it as if it were a *katana* and facing the *grendel.*

No, please, thought Ruth in sick terror, because the intellectual sophistry of accepting inevitable death is a far cry from watching it happen in front of you. *Not Naomi. No.*

The *grendel* reached out to take its Sword back, to slay this impertinent trespasser, but all there was to grab was blade—blade which cut, and stung, and flickered out of its grasp to cut again. Naomi backed frantically, trying to stay out of reach, making useless parries at the grasping taloned hands. Parries which did not kill.

But at last the *grendel* did what every lesson swore it would, and rushed her so heedlessly that Naomi had time to step aside; presented its unprotected ribs when there was time and all the world to strike, to shape the blow that struck and sank deep, deeper, and the monster hurt at last; turning, raging, swatting at the beloved object which had become its tormentor.

Then it was possible. Then the *grendel* was weak; gushing thick black fluid from its gaping side, sliced about the arms and chest, and, finally, sinking to its knees, misshapen arms dragging limp upon the ground as Naomi struck, and hard, at the scaled folds of flesh between head and shoulder. Struck one, and again, and then again, until that hideous head hung suspended only by a flap of skin.

Dead.

Then Naomi stood, exhausted and triumphant, bleeding and gore-spattered, resting the tip of the sword on the ground.

Ruth ran toward her.

"Get back!" Naomi whirled around to face her, holding the sword *en garde* as if it were weightless. Drops of liquid flew from the spinning blade. Her voice was high, her eyes wide and mad.

"You can't have it!" Naomi shrieked.

Ruth stopped dead.

Naomi retreated a few more steps, but even so Ruth could see the gleam of tears in her eyes. "So this is how it is," Naomi said, her voice softly wondering. "You can tell Melior he was right about everything, Ruth. It works just like he said—and it's fast. Oh, God, it's so fast. Don't let anybody else—" she broke off.

"Naomi?" Ruth said. "Don't do—"

"What you know damn well is the only thing I can do, now?" Naomi's voice was ragged; her breathing faster now than even exertion had made it. "Get out. Go on. There's a way out around the car. Use it."

"Come with me," Ruth said. "Naomi—"

"God dammit, Ruth." The words were evenly spaced, inflectionless, read off like the ingredients of a recipe. "Melior was right. The sword *wants*—" She broke off. Ruth could see sweat trickling down Naomi's face, her teeth bared in a grimace of effort. "Anyway. This is no time to—to be as Ruth and Naomi, Ruth." Naomi managed a ragged laugh. "Get out of here. Go on."

It should have been me! Ruth shook her head, wordless with the pain, but Naomi retreated into the shadows with the sword, leaving Ruth access to the way out.

If she could take it.

The *grendel*'s—the *FIRST grendel*'s—body was already liquefying, melting like a Popsicle dropped on a hot summer's sidewalk. The stench was unbearable. In the silence of this man-made cave, the only sounds were Naomi's ragged panting and the drip-drip-drip of fluid over the side of the platform.

Ruth looked back. She could not see Naomi, except as a deeper darkness surrounding the Sword. She jumped down onto the tracks.

There was less than a foot of space between the body of the carriage and the tunnel wall. Ruth pressed her back against the wall and slid along it, into the darkness, eyes closed so she would not have to see what was inside. There was a bare two foot expanse between the nose of the gondola and the wall.

At first Ruth was sure the wall was solid, but then her groping hands reached an opening, a window onto nothing, rough-hewn into the solid rock. *Ventilation tunnel,* the certainty from her recent reading came.

But whether it reached the surface, or whether Ruth could follow where the *grendel* had been able to lead, she did not know.

And she would not leave Naomi.

The conviction—as stupid as it was comforting—steadied her nerves and stopped her hands shaking. She was not going to leave her friend.

And besides, the sword would be sharp.

"I have a little neck—" Anne Boleyn's reputed words mocked Ruth's nobility. It wasn't easy to die.

But she wasn't leaving Naomi alone.

She had already made up her mind and turned back when she heard Naomi's indrawn gasp of pain, amplified by an architectural trick of acoustics. She groped her way back around the end of the car, then along its length, and at last was in view of the platform with its scattershot harlequin lighting.

She could see Naomi now. Naomi knelt on the damp-splotched marble next to the fountain that stood beneath the rotunda. The sword's hilt was balanced on the carved lip of the fountain, the blade pressing awkwardly against Naomi's lap.

And even in that dimness Ruth could see the bright red welling; the running of the fast blood.

Ruth climbed up onto the platform again.

"Get the *fuck* out of here!" Naomi snarled. "Do you want to be next?"

Ruth started toward her. Naomi warded her off with glistening red hands. "It hurts," she whimpered. "It slipped. It *hurts*, Ruth."

And it wouldn't kill her, Ruth thought with sickening clarity. The sword's spell was too clever for that. It would keep her alive, somehow, and incapable of breaking free before the sword finished the work of binding her will to its.

Or to something.

"I'm going to get you the canteen." Ruth said.

Melior had gone first, and even taken Michael's flashlight to light the tunnel. Both men moved crabwise, crouching, muscles of head and neck and shoulders screaming protest. If the *grendel* came upon them from either direction, they were dead. Left alone, Michael might have turned back—not from cowardice, precisely, but from a growing feeling of futility and time wasted—but Melior forged on; if not tireless, at least determined.

Slowly the passage changed its shape, from a slit eighteen inches wide in which a man might almost stand upright to a square box-shape, angling perceptibly downward, through which they must creep upon their stomachs. Now Melior put out the light and passed it back to Michael; there was simply no point. Even the rats had deserted them, and all the world dwindled to the excruciating, abrading procession through the dark.

At last Michael ran, face-first, into Melior's boot soles. He shoved. Melior kicked back, an irritated semaphore of caution. After a pause, he slid swiftly forward, the intermittent rasp of his swordbelt on the rock escalated to a continuous singing rasp. Then he was gone.

"Come, Michael." Melior's voice, low, from what must be the tunnel's end. The silvery radiance, absent in the tunnel, grew about him again, and in the light Michael could see the opening, square-cut like a picture frame, showcasing Melior.

There was a scream.

Ruth.

Michael dragged himself forward.

She had pushed the canteen toward Naomi—pity, if nothing else, kept Ruth from coming too close. Naomi drained the canteen, and then worked the Sword away from the wound in her side.

That done, she lay with her forehead pressed against the cool marble, cradling the Sword of Maiden's Tears as if it were a child.

Ruth sat, as close as Naomi would allow her, and waited with her. There was nothing else to do.

"You know what my middle name is?" Naomi said after they had sat there a very long time. Ruth jumped, but her voice was steady as she answered.

"No. What?"

"Francesca. Naomi Francesca Nasmyth. I guess I got off lucky; Mom married some Wasp yuppie from Connecticut named Caldwell Kettering Chesterfield Nasmyth the Third. Duration: seven years, product: me; and then we went back to being Jews. What about you?"

"Ten generations of Ohio Methodists," Ruth replied. Her secret—the truth she had always owed Naomi—swelled in her throat, but to tell it now in the face of this disaster would seem like plea-bargaining for sympathy; a consumer-comparison of dooms. "Nothing special. I was an only child."

"So was I. You should have seen what he sent for my *bat mitzvah*. A Barbie and three trunks of clothes."

She must mean her father, Ruth guessed. Naomi's voice was slurred, now, sleepy. Perhaps she would bleed to death after all. Maybe they'd get lucky.

And maybe they wouldn't. The pool that Naomi's blood had made on the marble was beginning to dry. It had gotten no fuller. The bleeding had stopped.

"You can tell Paul. . . ." There was a long silence, until Ruth thought Naomi had forgotten she'd spoken. "Tell him I figured out the answer," Naomi said.

"I will," Ruth said. She wasn't sure Naomi heard her. The silence stretched again.

Then Ruth heard the sliding, dragging sound; scales against rock; and all her battered nerves could imagine was that the *grendel*, before it died, had somehow managed to re-produce.

There was a flare of white light.

Ruth screamed.

She saw the dark winged figure lunging for her and screamed again, scrabbling backward on palms and heels, but then Melior—Melior shockingly returned from death—had grabbed her, pulling her to her feet and holding her close.

Ruth struggled against him. "Naomi—" she cried, trying to pull free.

Melior turned and looked. He saw everything in a rush. Naomi, on her knees but trying to rise, face twisted in an unconscious grimace half of pain, half of hate as she regarded him. In her hand, glittering as she plied it as her makeshift crutch, was the Sword.

The Sword.

"Ah," said Melior, all on a breath. He held Ruth even more tightly, retreating into the darkness that was not dark to him. The cold silver light on his body flickered and died.

"Michael," he called softly. "Michael, I have Ruth and she is well, but come warily."

Michael came around the end of the subway car. He had his flashlight in one hand and, Ruth saw with some surprise, a gun in the other. He flicked the light around the platform, highlighting first Ruth, then Naomi.

And the sword.

"Oh, *Christ—!*" Michael breathed.

"Hi, Michael." Perhaps the worst thing of all was that Naomi's voice was still recognizably hers; weak, but holding to its casual tone by a gallant exercise of will.

Michael stopped. *Dangerous,* the cop instincts assured him. *But she's dying!* another part of his mind protested.

"Hi, yourself," he said back. He stopped where he was. The important thing now was to find out who could be gotten out, and how, without anyone else being hurt. "Anything going on down here that you want to talk about?"

"I killed the *grendel.* I— But the sword slipped," Naomi said, leaving Michael to piece the truth together. *Then I tried to kill myself, but the sword slipped.* "Would you guys take Ruth and get the hell out of here, please, okay?"

"No." Melior's voice was low and regretful. Michael twitched but didn't turn toward him.

"Never take your eyes off the perp for a second, Cockie." Hoss had said that.

"She will not die, Michael. The Sword has her," Melior said.

"What if you take it away? What if you take it back to Elfland?" Michael's voice was even; concealing desperation with an effort.

"It will not save her," Melior's voice held infinite regret. "Give me your weapon, Michael."

"No." Ruth's voice was small as the realization sunk in. "No you can't. Melior, it's *Naomi.*"

"Michael." Melior's voice was patient.

"Where'd you get a gun, Michael?" Naomi's voice held friendly curiosity, nothing more.

"I helped you pick it out, remember?" Michael said, then: "There has to be another way," to Melior.

"There is none," Melior said. "She is *grendel.* I am sorry, Naomi, my friend."

"Will you guys stop talking about it and do it?" Naomi said wearily. "Please. *Hurry.*"

"Oh, please," whispered Ruth, meaning just the opposite. Melior turned her against his chest and she buried her face in his tunic.

"The gun, Michael," he said.

"You can't do it."

For a moment Ruth wondered who'd spoken, then realized the ragged voice must be Michael's.

Michael drew a sobbing breath.

"You've never fired a piece before. It takes practice. I've only got six rounds. You'd *miss!*"

His voice rose to an anguished shout, and over the echoes of his last words came the crashing sound of gunfire.

"You'd miss," Michael repeated. There was a sound, small and far, of something thrown striking rock far along the tunnel.

Ruth tried to turn and look, but Melior would not let her. And when he let her go, it was only so that Michael could take her, gripping her arms as if he did not know his strength, dragging her away toward the shaft in the rock.

Melior stood until they had gone, until the sound of Michael's voice as he forced Ruth into the shaft had faded. Then he reached for the Sword, still lady-bright despite being slicked along half its length with blood and ichor.

Only the Sword of Maiden's Tears could slay the *grendel* it had made. Michael's weapon could stop it for a time, nothing more.

But at least the one who had been the warrior-maid Naomi, who, for a brief time Melior had called "friend," would not know what he did now.

He took the Sword, and did what must be done. And when he had finished he wiped it clean, and slid it into its place in his swordbelt.

Then Melior turned, and began to follow the other two. Back toward the light.

CHAPTER 22

And Back Again

Ruth didn't have any truly clear memory of the time between entering the ventilation shaft and the time she'd seen open sky; a clear blue trapezoid at the top of the subway steps.

There had been no trouble reaching it, and no one to see them, since, oddly enough, the entire Lower Manhattan system seemed to have lost power.

And somehow Thursday morning had become Friday noon without Ruth's noticing—the sky was bright, the buildings pristine, the air clear and fresh and *open* as she walked through the concrete canyons of Wall Street. Reality was mocking in its normalcy. *Do what you like,* Lower Manhattan seemed to say, *it doesn't matter to me. In fact, nothing you can do will make any difference at all.*

Exhausted, battered, the three of them had caught a taxi back to Ruth's apartment. The driver hadn't wanted to take them, especially when he saw the sword, but Melior wasn't the only one who never wanted to see the subway again. Michael had convinced him.

And then there was the silence of the long ride uptown, with Ruth feeling Naomi's absence like an abscessed tooth; renewed pain with each rediscovery. She'd reached out, cautiously, for Michael's hand, and held it. He gripped her fingers as tightly as if he were trying to crush them, and she could feel him shaking.

None of them had very much to say.

Jane was waiting for them in the apartment. She'd been watching from the window and saw the taxi stop, seven floors below. She'd been holding the door open for them when they crested the last of the stairs, and had gone to put the water on for tea without saying a word.

She hadn't asked any questions. But later, after showers and blistering hot tea with brandy and too much sugar, Michael had reluctantly realized that Philip must be called, for mercy's sake, to tell him they were safe.

That most of them were safe.

"What do you MEAN she's dead? You must have made a mistake! You should have brought her back! We could have fixed it. You didn't have to leave her there!"

Philip stood in the middle of the living room, face red and white with incredulous anger, having broken all land speed records getting there from Amsterdam Avenue.

Michael turned away and walked off.

Philip stared after him, still furious and now hurt as well. He looked around for someone to blame and saw Melior, sitting quietly in a corner. The light flashed off Philip's glasses as he turned. And Melior looked up and saw him.

Ruth, grieving and exhausted as she was, was brought to painful alertness by the lightning-flash of unleashed emotion. But Melior, as he spoke, was gentle.

"Naomi was dead, Friend Philip. All that remained was *grendel.* There was no other way."

And no one, Ruth vowed, was ever going to know what that way had been. Not from her.

Philip's eyes were very wide, and for a moment Ruth held her breath, although what could Philip possibly do that would raise a ripple after everything else they'd been through?

"Mistress Naomi is dead, Friend Philip," Melior repeated with firm gentleness. "She gave her life in exchange for Ruth's and all who dwell in this realm, if that is any comfort. I and all my Line share your sorrow."

Philip still regarded him, unspeaking, and it came to Ruth, in a slow horrified dawning of realization, what the reason had really been that Philip hung around so much. The real reason that he listened to Naomi when he didn't listen to any of the rest of them. Naomi. *Naomi.*

Philip took a deep breath. "Well, sure," he said in a bright spurious voice. "That makes it all right. Since Nai turned into a *grendel,* I guess you had to do it. Considering her hobby was cooking, she'd probably have opened a restaurant or something. *To Serve Man.* Yeah, Elfie, I guess you didn't have any choices."

Philip didn't even bother to slam the door when he left. It

had hung open until Jane came out of the kitchen and closed it.

That had been Friday. And Saturday, following a notion of Melior's that seemed to be perilously close to wishful thinking, they—even Philip—had come down to the Brooklyn Subway Yards to see Melior off home.

And one of them was going with him.

"Why here?" Philip wanted to know. He hunched his shoulders against the chill, wearing a black leather jacket Ruth couldn't remember having seen him in before.

"If the subterranean way is Faery, then the approach to the subterranean way is the approach to the Morning Lands. And the Morning Lands are where we wish to go," Melior explained, patiently, for what might have been the first time. In fact, it was closer to the ten millionth time, and Philip hadn't liked the answer yet.

The moon was the traditional ghostly galleon, ducking behind cloud-wisps and painting the sky chill midnight blue. Jane and Michael, Ruth and Melior and Philip—*and never Naomi, never again*—stood outside the chain-link fence guarding the Brooklyn Subway Yards. Through the fence they could see acre upon acre of subway cars; some resting, some waiting for repair, some obviously beyond repair.

That was where they were going.

Jane and Melior, Michael and Philip and Ruth, all went down to the railway yards. To dance by the light of the moon, the moon, to dance by the light of the moon.

Have you danced with the devil in the pale moonlight? What was that from? Batman? No, something older.

The devil in the pale moonlight. . . Ruth looked at Melior beside her and thought of Coleridge: *For he on honey-dew has fed/And drunk the milk of Paradise.*

"I still wish you wouldn't do this," Michael said.

"I know." Ruth brushed her hair back; a nervous gesture. "I'm sorry, Michael."

He'd spent all morning—once she'd revealed that when Melior went home to Chandrakar she, Ruth Marlowe, intended to go with him—trying to talk her out of it. He'd called it running away. *"Naomi was my friend, too,"* Michael had said.

True. And it might be running away from people who, in

their own perverse dysfunctional way, loved her, but Ruth
didn't think so.

And if it was, she was doing it anyway. She had her biggest purse, and her toothbrush; four cans of Diet Pepsi, a
dozen Hershey Bars, and a paperback copy of *Gone With the
Wind.* All the things you'd take if you were leaving home
forever.

And over her favorite cashmere sweater and the Liberty
print skirt she never wore because it was "too good," there
was Naomi's Kinsale cloak, taken for a thousand reasons.

"When we are home, Ruth, my father's artificers will un-
bind the spell from the Sword, and you will be whole once
more."

Melior, trying to be comforting, and all his words did was
evoke more strangeness. Her soul. The silver cord that—so
Melior said—had pulled the Sword of Maiden's Tears into
the World of Iron: her soul, loosed from her grip while she
lay in her eight-year coma. She thought she could believe in
everything else before she believed in that.

She could even believe that Melior loved her.

He was dressed again as she had seen him first, and wore
the clothes that soon would not stand out in their strangeness, but would be the everyday garb of everyone. Melior
was going home to Elfland, and Ruth was going with him.

"How close do you have to get?" Michael asked. Who
would be practical, who would be organized, now that Naomi was gone? Would it be Michael?

Ruth would never know.

"Upon the iron road itself, I think, Friend Michael. We
must go within these gates." Melior gestured, offhandedly, at
the high chain-link gates, held together with chains and multiple padlocks, designed to keep trespassers out.

"What the hey; what's one more breaking and entering
among friends?" Philip said.

Why, feeling as he seemed to about Melior, Philip was
willing to be here at all was a Philip-mystery that Ruth
would never solve. Melior's signet ring still gleamed on
Philip's hand.

"You'll never know," Jane pointed out.

The paper bag she was holding crinkled slightly as she
held it. None of them knew what was in it.

"Well, come on, then," Michael said heavily. "Who's got
the wire cutters? Phil?"

* * *

The padlocks were beyond Michael's skeleton-key skills; in the end they went over the fence. The wire cutters had been only to remove a section of the razor-wire spooled along the top, and even in its absence—and with Michael's help—it was a difficult climb. Ruth was already battered from being dragged—*twice*—through the *grendel*'s tunnel less than two days ago. When she fell and skinned her knee, it infuriated her almost beyond speech.

Well, hell, it's been a rough week.

"Here?" said Michael.

"As good a place as any to begin," Melior agreed.

"And get this over with before somebody sees us," Philip muttered.

Melior turned and strode—there was no other accurate word for it—a dozen paces away. He stood between the iron rails—silver only where the rust had been scraped away—and looked expectantly back at Ruth.

Ruth looked at her friends.

"Here," Jane said. She thrust her paper bag into Ruth's hands. It was heavy. As the top gaped open Ruth caught the honeyed smell of beeswax.

"Candles," Jane said. "For the spell. There's a lighter in there, too." He round pale face gleamed in the moonlight, and it struck Ruth that of all the rest of them she'd miss Jane most. That Jane had wanted to be her friend, as much as Jane wished for anything she wasn't likely to get; Ruth's best friend, and not just one of a gang that happened to be all in the same place at the same time.

Jane looked at her, knowing what she knew, perhaps, or simply assuming that she knew it out of a lifetime's practice at informed assumptions. And not caring, because no amount of love and knowledge and caring and effort was going to make any difference now that the terms of Jane's reality had been set and the mind had been formed.

Knowledge was powerlessness.

"Thanks," Ruth said, and then, awkwardly, because this was not the sort of gesture there had ever been between them, she pulled Jane against her and hugged her tight. "Take care of yourself," she whispered, wishing there was someone, somewhere, who would make it their business to take care of Jane.

"Come, Ruth, we must away while the moon rides high."

Melior's cape billowed slightly behind him; his scarlet tunic was wine-violet in the cold blue light. He held his hand out to her.

"Ill met by moonlight, proud Titania." The tag was irresistible, but not apt; Ruth was no elf-queen, only cold and feeling irritable and foolish, just as she had when it had all begun. She trudged over to where he stood, hoping she would not sink High Romance entirely below the level of farce by tripping on the wooden cross-ties. She put one hand in his and held out the bag in the other.

"Candles," Ruth said.

"Ah."

Melior held his cape wide to shield the Bic lighter from the wind while Ruth struggled to light Jane's present, juggling two candles too thick to hold in the one hand she had to spare for them while trying to operate the lighter.

In the end it was Philip who rescued her, jerking the candles out of her hands and holding them like Frankensteinian electrodes while Ruth lit them.

"You're being a jerk, Ruthie," Philip said, low enough that it was meant for her ears alone.

"Shut up," Ruth answered wearily. She dropped the lighter into her pocket.

"Conservation of mass," Philip answered obliquely. He thrust the lit candles at her, and Ruth had to grab them hurriedly or drop them and have it all to do over again.

Then Philip turned his back on her and walked back to join the others. And though the night was not cold, Ruth felt cold, as if she were making some mistake she hadn't already taken into consideration and accounted for. Nerves, nothing more. *And who has a better right to them?* Ruth demanded of no one at all.

Hand in hand and each carrying a flickering beeswax candle, Ruth and Melior started down the tracks, toward the tunnel at the end of them.

There should have been more sound. Wind, carrying the far-off rhythm of subway trains on elevated tracks. Car alarms, emergency sirens; the sounds of the City, even in Brooklyn.

There was nothing. Only the prickling over her skin that Ruth associated with thunderstorms, and terror, and the last few minutes before the worst possible headaches. Melior's hand burned like cold fire over hers.

After a few moments of walking Ruth tried to look around and found she couldn't turn her head. Her muscles were suddenly painfully stiff and her field of vision had narrowed as abruptly as if she wore blinders.

Magic! And even the sudden realization that she, Ruth Marlowe, was smack in the middle of Real Magic was not enough to outweigh the fear.

Walking. Was she still walking? She couldn't remember how long this had been going on. She could not feel the weight of the candle she must still hold in her right hand. She was freezing cold, and the sweat was running off her skin like shower water.

Frightened, Ruth tried to open her mouth. Lips and tongue and palate were stuck together, immobile as if with the dust of the grave.

And Melior's hand burned, cold enough to sear flesh.

With a great effort Ruth jerked her head to the side and *saw* Melior a little ahead, walking with her hand in his down the tracks toward the tunnel ahead; blurred and shining; trailing luminous afterimages. He turned his head toward her and smiled; she saw the hot phosphor white of his teeth and the burning red of his eyes. His lips moved, though she couldn't hear what he said.

Demon lover, Ruth thought, and as swiftly another thought supplanted it. Tam Lin, and the lover claimed no matter what monstrous disguise he was enchanted into. She closed her left hand tighter over his.

Everything was fogged with halos; crisscrossing and multilayered in colors until she could hardly make out the subway cars that must be their basis. Everything was blindingly bright and much too dark to see all at the same time, and the rails of the tracks were a glittering hot-forged silver arrowing irresistibly toward a frozen nova terminus.

Now the ground—which had been perfectly flat the last time she had been able to see it clearly—was slanting upward beneath her feet. Now the footing was less certain than it had been before; still not treacherous, but a little slidey underfoot, and the gravel she kicked loose tended to roll—

—*where?*—

—downhill. Toward the World of Iron, which Melior was

trying to climb out of. Hadn't he said he'd fallen, that the Sword of Maiden's Tears had fallen, here?

And now he was trying to climb out. Back to the Lands Beyond the Morning. Home.

Ruth gritted her teeth and walked on.

Soon the road she and Melior followed—the Iron Road—was steeper and the air was winter-chill. Ruth was glad of Naomi's clock; the bare skin of her hands and face burned, chapped raw by some maleficent Frost King's breath. The frigid air was thin and painful in her laboring lungs: the clouds of her expelled breath added to the glittering ice-burning illusion which surrounded both of them.

But beneath it all, like cake under icing, she could see the Real World—the subway yards, the tracks and the tunnel. They weren't even halfway there.

Although she had never really been able to tell they were moving, Ruth was now aware they weren't moving as fast. Now Melior's grasp was nearly as much to pull her along as it was for comfort; without it, Ruth didn't think she would have been able to take another step. Her head spun giddily, and each step was a lead-weighted effort to defy gravity. Her mouth tasted of rust, metal, and salt, and her eyes stung with sweat.

Another step. Another. Ruth's arm arched as if her whole weight was suspended from it; as if Melior was drawing her up out of a well infinitely deep.

And if she felt this way, what must it be like for Melior, who had not only to carry himself out of the World of Iron, but her, too?

Ruth felt his muscles shudder as he fought to accomplish one more dragging step. Now progress was slowed to a series of halting baby steps, each bought at the cost of several seconds of agonizing labor.

Could he do it at all?

He'd said his magic was weak. He'd said that his only hope to return home was to ally his magic with that of the Sword of Maiden's Tears, and Ruth knew to her cost that the Sword's magic was cruelly strong.

But was it strong enough to take not only Melior back to his rightful place, but carry someone with him who didn't belong there at all?

Thin fires lanced up Ruth's arm to her neck; bruised mus-

cles, pulled tendons. Melior would not give up. She knew
that. He would not leave her behind. He would go on trying.

Could he do it?

What if he couldn't?

Did she have a right to let him risk his entire future? And
not only his, but his family's, everyone who depended on
him to come home with the Sword?

It was his decision to make.

And sometimes you had to decide things for yourself.

Ruth set her feet and hauled back hard against his grip.
She felt him check and stagger, almost sliding backward,
and that alone told her all she needed to know. Carrying her
weight as well as his own, Melior wasn't going to make it
home.

And he wouldn't leave her.

Ruth shouted at him, and could not even hear the sound of
her own words against the clamoring silence. In the corner
of her vision, the candle in her right hand glowed inferno
bright.

"Can I get there by candlelight. . . ?"

Ruth concentrated. Hard. And finally succeeded.

She dropped the candle.

And suddenly there was a roaring void on her right side,
chill blackness, savage and razor-edged, and here inside was
her sensible cowardly self shrieking that there were bad
things, worse by far than she had yet imagined, that could
happen to her in these forsaken spaces if she got careless.

But now Melior's hand was not quite so solid on hers.
And this time, when she pulled, her fingers slipped free.

"Ruth—!" Sound returned; she heard Melior's voice; terror and fear, longing and heartbreak, all mixed into one anguished howl but it was far too late to change her mind. She
felt him rise; soaring as if a great weight had been lifted
from his shoulders. Going home.

And Ruth fell, fell for hours, fell forever, fell as the
Sword had fallen, down into the World of Iron.

Philip was the first one to reach her; crouched on hands
and knees Ruth was treated to an intimate panoramic view
of his shoes.

"You're alive, right?" he said.

Ruth sat back and looked up at him. Her face burned, her

nose was running, and her lungs felt filled with pulmonary equivalent of hot green chile salsa.

"I'm alive, right," Ruth said. She located a handkerchief and blew her nose noisily. Around her the rail-yard had returned to rust, entropy, and iron. Melior was nowhere to be seen.

"What happened?" Michael, arriving, demanded. "Ruth, are you all right?"

"Physics," said Philip inscrutably. "Sure she is. She's breathing, isn't she?"

Yes. And Melior was going home. And there was too much riding on him for him to turn back, now that the hard choice had been made.

And it had been Ruth who had made it.

"So now it's really all over."

Jane, last of all to reach her, the statement flat and uninflected and just faintly accusing.

"Don't bet on it." Philip's voice had regained its accustomed sneer. "In books, magic strikes three times."

DAW

Elizabeth Forrest

☐ **PHOENIX FIRE**   **UE2515—$4.99**

As the legendary Phoenix awoke, so, too, did an ancient Chinese demon—and Los Angeles was destined to become the final battleground in their millennia-old war. Now, the very earth begins to dance as these two creatures of legend fight to break free. And as earthquake and fire start to take their toll on the mortal world, four desperate people begin to suspect the terror that is about to engulf mankind.

☐ **DARK TIDE**   **UE2560—$4.99**

In 1968, a freak accident at an amusement park saw three boys drowned, and the only survivor pulled from the ocean in a terror-fueled, near catatonic state. Years later, the survivor is forced to return to the town where it happened. And slowly, long buried memories start to resurface, and all his nightmares begin to come true.

Tanya Huff

VICTORY NELSON, INVESTIGATOR:
Otherworldly Crimes A Specialty

☐ **BLOOD PRICE: Book 1**   UE2471—$4.99
Can one ex-policewoman and a vampire defeat the magic-spawned evil which is devastating Toronto?

☐ **BLOOD TRAIL: Book 2**   UE2502—$4.50
Someone was out to exterminate Canada's most endangered species— the werewolf.

☐ **BLOOD LINES: Book 3**   UE2530—$4.99
Long-imprisoned by the magic of Egypt's gods, an ancient force of evil is about to be loosed on an unsuspecting Toronto.

☐ **BLOOD PACT: Book 4**   UE2582—$4.99
Someone was determined to learn the secret of life after death—and they were about to make Vicki Nelson's mother part of the experiment!

THE NOVELS OF CRYSTAL

When an evil wizard attempts world domination, the Elder Gods must intervene!

☐ **CHILD OF THE GROVE: Book 1**   UE2432—$4.50
☐ **THE LAST WIZARD: Book 2**   UE2331—$3.95

OTHER NOVELS

☐ **GATE OF DARKNESS, CIRCLE OF LIGHT**   UE2386—$4.50
On Midsummer's Night the world balance would shift—but would it be toward Darkness or the Light?

☐ **THE FIRE'S STONE**   UE2445—$3.95
Thief, swordsman and wizardess—drawn together by a quest not of their own choosing, would they find their true destinies in a fight against spells, swords and betrayal?

DAW

Eluki bes Shahar

THE HELLFLOWER SERIES

☐ **HELLFLOWER (Book 1)**   UE2475—$3.99

Butterfly St. Cyr had a well-deserved reputation as an honest and dependable smuggler. But when she and her partner, a highly illegal artificial intelligence, rescued Tiggy, the son and heir to one of the most powerful of the hellflower mercenary leaders, it looked like they'd finally taken on more than they could handle. For his father's enemies had sworn to see that Tiggy and Butterfly never reached his home planet alive. . . .

☐ **DARKTRADERS (Book 2)**   UE2507—$4.50

With her former partner Paladin—the death-to-possess Old Federation artificial intelligence—gone off on a private mission, Butterfly didn't have anybody to back her up when Tiggy's enemies decided to give the word "ambush" a whole new and all-too-final meaning.

☐ **ARCHANGEL BLUES (Book 3)**   UE2543—$4.50

Darktrader Butterfly St. Cyr and her partner Tiggy seek to complete the mission they started in DARKTRADERS, to find and destroy the real Archangel, Governor-General of the Empire, the being who is determined to wield A.I. powers to become the master of the entire universe.

Cheryl J. Franklin

☐ **SABLE, SHADOW, AND ICE**   UE2609—$4.99
The Mage's cards had been cast—but could a destiny once foretold ever be overturned?

The Tales of the Taormin:

☐ **FIRE GET: Book 1**   UE2231—$3.50
Only the mighty sorcerer Lord Venkarel could save Serii from the Evil that threatened it—unless it became his master. . . .

☐ **FIRE LORD: Book 2**   UE2354—$3.95
Could even the wizard son of Lord Venkarel destroy the Rendies—creatures of soul-fire that preyed upon the living?

☐ **FIRE CROSSING: Book 3**   UE2468—$4.99
Can a young wizard from Serii evade the traps of the computer-controlled society of Network—or would his entire world fall prey to forces which magic could not defeat?

The Network/Consortium Novels:

☐ **THE LIGHT IN EXILE**   UE2417—$3.95
Siatha—a non-tech world and a people in harmony—until it became a pawn of the human-run Network and a deadly alien force. . . .

☐ **THE INQUISITOR**   UE2512—$5.99
Would an entire race be destroyed by one man's ambitions—and one woman's thirst for vengeance?
